GAME OF DEATH

David Hosp is a trial lawyer who has spent a portion of his
ti working pro bono on behalf of wrongly convicted indi-
v   ls. He finds time to write his novels on his daily commute
b   at across Boston Harbour. He lives with his wife and
fa   outside the city.

Acclaim for David Hosp

'   Next of Kin] is one of the best thrillers I've read in a
l   ne, reminiscent of John Grisham, but, I think, better
a   a stronger, more sympathetic cast of characters . . .
A   absorbing page-turner'

Richard & Judy Book Club review

'   etail and subplots make Hosp such a gripping writer
.   is growing and developing with each new book'

Daily Express

'   It is a knockout; Grisham with passion, even a touch of
t   at Michael Connelly thrown in . . . It crackles from the
fi   ge to the last and never lets up for a second'

Daily Mail

'   is a born storyteller, a master of quirky character and
detail who enthrals through the simple, but elusive, expedient
of never seeming to write a dull sentence'

Daily Telegraph

Also by David Hosp

GAME
OF
DEATH

DAVID HOSP

MACMILLAN

First published 2014 by Macmillan
an imprint of Pan Macmillan, a division of Macmillan Publishers Limited
Pan Macmillan, 20 New Wharf Road, London N1 9RR
Basingstoke and Oxford
Associated companies throughout the world
www.panmacmillan.com

ISBN 978-0-230-76109-4

A CIP catalogue record for this book is available from the British Library.

Typeset by Ellipsis Digital Limited, Glasgow
Printed and bound by CPI Group (UK) Ltd, Croydon, CR0 4YY

Visit **www.panmacmillan.com** to read more about all our books
and to buy them. You will also find features, author interviews and
news of any author events, and you can sign up for e-newsletters
so that you're always first to hear about our new releases.

For my family

GAME OF DEATH

PROLOGUE

I'm floating. I take a deep breath to quiet the feeling of claustrophobia. It's like a drug – paralytic – someone else controls my every move. My senses are sharp and alive, though, as I go with him, a silent partner in his world, unseen and unknown.

He walks down a long corridor. The walls are stark white, the wood floors stained black. I see through his eyes as his head turns, taking everything in, as if he wants to remember every detail, every image, every moment. He looks down and I can see his shoes – black cap-toed boots. The pants cover them to the ankle, and with every step they ride up ever so slightly, so that I can see the bottom edge of the patch of elastic on the side that allows the boots to be slipped on without laces and still fit well. He reaches out and drags his fingers lightly along the wall and I can feel the tingle on my fingertips. The shirt flows loosely over his shoulders.

He pauses as he looks up and sees the door at the end of hallway. It's red, and it stands out against the sea of this otherwise colorless world. I hear his breathing grow heavy, and in my wrists I am aware that his heartrate has increased. He starts

1

walking again, hesitant at first, but each step like a gathering storm.

When he reaches the door, he waits there for a moment, listening. I hear faint moans – no words, only the guttural sounds of animal desire. He reaches up and runs his palm along the edge of the door, his head tilting. He's panting now.

The door opens and he stands there, scanning the room. It, too, is white, with fifteen-foot ceilings and ten-foot windowed doors that lead out to a balcony. The doors are open, and a gentle breeze blows the gauzy window dressings in. They billow and fall and turn as if dancing on cue, giving only a glimpse of the world outside. The room is barren except for a large four-poster bed with a loose canopy that matches the curtains on the window. It rustles nervously against what remains of the breeze inside the room.

He wipes his forehead and turns to the bed. I feel his sweat on my hand. Through the canopy I can see the outline of a woman. Soft cries of desire waft across the room. They are so quiet they are difficult to hear, and yet they reach down with an ancient yearning to some core instinct in both of us; some primal drive that is base and male and irresistible.

He walks slowly over to the foot of the bed and pulls the thin curtain aside. She is there, lying on the bed. The first thing I notice is her face. It is so perfect it seems unlikely that it could ever exist in the real world. Her white skin is flawless, her features perfectly symmetrical, her lips red and wet and full, parting with every gasp. It is her eyes that hold me, though. They are a shade of blue I have never seen, with flecks of gold and crystal, and they are so penetrating it feels as though they are reaching out straight through his eyes into mine, begging me for . . . something I can't quite make out. It's like those eyes have captured the dialectic of every human emotion that ever mattered – love and hate; ecstasy and terror; comfort and jealousy – and rolled them into a single glance that could level entire cities. I am slaughtered.

His eyes travel the length of her body. Her hands are bound to the headboard with leather straps. She wears white lace and a matching bustier that ends just below her nipples, which are small and erect. Sheer white leggings cover sculpted, perfect calves and thighs, kept taut by a satin garter and stockings. Her dark hair is spilled out over the pillow.

He moves to her and as he approaches her breathing quickens, matching his. Her moaning gains volume as he reaches out to caress her legs. I can feel her skin on my hands, warm and smooth, like the finest velvet ever woven. He slides his hands up the insides of her thighs and I can feel the heat she gives off intensify. He slips her panties down, over the garter and leggings, over her feet. She gasps and writhes from side to side in anticipation, as though given over wholly to his spell.

He stands before her, slipping down his pants. Then his hands are on her again, and her skin is like fire. He crawls over her, so that we are both looking down at her now, her face so close I can feel her breath. She smells of jasmine and musk. Her eyes are so large, so mesmerizing, they are all I can focus on. I sense his rhythm, and the way she matches it, her gasps now synchronized to each thrust of their hips. And yet still all I can see are those eyes. Eyes so deep I fear that I may be lost here forever.

His hands slide up her body, over her breasts, under her

arms. Her hands are still bound above her head, and he runs his fingers up over her elbows to her wrists, and then back again to her shoulders. My fingers go along for the ride.

Their rhythm is mounting now, and her gasps have become loud cries. His hands move from her shoulders to her neck, caressing the soft skin below her perfect jaw. He is holding her tight, and I feel his hands and mine close on her throat. She is still matching each thrust, but something is different. I can see it in her eyes. Those pools of wonder and trust darken with fear and doubt. I want to scream out. I want to stop it, but I am powerless. Our fingers grip her throat tighter. She writhes and I can no longer tell what she is feeling. I can sense what he is feeling, though. His heart is pounding in my wrists, and his rhythm is gathering speed and losing consistency, his control slipping as the end nears. Her face is flushed, her eyes bulging, and I know she cannot breathe.

The end comes with an explosion that shatters the world. They spasm and recoil. He screams. Her mouth is open, as though she is trying to call out, but no sound escapes. For both of them, every muscle contracts with such force it seems as though their bones will snap.

The room is quiet and I look down. She is still there, but no longer. She is limp and lifeless, and the fire that was in those eyes – those eyes I lost myself in – is gone.

The screen explodes in a flash of light that recedes into the center of the world until the monitor is black.

CHAPTER ONE

'Yo, Slick!'

The slap on my shoulder shoots adrenaline through my overwrought body. I jerk forward in my chair, ripping the sensory unit off my face. Yvette looks down over her nose-ring at me with a conspiratorial smile. Everyone I know is captivated by her looks. She has none of the attributes of conventional beauty: her nose is slightly askew; her eyes a bit too large and spread; her ears stick out when her hair is pulled back; and the hair itself . . . well, it would take a page for every day of the year to describe the ever-evolving, multicolored, kaleidoscopic mess that is her hair. She has a way of holding others with her piercing hazel eyes, though, that makes them feel at once understood, evaluated and dismissed, all before she's even blinked. In short, there is nothing soft about Yvette Jones. And yet her sharp edges are compelling. She is a challenge, and I can understand those who see the prickly exterior and yearn to unlock the vulnerable little girl trapped underneath. I have known her long enough to be sure that the little girl doesn't exist. Yvette is exactly who she appears to be; that's one of the reasons I trust her more than anyone else I've ever known.

'Shit, 'Vette,' I say, shaking off the remnants of the LifeScene I've just left. 'You could give someone a heart attack pulling them out of a GhostWalk like that?'

'Walk was over, Nick,' she says. 'I saw the feed go dead. You were just sitting there like you needed a cigarette.' The smile is there again. 'That good, was it?'

I roll my gloves down from the elbows and put them with the sensory unit carefully on the stand next to the computer. 'Don't you have any shame?'

She laughs. 'What do *you* think?' She leans in and whispers, 'Who was it?'

She knows we're not supposed to share information about our subjects' identities. Keeping our research double-blind is the only way to prevent bias, but it's a rule that's never been strictly followed or enforced. I suppose it doesn't really matter anyway; the names are all fake, and it's not like we're curing cancer. Besides, I'm technically her boss – though it doesn't always feel that way – and it's not likely that she's ever going to get me in trouble. 'The Marquis,' I reply.

She gives me a knowing nod. '*De Sade*. I walked one of his a few weeks ago. Very impressive graphics.'

'The graphics were spectacular,' I agree. 'But the scene was a little too hardcore for my tastes.'

'Sex too hardcore?' She laughs again. 'For you?'

I make an annoyed face. 'It's not the sex; it's the killing I could do without.'

Yvette shrugs. 'He did the same thing in the one I walked. He took it too far, but it doesn't change the technical brilliance of what he's doing.'

'It's pretty fucked-up. I wasn't expecting it.'

'She's an avatar, Nick,' Yvette points out. 'She's not real. She's not even someone else's avatar, she's one of his.'

'Still, he gets off killing her,' I say. I understand Yvette's nonchalance, and yet it bothers me for reasons I can't explain. Fake or not, there was something about the girl in the scene that I can't treat with my customary dispassion.

'He does,' she admits. 'And millions of people get off killing other fake people in war games.'

'That's different.'

'How? Have you ever watched a twelve-year-old play Mortal Combat? It's disturbing. What *De Sade* does in his LifeScenes is actually pretty tame compared to some of the other shit people use the platform for. You've been in management too long, and you're not out there anymore doing the daily GhostWalks. It's hard not to get jaded. There's some seriously vile crap I've seen out there that's real misogyny: uninspired assholes who are too dumb to do anything but create half-baked dungeons . . . tie girls up . . . beat them . . . humiliate them . . . crap like that. That's not *De Sade*'s thing. He takes his time, and comes up with some really innovative concepts. I give him some credit for that, at least.'

'Even if he kills them?'

'Like I said, they're not real, Nick, and you've been in this business too long to start judging people's fantasies now. Morality gets left at sign-in, remember? It might as well be right there in our Terms of Use. You told me that when you hired me.'

'Did I?' I remember that, and it's always been my view. Something is different in this case, though. I just can't explain why. 'This guy's taking it to a new level.'

'What do you expect from someone who chooses *De Sade* as his username? The Marquis de Sade was the king of sick pornography back in the nineteenth century.'

'He was more than that,' I say. 'A lot of people credit him with being the father of the Nihilist movement. They say that Nietzsche and others who followed were just picking up on the amoralism that De Sade explored.'

'Look at you with the big words.'

'I took a philosophy class once,' I shrug. 'Anyway, the original De Sade would have loved the Internet – the ultimate amoral world. Maybe this guy's our perfect user.'

'Look, he's clearly got some serious issues, but you've got to admit, until the end, his scenes are pretty erotic. In the LifeScene I was in a few weeks ago he had the girl tied to a chair, and he was switching off between whipping her lightly with a cat-o'-nine-tails and tickling her with feathers. Hundreds of thousands of them. He kept adding more and more, fluffing them over her skin while he touched her, and she was talking to him, telling him how much she loved it . . . how much she loved everything he was doing to her.' Yvette flushes a little as she recalls the scene.

'A fantasy of yours?'

'Is now. I'd never imagined the kinds of things someone could do with a feather.'

'It sounds very special.' Sarcasm is my native tongue.

'It was.'

'What happens in the end?'

She frowns. 'He wraps cellophane over her face.'

I look hard at her, wondering exactly how jaded she has become. 'Lovely.'

'Better that he's working out whatever issues he has on the NextLife platform, instead of doing something about it in the real world.' She looks at me. 'There weren't feathers in the one you just walked, were there?' She almost seems hopeful.

I shake my head. 'It was simpler. White room, lace panties.'

'Was there bondage? He's really into bondage.'

'Yeah, but not over-the-top. Just the wrists tied to the head-board. Not some of the really twisted shit he's into.'

'Simple, clean,' she comments.

'It's not the scene, it's the graphics. I've never seen anything like them. The girl in this one is just . . . ' *I'm seeing her. The vision of her on the bed is locked in my mind.* 'I mean, I've been doing this a long time, and I've seen a lot of good visuals before, but this girl is . . . ' I lose my words again, and it takes me a moment to realize it. I glance up and Yvette is giving me a look. She raises an eyebrow, and I can feel myself squirm. Honesty is dangerous with her. She is like a dog with a fresh joint when she senses the core truth in any personal revelation. She will gnaw on it for hours, sucking the marrow out of every emotional implication until there is nothing left but inert bone, all of the meat chewed out of it. It's an exhausting process that usually requires several shots of tequila, and I'm not up for that at the moment.

'He's just a very accomplished technologist is all,' I say with a wave of my hand.

Her face pinches like a dart aimed right between my eyes. '*He's a very accomplished technologist,*' she repeats in her best nerd voice. 'Nick, admit it: the man creates some of the most erotic LifeScenes you've ever seen, and you call him an "accomplished technologist"? That's a little like calling Leonardo da

Vinci a "proficient portraitist". The man is a genius. A twisted genius, but – shit! – Van Gogh didn't cut off his ear because he was stable.'

'He's an artist,' I concede. I have no interest in dragging this conversation out. 'You had dinner yet?' It's one o'clock in the morning, but the office is busy. We're in the basement of an industrial building off Massachusetts Avenue in Cambridge. It's an open 4,000-square-foot span with 200 computer stations, each outfitted with comfortable chairs and full sensory units. The people here monitor nextlife.com's heaviest users – the most active 10,000 or so – to get a good sense of what people want out of the LifeScenes. That way, we can figure out what changes to make; figure out what people will pay for. They don't know we're there, in the LifeScenes with them, and we don't know their real-life identities, but it still gives the company a good idea of what's happening on the site, and lets us stay ahead of demand.

Most of the stations are manned around the clock. There is no set business schedule; employees are required to put in their research hours, but the company doesn't particularly care at what time of day those hours are done. Our members are online 24/7, so we are too. For obvious reasons it's a secure facility with no windows, which means it has the feel of a Vegas casino. Time has no meaning once you walk through the door. We get a steady stream of people working, and I oversee the operation. There are two small private offices at the far end of the space, and one of them is mine, though I spend little time there. I'm usually on the floor.

'I haven't even had *breakfast* yet,' Yvette says. It's not surprising. One of the things that she likes about the job is that it lets her conform to a vampire's schedule. It's the way she's been since she was fourteen and dropped out of school. She didn't need school anymore; she'd figured out how to hack the Charlestown municipal computer system and graduated with a B+ average without ever attending class. She could have made herself an A+ student, but she didn't want to set off red flags, and she never had any inclination toward higher education anyway, so why bother?

'Diner?'

'Diner,' she agrees.

'I'll get my coat.'

The Diner is our weigh-station; a stopover between work and the real world. When you spend your professional life hip-deep in the fantasies and fictions of other people's minds, it's helpful to have a buffer before jumping back into the physical realm. It gives you a chance to reframe things; pause and acknowledge the differences between what's real and what's not.

The place has a Sixties feel about it, but that's mainly because it's really old. They weren't trying for a 'feel' when they originally decorated; the stuff was contemporary back then. The throwback decor reinforces the sense that the place straddles the line between reality and dream. If James Dean and Marilyn Monroe were sitting in the booth behind us, it would complete the scene.

Yvette is sitting across from me behind two huge plates. One has a stack of pancakes so tall it looks like a television-commercial prop, with bacon, eggs and toast on the side. The other has a burger with onions, pickles and jalapeños and a bucketful of fries. It's hard to believe that all that food could possibly fit into her thin frame. Then again, my guess is that this is the first time in a couple of days she's bothered to eat anything of substance. That's the way she operates. Binge and starve. Not just with food: work, men, booze, et cetera. I have to hand it to her, when she turns her attention to something, she gives it all she's got.

She's leaning over her food, attacking it. In defense against the late June heatwave, she's wearing a pink tank-top with the words 'Man's Best Friends' plastered across the front. It's a loose top, and it hangs down as she leans over, exposing her cleavage and the black bra she's wearing. My eyes are drawn with unintentional lechery. I don't realize I'm staring, mainly because I'm not seeing Yvette at all; I'm back in the white room.

'See anything you like?' she asks without looking up.

'What?' My tone is defensive.

She looks at me. 'What's the big deal, Slick? You've seen 'em before.'

I laugh. 'When we were fourteen.'

'I was an early bloomer; they haven't gotten any bigger.' She leans and glances over at me. 'I hope, for your sake, the same isn't true on your side of the table.'

'Nice.'

'Just sayin'.'

'You get anything interesting tonight?'

She shakes her head. 'It was God-awful. I spent about an hour with this middle-aged woman who's managed to find an old high-school boyfriend. They meet in the same shared LifeScene over and over and over. They stand there in this

Eighties disco – not a very nice one, either – and trade stories about their kids and tell each other how unhappy they are in their marriages. They won't touch each other, though. Not even In-World. I'm like: *Jesus Christ, get it over with!*'

'Maybe they don't want to.'

'Oh, they want to. Her heartrate peaks at around one-fifty, and I can see the look he's got in his eyes. For whatever reason, though, they can't seem to get past it all. Don't they realize it's not real? I mean, it's not actually cheating.'

'Isn't it?'

'Don't get all philosophical on me – it's a fantasy.' She pauses long enough to fit half her burger in her mouth. 'It's harmless,' she muffles through the food.

I take a sip of my coffee. It's all I've ordered; turns out I wasn't hungry after all. 'Maybe it's not harmless to them. I mean, what made them look for each other after all this time? Both of them are married, right? They're middle-aged, they've got kids, they've got lives that are flying around them faster than they can deal with, and yet they found the time to make this connection?'

'That's my point. Why not just dive into the full fantasy? That's what they're there for.'

'If they do that, it becomes real, doesn't it? At that point, they have fully admitted – to themselves and to each other – how unhappy they really are. And if they can take that step in NextLife, what's to stop them from taking that step outside in reality?'

'Well, first of all, she lives in Atlanta and he lives in Spokane.'

'Distance can be overcome.'

'It's totally different, though, Nick. Just because you do

something online doesn't mean you're gonna do it in the real world.'

'No, I suppose it doesn't,' I agree. I'm playing devil's advocate, I realize, and I'm getting tired. If I keep it up, we'll still be here two hours from now, and I've got an important day tomorrow, so I can't let that happen. I have to cut things short. 'You going back to the office?' I ask.

She nods. 'I've got to. I've got another twenty hours I've got to make up before Friday or I'm gonna be short on my time sheets. You'd know that, if you were even a half-assed boss.'

'I've never worried about your ability to get the work done,' I say. 'You have better stamina than anyone I've ever met for crawling around in other people's fucked-up fantasies.'

'Hey, it beats working for a living. You going back?'

I shake my head. 'I've got a management meeting at ten, and I'd like to get a little sleep before then.'

'Management meeting, huh? We talkin' IPO?'

I smile at her. Some secrets I can still keep to myself. 'Come on,' I say. 'I'll walk you back.'

'Why? You think I can't take care of myself?'

She is a rare specimen. 'I'm not worried about you,' I say. 'I'm trying to protect the muggers.'

CHAPTER TWO

The drive home feels apocalyptic. It's nearing two in the morning, and the streets are deserted. The traffic lights blink from green to yellow to red without purpose, like lonely reminders of a civilization long passed. The people are gone, but the machines we have created to manage our lives move sadly along. I cross the threshold from the liberal college enclave of Cambridge into the working-class neighborhood of Charlestown, where generations have lived in proximity to the wealth of Boston, feeding off it, making their living as hard-working painters and plumbers and handymen to the elite on Beacon Hill and in the Back Bay. It's a town that's proud of its heritage and of its gruff, blue-collar ways; proud even of the strain of local criminal gangs that filters through the projects. It's a place where the hard are revered and the soft are swallowed.

No one is prouder of Charlestown and all it stands for than my mother. She's lived here her entire life, and has made it clear that she will never leave. Not while she's breathing, and not thereafter. She purchased her cemetery plot down by the O'Brien Highway in cash to make sure there are no issues with her being planted here for good.

I love Ma. I know it seems unnecessary to verbalize that; I mean, every boy loves his mother, right? And yet for me, it's not always as easy as that. Ma's a hard woman. Hard and demanding. Always has been. Her father was in the rackets back in the days when the gangs had real muscle. She grew up in that world, and it's where she's always felt most comfortable. My father was part of that world, too, until he was killed in an accident when I was seven. I was told he fell off a ladder on a construction job. I stopped believing that when I was ten.

Funny thing is, I think Ma was always disappointed that I never went that way. I could have. I started hanging out with a pretty tough crowd when I was younger, and I was respected. I could have ended up being a leader in what's left of that world, but discovered I was different. It wasn't fear; I think I was bred to disregard fear. It's just that I always liked school. I liked learning, and I loved computers. That's how Yvette and I first became friends. I actually think Ma was ashamed when I got the scholarship to MIT.

Truth be told, I didn't fit in much in college, either. The Massachusetts Institute of Technology is one of the most prestigious universities in America – a mecca for the offspring of the rich elite and wonder-geek geniuses alike. I fell into neither camp. I was a tough working-class kid dropping my 'r's and scratching my head at all the bullshit I'd never encountered before. I think my hard exterior made it a little difficult to make friends, and my hard interior made it tough for me to care. As a result, I dove into the work, and loved having the facilities to learn how computers really operate. In that sense, it was one of the best times of my life.

That's where I was four years ago, doing a joint program with split concentrations in computer science and business when the recession hit. The market crashed, and the savings Ma had from the insurance settlement she got after my father's 'accident' disappeared. Two months later she was diagnosed with cancer and, without any health insurance, it was clear that she wasn't going to survive alone. I quit school and moved back in to help out. Some mothers would have told their only child to stay in school and would have suffered through, in the quiet hope of a better life for the next generation. I would have been the first in my family to graduate from college. My mother, though, is a realist, and a firm believer in the debt children owe their parents. Like I say, I love Ma, in part because she is as hard as the town I call home.

I don't know what we would have done if it hadn't been for NextLife. The company literally saved us. I was the fifteenth employee hired. When I joined, I never haggled over my salary. The only thing I cared about was making sure that Ma would be on my insurance. They threw in the stock because that's what they assumed everyone wanted. And they were right for the most part; pretty much everyone else getting into the start-up was looking for the big score. Not me. I was looking for enough work to feed me and Ma. I took the stock because it was given, but I never thought about it. Sometimes you get lucky.

Soon we'll be able to move anywhere we want. If things work out the way everything is lining up, I'll be able to buy Ma the biggest townhouse on the top of Beacon Hill. A place so high up, we can look down on everyone around us. I'd like to do that for her – show her what her boy has accomplished.

Ma, of course, won't even talk about it. Like I said, she was born in Charlestown, and she'll die here; that's her view and she's sticking to it. As for me . . . well, we'll just have to wait and see. Sometimes I think it would be nice to go back and get my degree. It's something that still nags at me. I hate leaving things unfinished.

I pull into the driveway of the house I grew up in. It's a little clapboard two-bedroom set flush to the street about two blocks from the projects. The neighborhood is solid but gritty – a lower-middle-class Irish faux-ghetto wedged in between the projects and the posh townhouses up on Monument Square. When politicians talk about 'The Real America', this is the place they're talking about, and Ma is the person they're talking to. These days there seem to be fewer places like this, and fewer people like Ma.

I pull open the screen door and reach into my pocket for my keys, but I can see that the main wooden door is slightly ajar. I shake my head and push it in.

The television is on in the parlor. I can hear the chattering of some twenty-four-hour news channel, and around the corner I can see Ma's feet sticking out from the couch, resting on the ancient fraying ottoman. I grab a beer from the refrigerator and walk to the parlor entryway.

'They don't know what the fuck they're talking about!' Ma barks at me. She waves an angry hand at the screen. 'These people just don't fuckin' know!'

'Ma,' I say. 'It's two-thirty in the morning.'

'That makes it alright to talk shit on television?'

'What are you doing up?'

'I couldn't sleep. It's all the goddamned pills they've got me on. I swear, sometimes I think they don't know what they're talkin' about either, these doctors. They're children. They don't understand what it is to be old.'

'Fifty-four ain't old, Ma.' I slip into street dialect around my mother. It's weird, but I think it makes her feel more comfortable.

'It is if it's the fifty-four years I've lived.' She stirs in her chair, her hand going to her lips, forgetfully. Her fingers linger there for a moment, as though there's something they are supposed to be doing. I wonder: if I wasn't there, would she still be smoking? Even with the oxygen tank strapped to her face, the tubes running to her nose, the rumble in her chest like the approach of a loaded eighteen-wheeler, would she still be pouring the fire into her lungs? I think she probably would.

'Help me carry this thing up,' she says gesturing toward the oxygen tank. 'I can't watch this shit anymore.' I give her my arm and pull her to her feet. 'How's work?'

'It's okay.'

'Strange business.' She shakes her head. 'I'll never understand it. How do you people make any money doing what you do?' She gives me a sharp look. 'You make sure they ain't running a scam on you, you hear?'

'They're gonna make me rich, Ma. You'll see.' I smile at her. 'I'll be able to get you whatever you want.'

'What would I want?'

'I don't know. A better house?'

'You think there's something wrong with this house?' she demands. 'I love this house.'

'Then I'll buy you another one, just for fun. Maybe I'll buy you Mabel Mullarkey's house? You never liked her, right? So,

I'll buy her house and we can tear it down, just for spite. That'd cheer you up, wouldn't it, Ma?'

She laughs at that. 'It just might. That bitch, always makin' eyes at your father.' I follow her up the narrow staircase and into her bedroom. 'I'll read,' she says. It takes a moment for her to get situated, getting the oxygen tanks and tubes set just so.

'You want anything else, Ma?' I ask. 'Something to drink?'

'I'm fine,' she says. She looks up at me from her bed. 'You're a good boy, you know that, Nick? I had my doubts for a while, but you turned out okay.'

'Thanks, Ma. I love you, too.' I close the door to her room and pad down the hallway. I have an important meeting in just a few hours and I'd like to get a little sleep before then.

As I'm walking to my bedroom, my cellphone buzzes and I look at it. It's an automatic notification from the NextLife system, letting me know that *De Sade* is online again. One of the things we've learned in our research is that our users often go back to their favorite fantasies again and again to relive the scene – to make modifications and elaborate on them. I'm hoping that *De Sade* likes the LifeScene I was in today enough to go back to it, so before I left work I adjusted my administrator's settings to buzz me whenever he goes on the site. I'm desperate to see if he's with my girl. That's how I think of her now – *my girl*. It's a bad sign, and I know it, but I can't help myself; I have to see her again if I can. There's a part of me, even now, when it's nearly three in the morning and I'm fifteen minutes from the office, nagging me to go in; torturing me with the possibility that I might be missing a chance to see her.

I dismiss the thought and climb into bed. It's too late, and he'd probably be offline before I could even get to the office. I need sleep, so I turn off the light. I know, though, that I will spend the hours lying in bed, staring at the ceiling, thinking about my girl from *De Sade's* LifeScene, unable to get her out of my head.

I realize, to my chagrin, that I've become obsessed.

CHAPTER THREE

My meeting the next morning is at NextLife headquarters out in Brighton. It's just across the Charles, a couple miles down the river, but a world away. Because of the sensitive nature of what my research division does, we're kept separate, in the dark isolated basement of a nondescript building. By contrast, the company's headquarters is in a gleaming new, twenty-story structure out by the New Balance building. It towers over the highway with spectacular views of downtown Boston to the east. A green neon sign on the top of the building screams the company's logo. It's not very subtle, but that's the way it's always been with overnight online successes. It's all about branding. It's all about getting your name out there and making it 'top-of-mind' for every single human being when they log onto the Internet. Building the brand is paramount. Revenue comes later . . . hopefully.

To be fair, NextLife wasn't initially built solely on its brand. It actually has real technology behind it. It's an online portal that allows people to interact in ways they never dreamed of before. It's essentially Facebook, Second Life and Google all rolled into one. People can chat, talk, email and buzz each other. They can share interests and have video conferences at the touch of a button. But that's not the real draw. The real draw is the ability to create LifeScenes. In LifeScenes, people can essentially do whatever they want – be whomever they want. They can go diving off the Great Barrier Reef, or attend a Rolling Stones concert from the 1970s, or take batting practice against Babe Ruth – either by themselves or with others online – all while sitting on their couch. They can create other people to interact with using our templates, and they can explore their deepest dreams and their darkest fantasies in safety.

It's not like we invented the concepts – online communities using avatars that enable people to interact in real time with each other have been popular since the turn of the millennium. World of Warcraft had millions of users long before NextLife wrote its first line of code. NextLife, though, has come pretty close to perfecting the implementation. Our avatar technology and sensory units represent a quantum leap forward in development. They make the user-experience so realistic it can be difficult to tell the difference between a NextLife LifeScene and reality. Sometimes it's disconcerting how life-like it all seems. That is the key to the company's success.

And the success has been astounding. The company was started five years ago; within two years the company's estimated value rivaled Yahoo. When we added social networking as a component of the NextLife experience, the company grew even faster. We passed AOL in estimated stock value last year, and we're expecting to rival companies like Google and Facebook within the next two years. It's all been very exciting. On paper, even with my paltry holdings, I'm already worth somewhere between fifteen and twenty million dollars, depending on fluctuations in the daily market.

Of course, the phrase 'on paper' is the rub. I can't convert that to real money until the people who run the company figure out the long-term capitalization strategy. At one point we were considering a private sale to a combination of private equity funds. We've grown too large for that now, though, and it's likely that the only rational way out is an initial public offering. It makes sense, but it has everyone at the company anxious. It's a complicated process that involves the corporate equivalent of a proctological exam. As with all overnight Internet successes, there's a nagging question as to whether our valuation is rational. While we're rapidly becoming one of the most visited websites in the world, we're still figuring out how to translate that into actual revenue. The founders initially had the view that any revenue model – whether it was a pay-as-you-go subscription or the clutter of advertising – would kill the concept in its infancy. I'm not sure the word 'profit' was even uttered at the company for the first three years. Now that we are considering going public, it seems that it's all anyone can focus on.

Eight months ago the founders created a new division – the Division of Revenue Generation – headed up by Tom Jackson and tasked with figuring out the most effective way of translating the company's brand dominance into fiscal growth. Tom was the one who brought me into the company four years ago. He was an assistant professor at MIT, and one of my few friends when I was in college. He used to joke with me that he and I were the smartest two people at the university and yet we were two of the poorest. He seemed to find some righteous irony in this, but eventually watching others cash in on technological development became too much for him, and he jumped ship to the private sector to seek his fortune. When he heard about Ma's diagnosis and the fact that I'd left school, he pulled me into the company and has been a mentor to me since I started at NextLife.

Tom and I have worked closely on one aspect of the revenue initiative, called Project Touchpoint. The goal is to figure out what new additional sensory equipment people will be willing to pay for. We've extended the gloves past the elbows and expanded the headgear to include olfactory capability and better audio. We've also started marketing more intimate accessories for those who are looking for a more complete sexual experience In-World.

Figuring out what people will pay for involves digging into their most private fantasies and watching them do things they would never give permission for if they knew people were watching. It's a necessary evil, though. After all, you can't figure out ways of generating revenue unless you understand how it is people use the site. Besides, no one will ever know that they are being watched, and we take great pains to make sure no one's identity can ever be discovered.

Project Touchpoint is the only aspect of the company's plans that has actually managed to generate significant revenue at this point. I've been amazed at the rate at which people have been willing to shell out hundreds or even thousands of dollars for the most advanced sex toys for their online enjoyment. Today's meeting is to present Tom's results on other fronts. Even I don't know what to expect.

I park my six-year-old Corolla in the lot at headquarters.

I'm really looking forward to a new car. Don't get me wrong, the Corolla's a good, dependable vehicle. It's never let me down. But there are few people in the world with my technical net worth driving Corollas. I could easily get a loan for a nice car based on my holdings in the company, but that's not my way. I associate loans with the loan-sharking my father did, and with the spiral of failure those who take the easy option find themselves in. As a result, I won't buy what I can't pay for in cash.

I take the express elevator to the twentieth floor and step out into a blinding display of corporate success. The floor-to-ceiling windows of the reception area face east, out toward Boston, giving a sweeping view of the city. It's only eight-thirty, so the sun still hangs over the horizon behind the Prudential Center and streams aggressively through the glass, ricocheting off the gleaming white, frosted glass of the reception desk and the conference-room walls, attacking the eyeballs. The floors are hardwood, polished to a fine sheen. Everything is pristine. The reception area is filled with the twenty or so top executives.

You can tell what people do at the company just by their clothes. The head of the software-development team has on rumpled khakis, New Balance 574s and a flannel shirt buttoned to the top. It would be a quirky look even if temperatures weren't going to reach the nineties by noon. He clearly doesn't get out much.

The head of marketing is dressed in a lightweight suit with a cool-looking button-down shirt. His thick hair is slicked back, and he looks like someone you'd never trust, but would probably still buy something from, if he deigned to talk to you.

The finance guys are in pinstripes. They're dealing with investment bankers just about every day now, and it's like they've been infected with some weaponized germ developed in the back rooms at Goldman Sachs. They're turning into the corporate Borg before our eyes.

I look down at my own clothes and wonder what people assume about me, from the outside. I'm wearing jeans pulled down over the old leather boots I've had since I was eighteen. I was self-conscious enough when I left the house to put on a button-down shirt, and my leather jacket is old and beaten enough to look intentionally stylish. Beyond that, I still have the hard-raised look of a street kid.

The door to the conference room is closed, and those of us in management's second echelon mill about exchanging nods and smiles. The company has become so striated that I don't know half of their names. They look at me warily; they know I run what is known affectionately here at corporate as the 'black-ops' end of the business. I stand against the wall, letting the low hum of polite conversation blend with the song from the car radio that is still caught in my ear.

Suddenly there is a shout from behind the conference-room doors. It's an angry bark, the tone clear even though the words get lost in the thick oak. The executives waiting for the meeting go silent and look nervously at each other. Faces flush and eyes turn toward the floor.

Another shout follows, and then a tirade with the rhythm and intensity of the ocean beating on the shore during a hurricane. Now the uncomfortable smiles on those around me have turned to anxious frowns. Everyone is staring at the door, but no one is moving. I step slowly forward and those around me move back, their cowardice outbattling their curiosity. For me, that's a battle curiosity wins every time, sometimes to my detriment.

I am nearly to the door, and the shouting continues inside. As I draw close, I can make out a word here and there, but the nature of the conversation is still lost in the wood paneling. I reach out for the handle that runs the length of the door, and just as my hand touches the cold brass there is a crash from inside the room. It's like an explosion and I pull my hand back involuntarily. Everyone behind me gasps. I hesitate for just a moment, looking at the door. The shouting has stopped. I reach out again, grab the handle and pull.

The door comes open easily, pushed from behind, and Josh Pinkerton, the CEO and one of the founders of NextLife, stands in the door smiling, his arms wide, the reflection of the sun off his teeth bright enough to blind.

'Ladies and gentlemen!' he calls to everyone in the reception area. 'Thank you for coming! Please, come in.' He looks over toward the receptionist. 'Louise, we lost a vase. Can you have someone come in and clean?'

I am standing there, my hand still on the door handle, less than a foot from Pinkerton. No one in the reception area has moved. Pinkerton looks over at me, the smile still on his face, and I want to duck to avoid the reflection. I don't, though. Instead I flash my merely mortal smile back at him. It seems a poor trade, and Pinkerton claps me on the shoulder. 'Nick!' he says with more enthusiasm than is necessary. 'So good of you to crawl out of the basement for this! Please come in.'

'Thanks, Josh,' I say. 'Glad to be here.' I walk through the doors. Tom Jackson is in the room, as is Dr Santar Gunta, the mastermind behind NextLife's technology, and Heinrich NetMaster, NextLife's Dutch head of security. NetMaster is the name he chose when he came to this country, several years ago. He is an intimidating presence at six foot six inches tall and over 300 pounds. The rumor is that he got his start in security working with organized crime in Amsterdam.

I glance at Tom, and he flashes me a warning look that tells me I don't want to ask any questions. I take a seat at the long conference table, and watch as the others stream in and take their own places. The receptionist hurries in with a broom and a dustpan and quickly sweeps up the vase that lies broken in the corner like a murder victim no one wants to acknowledge.

It should be an interesting meeting at least, I figure.

'We're close,' Pinkerton says. He looks out at those around the table, smiling again, making eye contact with everyone. The sun has risen enough that as it streams through the window it no longer flashes from his teeth, but still casts a warm glow on his permatan. It makes him seem almost human. 'We're very, very close.' He looks at Tom Jackson. 'As you all know, eight months ago I appointed Tom Jackson to head up a new Revenue Generation Division. His first undertaking, Project Touchpoint, has been an enormous success, and the growth in our sensual hardware line has quadrupled the company's overall revenue. Of course, hardware will only get us so far, right? We need to generate other forms of revenue as well. We all know what the ultimate goal is: to launch our IPO as the most highly valued company in history. We can meet that goal if – *and only if* – we can show Wall Street enough income to justify our current value estimations. Tom, do you want to tell them where we stand?'

Tom clears his throat. 'Obviously revenue generation in an environment that is, by its design, as completely organic as NextLife, is a challenge. From the company's founding we have recognized that traditional methods of revenue generation are incompatible with the entire notion of what it is that we offer. Advertising, in the traditional sense, is likely to clutter both the site and the experience for our users, and turn people off. Similarly, a pay-per-use or paid membership scenario would, by our estimates, cut our users by seventy percent. That would be devastating to our profile at this crucial high-growth point in the company's history. We don't even know if the company would survive long-term in such a scenario.'

'We all understand the challenges,' Josh says sharply. 'What are the solutions?'

'We have several that are in development,' Tom says. 'The first is a new spin on advertising. It would be an ad-insert tool that would allow us to actually place product endorsements within users' LifeScenes – advertising which the user wouldn't even know was placed there. They could be walking down the street in the LifeScene, and a sponsor's car could drive by. It would blend into the scene, but give advertisers a way of reaching subliminally In-World. A sign on a wall in someone's LifeScene would have one of our advertisers' ads. It would also be targeted based on the information Nick Caldwell and his black-ops team could supply about particular users and groups of users, so that someone who is an outdoor adventurer in the LifeScenes would be matched with outdoor products, while someone who attends virtual concerts would get music-related advertisements.'

'What have advertisers' reactions been?' Pinkerton asks. I can tell he already knows the answer.

Tom hesitates before answering, glancing at Josh with impotent frustration. 'It's been luke-warm. But I think it will grow . . . '

'Just give us the numbers.' Josh's words are like tacks from a pneumatic gun, pinning Tom to the wall by his clothes.

Tom looks around the table. I can tell from the expressions that the primary sentiment of those seated is relief that they are not Tom at this moment. Tom takes a deep breath. 'Six percent on the high side.'

'Is that number for potential interest, or actual purchase?'

'That's interest,' Tom says heavily.

'And purchase? What's that number?'

'It's not something we have pushed . . . '

'What's the purchase number?'

Tom pauses for a long moment. 'Zero.'

'Zero,' Pinkerton repeats. The word falls like a dead skunk on the table. Everyone just stares at it, their eyes glazed, their collective breath held.

Josh Pinkerton stands, walks over to the window and looks out at the Boston skyline. No one speaks. His hands are behind his back, and he is rocking back and forth on his heels. Finally he begins, his voice so quiet that I think at first he's talking to himself, and those around the table have to lean in to hear.

'I could blame Tom.' I look over at Tom and watch his head fall. 'That would be the easy thing to do. Blame Tom. Fire him.

Tell the world that we are waiting another year to go public. I could do that, but it wouldn't be fair.' He takes a deep breath. 'Do you know why that wouldn't be fair?'

No one responds. After a moment he turns and looks at those gathered around the table. 'Because incompetence at this level cannot be blamed on one person,' he says with a quiet intensity. 'Tom's failure is your failure. Each and every one of you shares in this, and if I fire him, I will have to fire every single one of you, do you understand?' He just stares at us, moving from person to person, meeting everyone directly in the eye. Then he walks slowly over to the table in the corner of the room and picks up a vase on the table next to the window – it looks like the twin of the one carried out in pieces a few moments before – and he hurls it across the room. It misses the head of one of the finance guys by a couple of inches and explodes against the far wall.

'As of this moment, revenue generation is priority one for everyone around this table, do you understand?' he asks in a voice so soft I can barely hear him. 'We don't need much; the Street has a hard-on so fucking big for this company, it's ready to cum cash all over us. All we need to do is show them there is a chance – some possibility that we will eventually be able to generate revenue. We have more traffic than most sites in the world, and if you people can't figure out how to translate that into revenue, you don't deserve to be here.'

With that, Josh Pinkerton, the CEO and founder of NextLife, walks out of the conference room. NetMaster follows him. Slowly the people around the table start to get up to leave. 'I need to see all department heads,' Tom Jackson says. 'Downstairs in ten minutes. We need to map out a strategy.'

No one responds. I walk over to Tom and pat his shoulder. 'It'll be alright.'

He nods. 'It will be.' He doesn't sound convinced. 'Ten minutes? Downstairs?'

'I'll be there.'

I walk out of the conference room and head toward the elevator. As I pass the receptionist's desk I look at her. 'Louise,' I say, 'We lost another vase in there.'

CHAPTER FOUR

'Two vases?'

Yvette and I are sitting down at the edge of the harbor in Charlestown in the old Navy Yard, near where the USS *Constitution* is docked. The *Constitution* is the oldest warship still in commission, having been the pride of the fleet during the Civil War. She stands at her dock like a proud Brahmin looking down her sails with disdain upon the newer, flashier yachts that surround her. Yvette, who is in starve-mode, has a giant coffee on the bench next to her and a newspaper spread out on her lap.

'Two vases,' I confirm. 'One before the meeting, and one just before he walked out.'

'Shit!' she says. 'That's bad.'

I shrug. 'We'll get it figured out.'

She takes a long, scrutinizing look at me. 'You really don't care about the money, do you?'

I scoff. 'I'm as interested in a buck as anyone else.'

She shakes her head. 'No, you're not. You'd be happy with the money, but it's not what drives you. In fact, I sometimes think you're afraid of the money.'

'You think?' I consider it for a moment, wondering whether she's right. 'So, what drives me, then?'

'I don't know. I haven't figured that out, yet.'

'Fair enough. You've only known me for two decades. Give it time.'

She chokes out a laugh. It's a distinctively unladylike sound, but it's conspiratorial and sexy. Two middle-aged men jogging along the pier hear it and look at her, their glances lingering as they approach. She is *dressed for the heat*, as she likes to say, which is a polite way of saying she is wearing very little. An extremely short, light cotton sundress hangs lazily from her shoulders, draped over her bra-less chest, revealing the athletic body she is secretly proud of. The joggers are enjoying the view, and I think she appreciates their lascivious stares.

'Keep going, boys!' she calls to them as they pass. 'You've got a lot more running to do!'

I laugh as they move on. 'You're a hard woman.'

'I am. Speaking of that, don't even think about backing out tomorrow.' I say nothing. It's been on my mind all day. 'I'm serious,' she says. 'If I show up there and I'm alone, I'll kill you. Literally hunt you down and put a bullet in your head.'

'You don't own a gun.'

'No, but I could find some other creative ways to bump you off. Seriously, you've got to face this, one way or another.'

'I'm not sure why.' She glares at me until I crack. 'I'll be there.'

She goes back to her newspaper. There is something intoxicating about sitting in public with an attractive girl, even if she is only a friend. Every man who passes thinks you're having sex with her, and the envy radiates from them. It makes you feel powerful.

I lean back into the bench and sip my coffee, looking out at the Boston skyline. I sometimes feel as though I'm always looking at the city from afar – like I'm here, but I'm not really a part of it. As someone who grew up just outside of the city, I idealize Boston. I look at the crisp, clean lines of the buildings rising from the edge of the water and I wonder what it would be like to really belong in a place like that. Boston is for other people, I think. Better people.

'Holy shit!' Yvette exclaims, disturbing my idle self-doubt.

'What?'

'Look at this.'

She holds the paper up so that I can see the headline. '*Model Murdered*,' I read. There is a blurry newsprint photo of a young woman, and I squint to make out her features. I don't recognize her. She is attractive, but not my type. 'I don't get it,' I say.

'You don't get it?' Yvette grunts, turning the paper back around so that she can read the story aloud to me. 'Listen: "The body of Amanda Hicks, 26, a part-time model and waitress, was discovered yesterday morning in her West Roxbury apartment. The specific cause of death is unknown, but the police are treating the matter as a homicide. Ms Hicks' body was found by a neighbor bound to a chair, covered in feathers."'

I get it now. 'It's just like the GhostWalk you were telling me about the other day,' I say. The similarity is clear, but I reflexively dismiss any connection. 'It's just a coincidence.'

Yvette rolls her eyes and whaps me on the head with the newspaper. 'It can't be a coincidence!' she says. 'I mean, come on! Feathers and bondage? It's not like that's a common sexual theme.' She looks at the face in the paper for a long moment. 'Jesus, this girl even looks like the avatar in the fantasy. You think it could be *De Sade*?'

My mind rebels at the notion that someone could have used our technology to rehearse a murder that they then actually carried out. 'Like you said the other day, just because someone does something in NextLife doesn't mean they're gonna do it in the real world.'

'That's true,' she agrees. 'But it doesn't mean they're *not* gonna do it in the real world, either.' She chews a fingernail for a moment, staring out at the water. 'What do you think we should do?'

She's right that it's a remarkable coincidence. I feel slightly sick, though, at admitting the possibility that the murder is somehow connected to the LifeScene. 'We could tell someone,' I finally concede, my voice hollow and unconvinced.

'What, just call the cops and blurt it out?'

I shake my head. 'No one will ever pay attention, if we do it that way. They'll think we're cranks. Besides, I don't want to have to go into a lot of detail about all the research we're doing on our users. If that got out, it'd cause some real PR problems.'

'We have to do something! We're talking about a murder. You have a friend who's a cop, right? The guy who handled security for the last company party? What was his name? Paul – something . . . ?'

'Killkenny. Paul Killkenny.' I frown. Paul's a guy I knew growing up. One of those tough guys who liked to mix it up, and ultimately had to choose a side in the real-life game of cops and robbers. Now he's a homicide detective in the BPD.

He and I have stayed friends, and I've hooked him up with a few sweet gigs organizing outside security for a few company events. Triple-time. I might be able to talk to him and hint around the edges, at least get a take on how serious he thought it was. 'I'll think about it,' I say.

'Nick, *De Sade* has other LifeScenes where he's killed women,' she points out. 'You've seen some of them.'

I catch her meaning. If he's carried out one of them, there's no reason to think he wouldn't carry out others.

'I said, I'll think about it.'

'Think quickly.' She folds her newspaper, leaves it on the bench and stands up.

'Where are you going?'

'Back to my apartment.'

'You don't have to get pissed.'

She doesn't turn around as she walks away. 'You do what you think is right; and do it soon.' She pauses. 'Oh, and make sure you show up tomorrow. I'll be pissed if you wuss out.' She has a brilliant way of making me feel belittled when she wants to. It's a gift, really. Her certainty about what is right and what is wrong is rock-solid. *Often wrong, but never in doubt,* as she likes to say. I can usually ignore her little tantrums, but in this instance something nags at me.

'And what if I'm not there?' I yell out at her, trying to take back a little more control.

She looks at me; her eyes are lasers. 'You'll be there.' She turns and continues heading away.

'Shit!' I mutter to myself. I've been sitting here having such a good time, relaxing, enjoying being with an attractive friend on a warm day down by the water. Now I feel nothing but terrible. I stand up, thinking about going home, but sit down again. Ma is at home, and her coughing has been getting worse. I feel like I need a break.

I look down at the paper lying on the bench. The dead girl's face is staring up at me. It's a picture that must have been taken at a graduation or a prom, or some similar seminal event that evokes the promise of limitless possibilities. She is smiling like she's made a list of all the secrets she plans to ration out to boys over the course of a lifetime. I wonder how many she managed to share before the life went out of her. I think about the beautiful avatar from De Sade's fantasy in the white room. I can see her eyes in my mind, and remember the moment when she realizes that it's all going wrong. She's not real, I know; she's just a series of millions upon millions of electrical impulses sliding through silicone. And yet there is something in that look that feels so real. The fear in it. The understanding. There's nothing synthetic about that look.

I look down again at the girl who was killed. 'Damn!' I mutter. I pick up the newspaper and tuck it into my back pocket as I head up the hill, away from the water. Ma is waiting for me, I know. I can figure the rest of this crap out later.

CHAPTER FIVE

I said before that I'm not really afraid of anything. That's not exactly true. There is one thing I am afraid of: heights. Always have been. It's not really a problem for me; I stay away from balconies and ladders, and I've never had to travel, so planes have never been an issue. Cape Cod – that's about as much of the world as I've seen outside of the greater Boston area. I don't feel deprived. I know there's a whole world out there that I know nothing about, but that's fine with me. Charlestown is my world, and I don't need to fly to see any of it.

Others take a different view. I made the mistake of sharing my phobia one night with Yvette when she was in a meddlesome mood, and she immediately embarked on a mission to cure me. Most people, in approaching that sort of process, would start by taking me through a series of desensitization exercises. Perhaps start with a walk up a tall hill. Go to the roof of a high-rise and look out. Take a ride on a roller-coaster. There are an infinite number of places she could have started to get me used to the concepts of height and speed and falling that might – just might – have eased my tension about heights gradually.

That is not Yvette's way, of course. As a result, that Sunday I find myself bent over in a stripped-down tin can with wings, a helmet and goggles wrapped around my head, a parachute strapped to my back, my heart pounding so hard I can feel it in my teeth. The noise is so loud it may be the only thing that will cause me to jump.

Yvette is there, too, laughing with the skydiving instructor who spent the morning with us. She leans her head out the open door and looks down, and the sight of it makes me throw up a little in my mouth. 'Get back!' I scream.

She looks at the instructor and the two of them laugh. 'You couldn't be safer!' he screams to me.

'Than what?' I shout back.

Yvette shuffles over to me, takes my arm. 'I know you're freaking out,' she says. 'But we're going to do this.'

'Why?'

'Because the Nick I grew up with wasn't afraid of anything. He wasn't afraid of the other kids on the street, he wasn't afraid of getting into fights; hell, he wasn't even afraid of school – and that's what the rest of us were most scared of. He just went out and did what needed to be done.' I look down at her, and she locks eyes with me. It's odd; her eyes are generally deep pools of cynicism, but at that moment they seem warm and genuine. For just this moment I forget that I am 10,000 feet off the ground with a glorified bed sheet strapped to my back, about to step out of a nominally functioning airplane. She screams, 'I don't want to see you scared of anything, understand?'

I nod.

'Are you going to call your friend about the girl who was killed?' she goes on.

'I'm still thinking about it.'

'Like I said, you're the one who does what needs to be done, no matter what,' she says. 'Remember that, as you're thinking it over.'

I put an arm around her. 'I hate you, you know that?'

'Yeah, but you still can't live without me. I make your life too interesting.'

'We're coming up on the drop-zone!' our instructor yells. We move over to the open door. He looks at me. Hanging this close to the door, every word has to be screamed. 'You go first!' he hollers. 'Yvette will follow three seconds later, and I'll be right behind her. I'll catch up to her, and then we'll make it down to you! We have around forty seconds total before we have to pull the 'chutes, got it?' My head nods, but I don't know whether it's an acknowledgment of agreement or a terrified spasm. 'Okay!' He turns me toward the door and I hold on to the sides. The wind shear is so strong I can barely breathe. Our instructor yells from behind, 'One! Two! Three!'

I hold my breath and jump.

There is no way to adequately express what it feels like the first time you step out of an airplane. Imagine that you're sucking on a giant fire hose, and out of that hose is shot all of the most intense emotions you can comprehend: terror, exhilaration, regret, hope, joy. It is literally like drowning. It's hard to breathe; it's hard to think; it's hard to comprehend what's happening. I relax my legs and put my arms out to stabilize my body position against the fall, as I was taught in a morning's worth of lessons. And all the while the curve of the Earth flattens more and more as the ground rushes toward me with unrelenting speed. I assume I'm screaming, but it's hard to know because the roar of my body rushing through the atmosphere is so loud. My hand goes to my ripcord, just to make sure I can find it.

I feel a tug at my arm, and it freaks me out. I know that our instructor told me he and Yvette would catch up with me, but it just seems so incongruous for them to be here, now, as I hurtle toward the world. It feels like I should at least be left alone in my own little hell. But I look over and they are both there, smiling brightly and giving me the thumbs up. I give them my best Fonzie back, though it feels insincere. I tap my wrist and pantomime pulling the 'chute, but they both shake their heads, still smiling as though they have a secret they haven't shared with me yet.

'When?' I scream.

Yvette reaches out and takes my arm and pulls my falling body toward hers until our heads are right next to each other. 'Relax!' she calls to me. 'Enjoy the ride!'

A horrible thought occurs to me. 'We're not wearing parachutes, are we?'

Her smile remains.

'Oh God!' I scream. I start pulling desperately at the ripcord, but nothing happens. I start to hyperventilate. 'No! Oh, God, no!' I start to struggle against the fall, and my body loses its stability, tumbling and rolling, but Yvette and the instructor grab me and settle my position again. I still can't breathe and I close my eyes. Yvette puts a hand on my back. 'Look at me,' she calls. I open my eyes and look at her. 'There's nothing you can do!' she yells. 'It's out of your hands. Just enjoy the fall!' She nods below us at the ground coming up.

It is, I must admit, a beautiful scene. We took off from an airfield fifteen miles outside Boston, and below me the landscape is laid out like a suburban jigsaw. From my fall, I can see how it all fits together. I've never seen it from this angle. There is an intimacy with the land, looking at it from this vantage point, seeing it the way it once was in its natural state, and the way that the inhabitants have molded it, sculpted it to their needs. That intimacy is intensified by the fact that it is still rushing toward me, intent on crushing me.

That's when it happens. I become calm. I see what is happening for all that it is, and nothing more. As we get closer to the ground it feels as though we are speeding up, but I'm okay with that now. My phobia, it seems, is gone.

'You tricked me!' I yell to Yvette.

'You needed to be tricked!' she yells back.

'You're a terrible person, but I owe you one!'

'I'm collecting!'

'I'll call Killkenny tomorrow,' I scream. I see her nod in a self-satisfied, serious way.

I turn and focus on the spot where I will make impact. It's a field near a school, white lines painted on green grass. It is rushing up to greet me, to absorb me. 'I'm ready!' I call out in terror and delight. I can hear Yvette and the instructor screaming next to me, their high-spirited whoops of joy and release adding to the thrill. The last twenty seconds go by so quickly it is breathtaking, the ground overtakes my vision and perspective.

And then I hit.

It doesn't hurt, and yet it feels like I have been blown apart, my being shattered into a billion flashes of light that spread out through the universe like giant fireworks in slow motion. It lasts for only a split second, but it is beautiful.

Then the bits of light coalesce. The screen explodes in a flash that recedes into the center of the world until the monitor is black.

CHAPTER SIX

I've known Paul Killkenny for most of my life. We're the same age, and he grew up a block closer to the projects in Charlestown, in a three-bedroom shared house with five brothers and two sisters. His father was in the game, but at a much lower level than my father. Growing up, we were pitted against each other for no reason other than that we were a fair match at everything we did: stickball, street hockey, little league, brawling. I think the adults in our parents' circle viewed us as the two who would carry on the traditions of the old ways. I can only imagine the collective disappointment they felt when we both walked away.

My defection from the neighborhood was viewed, I think, with a sense of confused acceptance. Few from our group made it into the world of higher education, and so I was considered somewhat of an alien. Paul's departure, by contrast, was viewed as a betrayal. He not only failed to carry on the traditions of the gray-market world of hustlers where we grew up, but he became a cop. That might have been okay if he'd decided to walk a beat in Charlestown. We had plenty of insiders who did that: young men who understood the way the system worked, and who protected our turf from outside influences, while leaving the internal system intact. Paul, though, went big-time. He left Charlestown altogether and became a detective in Boston. That was viewed as 'going Hollywood' by the townies, and it was not appreciated. I'm one of the few from the old neighborhood that he keeps in touch with.

Paul agrees to meet me at a bar near Fenway Park at around five o'clock on Tuesday. It's a hole in the wall and it's empty when I arrive, except for two men in their sixties who sit motionless at the end of the bar, staring forward like zombies. I wonder, as I sit there waiting on Paul, whether they are wax statues – decorations to make the place feel more crowded. Only when one of them moves a hand to tip his whiskey into his mouth am I sure they're alive. Even still, he moves with a stiffness that makes it seem as though he might merely be mechanized at a rudimentary level.

Paul walks in ten minutes late, pauses at the door to let his eyes adjust to the dark. He's about my height, just under six feet, with thick black hair pulled back from an angular forehead. He's good-looking in a street way, with a square jaw and symmetrical features thrown off only by a nose that's been broken more than once. We often competed for girls when we were younger, and I still feel that rivalry.

He scans the room, seeming to scrutinize the place. When he sees me, he walks over, moving with a loose, confident gait. It's the same walk I've seen over the years from so many cops on the street. Something in the way they carry themselves lets people know that they not only enforce the law, but, when the spirit moves them, they are the law. They are, at some level, untouchable. It comes through clearly in their every move and every word. I suppose it's a fair trade for all the crap that cops have to put up with.

'Nick,' he says as he slides into the booth across from me. He nods at the bartender, who watched him enter. It seems they know each other. 'Scotch,' he says. The bartender moves quickly. Paul turns back to me.

'You on duty?' I ask, looking at the bartender as he pours the drink.

'You gonna report me?' He smiles, and it occurs to me that, friend or not, Killkenny would be a bad person to be on the wrong side of. 'How's it goin', Nick?'

I shrug. 'Can't complain. Business is good.'

'So I've seen.' I look at him with a raised eyebrow. 'I read the financial pages,' he says with a laugh. 'It's the new BPD. You can't just follow the Sox if you want to get ahead; you've got to be able to talk business and politics and art and shit.'

'Brave new world,' I say.

'Well, new, anyways.'

'You get back to the old neighborhood at all?'

He shakes his head. 'Not recently. I stopped by my folks' place back around Christmas, but you know my dad. He wasn't all that thrilled to see me, so I didn't stay long.'

'He always was a pisser.'

'Yeah. Still is.' Killkenny spits out a bitter laugh. 'He pulled a gun on me. You believe that shit?'

'Pulled a gun?'

'Yeah. He said he didn't want any cops in his house. I told him I was just going in to wish Ma a merry Christmas. He stood on that porch and pulled his piece out. Told me to get off his property.' He laughs again. 'I swear to God, I almost shot the old fucker. Hand to Christ.'

I laugh with him. 'Shit! What happened?'

'Ma came out screaming. He's waving his gun around, probably ten Jamesons into the evening; I'm reaching into my jacket for my piece, just to show I'm not afraid of him, like I was when I was a kid; neighbors are starting to come out to watch. It almost turned into an ugly scene.'

'Almost,' I say without irony.

'Ma starts beating on him, asking what the fuck he's doing, until he finally goes out the back, gets into his car to drive to O'Malley's.'

'Close call.'

'You don't know the half of it. I almost got into my car to pull him over for drunk driving, just to fuck with him. I was so pissed.' He smiles and sips the drink the bartender has placed in front of him. 'It was good to see Ma again, though. It'd been a while. And Theresa Pesci poked her head out on her porch to watch the whole scene. I got a smile from her.'

'Oh, yeah,' I say, closing my eyes. 'Theresa Pesci. God, she was hot back in the day. How's she looking now?'

'Not bad. She's got two kids, but I'd still throw a shot into her if I had the chance. She's still got those tits.' He takes another sip of his drink. 'So, how's your ma?'

I shake my head. 'She's not good.'

He's silent for a moment. 'Life's a cold bitch. You got a sense of timing?'

I shake my head. 'She's a tough old broad.'

'She is that,' Killkenny agrees. 'If anyone's gonna tangle with death and come out on top, my money's on her. If there's anything I can do . . . '

'Thanks, we're good.'

'So what's this all about?' he asks directly. 'You didn't ask to meet me to reminisce about our childhood. You got another security gig for me?'

I shake my head. 'Nothing in the immediate future, but I've got you on the list if anything comes up.'

'Do that,' he says. 'That party you put me in charge of last year got me the down-payment on my car. Dealing with that prick Net-Minder, or whatever-the-fuck his name is, was a pain in the ass, but it's hard to turn down that kind of money.'

'NetMaster,' I say.

'Right, him. A real asshole, he is. But like I say, money's money. So what's this about, then?'

I decide to put my toe in the water. 'You know that murder that happened the other day in West Roxbury?' I ask. He frowns as he looks at me. 'The one with the girl tied to the chair with the feathers?'

'Yeah,' Killkenny says noncommittally. 'One of the guys in my unit caught that.'

'I might have some information on it,' I say hesitantly. 'Off the record. I mean, it's possible, but I don't know for sure.' All of a sudden, I feel a little foolish. After all, what do I really know?

'What kind of information?'

'It's probably nothing, but there is a guy who goes on NextLife pretty regularly. You know how the site works?'

'A little,' he says. 'I'm not big into computers, but I get the idea. It's like all that fake fantasy shit, right?'

'Right. Well, this guy goes on all the time. He's someone we refer to as a High Use Member – we call them "Hummers".'

Killkenny smiles. 'Nice.'

'Anyway, this guy, this Hummer, he's got this one LifeScene he created where he's with this girl – a fake girl, an avatar he created – and he ties her up and teases her with these feathers.'

'And he lets people watch him?'

'Not really,' I say. This is where it's going to get a little dicey. I knew that going into the conversation. I don't want to say anything that's going to cause a problem for the company. 'It's a private LifeScene, so it's one that's just for him, but we do some research on how people use our system. It's to gather information to make the technology better, and offer more things that people would like. Things like that. It's all harmless.'

'And he knows you're there?'

'Probably not. But it's in our Terms of Use, so technically he's agreed to it.'

'Yeah, in tiny letters at the end of forty pages of legal bullshit,' Killkenny says skeptically.

'Legally binding bullshit,' I point out.

He raises his hands. 'Like I care? People who want to go online and do freaky shit should know that someone's watching, always. That's my view.'

'Yeah, but that's why this is sensitive. This is all allowed under our Terms of Use, but we still don't want people to focus on the fact that we're doing this. It would cause a major public-relations hassle.'

'Yeah, I get you,' Killkenny says. 'Still, it doesn't sound like much. I mean, feathers are a little different, but not unheard of. It's probably just a coincidence.'

'That's not it,' I say. 'He's got her tied to a chair, and he's whipping her and then using the feathers, on and off, and when he's done, he kills her.'

'Oh,' Killkenny says. He sips his drink contemplatively. 'Yeah, that's a little more interesting,' he says after a moment. He frowns and goes quiet again, considering the information. 'Look, it's still probably nothing. But I'm happy to pass the guy's name on to my guy, and he can check the guy out. That'd be the best thing, just to make sure.' He takes out a notebook and a pen and looks at me expectantly.

'I don't know his name,' I say.

'Can you get it?'

I shake my head. 'There's no way to find it out.' I can see he looks puzzled. 'The system's designed for complete anonymity; that's one of the things we offer.'

'I thought you could track anything through computers,' Killkenny says. 'You have to be able to find something, right?'

I shake my head again. 'When you log on, you are run through a series of dummy servers that hide the IP address. It uses algorithms that even we can't crack. That's the point. People need to know their identities are hidden, particularly with respect to the LifeScene part of the site. I mean, people are also using this for their email and their networking and their online shopping. Every aspect of their lives is in our system. If someone had the power to put all the pieces together, they could know literally everything about that person. And not just that person, but everyone they know. You could end up with a complete map of everyone on the system – what they buy, who they know, what they like – everything. Add in the LifeScenes, and you now have their deepest fantasies.'

Killkenny lets out a low whistle. 'That's a little frightening.'

'That's why the system is designed the way it is. No one – including the company – knows anything other than what a user wants to tell us about themselves, and there's no way to match that up with anything else. It's the safest way.'

'So what good is this information you've got about this guy's fantasy? We can't even use it to find him.'

I shrug. 'Maybe it's no good at all, but I felt like I should tell someone. Like you say, it may just be a coincidence.'

'Probably. Either way, without anything more, I'm not sure there's anything I can do. I'll mention it to my guy, and maybe if he gets desperate he'll follow up.'

'Thanks. I just wanted to make sure that someone had the information, in case it turns out to be important.'

He finishes his drink. I'd finished mine a few minutes before. I reach into my pocket to grab my wallet, but he stops me. 'Don't bother,' he says.

'I'll expense it,' I say. 'I asked you to come here. I'm not gonna let you pay.'

He shakes his head. 'You don't understand. I don't pay for drinks in here.' I look up at the bartender and notice that he's still casting furtive glances our way. Killkenny follows my gaze and nods at the bartender, who looks at the ground. 'I helped him out with something a couple years back,' Killkenny says. 'He won't let me pay now. It's like that at a bunch of places around here.'

I look at him and I can see that he's studying me, gauging my reaction. 'Must be nice,' I say.

'One of the few perks.' I put my wallet away and we start toward the door. 'By the way,' he says, 'how'd he do her?'

'What?'

'The guy on the computer with the feathers. You said he killed the girl, but you didn't say how? Did he shoot her? Stab her? What?'

I look at him. 'Why?'

'Professional curiosity.'

'I didn't see it; it was one of my employees watching. She said he wrapped her face in cellophane.' I am walking through the door, headed out onto the street. Truth be told, I'd like to get out of the conversation as quickly as possible. There's a part of me that is sorry I decided to bring this up.

I feel Killkenny's hand on my arm. He's strong. I'm not a small guy, but his fingers feel like a vice-grip. I turn and look at him, and I can see the mixture of surprise and excitement in his eyes.

'What the fuck did you say?'

'He put cellophane over her face,' I repeat. 'Suffocated her.'

He looks like a shark with the taste of fresh blood in the water. 'Are you serious?' he demands.

'Yeah. Why?' I ask the question, but I already know the answer just from the look on his face, and it makes me feel sick to my stomach. 'It's him,' I say. 'It's the same guy, isn't it?'

He holds my gaze for a moment. Then finally he says, 'I'll get back to you.'

CHAPTER SEVEN

'He's looking into it.'

Yvette and I are sitting in my office in the bunker in Cambridge. It's a strictly utilitarian space with a steel desk and three chairs. There is nothing on the walls; I've never viewed the place as an extension of my personality, the way some do. It simply provides the privacy that is occasionally required by the responsibilities of management. Yvette is hunched over, her elbows on her knees, looking like she might get sick. I don't blame her; I've been feeling the same since my conversation with Paul Killkenny.

'When is he going to get back to you?' she asks.

'He didn't say. It should be soon. It's a murder investigation, after all.'

She is staring at the floor. 'Do you think they'll want to talk to me?'

'I'd think so. I didn't GhostWalk the Scene with the feathers. I can tell them about the other scene, but that doesn't really help them with the murder of the girl.' She sighs heavily and sits up, rubbing her neck as though all her muscles have stiffened. 'What did you think was going to happen when I told him about this?' I ask her. 'You were the one who was so convinced these things were connected. Did you think they wouldn't look into it?'

'I don't know,' she says. 'I wasn't sure they'd take it seriously. I don't know that I was taking it seriously, but . . . shit!'

'Yeah, well, for the moment they appear to be taking it seriously. Are you ready for that?'

She takes a deep breath. 'Yeah, I guess I am.'

The beeper on my phone goes off, startling both of us. I take a look and see that it is the notification I set up to let me know when *De Sade* logs on to the system. I'm embarrassed. I set the notification because of the obsession I'd developed over the girl in the LifeScene, and I'm not sure how to explain this to Yvette.

'What is it?' she asks.

'It's him,' I say. She looks at me with an expression of confusion. '*De Sade*. I set an administrative alert so I'd know when he was getting on the site.'

She raises an eyebrow. 'You did?'

'Yeah, I figured it would make sense, if we were really interested in what was going on with the guy,' I lie.

'Oh.' I can't tell whether she's buying it or not. 'Okay. Well, let's see what he's up to.' I have a full sensory-unit station set up in my office, though I never use it. There's something that feels creepy and voyeuristic about trolling around in someone else's fantasies when you're in a private place. When I GhostWalk, I do it at a station out on the floor; it makes it feel more like legitimate business.

'You want me to GhostWalk his Scene? Now?'

'Either that or I can,' she says. 'Whichever. But if we're

really thinking that he's connected to a murder and we're gonna help the cops go after him, then I think we need to know as much as we can about him.' She pushes the sensory unit toward me, and I take it reluctantly.

I sit in the comfortable chair by the computer and slip the headset on. It covers my entire face and I can hear my own breathing – like Darth Vader. She hands me the gloves and I slip them on. 'Do you want anything else?' Yvette asks with false lasciviousness. I realize that there is a prototype 'personal stimulation' unit on a nearby desk. I've never used it myself, but I helped collect the research for the development.

'Thanks, I'm good,' I say. I can hear her grunt a nervous laugh and I'm glad I have the mask on so that she can't see the blood in my cheeks. I pull the keyboard onto my lap. The screen on the sensory unit is curved and provides three-dimensional feedback. At the moment a prompt hovers in front of my eyes. I type in my administrator's code and start a search for *De Sade*. It takes less than two seconds for the system to access his ongoing LifeScene. Once located, it is highlighted, and two prompts hover below it, one reading OBSERVE and the other reading INTERVENE. When development on the system began, there was consideration given to whether the company wanted the power to unilaterally join a member's LifeScene. We decided, though, that the practice would lead to too many questions, and members would inevitably learn that their fantasies were being observed. As a result, only GhostWalking – where the administrator is passive, and merely sees and feels what the member is feeling, without any control or possibility that the member will become aware

– is permitted. Most of the sensory units in the lab don't even have INTERVENE as an option.

I reach out with a finger and tap OBSERVE. Immediately the visual field begins to shimmer, like the scales of a fish on a sunny day. It sparkles and shines, and begins to take shape. I can feel the sensory pads in the gloves coming to life, and it feels a little like insects crawling over my skin. I begin to get that claustrophobic feeling of being trapped. And then . . .

I am standing in the hallway again. It is the same hallway I was in before. The white walls . . . the red door at the end. He is breathing hard, but this time I'm breathing harder. I feel like I'm going to be sick. The walls look like paper – as though I could push a finger through them with no effort at all. Just out of his line of sight I feel like there are demons from which he is averting his eyes. I want to turn to look, but I see only what he sees, and he won't look there. He is focused on the door at the end of the hall, and he is hurrying toward it. We are both sweating now and, when the door opens, I can see her. She is there, on the bed, exactly as she was before. She looks at him, and I feel like she sees me. Those eyes are as they were before, brilliant and burning and full of life. This time, though, the fear is there from the start. She moans, but now it seems a desperate charade.

As he moves toward her, I can hear the two of them breathing, but there is something else as well – something in a corner of the room where he refuses to look. It sounds like the whispering of a thousand ghouls, urging him on so softly that they can barely be heard. They are saying something, but I can't make out the words.

Now we are on top of her. We are touching her, and their breathing swallows the sounds from the rest of the room.

She is perfect. As my hands caress her with him, I can feel her beauty – her human beauty. There's something even more real about her now than before. I can tell that the avatar programming has been tweaked – improved in a way that is subtle, but central at the same time. I am looking into her eyes, and it is like she is looking through him to me. Her eyes don't move; they bore into me. He is thrusting inside of her, and she meets his rhythm as before, but there is something different this time. There is a part of her that isn't with him; there is a part of her that is with me. Behind me, the ghouls are audible again. They are hissing and spitting, their excitement approaching a crescendo as *De Sade* reaches the end. For a moment I think I can understand them. For just a moment it sounds as though they are saying, 'Help her!'

And as I look down at her, our hands are still on her breasts, her hands above her head. He is moving his fingers up her arm, and I know eventually they will come to rest on her throat. As he touches her, I see the tear forming. It starts at the corner of her eyes and gathers quickly, spilling over and down the side of her face. At that moment, I am convinced that she knows. Even before he has reached her throat, she knows what is coming. I think: *maybe not this time*, but I know I'm wrong. Slowly, surely, our hand moves down her arm to her jaw. I see her take a deep breath, almost as though she knows it's her last.

'No!' I scream. The sound echoes in my sensory unit, but goes unheard in the LifeScene. Our hands tighten on her throat, and I can feel him begin to spasm inside of her. She is looking at me, the tears rolling freely now.

'No!' I scream again. I flail my arms uselessly, as though there is something I can do. I scream out as the two of them climax and her eyes close – a wordless, guttural, primal scream of despair.

The sensory unit is ripped off my head and Yvette stands over me, looking down with genuine concern. I can feel myself shaking, and I am covered in sweat. I am breathing so fast it feels as though I've just run a marathon, and my heart is pounding in my ears.

'Jesus!' she says, her voice the breathless gasp of someone viewing a corpse for the first time. 'What the fuck happened in there?'

I search for the words to explain. I can't even understand it myself. The woman in the LifeScene is so real to me, so tender and perfect. How can I possibly make anyone comprehend, when it doesn't even make sense to me? 'We have to stop him,' I whisper.

'What?'

'We have to stop him,' I say again. 'He's still working on the programming. He won't be satisfied until they're real.'

CHAPTER EIGHT

Yvette and I are sitting in the police station for Division 1-A in Boston's Back Bay, in a barren, cement-walled room with a faux-wood laminate table and three plastic chairs that look like they were found at the edge of the highway. The cement is painted, I think, though any hint of what the original color was vanished years before. It's streaked with the sweat of an endless parade of nervous innocence and squirmy guilt. The place is fetid and pocked with mildew – the kind that cannot be cleaned.

I look at Yvette, and I can see that she's nervous. That's unusual for her. I can't remember ever seeing her scared before. She hides it well, of course, cracking a few quiet, inappropriate jokes, but I know her well enough to see the tension in her upper lip.

'They'll be back,' I say.

'I know,' she says. 'Nearest donut shop's three blocks, though. It could take them a while.' She forces a smile.

'They're taking it seriously. That's good.'

She shrugs. 'I guess that depends on your perspective. How

do you think they're going to handle this back at the office? You think they're gonna like this?'

'They'll like it better if we head it off before the public finds out. We leave it and it becomes a bigger problem, then we're all screwed. As long as we keep the company out of the public eye, it'll be fine. Besides, either way, people are in danger.'

There is a quick knock at the door and it opens before we can respond. Paul Killkenny walks in, followed by a short, round, balding man in his fifties with the look of someone who gave up caring about life before I was born. The bags under his eyes are dark and puffy and wet.

Killkenny is carrying a manila file and nods to us. 'Nick, Yvette, thanks for coming in. This is Detective Sergeant Tom Welker.' The older man nods at us, but does not offer a hand and moves no closer. 'He's in charge of the investigation into the West Roxbury murder, at least for the moment. I'd like you to tell him what you told me.'

Yvette regards them carefully. When she speaks, she is deliberate. 'We don't know anything for sure,' she says. 'We just figured we should talk to you. Y'know, just to be sure?'

Killkenny sits down across the table from us, puts the file on the table. 'I know, and we appreciate it. I wouldn't have called you in unless we thought there was a chance you could actually help. Why don't you tell the Detective Sergeant about the fantasy with the feathers.'

'Hold on,' I say. I'm determined to help them, but I don't want this going too far down the road without getting some assurances about where that road may take us. 'We've come forward voluntarily, but we need to know that our company is going to be protected.'

Killkenny has been focusing on Yvette, but now he turns to me. He holds my gaze for a moment, then smiles, shaking his head at me like I'm an idiot. 'What kind of assurances are you looking for, Nick?' he asks. 'This is a *murder investigation*.' He lets that phrase hang in the air for a moment. 'You understand that, right? A girl *was killed*. Now, do you want to help, or don't you?'

'We'd like to help,' I say. 'But I need to know that our names, and the identity of the company, will be left out of it. I don't think that's unreasonable.'

'You don't?' Killkenny sits there looking at me. He opens the file and puts three pictures on the table, face down. I'm staring at the backs of the pictures with dread, and I'm not even sure why. When I was young I was arrested several times for petty stuff – usually for things that others had done, and nothing that I was ever charged with, but I've had enough experience to recognize the stagecraft of a police investigation. I understand that Killkenny's goal is to keep me off-balance. It's an effective tactic.

He flips over the first picture and reveals the image of a young woman. She is covered with a sheet from just below the armpits, her eyes are closed and her blonde hair is spread out on a steel table. She would be beautiful were it not for the dark-blue stains around her lips and under her eyes.

'Her name was Amanda Hicks,' Killkenny says. 'She was a local girl, grew up in Marlboro. Good kid, from what we can tell. Worked as a part-time secretary and model, and she was trying to make it in the local acting scene. She'd done some small local roles and was thinking about moving to New York to give it a real try. That's not gonna happen now, you understand?'

'I'm sorry for her,' I say.

'That's mighty fuckin' white of you, Nick.' Killkenny looks at Yvette. 'From what Nick told me, I'm guessing she looks an awful lot like the girl who was in the snuff-scene you saw, right? She was found strapped to a chair, covered in feathers.'

I look over at Yvette. She is staring down hard at the picture, and while she's holding herself together, I can tell that she is horrified. The clarity of her memory is etched on her face. Killkenny sees it, too, I have no doubt.

'Four and a half years ago she told her friends she did a "modeling" job for a little company called NextLife. Got paid a thousand bucks. From what we can gather, it was her biggest modeling paycheck ever. No one ever saw any advertisements with her in them.'

Yvette and I are both staring at Killkenny now, not comprehending. He has us, I know, and there is nothing I can do about it. I have to know more; I have to understand.

He flips the next picture over. Another young woman stares up at us in the same pose, against a similar steel table. This one has darker hair and finer features. A deep-purple bruise on her neck runs around from just under the ears. There is a pattern to the bruise, diagonal lines through it. 'Her name was Janet Schmidt. College girl; played field hockey over at BC. Good student, very popular. She was found hanging in her apartment over by the college two months ago. She was wearing black hip-boots and a variety of restraints. The assumption was that she probably got mixed up in a BDSM scene that went wrong, and the others there just ran. You'd be amazed what college kids in the big city get themselves into these days. We've been working the case, running down the pervs in the local latex scene, but we've come up with nothing. Thing is, though, after I talked to Nick, I had them pull her financial records and go through them. You know what we found?' I have a bad feeling about what he's going to tell us. 'We found a thousand-dollar deposit from NextLife, right around the same time Amanda Hicks was doing her modeling for the company. We don't know for sure yet what the check was for.'

He lets that sink in for a moment, then flips over the last photograph. 'She was the first, as far as we can tell,' he says. The woman in the picture has deep bruises on the side of her face, and a bad cut on her chin. I have the impression that she was probably very attractive, but it's difficult to tell because it looks as though her skull has been caved in on one side, so her appearance has no symmetry to it. She reminds me of a Picasso painting of a beautiful woman. 'Patricia Carnes. She was killed more than a year ago. The violence here was so bad, we've always figured it was just a straightforward random act of sickness. We never had any leads; never had any suspects. Doc tells us she was raped twice. Once after she was already dead. You wanna guess what we found when we went back and looked in her bank account yesterday?'

I'm looking at pictures, my mind spinning. I'm still not sure what it all means.

'What are you saying?'

Killkenny leans back in his chair. 'We don't know at this point. All we can tell is that these three girls were all raped and killed, all three of them got paid the same amount of money around the same time by your company four and a half years back.'

'That could be a coincidence,' Yvette says.

Killkenny looks at Welker, who still has neither moved nor spoken. 'It's possible,' he says. 'But we're cops. We don't believe in coincidences. And we sure as shit don't believe in them when we're talking about a connection like this between three dead girls. Plus, you add in the similarities between the NextLife cyber-fantasy you saw . . . It's something we have to look into.'

'But what's the connection?' I ask.

Killkenny shakes his head. 'I have no idea. That's why we're looking for your help. We need to know exactly what these girls did for the company. We need to find out as much as we can about the person whose fantasy Yvette was watching. You need to help us put the pieces together to figure out what the hell is going on here.'

I'm looking at the pictures, thinking about what the girls must have looked like while they were alive, thinking about what they must have gone through when they died. I'm also thinking about the eyes of the girl in *De Sade*'s fantasy that I've walked twice, and the way the spark in her eyes went dead. 'If we help you with this, will you try to keep our involvement out of the papers? Keep the investigation quiet for now?'

Killkenny glares at me. 'We're not looking to jam you up with your company, Nick,' he says. 'We're just trying to figure out who killed these girls.'

'I need some assurance,' I say.

'I can't promise anything,' Killkenny says, 'But to the extent possible, we'll keep the investigation quiet. I'm going to be joining the investigation formally, so if you've got any concerns as we move forward, you can come to me.'

I look over at Yvette. She is still staring at the first picture, the one of the girl from the feather fantasy. She nods.

'Okay,' I say. 'We'll tell you what we know.'

CHAPTER NINE

Mine is the first generation raised online. I was six years old when Tim Berners-Lee created the World Wide Web, simplifying navigation on the growing but still largely underutilized and esoteric Internet. By the time I was sixteen the dot-com bubble was getting ready to pop, and the entire world was plugged in. I sometimes wonder whether the early innovators had any concept of the Pandora's Box they were opening when they set out to create our entirely new world. I suspect they viewed the free availability of information as only a good thing. And, indeed, it has brought much good with it. It has allowed for the education of millions upon millions of children who had previously been cut off from information and opportunity. It has facilitated the exchange of knowledge and research that has sped development of medicines and useful technology. It has provided an outlet for the free expression of ideas and dissent, and been a key ingredient in the overthrow of some of the worst dictatorships in history.

Every good must have its evil, though. Ease of access to information has also led to an explosion of new crime. With the push of a button, criminal organizations can transfer funds from their illicit activities to safe havens around the world, or steal someone's identity and confiscate their entire net worth, or wipe out businesses or even governments.

Technology has also weakened the tangible human connections that form the basis of societal cohesion. Those of us in the connected masses indulge in a depth of electronic navel-gazing and self-fascination that the world never before knew was possible. Actual experience no longer seems paramount; posting *evidence* of experience online for the world to see is what matters now. People these days upload the images of their exploits literally as they happen, without taking the time to fully enjoy the moment. It's as though they can't quite distinguish between what happens online and what happens in the real world. It seems unlikely that the inventors of these technologies foresaw these consequences of their innovations.

And there is no chance that those early pioneers could have anticipated the economic turmoil their creations would bring. In the second half of my short life I've seen the rise and fall of business empires that, in times past, would have taken decades to build, and longer to crumble. It was only a few years ago that we all believed AOL would never be challenged as the dominant player on the Internet, and MySpace was the definitive social networking platform. Companies like Pets.com, which at one point seemed to have created the definitive platforms in their respective spaces, are now distant memories. Today fortunes are still willed into existence overnight, and disappear with as little effort or warning.

No one understands this better than Josh Pinkerton, the founder of NextLife. At thirty-nine, he is a veteran of the Internet business battlefield. NextLife is his third company. He started the first – Boats.com – in early 2000, when he was in his mid-twenties and angel financiers were desperate to shower millions upon every entrepreneur with a domain name and a half-baked business plan. He raised ten million dollars in his first round of financing; twenty in his second. It was all gone within six months, washed away along with more than six trillion dollars in investments in similar start-ups when the bubble burst. Pinkerton went from being a pauper to a millionaire and back to a pauper in a matter of weeks, and the experience taught him to make sure that, no matter what happened to any company he was involved with, his financial position would be protected.

He applied that lesson to his second start-up, which sustained its success for long enough that Pinkerton was able to pull three-quarters of his equity out of it before it crashed. It was a company called Adspace, and it promised to revolutionize the manner in which Internet companies would be able to track and target advertising. At the time it was acquired by Google in 2006 industry insiders predicted that the technology it had developed would be the answer to the prayers of website developers and CEOs from Silicon Valley to Boston's Route 128 corridor. The predictions were overblown, but the technology did help Google begin to develop strategies that would result in a moderate advertising profit. In exchange, Pinkerton walked away with sixty million dollars in cash and Google stock.

He was happy . . . for about a month. But he quickly discovered that while sixty million dollars might make him comfortable, it would never make him a player. Not a *real* player. Not the kind of player who could grant or crush dreams with a smile or a frown. He found that he was unsatisfied with the metaphorical pat on the head the real deal-makers gave him, and so he set out to create a company that would change the rules; something that would make people gape in wonder, and would make him a legend with resources beyond those ever contemplated by a single individual.

NextLife is his chance of fulfilling that goal. It's widely recognized as a company of breadth and vision, which will either succeed in changing the way everything online works or will lie upon the scrapheap of the Internet junkyard – the largest wreck in the short but spectacular history of Internet failures.

I know this. I understand the pressure Pinkerton has put on himself – and that he therefore places on others. And so I am also fully aware of the wrath that my cooperation with the police will bring forth. It's not that Pinkerton is a bad guy *per se*. It's just that he's so singularly focused on NextLife's success that he regards anything which threatens that success as anathema. No, more than that: he views any such threat as an enemy . . . a living, breathing foe to be vanquished at all cost. I get this, and so I am careful when I approach him to explain that the threat is the fact that the murders may be connected to the company, not the fact that the police have become aware of the possible connection. I also stress that I am friends with one of the detectives who will be coordinating with the company. I think this will mitigate the concerns he'll have. I am wrong, of course.

I'm in his office, a 1,000-square-foot palace perched on the top floor of the NextLife building, on the southeast corner. I'm standing in front of his desk. NetMaster, Pinkerton's gargantuan head of security, is standing to my right, just slightly behind me, as if he's there to prevent me from running. The views, like those in the conference room a floor below, are spectacular, but one hardly notices them. The room itself is so overwhelming in its eclectic ostentation that even with the floor-to-ceiling windows, anything beyond the boundaries of Pinkerton's base of operations seemingly ceases to exist. It's like the decorator was given an unlimited amount of money and instructed to satisfy equally both a well-heeled captain of industry and a nine-year-old boy with ADD and a twisted sense of humor. Modern art, loosely representational in style, with bold strokes of outrageous color covers one wall. They are expensive works – I recognize at least one Picasso in the center – and they assault the senses with their contrasting interpretations of the human form. It's like a ten-million-dollar collage made up of the fractured dreams of a dozen disturbed geniuses.

There is a bar along the second wall. Not the heavy oak kind one might expect to find in the office of an indulgent CEO's office, but an Art Deco stainless-steel version of a 1950s soda fountain. The furniture throughout most of the space is a mix of 1960s high-end design – where function has been sacrificed entirely to form, with low-slung chairs that force the spine into an uncomfortably prone position and sofas with no backs. They are placed in a deliberately chaotic arrangement, all facing the centerpiece of the room: a gigantic crystal desk angled in front of the corner where the two giant walls of glass meet, looking out and down upon Boston's skyline.

The desk is magnificent and bizarre and alarming. It has the general design of what one might expect in a desk – drawers, a writing surface, places for pens and papers and personal items, both trivial and precious – but it is entirely transparent. It looks as though it might have been carved from a single block of perfect crystal, and there is no way to tell how the drawers and working parts came together in a way to make it functional. Pinkerton keeps nothing in the drawers and so, standing before him, it's like he is some sort of magic force – some deity hovering, suspended between a world that's real and one that's nothing more than a figment of his own imagination. I confess that I have always admired the impact the office has on most people, and the forethought it must have taken to put all of it together. I can also say, truthfully, that I have never found it particularly intimidating myself. I think that goes back to where I grew up. In Charlestown the guys with real power – the guys we knew we had to be worried about – didn't need illusions to make their point. You just knew not to fuck with them from the way they looked, and the way they stood and made you feel just being around them. Pinkerton never really had that, and so I'm not intimidated by him. The worst he can do to me is fire me, and I feel secure enough now to believe that I'll find another job with medical benefits for Ma.

Still, that doesn't mean I'm thrilled that I have to have this conversation, particularly with NetMaster standing there behind me. I haven't been around him enough to know how full of crap he is, but his mere size is intimidating.

I talk slowly and clearly to Pinkerton, laying out exactly what the police are looking for. I explain that they've agreed to keep the company's involvement with the investigation out of the press, and to keep a low profile, so that there is no damage done to NextLife's reputation. Pinkerton is quiet as I talk, and he lets me get the whole story out. Part of the reason he has been so successful in business is because he has always been able to keep his thoughts to himself. He's impossible to read.

'What assurances do we have that the company's name will be kept out of it?' he asks.

NetMaster gives a deep snort. 'We have none, that is clear,' he says. He reaches out and pushes me hard in the shoulder. His hand feels like a Volkswagen.

I turn and look at him. 'Don't ever fuckin' touch me again,' I say. He smiles back at me, and I can see three gold teeth. It's the first time I've ever seen him smile, and now I can understand why; it's not an attractive sight. My attention goes back to Pinkerton. 'I know one of the detectives who's working on the case,' I say. 'He's a straight shooter. He's done some security work for us before.'

'What's his name?' Pinkerton demands.

'Killkenny.'

Pinkerton looks again at NetMaster, who nods. 'He was assigned to the million-user party we had last year. He was in charge of the doors.'

'Right,' I say. 'So he's not antagonistic to the company, and he said he's going to try to keep the company's name out—'

'*Try* . . . ?' Pinkerton's stare intensifies as he cuts me off. 'He's going to *try* to keep our involvement in the investigation out of it?'

As Pinkerton is talking, NetMaster reaches out and pushes me again. I whirl on him quickly, swinging my elbow with as much force as I can, landing it directly in his solar plexus. He makes a noise that is somewhere between a pig-squeal and a grunt and doubles over, gasping for breath. I stand over him with a fist cocked. 'I told you not to touch me.' He's looking up at me with hatred in his eyes, still unable to stand. 'We done here?' I ask.

There is silence for a moment, and then Pinkerton says, 'You're both done.' NetMaster looks angrily at his boss, but Pinkerton waves him off. 'We have more important things to deal with,' he says. 'Tell me about this policeman.'

'He has no reason to jam us up,' I say.

'I find that so reassuring.' Sarcasm drips from his lips as he leans forward, puts his elbows on his invisible desk, folds his hands together. 'You understand the danger, don't you?'

'Yeah,' I say. 'If someone's using the LifeScenes platform to practice murder, it's going to look pretty bad for the company.'

NetMaster grunts as he finally makes it to his feet. 'He understands nothing.'

Pinkerton shakes his head. 'NetMaster is right. You're talking about a minor risk. When people found out that a young man had used Craig's List in Boston to arrange meetings with hookers and then murder them, traffic on the site went up, not down. We have a population in this country that is obsessed by sex and titillated by violence. You put the two of them together – it's almost irresistible. I'm not worried about people finding out about that. The curiosity factor alone will drive up our users.'

'What are you worried about, then?'

'The real danger is that it will appear to our users that we are helping the police.'

I'm not sure how to respond to this. 'Helping the police to catch a murderer . . . '

'That's not how people will see it. They will see it as us helping the police to identify one of *them*. One of our users.'

'But under the circumstances—'

'There are no circumstances where it is not a betrayal of what we promise our users.' I'm staring at him, amazed at what he is saying. 'Don't get me wrong: if you were to poll them and ask whether we were doing a good thing, most of them would say "yes". But that wouldn't change the fact that they would cease using the site.' I blink as I consider this, and he sighs heavily, as though forced to teach a slow child basic math. 'Nick, people come to NextLife to explore those parts of themselves they are ashamed of; those parts they are afraid of even. Oh, they use the social networking tools – the email, the chats, the *respectable* parts of the site, too. They use our online shopping functionality to buy Mother's Day flowers and birthday presents for Grandma. But the real reason people are coming to us instead of the other sites that provide those same options is because we have the LifeScenes as well. They want the chance to be *dark*, and to be that way in safety and privacy. And for people to feel comfortable creating LifeScenes, they need to know that no one is ever going to know what they are doing. Even more important, they need to know that no one will ever be able to know their identity and link that identity to all of those things they are ashamed of. If they think there is any chance that the identity shield can be broken, they will stay away. They will go back to Google and Facebook and all the others. Do you understand that?'

'I understand what you're saying. I'm just not sure I agree.'

'One of the reasons the algorithms that protect the identities of our users are unbreakable is because I knew that otherwise there would always be a temptation to put the information together. It could be for good purposes – as in this case, to catch a murderer; or for bad purposes – for blackmail, or for identity theft. By making it impossible, I took those temptations away.'

'So it shouldn't be a problem,' I point out. 'If the algorithms are really unbreakable, cooperating with the police won't actually reveal anything, and no one can blame us for trying.'

'That would be true if reality were more important than perception. If there's one thing we have definitively learned in this business, it's that reality is no longer king. If people believe that we are cooperating with the police, even in the name of a good cause, this company will crumble.'

'It will destroy us,' NetMaster says in a low, menacing tone. 'All of us.' It feels as though he is getting closer to me again, leaning in toward my chair. I can almost feel him breathing on me. I clench my fists, readying for another confrontation, but Pinkerton waves a hand at him, and he eases off.

'So, what do you want me to do?' I ask. 'Do you want me to say that we won't cooperate with the investigation? Stop talking to the police?'

'You should never have gone to the police in the first place,' NetMaster growls.

'I think Nick understands that now,' Pinkerton says. 'But we are past that point. Now that we are here, we cannot refuse to cooperate. At least not overtly. But we must make sure that, as the investigation progresses, we are not violating the fundamental promise of privacy we have made to our users. Do you understand, Nick?'

I do, but I don't like it. 'Yeah, I understand' is all I say.

'Good. Make sure that you keep NetMaster in the loop. As head of security, he must know everything that is happening. You two seem as though you'll work well together.' Pinkerton gives an ironic smile.

I look up at NetMaster, and he is glaring down at me. 'Yeah,' I say. 'I got it.'

I start walking to the door and Pinkerton calls after me, 'Nick!' I turn to look at him. 'This is your home, Nick,' he says. 'I took you in because Tom said you were one of the good ones. I trusted him, and I've trusted you.'

'I appreciate that,' I say.

'Do you?' He stands and turns his back to me, looking out the windows toward Boston. 'I guess now we'll see if that's really true.'

CHAPTER TEN

'So, explain to me how this works.'

Paul Killkenny is sitting in the sensory chair in my office, looking at the computer in front of him with suspicion. Yvette and I are on either side of him, and we can both tell that he has had relatively little experience with computers. I shoot her a look and she shrugs her shoulders. When he arrived I asked how he wanted to proceed, and he said that before he got into the investigation itself, he needed to have an understanding of how the technology functions, at least at the most basic level.

'Okay,' I say. 'This is our home page. You know what a website is, right?'

'Fuck off.'

'Good. A user types in our URL and then enters their user information. I take it you're not a member yet?'

He looks up sideways at me. 'Good guess.'

'Alright, so you're a new user and you have to create a profile.' I take the keyboard from him and begin to fly through the prompts, putting in Killkenny's name and walking him through each of the steps in the process – address, birth date, phone numbers, et cetera. When I ask him for his credit-card number, he pauses.

'I thought this was free.'

'Much of what we provide is free,' I say. 'But we have shopping sites where third parties are selling their goods. We always want to make sure that anything anyone does on our site that costs money is tied back to a particular credit card. That way, we don't have to get involved in disputes. It's easier if the card information is there to begin with.'

'What if I don't want to put in a credit card?'

'You can click here,' I point to a box below the prompt, where it says: *I do not want to use any pay services*. 'A lot of first-time users go for that option, but we've found that most of our customers ultimately put in a credit card. There's so much more that you can do on the site, it just makes sense.' I complete the profile information and press enter, and the member home page comes up. 'This is what you see if you have a normal computer screen, and you are just using that to log on. As you can see here, we've segmented the site into different areas. You have your email, your social networking – most people tie these together, though you don't need to. You have your interest rooms, where people can chat about topics or issues they have in common; you have your shopping sites; you have your gaming area. These are just the top-level site sections. As you dig down, you'll find that the site has just about everything anyone could want as far as traditional web-services go.'

'But you also have these LifeSpots,' Killkenny says.

'LifeScenes,' I correct him. 'Yeah, that's right. That's what sets us apart from other Internet providers.'

'How do I get in there?'

I pick up the sensory unit sitting on the small table by the chair. 'First, you put this on.'

Killkenny looks at the unit with what seems like disgust. 'What the fuck's that?' he demands.

'This is cutting-edge,' I say, holding it up. It looks a little like a thin, space-age bicycle helmet with a dark visor that protrudes two inches from the forehead and comes down to just above the upper lip. On the sides there are comfortable headphones that fit snugly over the ears. 'It's one of our latest, top-of-the-line sensory units. Try it on.'

He takes it from my hands and examines it the way I imagine he might scrutinize a piece of evidence from a crime scene. He slips it over his head reluctantly, and adjusts it until he looks as comfortable as I suspect he's going to be. I hand him a sensory glove and he pulls it on up to his elbow.

'What now?' he says with exaggerated volume that tells me his earphones are on securely. I can still see what is on the computer screen, and I use the mouse to tab onto the spot on the user bar that reads 'Three-D Experience!'

The reaction is instantaneous. Killkenny slides back in the seat, as though he's ducking from something. 'Holy shit!' he exclaims.

'It's a little startling the first time,' I say, recalling the first time I put on a sensory unit. 'The visor generates the image you're seeing, and the optics give a full sense of three-dimensions, even for the home page. Now, you can use your forefinger in the glove to control where you want to go, and you'll have the full experience wherever you go on the site. If you're shopping, many of the retailers we work with have developed fully integrated marketing materials that will allow you to see the products they are selling in 3-D, often with realistic video action. If you are shopping for shoes, you can pick the image up and examine it as if you were actually in the store. If you're a woman and you are shopping for a dress, you can not only see the dress, but you can access a 3-D video where you are sitting by the side of the catwalk as a model walks by wearing the dress, so you can see how it moves. If you're chatting with someone else who is also wearing a unit, you'll be talking to them as though they are directly in front of you, with video and audio that are so clear you will forget that they may be halfway across the country or the world.'

Killkenny is sitting still now, and I can tell that he is settling in, beginning to appreciate the quantum leap forward that NextLife technology represents. 'This will change the way people use the Internet,' he says.

'It will change the way people live their entire lives,' Yvette responds.

Killkenny, who has been flicking through the home-page menu with his finger, goes still for a moment as he considers that. 'It will,' he agrees at last. 'So how do I get into these LifeScenes?'

'Do you see the bright silver orb up to the right that says IMAGINE?'

'I see it.'

'Touch it.'

His hand goes up and to the right and he reaches out into thin air, the angle of his head following the slow movement of his arm. 'Whoa!' he says quietly.

'Pretty cool, isn't it? This is the promo that gives you an

idea of what's possible In-World.' I helped to design the intro-ductory segment of the LifeScenes site, and I'm proud of it. It puts you in clips from some of the more exciting LifeScenes that the developers at the company have created. Things like being on an actual moonwalk; being at the top of Mount Everest; deep-sea diving; being behind the wheel of a racecar. It gives a decent sense of what's possible. Of course there are images of attractive men and women smiling at you interspersed as well. It lasts around a minute, and Killkenny sits immobilized as he watches it. I can tell he's blown away.

'So, what now?' he asks.

'Because you're a new user, first you have to create your avatar.'

'How do I do that?'

'Start with the body type; that's the least complicated part. If you tap on the "create" menu and select "avatar", you start by selecting "male". Then click on the "body type" and you'll see there are hundreds of options. You can be anything from a bodybuilder to Laurel to Hardy. You can have a hairy chest or be bare. You can even modify the body type from there, once you make your selection. That takes a little time, though. Just select "athletic"; that's our most popular body type.' Killkenny follows my instruction.

'What now?'

'Now you need to choose a head.'

'Choose a head?'

'Yeah. Your face, hair, et cetera. The easiest way to do it is simply to choose the "me" option.'

'What's that?'

'That will use the images of you generated by the camera

either in the screen or in the sensory unit to map your face and head and create an avatar that looks like you. It's quick and easy.'

'Is it what most people do?'

'Many, but I don't know that I'd say most. A lot of people use the LifeScenes function to get away from themselves. Some people don't like the way they look, or don't want to be recognized online, so they create avatars for how they *want* to look, or how they *want* to be perceived, rather than how they actually look.'

'How do they do that?'

'Go to the headshot section and choose the menu. You'll see a whole catalogue of choices – again, hundreds of them. This is why it takes more time to create a new identity; you are literally designing a new face and head. You can mix-and-match eyes, noses, chins, cheekbones, hairstyle, the whole shooting match. There are some people who can take days designing who it is they want to be In-World. It's amazing, really.'

'I just want to get on the system,' Killkenny says.

'So, choose the "me" option. You'll have your own face in around thirty seconds.'

Killkenny taps the air with his gloved hand and there is a flash from within the sensory unit. A moment later there is a beep and the screen reads, 'You are ready!'

'I don't get it,' he says. 'I don't see me.'

'Of course not,' I say. 'You *are* you. What you chose is what other people see. You're in that face looking out. When you walk around in the real world, do you see your own face unless you're looking in the mirror?'

'No,' he admits.

'The whole point to this is that it is as close to a real-life experience as you can come. You've got an avatar that looks like you and has the fairly normal-athletic body type you've chosen. Now you just need to step into a LifeScene.'

'How do I do that?'

'There are a few different ways. The simplest is to choose one of the preset LifeScenes that are built into the system. We have thousands that range from pure adrenaline to purely social. Then we have tools that let you choose a fairly standard LifeScene and modify it, within limits, to your particular tastes. And finally, for those people who are proficient with a computer, you could create your own from scratch, using some fairly malleable templates. We have some people who have come up with some of the most amazing stuff you could ever imagine.'

'I'm sure.' There is a hint of judgment in his voice.

'Why don't you just choose one of the options off the main menu?' I tap a few times on the keyboard that is attached to the sensory unit and I can see the menu that appears on the screen, so I know what he is looking at. I watch as he lifts his hand and air-fingers through the menu, browsing. I'm curious what a man like him will choose.

Yvette tugs at my elbow. 'Ten bucks says he chooses Strip Club,' she whispers. I reach out and shake her hand to seal the bet. There are several hundred options on the main menu listed alphabetically, and I'm not convinced he's even going to get to S. I'm watching as the standard LifeScenes pass by. Most on the main menu are of the family-friendly variety. The really hardcore options that so many of our users seem to favor have to be searched for. They are usually two levels down on the menu, so we know that the people who get there are really interested in them. We have never been looking to entice people into the adult sections; it's just that's what so many people are looking for. It often makes me wonder about the true nature of the human race.

Killkenny is through P on the menu. He's passed favorites from 'Amazon Zipline' to 'Prehistoric Africa'. He's paused a few times, but just for a moment. It's possible that he's flipping through the menu to see all the options before going back to choose one. That's what I did the first time around. I went through all the options that were available at the time – there were considerably fewer back then, when we were still in Beta – and then I went back and chose 'Grand Canyon Excursion'. I'm still not sure why, other than it seemed the most foreign option to a kid who grew up on the street of Charlestown. I'd never been anywhere out of the area, and the pictures I'd seen of the American southwest had always fascinated me. The place seemed further away from where I was from than the moon. And I'll say that the hour I spent during that first LifeScene hooked me. I genuinely felt like I'd been out there, and it was all so beautiful. It took some time before I got my head around the fact that none of it was real.

As he scrolls to the end of S, Killkenny's fingers slow down. 'Strip Club' is one of the options right in the middle of the screen. 'No,' I whisper. I hate it when Yvette is right about something like this, and I know I'll hear about it forever.

His finger hovers for a moment, and I think he's going to move on. I am just starting to breathe a sigh of relief when he reaches out and taps his choice.

'Strip Club,' I say quietly to Yvette.

'You're all the same,' Yvette chuckles.

'You're painting with a pretty broad brush, don't you think?'

'My brush isn't broad; men are narrow.'

'Touché.' I look down at Killkenny sitting in the seat. It appears that he's settled in and his attention is rapt. 'I'm not sure I can watch this,' I say to Yvette. 'You want to grab a cup of coffee?'

'Sure. Twenty bucks'll buy a couple high-end lattes.'

I lean in toward Killkenny and speak loudly enough for him to hear through the headphones and the din of the virtual strip club he has entered. 'We're grabbing coffee. We'll be back.'

'Okay,' he calls back. 'This is remarkable!'

I stand and look at Yvette. 'Like I said,' she shrugs. 'You people aren't all that complicated.'

'Hopefully that'll make it easier to catch *De Sade*,' I point out.

'I doubt it,' she says. 'Every guy has something in him that's only a few ticks off *De Sade*. He could be anyone.'

'You think?'

'Trust me, I've GhostWalked enough male fantasies to know.'

She and I head out to get some coffee. As we walk in silence, I wonder if she's right.

CHAPTER ELEVEN

'It's impressive.'

We're back in my office, sitting around a conference table that's chipped and stained. It's the closest thing to a desk that I have in the room. The evening has progressed to the point where the commuter traffic outside has died down, and the foot traffic of the neighborhood, which crawls with college kids and locals even on weeknights, is picking up. Yvette and I are sipping our coffees; we brought one back for Killkenny, too, but he hasn't touched it. I can't tell whether he doesn't drink coffee or whether he is simply too overwhelmed by his first NextLife experience to take further stimulation.

'We have some impressive people working at the company who've developed the technology.'

'Clearly.' He looks at the coffee, but doesn't reach for it. 'And this guy – this *De Sade* – he created his own LifeScene involving the girl with the feathers?'

I nod.

'So, how does that work?'

'It's a little like what you just did; it's just more sophisti-cated. NextLife gives the user a huge amount of freedom in constructing their own LifeScenes. You're basically limited only by your technical ability. Take the strip-club LifeScene you chose from the basic template options: that's a fully realized LifeScene that anyone can step into. It's sort of the "beginner" level. Even with that, though, you have the option of making things brighter or darker, increasing or decreasing the volume – simple options that you can exercise. At the next level down, you could take the scene and change it in more fundamental ways. You could create your own dancers from the avatar options library; you could set the place in a different city; you could add a casino. As you break down the elements of a LifeScene further and further, you get to the point where the user is literally in control of everything.'

'So *De Sade* uses the design tools in the system to create these LifeScenes where he kills the girls he creates. Can't we just look up who he is on the system?'

I shake my head. 'The system isn't designed in that way. One of the things that we promise our users is complete anonymity – particularly when it comes to the LifeScenes. Without that assurance, no one would use the site.'

'How do you provide that anonymity?'

'It's complicated. When you sign up, you give your name and basic information, including credit-card information if you are going to use any of the pay services. At that point, you're assigned an internal identifier by the system, which is a series of letters and numbers that only the computer can recognize. That identifier changes every ten minutes, and the system overwrites the previous identifier. The system keeps track of each user's activities by category, not by specific action – so it can tell that you've used email, or that you have Skyped or been in a LifeScene, but because the identifier for your actions is overwritten, the system has no record of what you specifically did on the site. This provides a much higher level of security and anonymity than on a normal site.'

'How so?' Killkenny asks.

'Take a normal site, like Google or Yahoo. Say you use their email system, and you delete an email. That email is never really deleted. It can almost always be found in the system and identified with you. Most people don't really understand that. On our system, the email technically still exists – because data is almost never fully destroyed – but because of our encryption and the shifting identifiers, it can never be traced back to you.'

'How about if someone hacks into the system to crack the algorithm?'

I shake my head. 'Not possible.'

Killkenny mulls this over for a moment. 'Is there any way to trace *De Sade* by the LifeScenes themselves? Can you search for elements in the LifeScenes – feathers, for example – that would lead us back to him?'

'No,' Yvette answers.

'How can you be sure? Have you tried it?'

'It doesn't work that way. When someone creates a LifeScene, it doesn't exist on our servers – it's not stored here. The servers make the tools and the software available, but the data for a user's specific LifeScene actually resides on their own computer server. So even if we had things to search for, there's nothing on our servers to search. The only time the LifeScene is accessible by us is when the user is actually in it. The LifeScene is inoperable without interacting with the NextLife software.'

'But you can access it when he's actually in a scene?'

'We can GhostWalk through the interface with our system, but we can't access the code for the individual's LifeScene,' I say.

'Does he know you're watching him?'

Yvette and I look at each other. The tracking that we do is not only against our users' expectations, but there are also questions about the legality of the practice. 'He doesn't,' I admit.

'Can you track the signal back to him when he's on?'

'No,' I say.

'Why not?'

'The system is designed to obscure the IP address of our users.'

'I don't understand.'

'Every computer that connects to the Internet has an IP address and a computer identifier that is used to find it. When you "access" a website, what you are really doing is sending a request from one computer to another to send back the information on the webpage you're trying to access. In order for the information that's sent back to reach your computer, there needs to be identifying information. That's true whether it's a laptop or a smartphone or whatever. Our servers are set up so that the signals are routed through several dummy sites that obscure the IP address, so it can't be identified once the data is sent.'

'Yeah, but those are the company's servers, so they could reprogram them to identify the IP address if you wanted to, right?' His cop eyes bore into me. We're in a basement, and I have no windows in my office, so the place is musty and getting hot. I'm sweating a little, and I feel a bit uncomfortable.

'It wouldn't be possible without configuring the entire system for everyone.'

'But you could still do it.' It's like he doesn't need to blink. 'These are multiple murders we're talking about.'

'The company wouldn't put our users in that sort of a situation,' I say. It sounds a little weak to me, as the words come out, but it's the truth.

'Three girls are dead,' Killkenny says, as though I need to be reminded. 'You don't think your users can live with that sort of "situation" so that no one else dies?'

'It would disable the entire system,' I point out.

'I can't believe—' Killkenny's voice is rising, but Yvette cuts him off.

'Detective, even if we could reconfigure the system internally, it wouldn't help. Anyone with the kind of computer skills this guy has is already routing his signal through blind servers, before anything even gets here. For five dollars a month you can sign up for access through a Russian Internet service that will wipe the signal clean, and there's no way to trace that.' Killkenny stares at her now, but she isn't sweating. 'There must be another way,' she says.

We sit in silence for a few moments. 'Maybe we can start with the girls,' Killkenny says at last.

'What do you mean?'

'How does someone create one of these avatars – like if I wanted to create a new stripper, and I had a particular person I wanted it to look like, how would I do it?'

'You'd have to start with one of our templates. You'd find the one that looks closest to the person you're thinking of, and then you'd adjust it. I assume that's what he did – he designed avatars to look like the girls he wanted to kill, and then used those for practice.'

'Where do the templates come from?'

'We have a library of several hundred looks that people may want.'

'No, I mean how were the templates created?'

'I don't know,' I answer honestly. 'I wasn't involved in that process. I assume they used models.' As I say the words, their implication hits me. 'They used models,' I say again.

Killkenny is nodding. 'Amanda Hicks was a part-time model. Four and a half years ago she did a modeling job for NextLife. We found deposits from NextLife in the bank accounts for the other two girls right around the same time.'

'They were models who were used to create the templates,' Yvette says, grasping Killkenny's point.

'He doesn't create avatars to look like girls he wants to kill,' Killkenny says. 'He kills the avatar girls in the template library, and then goes out and finds the girls they're based on in the real world.'

'But how would he find them?' Even as I ask the question, I know the answer.

'He would have to have access to the company records at NextLife,' Yvette says quietly.

Killkenny is nodding. 'Yeah, he would.'

CHAPTER TWELVE

It's late. The records for the models who were used to create the templates for the NextLife avatars wouldn't be at the basement facility in Cambridge; they'd be at the corporate offices in Brighton, and that office is closed, so Yvette and I agree to meet Killkenny there in the morning. Yvette lives just a few blocks down from Ma's house, so I give her a ride back to Charlestown. We're both quiet for the first half of the ride. I'm watching the road; she's looking out the passenger side window, watching the Charles River roll by, the lights of Boston rising above it on the other side, like Oz.

'It's got to be someone at the company,' she says at last. I was kind of hoping she wouldn't voice what we were both thinking.

'We don't know that,' I say.

'You've got a better explanation?'

'You want me to make rational sense out of murder? Who would do something like this? Why? I can't answer any of those questions.'

'We have to find him,' Yvette says.

'The police have to find him. That's their job,' I point out.

'Maybe,' she concedes. 'But the police didn't create him; we did.' I glance over at her and study her face for a second. Her profile is lit by the street lights, and the silhouette looks almost regal. Her chin is set, and I can tell that she has taken this on as a mission of hers. She is clear that if we do not find *De Sade* she will view it as her fault.

'That's bullshit,' I say. 'We didn't create this sick asshole. If NextLife didn't exist, he'd still be killing girls; he just wouldn't be practicing.'

'We're making it easier.'

'How? He still has to go out and find them. He still has to actually do the murders.'

'I'm not talking about logistics,' Yvette says. 'I'm talking about mentality. We're making it easier for people to see what it's like; to see whether they like it.'

'You could say that about almost every technology on the Internet.'

'Maybe that's right.'

I shake my head. 'I want to catch this guy as much as you do, but I'm not putting this on you or me, or the company. This is all on the guy who's doing it. It stops there; we're not responsible for how people use the site. You understand that?'

'Yeah,' she says. 'I guess.' She doesn't sound very convinced. 'We still need to catch him.'

Yvette gets out of the car at my house and comes in for a drink; we both need one. Ma is awake and sitting in the kitchen, her oxygen tank parked next to her chair, the hose slipped over her back and snaked around under her nose. I'm thankful, at least, that she is wearing a housecoat. Not that it would make much difference to Yvette; she's known Ma a long time.

'Hey, Mrs C.,' Yvette says as she walks in, goes over to the refrigerator and pulls out two beers. 'How's it going?'

'Help yourself,' Ma says. There's a tone in her voice, but I know it's for effect. It took some time, but Ma eventually came around to liking Yvette years ago.

'Thanks,' Yvette says, ignoring the tone. She walks over and sits at the table with my mother, looks at the mug between my mother's hands. 'Coffee at night?'

'Helps me sleep.'

'Decaf?'

'Irish.'

'Ah.'

I shake my head. 'Ma, the doctors said you're supposed to be off that stuff.'

'Doctors said I was supposed to die last winter. You want me to start doing now everything they tell me I'm supposed to do?' She looks at Yvette. 'I never had much use for rules,' she says with a shrug.

'One of the few things we have in common,' Yvette says with a wry smile.

My mother narrows her eyes at Yvette, examining her face. Yvette stares back, refusing to back down. I think this might go on all night. 'You having sex with my son?' Yvette is taking a sip of her beer when Ma asks the question, and she snarfs some of it up on the table, drawing a look of satisfaction from my mother.

'Ma!' I yell.

'What?' She gives me the look of the falsely accused. It's

one I'm sure she practiced in the mirror for hours when she was younger, for all manner of occasions. She looks back at Yvette. 'Well?'

Yvette has recovered and waves me off as I begin to protest again. 'No, Mrs C. We're not having sex.'

'What, you don't like my boy?'

'I like him fine.'

'You just like girls better?'

That draws another laugh from Yvette. 'That would be easier, wouldn't it? No, I like guys, but we're just friends.' She looks at me. 'And he hasn't tried.'

I am starting to feel very uncomfortable with this conversation. 'We've got a long day tomorrow,' I offer, in a futile hope to move off the subject. Ma is having none of it, though.

She turns back to me. 'You ain't tried?' she barks at me. 'Why not?'

'Ma—'

'Don't *Ma* me.' She gives Yvette an evaluating look. 'I'm not sayin' she's exactly my cuppa tea, but she's got a decent face, and with that hair she's gotta be easy.'

'Excuse me?' Yvette protests, but I can tell she's more amused than upset.

'You spend enough goddamned time with her,' Ma continues. 'Shit, the last girlfriend you had was that uptight little bitch from that college you went to. And that was – what, three years ago?'

'We're done with this conversation,' I say.

'I'm just sayin', I don't want people in the town thinkin' you're a faggot.'

'Ma!'

'I got nothin' against them. Jimmy – Ethel's boy – the one who cuts the ladies' hair down on Warren Street, I like him. Funny. But gay as the day is long, and that's fine for him. But you don't have his style.'

'Nick's not gay,' Yvette says. I look at her, and she gives a smile that is impossible to read. 'That much I'm sure of.'

Ma looks back and forth between the two of us. 'So?'

'Go to bed, Ma,' I say. 'I'll be up to check on you in a little while. After I make sure Yvette gets home.'

Ma shakes her head as she stands and maneuvers her oxygen tank toward the stairs. 'Ah, shit, I don't get you young people these days. When we were your age we knew how to spend our time, and it wasn't talkin'.'

'Ma!'

She disappears around the corner, calling out behind her, 'I'm just sayin'!'

Yvette's house is walking distance. I go with her, just to make sure she gets there okay. She protests that she doesn't need me to be safe, and I know it's true, but I go anyway. Chivalry still exists on the streets of places like Charlestown. It's a place where people take pride in doing things the way they're supposed to be done – for good or bad. The honor code that's followed here is cracked and dented, and at times runs counter to the way things should be in a perfect world, but it provides a set of rules that people understand.

'Sorry about Ma,' I say as we walk. We've been quiet for the first block or so, my mother's comments hanging between us like the scent of opportunity.

She shakes her head. 'She's an original.'

'She is that.'

I start to say something, but the words get caught in my throat. I know that she is waiting for me to do or say something – anything that will open the door between us – but I can't. And, knowing that I can't, I am at a loss for any sort of coherent expression. How can I possibly tell her that I can't focus on anyone else at the moment because I've become obsessed with a mirage? *I'm sorry, Yvette, you're great, but I'm obsessed with a computer-generated girl who gets killed in an online snuff-scene* . . . I'm embarrassed just thinking about it.

We are standing there, so close together that I can feel the heat coming off her body. She's looking at me with curiosity. 'I've always wondered,' she says.

'We have to meet Killkenny early tomorrow. We should get there before him, just to prep people; make sure they don't freak out.'

'Yeah,' she says. 'I should probably go in.'

We are standing at the edge of the sidewalk in front of her house, looking at each other, neither of us knowing quite what to say or do next. She leans in toward me, the way she might if she was going to kiss my cheek, except that she doesn't turn her face the way she would if the target was really my cheek. I lean in, too, the reality of the moment overcoming the loyalty I feel to my other fantasy. I know we are about to kiss and that, once we do, it won't stop, but I don't have the energy to fight it. It's like there is a collision of emotions in my head, and it sounds like the tearing of metal and the screeching of rubber. I lean in further, but she isn't there.

I open my eyes and see that she is still in front of me, but no longer looking in my direction. Instead she is looking off down the street, her face frozen in shock. I turn and I see the headlights streaming down the narrow street toward us, the car's right wheels up on the curb. It takes just a flash before I realize that the sounds of tearing metal were not in my head. The car coming toward us is out of control, tossing metal garbage cans against the houses like paper cups.

'Look out!' I scream. I grab for Yvette, but I am the slower of the two of us and she has already hurled herself against me, knocking me toward her house.

We fall over the scrub bush that hides the cement foundation. The 'yard' is a strip of weed-infested dirt no wider than a couple of feet. We fall onto that strip, she on top of me, just as the car passes us by, close enough to rip out the scraggy bushes we've just fallen over; close enough for me to feel the exhaust on my face as the rear bumper comes within a couple of inches of my forehead; close enough to smell the burned rubber as the tires narrowly miss Yvette's leg.

The car looks as though it might crash into the telephone pole up the street, but after jockeying wildly for a moment, taking out several more garbage cans and two mailboxes, it rights itself and lands unsteadily back on the road. It takes the next corner with enough speed to let out an anguished scream of rubber on cement, and then it is gone.

The street is quiet. One might expect that neighbors would quickly rush out to find out what caused the commotion, and perhaps offer help. They're good people here, and that's probably their first instinct, but we're close enough to the projects that gang violence is not unknown. There have been drive-bys within a few blocks of here in recent years, and while there were no gunshots fired in this particular instance, it's likely –

and understandable – that the people in this area will wait to make sure there are no reprisals coming before venturing out to see what assistance they can be.

'Are you okay?' I ask Yvette. She is lying on top of me, her head swung around looking in the direction where the car disappeared.

'I didn't see the license plate,' she says angrily.

'Who are you, Columbo? I didn't even see what kind of a car it was.'

'I didn't either,' she admits. 'It looked like a sedan, but I couldn't really tell.'

'He keeps on the road that drunk, the cops will find him eventually. Wrapped around a tree, probably.'

'You think?' She sounds skeptical. No, that's not right – she sounds suspicious.

'What is it?'

She shakes her head. 'Nothing.'

She's still on top of me as we lie in the dirt, and she turns back around and looks at me. Her face is so close to mine, and even in the dark I can make out her eyes. They are pretty eyes – deep green, warm and lively. But as I look into them, all I can think of is the fire within the eyes of my girl from the LifeScene.

'We should call the police, just to file a report,' I say.

'Yeah, we should.'

'And then I should go.'

There is a moment before she answers when she is just looking at me, a mixture of hurt and anger in her eyes. 'Yeah, you probably should,' she says.

CHAPTER THIRTEEN

The next morning Yvette acts as though nothing passed between the two of us the night before. I'm grateful for that. We're dealing with enough at the moment that recriminations over a near-kiss would just complicate matters. If there's something between us that's real and goes beyond friendship, it will still be there when things calm down.

I pick her up in the morning and we drive to the NextLife headquarters. We park in the back, and sit in the lot waiting for Paul Killkenny. She's sipping a coffee out of a Styrofoam cup that's large enough to shelter kittens. The aroma of French vanilla swirls in the car, overpowering the acid sting of the small cup of black dark roast that I've almost finished.

'Any word from the Charlestown cops?' she asks.

I shake my head. 'I checked in with them this morning. There were no other accidents reported last night, so at least whoever it was got home without killing anyone.'

'Lucky,' she says.

'Yeah,' I deadpan. 'Lucky.'

At that moment Paul Killkenny pulls into the parking lot. He's driving a black Chevy SS with dark tinted glass that rumbles low and fierce as it pulls around the tarmac. He sees my Corolla and pulls in next to us. I get out, looking over his ride. 'Subtle,' I say.

'More effective than a black-and-white,' he says. 'The bad guys know not to fuck with me.'

'I bet they see you coming, too.'

'I don't work undercover,' he says. 'I want them to know when I'm in the neighborhood.' He looks at the Corolla. 'I see you're still all about impressing people.'

'That's how I roll.'

Killkenny looks at Yvette. 'Sounds like you two had a close call last night. Hope you're okay.'

'How did you hear?' Yvette asks.

'Nick texted me this morning. Said you'd both been up late last night filing the report.'

'It's not the quickest process I've ever seen,' she concedes.

'I hope they catch the guy. Sounds like he could have killed you.' She doesn't respond. He looks up at the NextLife building, which towers over the area, coated in blue glass. 'Speaking of subtle . . . ' he says. 'When did they finish this?'

'Last summer. We've been in since October.'

'What's here?'

'Pretty much everything except our server-farm, which is out in Hopkinton, and my division.'

'Which they keep hidden in a basement.'

I nod.

'So, what now?'

'Let's get you checked in and we can go see HR, see what we can find out about the murdered girls.'

The lobby is gleaming chrome and glass, with a reception

desk that looks a little like an inverted shell. There are two security guards there. One is an attractive brunette in her twenties, the other is a six-foot-two soup-can with a head. He hangs back and lets his partner deal with us. She smiles as she scans my ID, and then Yvette's. Her smile hiccups for a second when Killkenny presents his badge, but she recovers nicely. 'He's with me,' I say. She nods and presses a button to let us through the turnstiles that lead to the elevator.

We head to the third floor, where most of the administrative offices are. I ask to see Helen Jimenez, our head of Human Resources. Because of the nature of what my department does, most of my people are vetted fairly heavily, and I have regular meetings with Helen. I like her, and I've managed not to annoy or offend her, which means that she's probably one of my biggest fans at the company. I wait with Yvette and Killkenny in the reception area for about five minutes before Helen emerges.

'Nick,' she says pleasantly. She comes over to me and takes my hand, leaning in close enough to make the handshake seem almost like a hug. 'No problems with the new hires, I hope?'

'No, Helen, everyone seems to be settling in. You know Yvette Jones? She's in my department.'

Without answering the specific question, Helen smiles at Yvette and extends her hand. 'Yvette,' she says.

'And this is Paul Killkenny,' I say. She shakes his hand as well. 'He's a detective with the Boston Police Department.' She withdraws her hand a little more quickly than I think she might normally, raises an eyebrow.

'Really? A detective.' She tries to make her voice sound impressed. 'What brings you all out to Brighton today?'

'We're looking for some information about three women who did some sort of work for the company a few years back,' I say.

'What kind of work?' Helen asks.

'We're not entirely sure,' I say. 'We know one of them did some work as a model, but we don't know specifically what she did for the company.'

She looks at Killkenny. 'We don't normally give out any employee information to the police without a warrant,' she says hesitantly. 'It's a policy.'

'I know,' I say, 'but in this case it's probably better for the company if we bend the policy just a little bit. At least for the moment.'

'Why? What is it that the police are investigating?' She looks at Killkenny, and he stares evenly back at her.

'All three of the girls were killed,' he says in a cold, flat voice. 'I'm investigating their murders.'

Helen's smile fades, and her face drains just a little bit. There is a receptionist in the waiting area and her head swivels at the use of the word 'murders'.

'Maybe we should continue this discussion back in your office,' I suggest.

'Yes,' Helen agrees. 'Yes, that might be best.'

Helen's office is a large corner spot with luxurious furnishings and a separate sitting area set away from her desk and work space.

'I'm not comfortable with this,' Helen is saying as she taps away at her computer.

'None of us are,' I reassure her.

'I could get a subpoena,' Killkenny says. That gets Helen's attention. She looks up at him, glaring. 'I don't want to, but I will if I have to.'

'It isn't necessary,' I say to him. I look at Helen. 'He could, though. We're trying to keep the company's involvement in the investigation quiet. I can't imagine there's much information the police need from us. We can simply provide a little help and be done with it.' I don't know whether Helen believes me, but I doubt the words even as they leave my mouth.

'Here it is,' she says. 'Amanda Hicks. All I have is a contract, nothing more.'

'What's the contract for?' I ask.

'Looks like a fairly standard modeling contract and release. It was four and a half years ago, just after the company started. They clearly didn't have many record-keepers back then. Frankly, I'm surprised we found this.'

'There are no other records that mention her?' Killkenny asks. Helen shakes her head. 'How about the others? Janet Schmidt and Patricia Carnes?'

Helen taps some more on her keyboard. After a moment she nods. 'Janet Schmidt had the same contract. No further information.' She goes back to her tapping. 'Patricia Carnes, too.'

'But you have no more information?' Killkenny asks. There's an edge in his voice.

'None.' Helen's tone is cold.

'Like I said, I could get a subpoena,' Killkenny shoots back.

'I'm sure you could, Detective, but you won't get any additional information from that. I can't create documents that don't exist. Apparently these women did modeling for the company when it was starting out. I know nothing more than that.'

Killkenny looks at me. 'So, that's it? That's the extent of the cooperation?' He shakes his head.

I'm frowning as I look back at Helen. 'These are contracts with the company, right?' I say to her.

'Yes, as I said.' It's clear that she is getting annoyed with the process. I may have burned any goodwill I might once have had with her.

'Who signed on behalf of the company?'

She looks at me for a moment, then turns back to the screen and scrolls through the document. I can see her come to rest toward the bottom, and she sits there for a few seconds, just staring. Then she looks up at me. 'Tom Jackson,' she says. 'He signed on behalf of the company.'

CHAPTER FOURTEEN

'They're modeling contracts.'

Tom's office is one of the ones on the executive floor. He could have one of the corner offices, given his seniority, but it's not his style to push for perks like that. As a general matter, he's not particularly concerned what people think about him; he's not a people person. He's an exceptional technologist, though, and he's smart enough that he was able to transition to the business side of the company early. His particular gift is in figuring out how technology could be monetized based on the way people behave online, and how much they are willing to pay for a variety of services. He went through the process with several start-ups early in his career, and had enormous success. NextLife, though, is turning out to be more of a challenge.

'Yes,' Killkenny says. 'They're modeling contracts. That much I could see. But what were they modeling?'

Tom's sitting behind his desk, a plain slab of Formica that the company leases for all the offices. There are few personal items in the office, and the desktop and credenza behind him are dominated by three large computers, two with oversized screens. He's a lot like me; he's here to work. That's one of the reasons we get along so well. He picks up the contracts again and looks them over. 'They're from four and a half years ago,' he says. 'We were in the development stage at that point, so it wasn't for any type of media.'

'No?'

Tom shakes his head. 'No, we didn't have anything to sell at the time; we weren't in the market yet. We certainly weren't doing any advertising.'

'What kind of modeling were they doing for the company then?' I ask.

He looks at me, shifting in his chair just enough to make it clear that he isn't entirely comfortable with the question. 'That's sensitive company information, Nick. I'm not sure we should be sharing that with anyone outside of the corporate structure.'

'It's important,' Killkenny says.

'Why?' Tom asks. He looks at me, then at Killkenny. 'What's this all about?'

'It's about three murders,' Killkenny says. The effect is pronounced. Tom's face goes white, his mouth dropping open. 'All three of these girls have been murdered, and the only thing we can identify that they have in common is that they modeled for this company at around the same time four and a half years ago.'

'I'm sorry,' Tom stammers after a moment. 'I had no idea.'

'No reason you should have,' I reassure him. 'You see why we need to know, though, right?'

He nods slowly. 'I do.' He takes a deep breath and rubs his hand over his face. 'They were prototypes,' he says at last.

I stare at him, blinking, and it takes a moment for me to understand. 'Prototypes,' I repeat, the meaning sinking in. 'I never put it together,' I say. 'Prototypes,' I say again, like I am exploring a new term.

'Prototypes?' Killkenny says. 'What the hell does that mean?'

'Come with me,' Tom says, standing. 'You need to talk to the Doc. He'll be able to explain this better than I can.'

The computer lab is on the fourth floor, and it's entirely an expression of Dr Santar Gunta's personality. While many companies in the technology sector have adopted a loose, informal atmosphere, particularly for their programmers, Dr Gunta considers himself first and foremost a scientist. As a result, he has been unwilling to give up the clean-room feel. The entire floor is open, and the sunlight streams through the huge glass windows on all sides. The floors are white tile, the walls freshly painted, the desks and computer equipment all shiny bright white plastic. Everyone in the room is wearing a lab coat, giving the place the feel of a bright, sterile medical facility, or perhaps a NASA mission launch.

There are a hundred programmers at their computers, all their attention trained on the screens in front of them, tapping endlessly on their keyboards. Every once in a while one of them will print out a sheet of programming and take it over to a supervisor, discuss programming strategy in hushed tones and then head back to his computer. Looking around the room, I notice that none of the programmers are women. Not one. In fact, Yvette is the only woman on the floor. I guess I've probably noticed the prevalence of men in the programming business before, but it's never struck me as directly as it does standing in this room.

'It's impressive, isn't it?' Tom says. It takes me a moment to realize that he's talking to Killkenny, not me.

'What are they doing?' Killkenny asks.

'Programming,' Tom replies.

'Programming what? The system's finished, isn't it? It's up and working.'

Tom lets out a little chuckle. 'The system's never finished. Not if we want it still to be relevant six months from now. Technology moves at light-speed, and no one who wants to survive can sit still. Our competitors are out there right now, trying to come up with something even more impressive than NextLife; something that will blow it out of the water. We have to beat them to whatever that is. If anyone is going to make our current technology obsolete, we want it to be us. We learned that from Steve Jobs. At most companies they'll kill any new project that cannibalizes their most successful product lines. At Apple, they encourage it. It's what keeps them fresh, keeps them sharp. We're trying to emulate that here.'

I can see Killkenny scanning the room, and his eyes light upon a large desk at the center of the room. It's twice the size of any other desk, and it's raised up so that the man sitting behind it can survey the entire room at a glance. The man in the chair is in his mid-fifties, with dark skin and thin, close-cropped gray hair. He has a serious, studious expression on his face as he scrutinizes two giant computer screens on his desk.

'Who's that?' Killkenny asks.

'That's the Doc,' Tom says. 'Dr Santar Gunta. He's the technological genius behind all of this.' From a distance, Tom looks at Gunta with something like awe. 'Do you want to meet him?'

'I guess I have to,' Killkenny says.

We walk over to the center of the room. Next to the raised desk, nearly connected to it, is a smaller workstation. Sitting there is a strikingly attractive young man in his late twenties. He watches us as we walk toward them. He is thin, with dirty-blond hair and bright-blue eyes. He's looking at us, seeming to evaluate each one of us.

Gunta doesn't look up from his work until we are standing next to his desk. I see that the desk actually rests on a platform nearly a foot off the ground. As a result, even seated, Gunta is almost looking us in the eyes when he turns and regards us with evident surprise.

'Tom,' he says, nodding to the company's head of Revenue Generation. He looks at me with suspicion. 'Nick.' When his eyes fall on Yvette I can sense a hint of disgust at her presence. 'What are you doing here?' he asks us. His voice is quiet and self-possessed and has the gentle lilt of the small village in India where he was born and raised.

'Doc, this man is with the police,' Tom says. 'Nick and Ms Jones are helping him with an investigation, and they need some information from you. Can we have a moment of your time to talk?'

Gunta's voice remains quiet, but I think I can sense some hesitation. 'I have a great deal of work to do today,' he says.

'It won't take too long, I don't think,' Tom says, trying to put Gunta at ease. The scientist doesn't look convinced. 'It's important,' Tom presses.

'I have an office.' He nods to the far corner of the floor, where there is a span of three doors. He stands and steps down from the platform where his desk sits. He's a man of short stature, and stepping off the platform has a transformative impact. From his perch he seemed authoritative – imposing, even. Now he seems intimidated. He walks over to one of the doors, opens it and walks in. Killkenny, Tom, Yvette and I follow.

Gunta's office has a strange feel to it. The floor is the same bright tile as the main lab, the walls whitewashed, the windows framed by white, industrial treatments. His desk, though, is antique with elaborate inlay and a leather top. Behind it stands a matching credenza that reaches almost to the ceiling. Scattered throughout the many shelves are mementoes from the Far East.

Gunta walks to the far side of the desk and sits. He waves toward the pair of metal and plastic chairs on the other side of the desk. Tom sits in one, Yvette in the other. Killkenny and I remain standing.

'How can I help you?' Gunta asks. I think I hear a slight quaver in his voice.

'As I said,' Tom begins, 'Detective Killkenny is with the Boston Police Department. He's investigating a murder.'

'Three murders,' Killkenny corrects Tom.

'Yes, right,' Tom agrees. 'Three murders.'

Dr Gunta's expression changes only slightly. He seems less surprised than one might expect. 'What do these murders have to do with me?' he asks.

'Nothing,' Tom reassures Gunta quickly. 'It's just that all three victims seem to have a connection to NextLife. It could

be a coincidence, but the police need to look into it, you understand.' He seems almost apologetic in his approach to Gunta,
and the computer genius stares back at him without expression.

'We're not sure it's a coincidence,' Killkenny says flatly.

Gunta looks at me, and then at Yvette. 'And what is your
involvement in this?' he asks us.

'Nick and Ms Jones were the ones who discovered the
connection. They did the right thing and notified us,' Killkenny
says.

'Did they?' He takes a breath. 'Should Mr NetMaster be
involved in this?'

'He's been informed, and I'm keeping him in the loop,' I
say. It's only a partial lie. 'I also spoke with Josh, so he's fully
aware of the situation.' My tone is neutral, but my glare at
Gunta is sharp. I respect the man's abilities, but I've never fully
trusted him. He returns my look with a sour expression.

'Still, it might be better if he were here,' he says. He picks
up the phone on his desk and presses a button. 'Michael, will
you please have Mr NetMaster found and sent to my office?'
He hangs up quickly. The room is silent for a moment.

'If it's helpful, we can do this down at the station,' Killkenny
says. It's clear that he is intent on reasserting control over the
situation.

'No, no,' Tom says, 'that's not necessary.' He looks at Gunta
with a pleading expression. 'We're just looking for a little background. Dr Gunta will be happy to cooperate, right?'

It takes a moment for Gunta to nod slowly. 'What connection do these women have to NextLife?' he asks.

'All three were prototypes from our original sessions,' Tom

says. 'I wasn't involved in the process, other than that I signed the contracts, so I thought it would be helpful to have some background from you.'

Gunta looks at Killkenny. 'What is it that you would like to know?'

'Well, first of all, what the fuck is a prototype?'

'There's no need for swearing, Detective,' Tom says sharply.

'I don't know about that,' Killkenny shoots back. 'Three girls are dead. Seems to me that justifies some choice language.'

'It is okay, Tom,' Gunta says quietly. He looks at Killkenny. 'A prototype is a model we used as a baseline for creating our library of avatars for the system.'

'What does that mean?' Killkenny asks.

'It means exactly what I said.' Gunta is quiet for a moment and then rolls his eyes slightly. 'Computers only function based on the information that is fed to them. No one would be able to create a convincing avatar from scratch; the computer would have no effective frame of reference. Oh, if you were skilled you could create the kinds of avatars they have in video games – those that look somewhat lifelike and mildly realistic. But that has never been our goal. Our goal has always been to create a world that is virtually indistinguishable from reality. To do that, we had to begin with detailed photographs mapping the exteriors of various subjects that served as models – what we call prototypes.'

'Detailed photographs?' Yvette, who hasn't said a word since we entered the lab, stares at Gunta. It is as though the cadence of a woman's voice has never been heard on this floor. Gunta glares at her, his mouth drawn down in embarrassment. 'How detailed?'

It takes a few beats for him to answer, and he averts his eyes as he speaks. 'Very detailed.' He looks at Killkenny. 'It was part of the process. All of the models gave releases, and all of them knew what they were being asked to do. They were well compensated. There was nothing improper done.'

'Of course not,' Tom says. 'No one is suggesting that.'

'No,' Killkenny agrees. 'I'm not suggesting that there was anything improper about the process. But three of them have been murdered, so I need to have a sense of the process. How did it work?'

Gunta shrugs. 'This was very early in the company's existence. Even before Nick joined us. We put ads in some of the local papers, explaining that we were looking for models for a computer simulation. You understand, we had more people volunteer than we could even use. Literally thousands sent in pictures. It was quite remarkable.'

'How many did you use?'

'To start out, two hundred. Over the past few years we have expanded the database, but we started with a manageable number.'

'All women?'

'No, seventy-five percent women. That ratio has held even as we have expanded the database of prototypes.'

'Why the disparity?' I ask, genuinely curious.

He fidgets behind his desk, as he starts to answer. 'We have found—' He stops talking, as though he's searching for words. 'Our customers . . . men generally—' He cuts himself off again.

'What?' Killkenny pushes.

His sinks toward his chest and looks up hesitantly at Yvette. 'It is indelicate,' he says.

She smiles at him, and I wonder whether he can tell that her look is one of pure condescension. 'Don't worry about it,' she says. 'I'm indelicate.'

He frowns, but continues. 'Men tend to be more visually demanding,' he says. Yvette barks out a laugh, which clearly makes Gunta even more uncomfortable. 'To be clear, we have found that men have more particular tastes, and have a wider variety of interests in the way women look. Both with respect to their facial appearance and parts of the female anatomy. As a result, we provide a wider baseline of the female form.'

'I'm guessing very few men are looking for a wider base line when it comes to the female form,' Yvette cracks.

This, at least, draws a wry smile from Gunta. 'You'd be surprised.'

'So, basically, you needed a bunch of hot women to entice men to the site, is that it?' Killkenny says.

Gunta shakes his head emphatically. 'No, Detective, that is most certainly not it. Do you know what this technology was originally developed for?'

Killkenny shakes his head. 'No. I assumed it was for the company to use on its website.'

'The company has funded the expansion of the technology – the commercialization of it. But I developed this technology for the criminal-justice system. The original concept was to use this technology to train convicted prisoners to deal with real-life situations before they were released, and to pre-screen for recidivism to aid the parole board in determining who was ready to be out in the world.'

'I never knew that,' I say.

Gunta nods. 'It is not something the company publicizes

widely, though I'm not sure why. It will ultimately be of great benefit to society.'

'How does it help?' Killkenny asks.

'You must understand,' Gunta begins, 'prisoners – particularly those who have been incarcerated for an extended period of time – have lost all sense of how to behave in the real world. They have been isolated, and they have learned to function in accordance with a very different set of rules and behavioral norms – one that often rewards violence. If we can begin giving them some experience in more normal situations, even if they are computer simulations, it can help them relearn appropriate behaviors. It also allows us to observe their responses to stimuli. It can test them to see whether they will react with violence; by seeing whether they are capable of resisting baser instincts – how they react to women, for example – we can start to determine who really presents a risk upon release.'

'Has it been implemented?' Yvette asks.

'Only in testing over the past several years.'

'Has it helped?' I ask.

Gunta purses his lips. 'I believe it has. It is, of course, difficult to track on a scientific level, and there are those who say the evaluations are inconclusive, but I believe it has been helpful in many instances.'

'Is this testing done in connection with NextLife?'

Gunta nods. 'The company has been very generous in allowing us to use the facilities. The technology that you use, Nick, in tracking our customers was originally designed to give us visibility into our experimental subjects' actions – so we could observe how they reacted to different situations and actually feel what they were feeling.'

'When the models were hired, was it for the company, or for your experiments?'

'Both,' Gunta says. 'At that point we were working on parallel tracks. What we learned on the technology side, we implemented in both systems.'

'Who was involved in the hiring process?' Killkenny asks.

Gunta looks at him, his eyes narrowing slightly. 'As I said, we were a very small company at the time.'

'Which means you were personally involved,' Killkenny says. It's not a question.

'Yes, I was.'

'Were you involved in the photo sessions as well?'

'I don't understand what you are implying!' Gunta protests. His voice is raised at least an octave.

'I'm not implying anything,' Killkenny says smoothly. 'As I've said, I'm trying to get the facts. And, in particular, I need to identify anyone who had actual contact with these women. Were you involved in the photo sessions?'

'It was necessary!'

'I'm sure it was.' Killkenny takes out a notebook and smiles as he makes a few jottings. 'Who else was involved? There was a photographer, presumably?'

Gunta is flustered, but seems more relaxed as the discussion turns away from his involvement. 'Yes, of course.'

'Was he someone from the company?'

'No. We hired a professional photographer. I don't recall his name, but I am sure we have his contact information somewhere in our records.'

'That would be helpful,' Killkenny says. 'Who else was involved?'

119

'We had two assistant programmers at the time. They had some contact with the models, but very little.'

'I'll need their names as well. Anyone else?'

'Not that I can recall.'

'Was Josh involved?' I ask the question without thinking; it just seems very odd that at that stage Pinkerton would have relinquished complete control. And, frankly, he seems like the kind of a man who would have trouble forgoing an extended photo shoot with a series of beautiful women.

Gunta glares at me as though I've transgressed.

'Was he?' Killkenny asks.

'Yes,' Gunta says, his eyes still on me. 'He was.'

'Anyone else?' Killkenny presses. 'Anyone at all?'

Gunta shakes his head.

'Have you had any contact with any of the models since their photo sessions?'

Gunta looks offended. 'No! Why would I have?'

'None whatsoever?'

'No, Detective. None whatsoever.' Gunta's voice has turned cold, and he is no longer fidgeting in his chair. He now looks straight at Killkenny, his eyes clear.

'Do you know Amanda Hicks?'

'I've never heard of her,' Gunta says. 'Who is she?'

Killkenny pulls out the photograph of Amanda Hicks on the coroner's slab, puts it on the desk. Gunta looks at it, flinches slightly and looks away. 'As I said, I don't know her,' he says.

Killkenny pulls out the pictures of the other two dead women, puts them on the desk. 'How about Janet Schmidt or Patricia Carnes?'

Gunta keeps his eyes averted. 'I don't know them.'

'Maybe you could look at them, just to be sure.'

It takes a moment for Gunta to turn his head and glance briefly at the images. When he does, it's as though the pictures burn his eyes and he turns away almost immediately, his fist going to his mouth. 'I don't know them!' he says. 'I told you!'

The room is silent for a moment. Killkenny, Yvette and I are staring at Gunta. Tom is staring at the floor. Suddenly the door swings open and we all turn to see NetMaster standing at the threshold, scowling. Michael is standing, barely visible, behind him, looking protectively at Dr Gunta. 'Why wasn't I informed of this interrogation?' NetMaster demands in his thick Dutch accent.

No one says anything for a moment. 'It's not an interrogation,' Killkenny says at last. 'Just a friendly conversation.'

NetMaster's eyes narrow as he looks at Killkenny. 'I know you, no?'

Killkenny nods. 'Yeah, we've met. I organized security on the police side for a corporate party the company had a little while back. Name's Killkenny. Detective Killkenny.'

'Yes, Detective. I remember now. You were paid well, yes?'

'I was paid the going rate.'

'The going rate is more than you make for the police?'

Killkenny doesn't reply.

NetMaster scowls at me. 'Nick Caldwell, you were to keep me involved in all aspects of this . . . cooperation . . . we are providing. Why was I not informed that you would be talking to Dr Gunta?'

'It wasn't on our schedule, initially,' I reply honestly. 'We were talking to Tom, and he suggested a conversation with the Doc. I had no idea you wanted to know every time we talked to anyone.'

'I must know everything,' NetMaster says. 'Everything.'

'I'll keep that in mind, now that I know.'

'You are done with the Doctor,' NetMaster says to Killkenny. His inflection is ambiguous enough that it could have been either an order or a question. From the violence simmering under his demeanor, I am assuming NetMaster meant it as a directive.

'Yeah, sure,' Killkenny says. 'I'm done with him for now. I may have a few follow-up questions later, obviously, but for the moment he's been very helpful. Thank you, Doc.'

'You are welcome,' NetMaster answers for Gunta. 'If you have any further questions, please let me know, and I will arrange to have them answered.' He makes clear that any additional access will have to come through him.

'Sure thing. I'll need the name of the photographer, as well as the names of the two programmers who were involved in the process as well.'

'Of course, Detective,' NetMaster says. 'Anything else?'

'Yeah, actually. I need a list of all the models who were hired, and pictures of them matched to their names.'

'Why?' NetMaster demands.

'Because, at the moment, we still have a killer out there who is choosing his victims from your company's prototypes. I think it's only fair to warn them, don't you?'

CHAPTER FIFTEEN

'What did you think?'

Killkenny, Yvette and I are out in the parking lot at NextLife's headquarters. It's a little after noon, and the sun is shining in that crisp way it does in New England. Even from ground level, we can still see the tallest buildings downtown peeking over the smaller buildings in Brighton. I know Killkenny is going to ask me the question even before it comes out, and I'm not sure exactly how to answer it. I'm still a top executive in the company, and complete honesty isn't necessary or appropriate in that role.

'Interesting,' I say. It's noncommittal enough, I figure.

'That's one word for it.' Killkenny takes out a pack of cigarettes, slides one out, puts it between his lips. He holds out the pack in our direction. 'Either of you smoke?'

'Only when I'm drunk,' Yvette says.

I wave him off. 'I'm good, thanks.'

'Is he normally like that?' Killkenny asks.

'Who?'

'Gunta.'

'Like what?'

He takes a long drag off his cigarette, looking at me carefully as he takes it into his lungs. 'You know what I mean,' he says as he exhales. 'When we started talking about the girls, he looked like I had his nuts in a vice and was turning the screws.'

'Some people are uncomfortable talking about murder,' I offer. It's clear from his expression that Killkenny isn't buying it.

'Maybe,' he says. 'Seemed like something more to me.' He looks at Yvette. 'How about you? What's your take?'

'I think he's a creep,' Yvette says. I close my eyes and shake my head; she's never been one to sugarcoat her views. 'What?' she demands of me, noting my reaction. 'He is; he's a creep. He looked at me like my vagina offended him.'

'You think he could've killed those girls?' Killkenny asks her. I think about interjecting to keep her from saying anything more, but it's unnecessary. She shakes her head.

'He's creepy, but he's not *De Sade*. A least, he sure as hell didn't create the LifeScene that I walked. Whoever created that scene is conflicted – completely fucked-up, actually – but they're also obsessed with women. There's an aspect of pleasure that I sure as hell don't see in Dr-Stick-Up-His-Ass.'

'Maybe that's a cover,' Killkenny suggests.

'Maybe,' she says. 'But my impression is that anyone Gunta's obsessed with probably has a dick between his legs.'

I have the same impression, but I'm not going to express it.

'You think?'

'You see the way he was looking at the pretty-boy assistant?'

Killkenny thinks for a moment. 'I need you to talk to all of the people who work for you,' he says to me. 'I want to talk to anyone who has been into any of *De Sade*'s LifeScenes. You said he's a heavy user, right? What did you call them? Hummers?'

'He's one of the heaviest users,' I agree.

'So you keep a pretty close eye on him in that dungeon of yours, right?'

'He's on the list of people we track. That doesn't mean we've had someone in all of his LifeScenes, but many of them, yeah.'

'Okay, I want any of your people who have seen any of his fucked-up fantasies to look through all the models' pictures. Maybe we can get a handle on other girls who are in danger.'

'Makes sense,' I agree.

Killkenny gets in his car, tosses his cigarette butt out onto the tarmac. 'I'll be over at the Cambridge office at four o'clock,' he says. He hits the gas and peels out. For just a moment the sound gives me a flashback to the car that almost killed Yvette and me the night before.

The cigarette butt is still smoking on the ground, blowing back and forth in a gentle, swirling autumn breeze. Yvette walks over and stamps it out with her thick heels. 'You really didn't notice anything fucked-up about how Doc was acting in there?' she asks me.

'Yeah, I did. I just didn't want to get into it with Killkenny.'

'Protecting the company?'

'Maybe. Plus, like you said, his reaction was weird, but I just don't see him as the one who created those LifeScenes. It's not his style in a dozen ways.'

'I agree. But it raises a couple of related questions that you and I need to talk about.'

'Which are?'

She looks sideways at me, her eyes narrowed. 'How far are you willing to go to protect the company, and how far are you willing to go to catch this guy?'

'I'm not sure I understand the questions.'

'I don't think Gunta created those LifeScenes. But he knows something he's not sharing. The way he was behaving got me to thinking: we've been assuming that we can't piece together any of these LifeScenes because the Scenes themselves reside on the user's computer, so we can only access them when they are actually in the Scene – when they are hooked into our system.'

'Right,' I say. 'We have limited visibility into the user's computer.'

'That's true,' Yvette says. 'But what if these Scenes were actually created on a computer that's already hooked into the system?'

'What do you mean?'

'What if it's someone at the company and it's being done on a computer that's part of the NextLife system?'

I think about that for a moment. It's a long shot, but it's possible. 'Anyone who works here would know the risk, and even if they created them on their own laptops that are hooked into the system, they'd be smart enough to encrypt them so that we can't get at them.'

'They might be able to encrypt them so that *you* can't get at them,' Yvette says with a smile. 'I doubt they could come up with an encryption scheme that I can't crack.'

'It's still a one-in-a-million chance,' I say. 'In all likelihood, it's not someone at the company, and even doing the search will be a waste of time.'

'Maybe,' Yvette agrees. 'But it's my time. And I'm curious.'

'You're dangerous when you're curious,' I say. 'I know that.'

Her smile takes on a sad edge as she looks at me. 'Yeah, you do.' The wind blows her hair into her eyes, and she pushes it back off her forehead. 'Are you willing to live with what I find, even if it implicates someone at the company?'

I don't hesitate. 'If someone at NextLife is using the system to practice killing these girls, then, yeah, they need to be stopped. No matter what.'

She nods. 'I thought you'd feel that way. I'm going to start poking around, see what I can find.'

'Have a go,' I say. 'If anyone can find anything hidden on the system, it would be you.' I open the door to the Corolla and get in. She climbs into the passenger seat. 'One thing, though,' I go on.

'What is it?'

'Let's keep this between you and me for now,' I say. 'If you're wrong, I don't want it to come around and bite us in the ass. And if you tell Killkenny, he'll push it, even if there's nothing there.'

'It's his job to push it,' she points out.

'I know,' I agree. 'But until we know whether there's something there, there's no point in getting his hopes up.' I look at her. 'You agree? We'll keep this just between the two of us?'

She looks away from me, out the passenger side window. 'I'll add it to the list.'

CHAPTER SIXTEEN

I drop Yvette off at the Cambridge office and swing by home before going back to work. Ma was complaining this morning about a pain in her chest, and I want to stop in to see how she's doing. I'd call, but Ma wouldn't say anything over the phone; you had to see the pain in her eyes before she'd admit anything. Her motto since the days I was a little boy was always the same: *Life is hard; quit your bitching.*

Even at this time of day the traffic is light. A steady stream of runners and bikers and roller-bladers flows along the banks of the Charles as I head east to Charlestown. Most of them are wearing sweatshirts identifying them as connected in some way to the dozens of colleges and universities that make the Boston area their home: Harvard, MIT, Boston College, Boston University, Northeastern, Berklee College of Music, Simmons, University of Massachusetts, Tufts, and on and on. Too many to count. They're not all college students, clearly; many of them are too old for that. Professors perhaps, or alumni who loved the area too much to leave. It's one of the reasons that Boston is a hub of technological development and entrepreneurship, second only to Silicon Valley. There is such a rich pool of overeducated, hyper-motivated people coming out of school, it drives innovation and growth.

And yet Charlestown remains, in many ways, unaffected by it all. Genetically resistant to change and psychologically unwilling to accept outsiders, it juts its chin defiantly at the towns around it. It's hard not to notice every time I cross the border.

I pull the Corolla up to the curb in front of Ma's house because there is a truck in the driveway. A red pickup that is in some need of attention. I frown as I walk by it, wondering whether some contractor is preying on the old woman, trying to convince her that she needs a new roof, or new siding. Work has been hard to come by in recent years, and some of the more motivated home-improvement businesses have become relentless. I know that Ma is perfectly capable of turning them away, but it still bothers me.

My frown turns to a smile as I walk into the kitchen. Sitting at the table, beer in hand, is an energetic-looking man in his mid-fifties. He's wearing a weathered pair of Navy-issue khakis, work boots, a flannel shirt and a stained vest. A beaten cap with the emblem of the USS *Norfolk* sits askew on a balding pate. A fisherman's beard runs along his jaw from ear to ear, surrounding a face that is dominated by large, sharp eyes and a mouth that is constantly lost between a smile and a smirk.

'Look what the tides brought to us,' Ma says. I look over at her and I'm shocked. She's put on one of her best dresses, and fixed her hair. The oxygen sits in a corner, disconnected from her face. Even as thin as she's become, she looks great – maybe fifteen years younger than I've seen her look in the past six months. Her smile is a rarity, and it's good to see.

'Nick,' the man says. 'You look fit.'

'You too, Cormack,' I say, walking over and giving him a firm handshake. I've known Cormack O'Connell for my entire life, and he was the one who taught me when I was a boy: *always give a firm handshake.* It's one of the few lessons that has stuck with me. 'It's been a while.'

'It has,' he says. 'We've had a busy summer down at the harbor. Lots of work for a change. Good for the lads.' He still has a hint of the brogue he brought with him when his family arrived when he was five years old. These days he owns three tugboats that run much of the commercial traffic in and out of Boston Harbor. He was one of my father's best friends, and I've always assumed that he's heavily connected. That's the way many of the rackets are run here; those in charge have real jobs – often important jobs – that also serve as cover for their more illicit activities. It's never bothered me; that's how I grew up. Besides, of all of the people I've known in that world, Cormack has always struck me as the most legitimate, and the least violent.

'What brings you by?' I ask.

He shakes his head. 'Nothin' but neighborliness,' he says with a smile. 'How is the world of big business treating you?'

For some reason, the simple question catches me by surprise and I hesitate in answering. 'It's good,' I say after a moment.

He knits his eyebrows at me, though the smile remains. 'If one of my gaffers showed that little enthusiasm, I'd feed him to the stripers.'

'It's complicated at the moment.' I sit at the table with him and Ma.

'I'm sure.' He leans in. 'You be careful now, boy. You know

what your da used to say: *There's no one as crooked as a legit-imate businessman.* Much truth in that.'

'If it was just someone crooked, I could live with that,' I say.

Ma shoots me a hard look. 'What, then?'

'I can't talk about it.'

'The hell you can't.'

'Leave the boy alone,' Cormack says to Ma. 'His business is his business. Any man who can't keep to himself isn't worth a damn.' He looks at me. 'You just keep care of yourself, and understand that there's no one else who's looking out for you, understand?'

'Yeah, I understand.'

'You always were the smartest one here. Your father knew that, too. Even when you were young, he'd say to me: *That boy's made of different stuff. Smart.* He meant it, too.'

'I've never heard that before,' I say. I look at Ma, for some reason feeling as though she's been keeping information from me. 'You never told me that.'

'Like you needed someone else telling you how smart you are? You never lacked for confidence in your own brain.'

It's a fair comment, but it still annoys me. I'm about to start an argument about it, but I remember that I have to get back to work and I recall the reason I stopped by in the first place. 'How are you feeling, Ma?' I ask.

'Never stronger,' she says defiantly.

'This morning you were saying—'

'Nothing,' she says sharply. 'This morning I was saying nothing.' She steals a glance at Cormack. 'He worries. No reason, really. I'm feeling fine.'

I look at her and realize that she's wearing lipstick and blusher. I can't remember the last time she wore makeup.

'He's just lookin' out for you,' Cormack says. 'He's a good son.' He looks at her and smiles, and I can see the lust in his eyes as his eyes meet hers.

It's funny, when I was little I remember people talking about how beautiful Ma was. Other men used to joke to my father that they'd put up with her attitude just for one night with her. But when my father died, it was as though she aged decades overnight. Her hardness became heavy, and her edge became serrated. When the cancer came for her, it was like the last of her youth was scared off. Now, sitting here in the kitchen, for the first time in more than decade I can see the woman my father married and put up with, and I get a hint of why.

At that moment there is a buzzing of a text message on my phone. I take it out of my jacket pocket and look at it. There's an automatic notice from the NextLife system alerting me that *De Sade* has activated a LifeScene. I can feel my heart beating, and my throat goes dry. I'd like to think it's because I'm appalled at the notion that this creature could be practicing his next murder, but that's not it. Mainly I'm just devastated that there is a chance that he is in a LifeScene with the avatar I'm obsessed with, and I'm missing the chance to see her again. I go through a whole range of emotions as I look at my phone, before I realize I'm not alone in the room.

I glance over at Cormack. He's still smiling, and he tips his beer to me. The juxtaposition between the rush of desire I've just felt thinking about the woman in the LifeScene and the discomfort at the notion that my mother may be having a physical relationship with my father's old friend is dizzying.

I stand. 'I just wanted to swing by, but I've got to get back to work.' I feel like I'm stammering.

'It's good to see you, Nick,' Cormack says.

'You too.'

Ma's still sitting, so I stand there in limbo for a moment. 'There's a bunch of stuff going on at work,' I say. 'I'll probably be late tonight.'

'No problem,' she says. 'I've been looking after myself for long enough as it is. I'll be here.'

I walk out and get into my car, feeling sideways, somehow. Ma's not actually old, I realize, and it makes sense that she should still have feelings for men. And yet, for whatever reason, I just thought that part of her life was over. It strikes me at that moment how much of our lives are directed by our physical impulses. I think about the obsession I've developed over the woman in *De Sade*'s LifeScene. Then I think about *De Sade* and the twisted passions that he must feel, and I wonder – if he's not caught – for how long they will drive him.

I'm still unsettled when I walk through the door to the basement of the building in Cambridge. I head to the back of the open floor, passing dozens of GhostWalkers splayed out on their chairs, headgear and gloves on, peering in on our members' most intimate fantasies. The sight only makes me dizzier.

Yvette is at her station, back near the door to my office. She is sitting in her chair, gloves still on and rolled up above the elbows, but her visor is off, resting on her lap. Her face is flushed and she is glancing off into space.

'Yvette,' I call to her as I get closer.

She looks up at me, and the distant look remains for just a moment. Then she shakes her head and her eyes clear. 'I GhostWalked him again,' she says. 'We got a ping, so I went in.'

'I saw it,' I say. 'Was it one we already know about?'

She shakes her head. 'Not that I'm aware. It's not the one you've walked, and it's not one I've ever seen before.'

'What was it? What did he do?'

'She was standing,' she says, her voice just a little dreamy. 'It was a room with velvet walls, deep red, and her wrists were chained to the ceiling, her ankles to the floor. She had on the metal collar, and that was chained to the ceiling as well. She was blindfolded.'

'What did he do?'

'He had this . . . thing . . . I don't know what it was. It had this thin handle, like a pencil, and at the end of it was a wheel that had these little sharp spikes. And he was running this wheel all up and down her body.'

'You mean he was cutting her?'

She shakes her head. 'No, it was just giving her these little pricks – tiny little impulses of pain all over her body. And she loved it.' She looks up at me. 'She really did love it, that much was obvious.'

'How did it end?'

She closes her eyes. 'Not well.'

I'm not sure how to ask, but I have to know. 'What did she look like?'

Yvette opens her eyes. 'What did she look like?'

'Yes. What did she look like? Her eyes, were they blue with flecks of gold?'

'I don't know. I told you, she was blindfolded.'

'Right,' I say. 'Well, what else could you tell? What color was her hair?'

She thinks for a moment. 'Red. Almost as red as the velvet walls.'

I breathe a silent sigh of relief. It wasn't my girl.

'He left her hanging there,' Yvette says quietly.

'What do you mean?'

'In the end she was just hanging there, the metal collar digging into her neck.' I look down at Yvette sitting in the chair, and I see the tears streaking down her cheek. 'We have to catch him,' she whispers. 'We have to catch him before he can do this in real life.'

CHAPTER SEVENTEEN

'Seven.'

It's two o'clock in the morning and I am sitting in my office with Yvette and Killkenny, an array of ten photographs in front of us. Three of them are the headshots of the three murdered women. The other seven are of models identified as having been the prototypes for women who appeared in *De Sade*'s LifeScenes that have been GhostWalked by my people. They are all attractive and have the youthful, eager look of people who are about to be taken advantage of. In the middle of the bunch is my girl. Kendra Madison. She looks out at me from the image, her face unmistakable, her hair long and dark, her skin clear and light. The only real difference is the eyes. They stare at the camera without the sparkle and life that I have seen in them before, when I was inside *De Sade*'s head, looking down upon her, touching her, caressing her. Something about the image makes me feel cheated.

'Seven,' Killkenny repeats.

'That we know about,' Yvette says.

Killkenny looks up at her sharply.

'He's a Hummer, there's no doubt, so he falls into the category that we track with the most diligence, but that doesn't mean that we've actually been in every one of his LifeScenes. There could be others that no one here has walked. I'm just pointing it out.'

Killkenny frowns as he considers this. 'Is there any way we can make sure that someone is GhostWalking everything that he does going forward?'

'Already done,' I say. 'As soon as we started putting this together, I set an administrative watch to make sure we are notified every time he gets on the system.'

'When was the last time?'

I look at Yvette. She is staring at one of the images at one end of the picture array. 'About five hours ago.'

Killkenny looks at Yvette. 'You walked it?'

She nods. 'Taylor Westerbrooke,' she says, fingering the picture at the edge of the line-up she's been looking at. The girl has a flood of blood-red hair and wide blue eyes. Her smile says it all; for her, the modeling session had meant that she was on the edge of stardom. This was her breakthrough. I wonder how she would feel now to know that the thousand-dollar session had led to her being a fantasy plaything for a psychotic killer. It probably wasn't the type of fame she was looking for when she walked into the photo session.

'How did he do her?'

Yvette stabs a glare at Killkenny. 'Which part do you mean?'

'The pun was unintended. How did he kill her?'

'He hanged her,' she says. Yvette takes one last look at the image and then her eyes go to the floor.

Killkenny looks baffled. 'He hanged her?'

'Yeah,' Yvette says sharply. I can see that the investigation is wearing on her. 'You want to know the goddamned details?'

'It's my job,' Killkenny says. 'It may seem morbid to you, but yeah, getting the details is what makes it possible for me to catch him.'

She takes a deep breath and shakes her head, lets her eyes drop to the table. Her voice is barely audible. 'She had a metal collar that was chained to the ceiling. He was having sex with her standing up. When they both started to . . . to finish, he lifted her legs off the ground and pulled her down with her own weight. He was still inside her as she—'

'Okay, that's enough,' I say, cutting her off, putting a hand on hers. I don't know whether it was for her benefit or mine. I've lived in this world of dark fantasies for four years, learning more about the human psyche than I ever wanted to know, but it was all fake. I never thought of it as real. As the lines between NextLife and real life blur, I'm starting to feel nauseous. 'What do we do now?'

Killkenny takes a deep breath. 'Well, I keep the investigation going to find this asshole. In the meantime, though, we have to talk to these women.'

'To warn them?' Yvette asks.

'In part. But I also want to know if they've been contacted by anyone strange. If he's picking up the pace, he may be dealing with more than one of these women at a time. Maybe he's asking them out, or posing as a salesman to case their houses or apartments. If we can find any crossovers between people in the lives of these girls, it may help point the way.'

'We need to be involved in those interviews,' I say.

Killkenny looks at me as though I'm crazy. 'You? I don't think so.'

'I said when we started this that we are willing to cooperate as long as we can protect the company name. I understand that you need to talk to these girls, but I have to be there to hear what's said and to answer any questions that they may have of NextLife. There are liability issues here that I need to address.'

Killkenny laughs. 'I don't give a shit about your company's liability issues,' he says. 'I only care about finding this sick fuck, and making sure he doesn't kill any other woman. It seems to me that that ought to be your main focus as well, Nick.'

'It is,' I say. 'That's why we've been cooperating. That's why I'm running interference with the company when I can. But I do still have responsibilities to the company to know what's happening.'

Killkenny shakes his head. 'No can do,' he says. 'This is a police investigation, not a fuckin' PR campaign for NextLife.'

'Fine,' I say. 'Anything else you need from the company, you can get through proper channels. You need to take the full names and addresses for these women? Serve a subpoena. I'm sure you'll get the information within a few months, once the company's lawyers have had a chance to run the request through the usual legal rigmarole. The court process can be a motherfucker, from what I hear.'

'You really want to play that game?' Killkenny shouts at me. 'You really want to mess with these people's lives like that?'

'No, I want to fully cooperate and give you everything you

need, but like I said from the beginning, there are conditions to that.'

'I'll have you brought up on charges of obstructing justice!' Killkenny yells, standing.

I stand, too. 'Good. More work for the lawyers. Have fun with that!' We are at a stand-off across the table and I have a flashback from my youth – back in the days when all those a generation ahead of us in the Charlestown rackets used to like to pit the two of us against each other, just to see who was stronger. The years have passed, but the instincts we learned are not far from the surface. We are both breathing heavily as we glare at each other. I wonder whether one of us will throw a punch. Odd as it may sound, it's clearly a possibility. Fortunately Yvette steps in.

'Sit down, both of you!' she shouts at us.

It breaks the spell. We continue staring at each other for a moment, but then both sit down. 'We all have the same basic goal here,' she continues. 'And, Paul, you can't possibly feel that we have been obstructing the investigation with our presence. In fact, if it wasn't for us, it's fair to say that you wouldn't be half as far along as you are, right?'

He says nothing, and it answers the question.

'Good. We're both glad we can help. We're both offended that someone might be using our technology to practice killing these girls. And we both want to continue to help. We've also made clear that we have not – that we *will* not – put the interests of NextLife above the need to catch this man. But if you want us in on the investigation, we do need to know what's happening. I don't think it's unreasonable for us to be involved in talking to these women. Hell, if we wanted to we could go out and talk to them on our own, but then we could be giving them mixed signals. Doesn't it make sense to coordinate this, so that we all know where everyone is?'

Killkenny considers this for a moment. 'Alright,' he says at last. 'You can come to the interviews, but let me handle them – you got it?'

'Of course.' Yvette looks at me. 'Nick?'

'Fine.'

'Fine,' Killkenny says. He looks at his watch. 'It's two-thirty. Will you be ready to start at seven-thirty? We may be able to catch a few of them before they go to work.'

'I'm fine with that,' I say. 'I can't remember the last time I was actually able to sleep for more than four consecutive hours anyway.

Killkenny looks at Yvette. 'How about you?' he asks. 'Are you coming along as well?'

She shakes her head. 'I'll let you boys handle the unfortunate task of interviewing the hot models. I have some things that I need to look into here.'

'Things related to the case?' Killkenny asks.

Yvette shoots me a quick glance. 'No,' she says. 'It's something else work-related.'

She's lying, I know. She's going to start trying to hack into the system to see whether *De Sade*'s LifeScenes were created on any of the NextLife computers, but she's being true to our agreement to share that with no one. She is, I realize again as I sit there, the most trustworthy person I have ever known.

Killkenny nods. 'I suppose work has to go on.'

'It does,' she agrees. 'And I need to talk to Nick about what I'm doing before he leaves. He is technically my boss.'

Killkenny looks back and forth between the two of us. 'In name only, I'm sure,' he says. It occurs to me that he has no idea how close to the truth this is. He stands up, pulls his coat off the back of his chair. 'I'm going to grab a smoke and a couple of hours' sleep.' To me he says, 'Meet me in front of my apartment at seven-thirty, and bring the list of addresses.'

'Sounds good,' I say. I still can't bring my tone to be friendly, but it's neutral. That should be enough.

'Thanks, Yvette,' he says.

'You're welcome.'

He looks at me, nods and walks out of the office.

'Asshole,' I mutter under my breath.

'Yeah, you should be good together in that way.'

'Nice. You said you needed to talk?'

She walks over to the office door and peers out onto the floor. The place is three-quarters filled with my staff, reclining in their overstuffed chairs, peeking into the fantasies of the company's loyal users, no one knowing that they are being watched and catalogued to enable us to analyze and create new products to keep them coming back – to keep them pushing holes in the barrier between real-life daydreams. I can see Killkenny walking out of the main door at the far end of the floor. She watches him leave and closes the door.

'I just wanted to make sure you weren't making a liar out of me,' she says, studying my face as she speaks.

'What are you talking about?' I have an idea, but I want to hear it from her.

'I told Killkenny that your priority is to find this guy. That that is more important to you than protecting the company. I need to know that I wasn't lying; that it's the truth.'

'It is,' I say. 'It is the truth.'

I can tell that she is trying to decide whether or not she believes me. 'Why do you need to be there when Killkenny talks to these girls?'

'I said why,' I point out. 'We need to know what's happening. If they have any questions that they want to ask the company, then we need someone there to know that those questions are addressed. NextLife hired these girls, after all.'

'That's it?' she asks. 'It's not so that if you find out that someone connected to the company is contacting these people, you can warn the company and protect whoever it is that's doing this?'

'It's not so I can protect the company.' That much is absolutely the truth.

'Really?'

'How can you ask me that?'

She makes a face. 'What do you mean: how? I know how much stock you have in this company. I know how much that's worth if we go public. It's millions. Tens of millions, probably. Greater men have been tempted by less.'

'I've never been a greater man,' I point out.

'You know what I mean,' she says. 'I don't care how aloof you are, that's a lot of money. I couldn't blame you for wanting to balance the need to catch *De Sade* against your own inter-ests. No one would.'

'Yes, you would. And you know me better than that.'

'I thought I did,' she says. 'Once I really thought I did.' She's looking me right in the eyes and I find it difficult to meet her gaze. I force myself to, though.

'I haven't changed.'

'No? I'm not sure.'

'You worry too much.'

'And there's no other reason you want to hear what these women have to say?'

'None.' I hold her look with all the effort I can muster.

'Okay,' she says. We stand there for a moment, looking at each other. It's the first time I can ever remember being with her when I felt uncomfortable. I've felt other things with her – amused, frustrated, angry, annoyed, turned on, happy – but there's always been a level of comfort that sat as the bedrock of our relationship. Then again, I've never lied to her before. Now it feels as though a tremor is running through that bedrock and, as slight as the shift is, it still feels as though it could tear a building down.

'Are you going home?' I ask. 'I could give you a ride.'

She shakes her head. 'I'm not tired, and I want to get started hacking. It's quiet now, not a bad time to begin.'

'Okay. I'm gonna try to get a little bit of sleep.'

'I understand.'

I grab the handle to my office door, turn it. Before I can open it, though, she says, 'Nick?' I turn around to look at her. She is a beautiful creature, I'm reminded. Even now – at two in the morning, with her hair wild and streaked, in the same clothes she's been wearing for close to a day, no makeup, no pretense – she is beautiful and strong and hard. For the first time, though, I can see a softer side. A sadder side. Perhaps, even, a damaged side.

'What?'

'I'm here,' she says. 'I'm a friend, and nothing can change

that.' Her face is, as it so often is, set against emotion. And yet there's something else there, tugging at the corners of her eyes.

'I appreciate that,' I say. 'I really do.'

I open the door and step out onto the floor. I look around the strange invented world in which I spend my life and, for the first time in twenty years, I wonder how well Yvette and I really know each other.

My car is parked on the street, two blocks north of the warehouse. It's a clear night and the moon is in its ascendancy, just a few evenings from being full. With the stars, it casts a light that makes it feel as though it's not really nighttime. I think this must be what it's like up in Alaska or Greenland during the summer, when it never really gets dark, but only dims a bit.

There's no one around as the hour approaches three. It is the heart of the night, when the latest partiers have stumbled home and the earliest risers are still more than an hour from dragging their weary asses out of bed. I think of it as *the quiet time*, when only the night shift and the lonely are conscious. Many of the lonely are on our website now, strapped in, exploring who they might be in a different reality; looking for loves lost and hoping that they might, too, be looking for them; seeking out the random and the strange and the dangerous. It's a relatively high-traffic time of the day for NextLife, which is why we still have nearly a full complement of Walkers active. In Bombay it's early afternoon, and our outsourced support staff are taking technical calls. Here, the vampires of our emerging online world are crawling over the World Wide Web, looking for others like them, or others to prey upon.

I hear the noise, and it takes a moment for it to register. I assume it's merely some college kid getting an early start on the day's walk of shame, getting home from some random, ill-advised hook-up. Stumbling, head down, muttering to himself . . .

Something about it, though, raises an alarm in the back of my head. I think there's something about growing up on the streets of a rough neighborhood. Of necessity you develop an inexplicable instinct about the world around you: what fits, and what doesn't; which movements are harmless, and which could be a threat.

I turn quickly and see a shadow duck into an alleyway ten yards up the street. 'Who's there?' I call, but there's no answer. I hear a bottle being kicked down the alley, rolling and bouncing loudly off the uneven bricks before it cracks. Against my better instincts I walk toward the alley, keeping my footsteps soft, creeping up on the corner as quietly as I can. I can feel my heart beating in my throat as I move.

When I get to the corner I plaster myself against the building, just out of sight from the alleyway. I stand there for a moment, listening. The silence is so overwhelming that it starts to wear on me, so I take a deep breath and stick my head around the corner, looking down the narrow passage. At the far end, I see a movement – running – and, without thinking, I take off after it.

There's a bend in the alley twenty yards down, and by the time I reach it, whoever is fleeing from me has reached the far end of the alley and has disappeared. I sprint to the end of the alley and stand on the intersecting street, looking both ways, searching for any movement, but there is nothing. The shadows are still, and the night is quiet again. I have no idea for how long I stand there, wondering whether I'm letting my imagination get the better of me. The images of the dead girls from the autopsy photos run through my head, and there is a buzzing in my ears as it dawns on me that this is no longer a game.

An explosion sends my heart nearly through my chest. It is a thunderous crash – a popping sound combined with a sprinkling of broken glass, coming from back up the alley in the other direction. I am frozen for a moment, unsure whether to follow the sound or to run in the other direction. Then a second explosion sounds, louder than the first, coming from the same direction, and I am moving back up the alley. It's not in my nature to flee.

I reach the far end of the alley, and everything is still and silent again. I look around, searching for any indication of where the explosion came from. It takes a moment, but then I see my car and I can tell something is wrong.

I walk over slowly, looking around me with each step, waiting for someone to emerge from a darkened doorway, or from behind another car, or from out of the sewer. Nothing happens, though, and as I come closer to my car I can see where the noises came from. My rear windshield and back passenger window have been smashed. The shards of glass are spread across the street and cover the back seat, sparkling blue-green at the edges in the moonlight, looking like rough diamonds or polished crystal meth.

'Shit,' I mutter to myself. The fear I had a few moments before is gone at this point – I'm angry now. I turn to the empty street. 'Who are you?' I shout. I wait a moment, almost as though I'm expecting a response. 'Who are you?' I shout again. In the distance, a woken dog barks an alarm.

I stand there for another few moments, looking around. I have the feeling that I am being watched by someone very close by. 'We're coming for you!' I yell out. 'We will find you!'

I think I hear some rustling, like a phantom shrinking back into the night, but I can't get a fix on the direction from which it is coming.

At last I open the driver's side door to the car and climb in. There is some glass on my seat, but I don't even bother to wipe it away. I turn the starter and put the car in gear, taking one last look around before I pull away.

'We're coming for you,' I say quietly again.

I step on the gas and head toward home.

CHAPTER EIGHTEEN

The next morning I pull up in front of Killkenny's apartment building. It's a renovated brownstone in an upscale section of the South End, close in toward the Back Bay. It's quarter after seven. I'm early, but that's just because I had trouble sleeping. My mind is in turmoil and I feel lost, but there's little I can do about it at this point.

I sit in my car as a warm morning breeze blows through my shattered car windows. The area is just starting to come to life, with people leaving early for work or heading out for a run before breakfast. Posh coffee shops and bistros dot the storefronts along the neighborhood. The residents are a combination of younger professionals and wealthy retirees, from the look of the people on the street. I know that apartments in the area start at seven figures, and I wonder how someone can afford to live in this area on a cop's salary.

Killkenny's SS is parked in front of a hydrant near his building, and I'm not surprised that there is no ticket on the windshield. I'm sure that the police department's parking cop for this area has been warned off messing with that particular car.

The detective emerges from his building at seven thirty-five, stands on his stoop and looks around. I climb out of my car and he sees me, comes my way. 'You ready for this?' he asks.

'Yeah,' I answer with more confidence than I feel.

He looks at my car windows. 'You had some work done, I see.'

'Cheaper than air conditioning.'

'What happened?'

I shrug. 'Not sure. Happened on the street last night.' For some reason I'm not eager to relay the entire story to him at the moment. Perhaps later, but not now.

'That's two bad nights for you in a row,' he comments.

'Bad luck.'

He raises an eyebrow. 'I try to stay away from people with bad luck,' he says. 'Maybe you shouldn't come today.'

'It only seems to come out at night,' I point out. 'We should be fine.'

He nods. 'Okay, but we're taking my car.'

'I don't have a parking sticker for this neighborhood,' I say.

'Good thing you know a cop who can take care of any parking tickets then,' he says with a crooked smile.

'I guess.' I look over my car, hesitating.

'What, are you worried it'll get stolen?'

'There are no windows,' I say. 'I can't lock it very effectively.'

He laughs. 'Trust me, no one's gonna steal that car. And if they did, I'm guessing you'll be better off. Insurance'll probably pay off more than it's worth.'

Sadly, he's probably right about that, but I've had the car

for a long time, so I still feel like I'm leaving a wounded comrade to die on the battlefield.

'It's a good neighborhood,' he says, clearly sensing my hesitation. 'Not like Chucktown. It'll still be here when we get back.'

I nod. 'Okay.' We walk over and get into his SS. It has a black leather interior and every extra feature you can imagine: rearview camera, Internet connectivity, Bluetooth, tricked-out stereo with satellite . . . the works. 'Nice,' I say.

'I told you, people judge a man by his car,' Killkenny says.

'You've done well for yourself.' I wonder whether he'll catch the implication in my voice, and regret having made the comment as the words tumble from my mouth. Fortunately Killkenny isn't self-aware enough to catch my drift. Either that, or he chooses to ignore it.

'Not as well as you'll do for yourself, when your company goes public,' he says simply. 'I just like to show it a bit.'

I leave it there; there's no point in pursuing it any further. He turns the ignition and the car roars into life. A few of the people on the street turn to look as Killkenny revs the engine. 'Where to first?' I ask.

Killkenny takes out a folder that contains the photos and information printouts of the seven models we've identified as having been the prototypes for *De Sade*'s LifeScenes. He flips it open. 'Jennifer Quincy,' he says. 'She lives relatively nearby.'

'South End?'

'Washington Street. Out by Mass. Ave.'

'That's still South End.'

He snorts. 'Barely.'

*

We pull up to the apartment at the address in Jennifer Quincy's file, on Worcester Square, just off Washington Street. It's three-story brick bow-front, probably built in the first half of the twentieth century. All of the buildings around the square are identical, facing out on a tiny patch of grass in the center that divides the traffic that flows to the northwest on one side and the southeast on the other. It's a mixed lower-middle class neighborhood a block from City Hospital. There are some young professionals trying to save money who have moved in, but the area hasn't given in to gentrification yet, and the people on the street stare at Killkenny's car with distrust as it glides to the curb in a no-parking zone.

I look back and forth between the photo in the file on my lap and the second-floor windows, which, from the address in the file, likely look out from Jennifer Quincy's apartment. Closing the file, I open the door and get out. Killkenny climbs out as well. We walk up the steps of the stoop and look at the list of names by the series of buzzers next to the front door. Killkenny reaches out and presses the button next to the names 'Quincy/Kimball' identified as living in Apartment 2A. We stand there for a while waiting. Nothing happens and Killkenny reaches out and presses the button again.

It takes twenty seconds or so, but eventually a woman's voice comes over the intercom. 'Yeah?' She sounds annoyed.

'Is this Jennifer Quincy?' Killkenny says, pressing the intercom button and speaking into the grille.

'Yeah. Who's this?'

'At least we know she's still alive,' Killkenny says to me. He presses the intercom button again. 'This is Detective Paul

Killkenny, Boston Police Department. Do you have a moment to talk?'

There's a long pause before the voice comes back. 'Talk about what?'

'I'd rather talk in person, if possible,' Killkenny responds.

The pause again. 'Fine. Just give me a couple minutes, okay?' For the first time I can hear the thick Boston accent.

We stand on the stoop, looking out at the neighborhood. Those who pass us look up with scowls. 'We're not popular here. They know I'm a cop,' Killkenny comments.

'What do you think gives it away?' I ask deadpan, looking at him. Everything about him – the aggressive stance, the sense of entitlement – screams 'cop'; he could be nothing else.

'You're my silent partner up there, right?' he says.

'Whatever you say, boss.'

'I'm serious about that. You're only here so I can avoid the hassle of a subpoena and dealing with your company's lawyers to get the information I need. If Welker knew I allowed you to tag along on this, he'd have my ass in a sling. If you or your girlfriend step out of line, we're done with this, and I'll consider bringing charges.'

'She's not my girlfriend.'

That draws a smirk from Killkenny, and I realize he was baiting me. 'Whatever,' he says. 'I just want to know that you're gonna keep your mouth shut.'

'Yeah, I'll let you do the talking,' I agree.

The front door opens, and a guy who looks like he's in his early twenties comes out. He's attractive, with dark hair and a brooding, unshaven look that women tend to like. His hair is disheveled, and he's tucking his shirt, which is inside-out, into his pants. He's carrying his socks and his wallet and his head is bowed, looking down at the ground. 'Excuse me,' he says as he sidesteps us on the stoop.

Killkenny and I turn and watch him walk away, down the street, as the intercom cracks and Jennifer Quincy's voice says, 'Okay, you can come up if you want.'

Killkenny smiles at the man walking down the street and chuckles. 'This should be interesting.'

'What's this all about?'

Jennifer Quincy is standing in the living room/dining room/kitchen of her 900-square-foot apartment, her arms crossed in front of a loose-fitting T-shirt with the logo of a band that I don't recognize emblazoned on the front. She is wearing striped leggings, and she's tried to pull her blonde hair back into some reasonable shape, but it's too unruly to be tamed without a great deal more effort. The apartment is small for two people, but relatively neat. The furniture is low-end IKEA, and there are candles lined up on the mantel above a non-working fireplace. Killkenny walks over to the mantel and examines the candles. They have burned down, and the wax has spilled out unevenly onto the mantel's white paint. It looks like they were probably burning the night before, likely to help set the mood with the guy who shouldered past us on the stoop. I look at Jennifer, standing there like a post-coital wreck, and it's hard not to notice how striking she is, with her tanned skin and light hair. Even her angry stance makes her seem all the more sexual. I feel a distinct pang of jealousy toward the man we saw leaving.

'The door outside says Quincy/Kimball,' Killkenny says. 'You have a roommate?'

'She's away on business.'

'What kind of business?'

'Commercial real estate. She's an intern. Is this about her?'

'I just wanted to know whether there was anyone else here.' Killkenny is walking around the room, looking things over. He picks up a picture of Quincy and a group of friends smiling broadly at the camera, all holding drinks raised in cheer. It looks like it was probably taken on some spring break within the past few years.

'There's no one else here,' she says.

'Not anymore.' Killkenny looks over his shoulder at her and gives her a smile that borders on lecherous.

'Am I in trouble?'

Killkenny puts the picture down. 'No, you're not. We're in the middle of an investigation, and we're here to ask you a few questions about a modeling job you did around four and a half years ago.'

She's looking blankly at him. 'A modeling job I did four and a half years ago?'

'Yeah. You were a model, right?'

She shrugs, and I see the shadow of disappointed expectations cross her face. 'I did some modeling,' she says. 'I don't know that it was ever steady enough to say I was *a model*. It's a tough business.'

'I'm sure,' Killkenny says. 'Lots of pretty girls out there.' She says nothing, but recrosses her arms, waiting. 'We wanted to talk to you about a job you did for a company called NextLife. Do you remember that one?'

Her arms fall to her sides as she exhales and her face goes

sour. 'Yeah,' she says. 'I remember that one.' She sits on the faux-modern orange couch against the wall. 'That was the one that got me out of the business.'

'How so?'

'What are you investigating?'

'Murder.'

That gets her attention. 'A murder? Of someone I know?'

Killkenny shakes his head. 'It's not likely. But it may have to do with NextLife. It would help if you could tell us about what you did for them.'

'Sure,' she says absently.

'You said it was the job that got you out of the business. How did it do that?'

Her eyes are directed toward the floor, but her focus is in the distance, on the past. 'I'd been trying to break in for a couple years. I got some modeling jobs in my senior year, up in Leominster. Some local-paper stuff for some of the manu-facturing companies. That convinced me to come to Boston to see if I could make it a steady thing.' She takes a deep breath and lets it out. 'I was naive.'

'How old were you?'

'I had just turned eighteen when I got to Boston.'

'And when you did the job for NextLife?'

'It was right before my twentieth birthday.'

'What happened?'

She leans back in the couch, crosses her legs and her shoulders seem to draw in upon her body. 'The first year I was here I got picked up by the Helena Agency. It's one of the smaller ones, but it had an okay reputation, and who was I to judge, right? Anyway, they got me a job here, a job there – usually catalogue stuff, a few fliers. Nothing that paid any real money. I had to get a job waiting tables to buy food and pay rent. They kept telling me that I could make much more money if I'd be willing to show a little more skin, but I'd always said that I wouldn't do nudity. I did some underwear stuff for a flier once, but it was pretty tame, and I'd always said that was as far as I'd go.'

Killkenny sits in an upholstered chair across the coffee table from her. He frowns and reaches underneath him, in the folds of the cushion, and pulls out a black lace bra. He holds it up on one finger. 'You had your standards, no doubt.'

She shoots forward, grabs the bra back from him and crumples it into a ball angrily, starts to put it in her pocket, but quickly realizes she has no pockets. She seems defeated and unfolds the bra on her lap, looking at it contemplatively. 'I had standards once,' she says quietly. 'After a year and a half the people at the agency sat me down and told me they were going to drop me. They thought I had the look, but I wasn't getting the jobs, and they had other girls they wanted to bring in.' She looks at Killkenny, her eyes pleading for understanding. 'You gotta realize, when I left Leominster I said I wouldn't go back until I was a real success. I didn't have any skills, I didn't have any money. So I begged them. I told them I'd do anything to get work.'

'So you started taking your clothes off.'

She nods. 'Just a little. No full nudity, but I had a few jobs posing for fliers that the hawkers for the strip-joints out on Route One give out. You know, the teasers? Those six-by-four postcards that offer free admission? They give them out in the city to try to get the business out there. Nothing too bad. Show a little bit of nipple, that sort of thing. And the money was better. The jobs I was doing before were paying a couple hundred dollars for the day, tops. These jobs were paying five, even six hundred dollars. So that was good.'

'How'd you get the job for NextLife?'

'Through the agency. They called and said they had this job that would pay a thousand dollars. They said it was full nudity, but the trick was, it was never going to be used as advertising or anything like that. They said it was just to help some programmers map the female body. So I figured it was low-risk, and no one would ever know. And the agency really wanted me to do it, and it was the best money I'd ever been offered, so I figured: what the hell – you know?'

'What happened?'

'It was like I was captured by fucking aliens, that's what happened,' she says angrily. 'Those people were freaks.'

'How so?'

'Well, to start with, at most photo shoots there's a set of some sort, and they have robes, and there are people there who are nice to you and try to make you feel comfortable. There was none of that in this case. There were about ten of us who were being shot all in a row, so we just had to sit there in this sort of laboratory of a place. There was one photographer, who was okay; he seemed to know what he was doing. But then there were these three or four geeks there who were directing the show. When it was my turn, they had me strip down – no prep, no explanation of what we were doing. And then they had me stand in front of this blue backdrop bucknaked, and the photographer took about a hundred pictures.

A few of them were full-body shots, but then they had him focus right up close on every part of me.' She pauses and looks at us both. 'You get that? *Every* part of me.'

'Yeah, we get it,' Killkenny says.

'I mean, it wasn't even like something from *Playboy*, where they try to be sexy. This felt like . . . I don't even know what.'

'That was it?'

'I wish. After that, they put these little dots all over me, and they told me to move from pose to pose while they took movies with this special camera. And, let me tell you, some of these poses . . . well, they didn't leave much to the imagination. The entire time these people there were looking at me like I was some sort of fucking lab rat. When I walked out of there I said: *fuck this*. Nothing was worth going back to do something like that again.'

'Do you remember anything about the people who were at the shoot?'

'Sure. It was such a freaky experience. The guy who was directing things was an older guy. An Indian – dot, not feather. I didn't like him; he had no warmth. If anything, he almost seemed angry. It was like he thought I was unclean, when he was the one having them take the goddamned pictures of me.'

'Was his name Gunta?'

She gives a derisive laugh. 'I never got their names.'

'Who else was there?' Killkenny asks.

'There was another guy there who was younger than the Indian, but who seemed like he might have been the Indian guy's boss. Nice clothes. He seemed more normal.'

'More normal – how?'

'Well, he was at least talking to a couple of the girls,

trying to make them feel comfortable. Maybe even hitting on them.'

'You find that normal?'

'Yeah, Detective, I do. If there's a roomful of models who are all taking their clothes off, I think a normal guy might think to strike up a conversation. What do you think you'd do?' Her tone is sharp and biting, and it makes me like her more. Killkenny deserved to take a little back for all that he'd been giving her.

He nods. 'Fair enough. Did you talk to this guy enough to get a name?'

She shakes her head. 'He might have said a quick hello to me, but he was focused on a couple of the other girls. One in particular, with a totally different look from me.' She looks at Killkenny. 'Not everyone's into blondes, y'know? I'm okay with that.'

'Anyone else?'

'There were two guys sitting behind laptops, tapping away as the pictures were being taken. I have no idea what their job was.'

'Can you describe them?'

'Not really. By the time I had any exposure to them – no pun intended – I was so freaked out that I was just trying to get through it. I have a vague recollection that one of them was decent-looking, and he seemed to have some sympathy for what I was going through, but that's about it.' The room is quiet for a moment. 'What are these questions all about? What do they have to do with a murder?'

'Three murders, actually,' Killkenny says.

Her eyes go wide. 'Three murders? What do they have to do with the modeling job?'

Killkenny leans forward in his chair. 'Do you know how they ended up using the images they took of you that day?'

She shakes her head. 'I wanted nothing to do with it after that. I've never seen anything that's used them.'

'Have you ever gone on NextLife?'

'No. I know about them, now. Who doesn't? But I've got no interest, after my experience with the company. Why? How did they use the pictures?'

Killkenny looks at me, and I can't tell whether he wants me to speak now. It would be just like him to let me handle the worst part of the discussion. He doesn't, though; he turns back to her. 'The company has a portion of the website where you can create your own world and you can populate it with people. When you design those people, you go to a library of different looks that they have. You're one of the prototypes for those looks.'

'Oh.' For a moment, she seems to accept this without concern. 'So I'm like a backdrop?'

Killkenny frowns. 'That's one possible way the images can be used.'

She stares at him, her expression darkening as she starts to connect the dots. 'Of course if that was it – that I was just going to be used as a backdrop – why would they have needed to take pictures of me naked?'

Killkenny says nothing.

'Great,' she says. 'Motherfuckers! They said the pictures were just to train the computers.'

'That's true,' Killkenny says, an obnoxious smirk on his face. 'They trained the computers to create an image that looks like you.'

She leans her head back and looks at the ceiling. 'Goddamnit! I'm such a fool!' she screams.

'If it makes you feel any better, I think you're generally a starting point. From what I've been told, most people mix and match different features and body parts, so there's probably very few times where you're used in full. And there are several hundred others, too.'

'It's still fucked-up,' she says. 'And what does it have to do with these murders?'

'The three murdered girls were also models for the project,' Killkenny says. 'We wanted to talk to you and let you know that.'

She just stares at him for a long time. 'So, am I in danger?' she asks at last.

'We can't say that for sure.'

'You can't say for sure? Is that supposed to make me feel better?'

He shakes his head. 'No. But it might help us to know whether you've had any contact with anyone from the company recently.'

'You're kidding, right? After the way I described my experience, you think I'd have anything to do with anyone from that company?'

I have to bite my lip as I listen to her. I want to apologize for my company. I want to defend my company. I want to tell her that the company I've spent the last four years working for – the company that pulled me and Ma back from the brink of despair – is not the same company she's talking about. I keep my mouth shut, though, and bear her justifiable rage in silence.

'How about anyone else? Any random men you've come into contact with who've expressed more than casual interest?'

'How do you define casual interest?' she asks, an eyebrow raised.

'I mean more than conversation. Random men who seem to want more from you, particularly in a sexual way, for example.'

She laughs ruefully. 'Seriously? Do you go to bars, Detective? I don't think I've spoken to a random guy in the past ten years who didn't want something more from me – particularly in a sexual way. That's the way of the world.'

'Fair enough.' Killkenny gets up and walks to the window, looks out on Worcester Square. 'And the guy you kicked out before letting us in?' he asks.

She straightens. 'I don't know what you're talking about.'

'Yes, you do.'

She's looking at his back, and he turns around and meets her gaze. She tries to hold the look, but it lasts less than ten seconds before she looks away. 'He's . . . he's a friend.'

'For how long?'

'He's okay.'

'For how long? Last night?'

She looks back up at him. 'Night before last.'

'You got a name?'

'He's okay.'

'I guess that's your call. I can have him checked out if you want, but if you want to keep it to yourself, there's nothing I can do. I'm just trying to help.'

She looks down at the floor. 'You really think he could be dangerous?'

'I have no idea, I do know that there is someone out there who is dangerous and who has murdered three women who were involved in the same modeling project you participated in. Do you really want to take a chance?'

'I can't believe this is happening,' she mutters, shaking her head.

'Like I say, it's your decision.'

'Jake,' she says after a moment. 'He bartends down at a bar called the Sandstone.'

'Last name?'

She shoots Killkenny a look like he's an idiot.

'Right. No last name.'

'I live my life,' she says.

'So I gather.'

She is still holding her bra in her hands and she looks down at it, spreads it out and smoothes it out on her lap. 'I live my life,' she whispers, more to herself than to us. She takes a deep breath and looks up at Killkenny. 'So what happens now?'

'What do you mean?'

'I mean do you provide me with some kind of protection?'

'You strike me as the kind of girl who keeps plenty of protection handy.'

'Fuck you, I'm serious,' she says. 'Are you gonna have someone watching the apartment, at least?'

He shakes his head. 'That's not possible. We don't have the manpower.'

'So, you just show up and tell me that I'm in danger, and then you do nothing?'

He reaches into his pocket and pulls out a business card,

hands it to her. 'You call me if anything out of the ordinary happens.'

She looks at the card. 'What do you consider out of the ordinary?'

'In your case I have no idea.'

She looks at me. 'Can I get your partner's card, too?'

'You call me, I'll answer,' Killkenny says.

'Your partner's better-looking,' she says, still looking at me. I give her a half smile, mainly because I know she said it primarily to annoy Killkenny and I appreciate the spite. She returns my smile, and I can see the weariness in it. 'He's awful quiet, though.'

Killkenny walks toward the door. 'That's him, the strong, silent type. C'mon, Gary Cooper, we have other fans of yours we need to talk to.'

I nod to Jennifer Quincy. 'Ma'am,' I say, figuring I might as well play up the stereotype now that it's established.

'Bye, Gary,' she says, watching me leave. 'I waitress at the Nines down in the Back Bay, if you're ever hungry.'

I give her the half smile again, touch the brim of my imaginary hat and walk out the door.

CHAPTER NINETEEN

'You were pretty rough on her, weren't you?'

Killkenny and I are back in his car, headed to the home of the next woman on the list, who lives in Brookline, around five miles outside of Boston. We travel north on Massachusetts Avenue, toward the Charles, then peel off onto Commonwealth, inch our way through the traffic at Fenway and then pick up some speed out to the western suburb. It's about a fifteen-minute trip.

'She chose her life,' Killkenny says.

'Don't we all?'

'Yeah. But not all girls choose to pose nude and have a train of random guys trekking through their bedroom. She's getting what she asked for.'

'Right. And you strike me as the monogamous type.'

'That's different. I'm a guy.'

'So?'

'We're the hunters. They're the prey. That's just the way it is. It's nature. We're genetically programmed to spread our seed. Women – at least the ones who aren't screwed up in the

166

head – are programmed to nail us down. It's the way the human race has survived through the years.'

'That's the dumbest thing I've ever heard.'

'It's science. Don't you read?'

'They're the gatherers, not the prey.'

'What?' He looks over at me, confused.

'You want to get into the science – if you want to call it that – men were the hunters and women were the gatherers, not the prey. The prey was the wooly mammoths, or the bison, or whatever it was we were hunting. And by the way, there's evidence that the women participated in the hunt, too.'

'Huh!' He digests that for a moment, but it seems to have little impact. 'It's still fucked-up. All this bullshit about gender equality is just that. Men and women are different, and they should act different.'

I give up. 'I have to call Yvette.' I want to see what she's been able to learn. I pull out my cellphone and dial her number. It rings four times before she picks up.

'Hey,' she says.

'Hey. Where are you?'

'The office. Your office, actually.'

'Still?'

'I'm on a tear,' she says. 'You know how I get.'

'I do.' I glance over at Killkenny. He seems focused on driving, but I still don't want him to know that we are working a different angle without keeping him in the loop. I realize I have to be a little careful about what I say on the phone when he can hear me. 'How's it going?' I figure that's unspecific enough that it won't raise Killkenny's suspicions.

She hesitates. 'I don't want to say, yet. I still need to nail some things down. It's complicated.'

'That sounds promising.'

'It may be. I'm still not entirely sure, though.'

I can't deal with the suspense. 'Can you give me an idea of what we're talking about, at least?'

'You sound strange. Is Killkenny there?'

'Yup.'

'Ah, I get it.'

'Good for you. Can you give me a little more detail?'

She sighs over the phone. 'Fine. I've found pieces of *De Sade*'s LifeScenes on the system. At least I think I've found portions of them on the system. They're just fragments. If these things were created on the system, though, whoever did it did a damn good job of trying to wipe them out, or at least make it so that it would be awfully difficult to reconstruct them.'

'How?'

'Most frag programs simply unhook the data. Whoever did this went at least one step further.'

'I'm not sure I'm following you,' I say.

'Think of the data stream that makes up the LifeScene as a series of data packets that are hooked together, like a train. When they are transmitted over the Internet, or over any network for that matter, the cars in the train are decoupled so they can travel separately, which is way more efficient and necessary for the network to transport significant volumes of data from multiple sources. Each packet is given the information about the destination, and then they're also given a code at the beginning and ending of the packet, so that the stream can be reassembled at the other end. Most frag programs simply remove those identifiers, so it's hard to put the pieces back together.'

'But it's still possible to do, right?'

'Yeah, it just takes a little time and work. If you can find the data fragments and identify them by similar structures, it's possible to start reassembling them. At least, that's normally true. In this case, though, whoever created these LifeScenes seems to have gone further, so that even when I identify the fragments by their properties, I'm having trouble reassembling them because it seems like they're allergic to each other.'

'I don't understand.'

'I didn't either, at first. But whoever did this seems to have come up with a way to not only remove the sequence identifiers, but also make it so that the data fragments no longer want to be put together. It's like they're repelling each other. It's very sophisticated.'

'Can you fix it?'

'I think so. That's what I'm working on now. But if I'm right, and these data bits I've found are actually from *De Sade*'s LifeScenes, you know what it means, right?'

I cast a quick glance over at Killkenny. He seems to be listening to my half of the conversation, and I realize we're probably talking too much. 'Yeah,' I say. 'I've got a good idea.'

'It means that *De Sade* is here at the company – or at least that he has access to hardware that's connected to the company's system. And he's someone with some sick computer skills.'

'Yeah, I get it. Keep at it.'

'Will do, boss.' I can't tell over the phone whether there's sarcasm in her voice. 'How's it going there?'

'It's a barrelful of laughs.'

'Have you talked to any of the women yet?'

'One.'

'How did it go?'

'It was interesting.'

'I'm sure. How did the girl take it? Was she freaked out?'

'She wasn't happy,' I say. 'Who would be, when a cop shows up in the morning to tell you that there's a psycho out there who might be interested in making you his next victim? At least our good detective here was extremely sensitive.'

'I'm sure his bedside manner is just great.'

'He's a regular Florence Nightingale.' Killkenny looks over at me. 'And his views on women are very enlightened.'

'I'm shocked,' Yvette says.

'Fuck off!' Killkenny says quietly.

'I've got to go,' I say. 'He seems displeased with me.'

'Let me know how the rest of the day goes.'

'Will do. And let me know how the rest of the research goes.'

'You'll be the first.'

'You mean the only.'

'Right. That's what I meant.' The line clicks dead. I put the phone back in my pocket.

'Sounds like she's working on something important,' Killkenny says.

'The company's business goes on.'

'I'm sure it does. Is this a new product?'

I look over at him. 'Sorry, it's proprietary. We're not allowed to talk about the things that we're working on.'

'That's smart. I usually operate under the same rules. I'm making an exception in this case, though, aren't I? I mean, here you are going on a ride-along with me on the investigation of a murder that involves your company.'

I decide to try to change the subject. 'Who is the girl we're talking to now?'

'Taylor Westerbrooke,' he says. 'Next one on the pile.'

I open the file and flip to the next image. The striking young redhead from the LifeScene that Yvette GhostWalked the day before stares out at me, her smile thick with enthusiasm and possibilities. 'With luck, this will go better than the last one.'

We arrive at the Westerbrooke residence on Hilltop Avenue five minutes later. There is a large stone archway that we pass through, which leads to a wide, circular, cobbled driveway. We park near the front door and get out, both looking up at the enormous house. It is a three-story stone Georgian building with two wings and columns out front. It's on at least two acres near the heart of the city.

'Looks like her modeling career is going well,' Killkenny says.

I nod, and we walk to the front door. We press the doorbell to the left of the door and we can hear the elaborate chimes sounding from inside. A moment later the door opens and we are greeted by a very attractive redheaded woman in her early forties. 'Can I help you?' she says.

I am holding the file and I flip it open to the page for Taylor Westerbrooke, glancing from the photo to the woman. It looks like her, but the age is off.

'Miss Westerbrooke?' Killkenny says tentatively.

'*Mrs*,' she says with emphasis. 'Mrs Westerbrooke, yes. How can I help you?'

'Taylor Westerbrooke?' I ask.

She frowns, the confusion apparently resolved. 'Meghan Westerbrooke,' she says. 'You're looking for my daughter.'

'Yes,' Killkenny says. 'Does she live here?'

'Just for the summer,' she says. 'She's home from school. She's a sophomore at Skidmore.' Killkenny and I look at each other; we've both done the math in our heads, and it doesn't add up. He takes out his badge and holds it up for the woman to see. Her frown deepens. 'What is this all about?'

'Can we come in?' Killkenny asks.

It takes a moment for her to respond and I can see her debating. 'By all means,' she says at last, stepping back. I follow Killkenny in. We're in a two-story foyer; a grand staircase sweeps up from one side, and archways lead in three directions – left, right and center. There is artwork on the walls that I'm guessing is worth more than Ma's house.

Mrs Westerbrooke leads us through the archway to the left, into a sitting room dominated by yellow florals. She motions us to sit on a deep couch, and sits across a glass-topped coffee table from us on a Queen Anne chair. 'What has she done now?' she asks with a sigh.

'She's not in trouble,' Killkenny says. 'At least, not in the way you're suggesting, and not as far as I know.'

'Oh.' She seems wrongfooted now. 'What's this about, then?'

'Taylor did some modeling for a company called NextLife a few years ago, is that right?'

She waves a hand. 'It's possible,' she says, wrinkling her nose as though she finds the notion distasteful. 'She used to model when she was younger. It was her father's idea; I never really approved. That was when she started—' She cuts herself off and looks at the two of us, realizing that she may be saying too much. 'That's when she started having more of an attitude.'

'The job we're talking about was a little over four years ago. How old was she then?' Killkenny asks.

She frowns. 'She's nineteen now, so that means she would have been fifteen back then. She'd already been modeling for a couple of years, of course. They like the girls to start young.'

Killkenny gives me a look of wonder, then turns back to her. 'Mrs Westerbrooke, do you know whether she did a modeling job for NextLife?'

'I don't, but I didn't keep track of what jobs she was doing back then.'

'When she was in her early teens? You didn't keep track of what modeling jobs she was taking?'

'Of course not.'

'Did you know she was modeling in the nude?'

She looks shocked. 'Don't be silly. Of course she wasn't. She was a child.'

'Yes, she was. You can see why I'm asking.'

She's silent for a moment. 'That's not possible,' she says. 'It would be illegal, wouldn't it?'

'Yes, it would. It's called child pornography.'

'There, just as I said. She couldn't have been modeling nude; the agency wouldn't have permitted it.'

We hear a door open and the sound of heels clicking on the marble foyer floor. A moment later Taylor Westerbrooke walks into the room. She has a mane of fiery red hair that falls about her shoulders in a deliberately untamed way. She's wearing a short skirt and a loose T-shirt, and she's carrying a giant coffee. She's wearing headphones, and large sunglasses cover half her face. She's a few feet into the room before she notices that we are there, and she pulls up short. 'Oh,' she says, and I hear her mother's influence in her tone. She scowls at her mother. 'I didn't know you were in here.'

She turns and starts back in the other direction. Her mother tries to flag her down. 'Taylor,' she says. The girl either can't hear her mother over the music coming out of the earphones or she ignores her. 'Taylor!' her mother calls louder. I think I sense a pause in her step, but she picks up her pace again with only a slight miss in beat.

'Excuse me, Miss!' Killkenny shouts. He's loud enough that it startles even me, and I think for a moment Taylor Westerbrooke may fall off her heels. She turns around and looks at all three of us. She reaches up and takes the buds out of her ears.

Mrs Westerbrooke, who is clearly also startled, stares at Killkenny for a moment. 'These men have a couple of questions they need to ask you,' she says.

The girl comes slowly back into the room, a look somewhere between annoyance and boredom on her face. 'What?' she demands in a tone that is pure teenage entitlement.

'It's about your modeling, dear,' her mother says. 'These men are under the impression that you posed in the nude when you were younger. I was just explaining that they were mistaken.'

The girl looks at her mother like she's an idiot. 'No, they're not,' she says.

Mrs Westerbrooke looks like she's swallowed gum. 'Of course they are,' she says. 'You were far too young to pose without clothes.'

'What are you talking about, Mom? Did you ever see the clothes they used to put me in on the runways? Shit, I was practically naked at fashion shows.'

For a moment her mother looks relieved. 'Oh, well yes, if you're talking about metaphorically, there were times when the clothes were probably more risqué than they should have been, but you never actually posed without anything on.'

'Sure I did.'

This time it looks as though the gum has gotten caught in Mrs Westerbrooke's throat and might choke her. 'You . . . did . . . not.' The words come out with emphasis and authority, as though that would be enough to make them true.

'Don't be such a prude, Mother. Sometimes I wore a school-girl outfit, too. That seemed to go over big.'

'You were a child!'

Looking at Taylor Westerbrooke, it occurs to me that – age aside – it's probably been a long time since she was really a child.

'It would have been illegal. No one would have let you.'

'I lied about my age,' Taylor says. 'We all did. If you wouldn't take your clothes off, you couldn't make any real money. My allowance only went so far back then.'

Mrs Westerbrooke tries to say something, but no sound comes out of her mouth. Killkenny takes the opportunity to gain some control over the direction of the discussion. 'Did you ever model for NextLife?'

She makes a face. 'That was a freakshow.' She tosses her hair back and puts one of her buds back in so that she can listen to the music as she talks to us. 'They had no class what-soever, and no idea how to treat the talent.' She emphasizes the word *talent*. 'I swear to God, the photographer might as well have been working a picture booth at the mall. There was no art to it at all. I was just standing there, and these old guys watched as he took pictures all up and down my body.' She shakes her head at the memory. 'They didn't even have decent coffee for us.'

Her mother listens, her mouth open. 'Taylor Westerbrooke!' she manages to choke out. 'How could you?'

'Oh please, Mother. I was working.'

'Without clothes?'

She looks at her mother with venom. 'It's not like it was the first time.'

'You did this more than once?'

'You're going to act now like you care what I was doing? It's a little late for that, don't you think?'

Killkenny jumps back in, trying to keep the mother–daughter spat from spinning beyond his control. 'It's the NextLife job we need to know about.'

The girl looks at him dismissively. 'Who are you?' she demands. Killkenny takes out his badge, holds it up. She looks past the badge and right into his eyes. 'So? I haven't done anything illegal. Not lately, and not that you'd know about.'

I hear Mrs Westerbrooke gasp. This conversation may be enough to keep me from ever having children. 'Child pornography is illegal,' Killkenny points out.

'And you're going to arrest the child? I'm the victim, aren't I?'

Killkenny shakes his head. 'We're not here to arrest anyone. But we do need to know what you remember about that photo shoot.'

'Like you could call it that,' she says. 'I've pretty much told you all I remember. It was cold, and there was no coffee. I was in and out, and they gave me a check. That was pretty much it.'

'Do you remember anything about the people who were there during the shoot?'

She shakes her head. 'There were four or five, I think, but I can't really remember. None of them stand out.'

'What is this all about, Detective?' Mrs Westerbrooke asks.

'Have you ever been on the NextLife website?' Killkenny asks.

'Goodness, no,' she says.

'How about you?' he asks the girl.

She shakes her head. 'No. I have friends who like it, but I'm not big into computers. I have a real life, you know?'

'Well, your images are part of a library of several hundred models that's used to create avatars. You understand what that means?'

'Sure. The fake people in computer-land, right?'

'Yeah, that's right. Well, three of the other women who modeled to create that library have been killed. It could be a coincidence, but we're investigating.'

Mrs Westerbrooke gasps again. 'Oh my God! You don't think my daughter could be in any danger, do you?'

'Probably not. Has anything out of the ordinary happened recently?'

'I wish,' the girl replies.

'No contact from men you don't know? No one reaching out to you, looking to get . . . involved?'

She thinks about that for a moment. 'There was a boy I

met at a bar a week or so ago. I was planning on going out with him; he's really cute. But that's it.'

'This is someone you don't know?'

'Yeah. Like I said, we met at a bar.'

'Taylor!' her mother says sharply. 'You're still only nineteen. You shouldn't be out at bars.'

The girl rolls her eyes. She asks Killkenny, 'Are you saying I shouldn't go out with him?'

'Until we get this straightened out, and we know what we are talking about, you may want to deal only with people you already know.'

'I'm not interested in any of the boys I know,' she says in a pouty voice.

'It's for your own good,' her mother says. 'Besides, you're grounded.' The attempt to enforce discipline draws a loud, sharp laugh.

'Your mother's right,' Killkenny says. 'It's better for now if you don't deal with anyone you don't know.'

'He's so cute, though!' The pout comes out again.

Killkenny stands. 'I think we've got all we need. We'll let you know if we learn more. And please, by all means, let us know if anything unusual happens.'

'We will, of course, Detective,' Mrs Westerbrooke says. She walks us back out through the foyer to the door. 'I'm sorry about Taylor's behavior,' she continues. 'She's always been . . . a difficult girl.' She looks at Killkenny nervously. 'You're not going to put any of what she said in any sort of an official report or anything, are you? I don't want her to get into any trouble.'

'Our files are not public,' Killkenny says. 'For the moment, ma'am, I would just keep an eye on your daughter. She could use some looking after.'

Mrs Westerbrooke shakes her head. 'You have no idea.'

CHAPTER TWENTY

As we pull out of the Westerbrooke driveway I turn and glance at Mrs Westerbrooke standing there, looking dazed and confused. For a moment, I wonder whether she'll even go back into the house. It seems just as likely that she'll flee; get into her car, leave it all behind, and drive. It constantly amazes me how rarely wealth translates into happiness. Growing up in my lower-middle-class neighborhood in Charlestown, we always assumed that money was the answer. It's what everyone chased back then. What they all still seem to chase. And we certainly all thought that those who made their money in legitimate ways – and those who'd had wealth all their lives – sat around in their safe, secure homes marveling at their good fortune. I never knew anyone who was really wealthy back then. It wasn't until I went to MIT that I started to have a window into the lives of the people I'd always thought of as privileged, and what I saw shocked me. I saw insecurity and bitterness and a lack of fulfillment that rivaled what I'd grown up with. It sometimes expressed itself in different ways, but it seemed, at its core, to be the same. And so many of my experiences with the rich people I'd come across since then, like the Westerbrookes and

Josh Pinkerton, had reinforced my suspicion that I'd been misled about the effects of money while growing up.

'Fifteen years old,' Killkenny says as he drives, interrupting my musings on wealth.

'Huh?'

'That's how old she was when those images were taken. Fifteen. Nice company you've got there.'

'She lied about her age.'

'And apparently the company didn't do anything to verify how old she actually was.'

I have no response 'Where to now?' I ask.

'We're headed north, up to Sommerville. The next girl.'

'Who is it?'

'Check the file.'

I flip open the file and turn to the next set of images. For a moment I can't breathe. My girl from *De Sade*'s LifeScene with the canopied bed is staring up at me. 'Kendra Madison,' I say quietly. I'm not even aware that I've said her name out loud.

'Kendra Madison,' Killkenny repeats. 'What do you think we'll find with this one?'

I'm staring at her picture, but I'm seeing her tied to the bed. In my mind, I'm looking down at her from *De Sade*'s eyes, watching her as the ecstasy builds in her face, feeling her move beneath me. 'I don't know,' I say. 'I really don't know.'

Sommerville was originally part of Charlestown. It split off more than 150 years ago, as Charlestown was urbanizing. Any hope that the split would maintain the rural feel of the area ten minutes due north of Boston, wedged between the northern corners of Cambridge and Charlestown, turned out to be a pipe dream: Sommerville is now the most densely populated municipality in New England. Bounded by the Seven Hills of the town, it was the first city to fly the Stars and Stripes; it was the first town where a residential phone line was installed – running to the laboratory where Thomas Edison did much of his work; and it was the birthplace of the revered American delicacy, Marshmallow Fluff. It was also the home of the Winter Hill gang, the Irish-American mob that ran most of the Boston area for decades through the 1990s.

As we drive through the narrow streets crowded with blue-collar workers and artists, deadbeats and homesteaders, I consider the path I have set out upon. Yvette asked me whether being present as a company representative – to know exactly what was said – was the only reason I'd demanded to accompany Killkenny this morning. I lied when I said it was. In truth, a large part of my motivation had to do with meeting Kendra Madison.

My girl.

I know how stupid that sounds. I've seen her twice in a fantasy constructed by another man – not just another man, but a psychopath. I haven't even seen her, but I've seen an avatar that was created based on pictures of her. There is no reason for me to have developed the obsession that has crawled over me and seeped into my pores. But that's the thing about obsession; it has no reason and obeys no logic. I tell myself that meeting the real woman is the cure – that's the reason I've put myself in this position. It's possible, but that's certainly not my driving belief. The truth is that I simply couldn't resist the possibility of meeting this woman. I've constructed fantasies about what might happen, which I would be embarrassed to share with anyone. It's like I'm fourteen, and the wave of unfamiliar hormones is flooding my veins again.

It's just past eleven o'clock in the morning when we pull up in front of her house in the nicer area of Sommerville, out west toward Cambridge. It's a large Victorian building with gables and turrets, and a covered porch out front. If you blocked out the bustle of the neighborhood, you could almost imagine the place as it was built, probably 120 years ago, in a sleepy rural area with land and quiet.

Killkenny and I walk up the steps onto the front porch. Neither one of us has talked for a while and I wonder whether he's noticed that I've gone quiet. I suspect not. Like most men, he strikes me as someone who accepts silence as a natural consequence of having little to say at the moment. He does not seem the sort to read into every conversational respite.

There is no bell that we can see by the door, so Killkenny reaches out and takes hold of the brass knocker shaped like a lion's head. A moment later the door is opened by a young woman with auburn hair streaked with blonde at the temples. She is compact, and she's wearing a T-shirt that accentuates her breasts. Below the waist she has on what looks like pink pajama bottoms.

'Can I help you?' she asks.

Killkenny asks, 'Is Kendra Madison here?' He holds up his badge. 'BPD,' he says.

She tilts her head at him. 'Is that real?'

He tilts his head back at her. 'Is she here?'

She looks at him for a moment, rolls her head back and

calls over her shoulder, 'Kenny! Cops are here for you!' She looks back at Killkenny and says, 'She'll be right with you.' She closes the door in our face.

'Interesting,' Killkenny says.

A moment later the door opens again, and she is standing there in front of us. Her face is almost exactly as it is in *De Sade*'s LifeScene. Her skin is smooth and clear and creamy, the lines of her jaw and her cheekbones even and perfect. Only her eyes seem different. I can see just a hint of fatigue in them – a world-weariness that is not evident in the fantasy – but other than that there is simply no denying that it is her. She's wearing a short black skirt and a thin silk blouse that clings to her skin. Her legs are covered to the calf in black leather boots. She's nearly looking me in the eyes, and I'm almost six feet tall, but from the look of it, she's borrowing at least three inches of that from the heels on the boots. Her black hair falls straight, covering her shoulders and spilling down to the swell of her breasts. Around her neck she's wearing a black satin choker with a small silver cross nestled in the cleft between her collarbones. She looks at both of us with a confident, unafraid expression and says in a clear voice, 'Can I help you gentlemen?'

'Kendra Madison?'

'My friends call me Kenny.'

'We're not friends.'

'Not yet.' She gives a mischievous little smile. 'What can I do for you?'

'We'd like to talk to you.'

'I'm all ears.'

Killkenny looks around the porch. 'Is there any chance we can come in?'

She considers this. 'For just a moment,' she says. She opens the door and we walk in. The house has narrow hallways, and small rooms. From where we are standing we can see down a long passage to a kitchen, where there are two or three young women talking. The girl who answered the door looks down toward us with suspicion and closes the kitchen door.

We are cramped in the entryway, and Kendra leads us into a larger room that looks like a sitting room. There are couches along the walls, and several tall tables with chairs around them. In a corner there is a small bar. 'What is this place?' Killkenny asks.

'It's my home,' she says. 'I rent out some of the rooms to other girls to help make ends meet. Gillian mentioned that you gentlemen are with the police department.'

'Boston Police Department,' Killkenny says. 'Not Sommerville.'

'Do you mind if I see your badges? I find them so impressive.' She smiles as she says this, but there is no mirth in her eyes. Killkenny takes out his badge and holds it up. 'Can I hold it?' she asks.

He hesitates, but hands it over. She studies it, comparing the picture on the identification to the man standing in front of her. 'Detective Paul Killkenny,' she says. 'Just as I said, very impressive.' She hands it back to him and looks at me. 'Can I see yours, too?'

'He's not on the force,' Killkenny says quickly.

She raises her eyebrows. 'No?'

'No, he's helping me with an investigation.'

She's looking at me, and I feel like she can see through my skin. 'Is he allowed to speak for himself?'

'I'm helping the detective with an investigation,' I say.

'We have agreement on that, at least. What is this about?'

'We just have a few questions, and then we can get out of your hair,' Killkenny says.

'Are you planning on getting into my hair?'

Killkenny smiles, but I can see that he's on the defensive now. 'As I said, just a few questions.'

'Of course.'

'You did some modeling for a company called NextLife a few years ago, is that right?'

She moves over to one of the raised tables. There's a pack of cigarettes there and she picks it up, slides one out and puts it between her teeth. 'Either of you have a light?'

I shake my head. It feels like she's stalling, though it's not clear why.

'I don't smoke,' Killkenny lies.

'A couple of regular Boy Scouts, huh?' She walks over to the bar and bends over, reaching across the wooden top and digging behind it, coming up with a pack of matches. As I watch her, there's a part of me that wants to scream that I'm not a Boy Scout. There's a part of me that wants to tell her exactly what I am thinking at that moment, but I keep quiet.

'Getting back to my question . . . ' Killkenny says.

She comes back to the table, lights the cigarette, takes a deep drag, holds it in her lungs and blows it back out. 'Yes,' she says. 'I did some modeling for them. It was a long time ago.'

'A little over four years ago, right?'

'That sounds about right.'

'Do you remember anything about the job?'

'Like what?'

'Like anything? Do you remember anything about the people who were there?'

'Sure. What do you want to know?'

'Do you remember who they were?'

She takes another drag on her cigarette. 'The photographer's name was Todd Pritzker. He's a local Boston guy, does pretty good work. Frankly, the job was a waste of his talents.'

Killkenny is visibly surprised. 'How so?'

'They weren't looking to interpret the female form,' she says with a laugh. 'They were looking to record it. They might as well have used a giant Xerox machine. I stood there, *au naturel*, as they snapped close-ups. Not exactly an Annie Leibovitz moment. Still, I suppose it served their purposes.'

'Which were?'

'Have you never been on the site?'

'Humor me, sweetheart.'

'I'm not your sweetheart.' She flicks the ashes into a tray on the table. 'Remember that, Detective.'

Killkenny laughs. 'I get the sense you're everyone's sweetheart. What were the pictures for?'

She scowls at him. 'They used us as the models for the LifeScene computer images. It's not all us, necessarily; it's more of a mix-and-match thing. You can take this girl's face with that girl's tits, and another girl's ass. Put them in a dress, or not, depending on what you're trying for. It's not the perfect substitute for reality, but as far as the technology is concerned, it's impressive enough.'

'You remember anything else about the shoot? Anything about the company people who were there? Anything at all, or have I taxed your brain?' Killkenny's tone is dismissive, and I feel somehow like I should come to her defense. It's a stupid instinct.

'I don't think I'll answer any more questions from you,' she says.

'Are you refusing to cooperate with the police?'

'I'm refusing to cooperate with you,' she says. 'I'll answer questions from your non-cop friend, if you want.' She looks at me as she puts her lips to the cigarette again. Killkenny looks at me, sweeps his arm, inviting me to take over.

I clear my throat. 'Do you remember who the other men at the photo shoot were?'

She smiles at me. 'I do,' she says. She doesn't continue.

'Who were they?'

'One of them was Dr Santar Gunta. He's one of the founders of the company, and he's the one who is primarily responsible for the development of the technology. He's Pakistani. Most people think he's Indian, because he's Hindu, but he grew up in Pakistan. Weird guy, not particularly warm and fuzzy. I got the feeling he found women distasteful – particularly when they were naked in front of him. I couldn't tell whether that was because he wasn't interested in women, or whether it was because he was too interested in women. Oh, yeah, and he smelled like good pipe tobacco, which I thought was weird because I didn't see him smoking.'

I look over at Killkenny as the details pour from Kendra's lips. He's looking at her in astonishment.

'Who else?' I ask.

'Let's see, there was Michael François. He was a programmer, I think, and Dr Gunta's primary assistant. He was the youngest of them there, and the nicest. Very good-looking too. There was another programmer as well . . . Sam something . . . I can't remember his last name. He didn't make much of an impression on me.'

'Is that it?'

She gives me a coy look. 'Is this a test?'

'I guess.'

'Well, I saved the best for last, then.' She takes a drag of her cigarette, closing her eyes as though it's a last rite. 'Josh Pinkerton,' she says, almost wistfully. 'The man behind the company. The CEO of NextLife, and God's gift to Internet companies. He's thirty-nine, good-looking – not as good-looking as you,' she bats her eyes mockingly at me, 'but nothing to sneeze at. He's a man who likes the ladies and isn't afraid to make that clear. He was in the background during the actual shoot; I don't think his skills lie in the technical functioning of the system, but he was every bit the face of the company. And he's worth hundreds of millions of dollars.' She closes her eyes, as if dreaming of the money.

'You have a remarkable memory,' I say. 'I'm impressed.'

She laughs. 'I think we can stop the games now, don't you?'

I look over at Killkenny, who shrugs. 'I'm not sure I understand.'

She looks back and forth between the two of us. 'C'mon, fellas, we're among friends, aren't we? Let's put our cards on the table.'

I'm confused, and it must show on my face. She gets a look on her face like she has said too much. 'How is it that you remember all that detail?' I ask.

'You really don't know, do you?'

'Know what?'

She polishes off her cigarette, stubs it out in the ashtray. 'How should I put this? We . . . dated,' she says.

'Who?' I ask.

'Me and Josh Pinkerton.' She looks up at me and I'm sure she sees the shock, and at least a hint of jealousy and disappointment, on my face. 'For almost four years.'

CHAPTER TWENTY-ONE

'You and I met once.'

I'm still digesting Kendra's story, and her words don't register at first. Over the course of the past fifteen minutes she's summarized her four-year relationship with Pinkerton, beginning with the moment he walked over to her as she was putting her clothes back on at the photo shoot. He was aggressive, she says, and always demanding in their relationship. He was also clear that, given his role in the business, and the need for him to keep up his profile, their relationship couldn't be public. In his view he needed to project youth, and that was more easily done by a CEO unburdened by public attachments. I'm still thinking about all this, and it takes a moment for me to hear what she's said to me.

'We met?'

'We did.'

I shake my head. 'I would have remembered that.'

'That's sweet. It happened, though. Josh used to get me into company events from time to time. We couldn't talk, of course, but he said he liked to look at me.' I sense a shudder from her. 'I thought you looked familiar when I first saw you. Now it's all making sense. You're Nick Caldwell. You were Tom Jackson's friend, and you were brought in a few years ago. You were going to work with him on product development and analysis, right?'

I nod. 'Yeah, that's right.'

'God, Josh had such high hopes for you. He said from what Tom had told him, and from what he saw in those first few months, that he thought you might end up running the company some day.' I look at her sharply, trying to gauge whether she's playing me. I can see no evidence of it. 'After he'd taken as much money out of the place as he could for himself, of course.'

That did sound like something Pinkerton would say. 'Of course,' I agree.

'What happened with you and Pinkerton that ended it?' Killkenny asks. It startles me; for a few moments I'd forgotten that he was still in the room. 'That's an awful lot of money to walk away from. I would have thought that a woman like you would have hung on to the death.'

She looks at him for a moment, and just for a brief instant I think she's not going to answer his question. She does, though, meeting his eyes as she speaks. 'Money's important to me, Detective,' she admits. 'I like to eat. I like to have a roof over my head. I like to feel like I can take care of myself. If you knew anything about how I grew up, that might make sense to you. But I'm not putting up with anyone's bullshit for any amount of money. Not if they think it means they own me.'

'So you ended it with him?' Killkenny sounds incredulous.

'Yes, I did. He began trying to run my life, and when I made it clear that I wouldn't play that game, he got violent.'

'Josh?' It surprises me. I've always known that he's a bit of an asshole, but I didn't see him as the type to beat women.

She nods. 'Him and that psycho who runs his security.'

'NetMaster?'

'Yes, NetMaster. Not a pleasant man.'

'What did they do?'

'It doesn't matter.'

'Yes, it does.'

She's looking down and her head whips around on me, her face deadly serious. 'No, it doesn't. I got away, that's all that matters.'

'And we're supposed to believe this?' Killkenny says.

'You can believe whatever you want, Detective. If you want the full story, you can ask Tom Jackson. He helped me get away, and he kept Josh from going off the deep end. I'm not saying it solved the problem, but it made it better. I'm pretty sure Josh keeps tabs on me, but I'm far more careful now, so I think I'll be fine.'

'Tom helped you,' I say.

'Yes. He's the only one there I'd ever trust. He's the only one who sees the company for what it is and what it could be – the good and the bad. You want some free advice, I'd keep your wagon hitched to his. He's the one who knows what he's doing.'

'He's a good man,' I say. 'He helped me when I was in trouble.'

'I know.' She smiles at me, and it cuts to my heart. 'I told you, we met.' She lights another cigarette and, as strange as it seems, I want to tell her to stop. I have some instinctive need to protect her, and as the flame touches the tobacco and the tip glows like the embers of an inferno, all I can think of is my mother strapped to her oxygen tank. I have to fight the urge to say something. 'So, you two really didn't know about me and Josh,' she comments. 'Which means you're not here investigating him. I assumed when you started asking about NextLife that you were going to ask me some questions about Josh.'

'Why would you assume that?' Killkenny asks.

She shrugs. 'I don't know. You read all the time about CEOs getting in trouble with the law. And think about the information they have – the chances for abuse.'

'What do you mean?'

'Nothing,' she says. Again, it seems as though she feels she's said too much. 'I just assumed you wanted to ask about Josh because we were together.' She blows a huge, perfect smoke ring. It hangs in the heavy air in the sitting room, swirling in an ever-expanding circle, losing its definition until I can't even tell whether it's still there. 'So if you're not here to ask about Josh, why are you here?'

'We're here investigating three murders,' Killkenny says.

'Murders?' She sounds shocked. 'Who was murdered?'

'Three of the other girls who were part of the modeling for the NextLife avatar library.'

She looks at Killkenny, clearly trying to judge whether he's telling the truth. He just nods at her. 'How were they killed?'

'They were all the victims of sexual assaults that culminated in their murders.' Killkenny relays the information in a cold, clinical manner. He could have done it with more tact, but I think he's getting back at her for refusing to answer his questions before. 'We think he goes on NextLife to practice the murders, and then when he feels he's ready, he goes out and does it for real.'

'How does he get the girls' names? It's not like they're on the website.' She's smart, and she's working through the implications quickly. 'Which means,' she continues, 'that he's getting the names from the company somehow.' It takes only a matter of seconds for her to make the next logical leap. 'Which means it's probably someone who actually works at the company and has access to the records.'

'We don't know that for sure,' Killkenny says. 'But it's certainly one possibility.'

'There have to be hundreds of girls who modeled for the project,' she says. 'Are you talking to all of them?' She's looking at me as she asks the question. I shake my head slowly. 'Great,' she says. 'So you have a particular reason to talk to me, which apparently has nothing to do with the fact that I dated the CEO.'

'We're just taking precautions,' Killkenny says.

'Has he practiced my murder?'

'We can't talk about specifics.'

For the first time I can see real vulnerability in her eyes. She's scared, and she's clearly not used to being scared. 'Has he?' she asks again. Now she is looking only at me, her eyes locked with mine. They aren't exactly the same as the eyes I've seen before in the LifeScene. They're missing the luminous flecks of gold and silver, but they have so much of the life that I've seen before, when looking down at her from *De Sade*'s vantage point as his hands go to her throat. Her eyes are begging now, just as they have when the oxygen is cut off. I've been powerless in the LifeScene, but I'm not powerless now.

I nod. 'He has.'

'Nick!' Killkenny shouts at me. 'This is a police investigation!'

'Am I the only one left?'

'Don't answer that!'

'No,' I say. 'There are at least six others that we know of. There could be more.' The news that she is not the only potential target left seems to comfort her slightly.

'That's it!' Killkenny shouts. 'This interview is over!' He stands up and takes my arm by the elbow. 'Nick, you're coming with me now, or I'll bust your ass for obstructing a police investigation.'

I stand and let myself be pulled away. I'm looking at her as we leave, and she is watching me go. I'm overcome with the need to do more – overcome with the need to protect her. 'I'm sorry,' I say as Killkenny pulls me out of the house.

'What the fuck was that?' Killkenny demands, still holding my elbow as he guides me toward his car.

I shake my arm free and make my way to the passenger side door. 'What are you talking about?'

'You were going to be my silent partner, remember?'

'Hey, you were the one who told me to ask her the questions, when she refused to deal with you. Maybe if you hadn't been such a prick to her from the start, she would have been willing to deal with you.'

'Oh, please? What, you think I hurt the whore's feelings?'

'She's not a whore!' The words come out of my mouth before I can stop them, and they fly with such force that I practically knock out my teeth as I spit them out.

Killkenny is on the other side of the car now, and we are looking at each other over the SS's roof. 'What do you think that place is, Nick?'

I look back at the tall Victorian house looming over the narrow sidewalk. 'What are you talking about?' I almost don't want to hear the answer.

'Shit, if I didn't know better, I'd think you grew up sheltered.' He nods back toward the front door. 'She's running a cathouse.' I stare in bewilderment at Kendra Madison's house. 'The girls, the sitting room – it all makes sense. I'm not saying it's organized or official, but you don't think there's something fucked-up going on in there?'

It makes me angry that I know he's right. There was something off about the place, and I could feel it as soon as we stepped through the door. What he's saying makes sense, and I know it, but I still can't accept it. 'There has to be an explanation.'

'There is,' Killkenny says. 'It's the oldest explanation in the world.'

'No, it's something else.'

'Jesus, Nick, don't feel bad. It's not like you're the first guy in history to be fooled by a hooker. Their profession is making the men they're with feel special. Any girl can fuck. Only the best can make the guy who's paying feel like the money has nothing to do with it. You think she wasn't into Pinkerton for a shitload of cash? Please, let's deal in the real world.'

I climb into the car, my head still reeling. 'Where are we going now?' I ask, absently.

'Back to Cambridge for you,' Killkenny says. 'I'm handling the rest of the interviews on my own.'

'Why?'

'Because we made a deal. You were gonna keep your mouth shut. I'm not gonna jeopardize this investigation for you; I don't care how far we go back, how much you care about your company or how infatuated you are with little-miss-tits, in there. You got that?'

I want to argue with him. I want to tell him that I'm necessary to these interviews, but I know I'm not. Besides, I no longer care. I've seen my girl in the flesh. The spell is broken, I tell myself; the obsession will fade away now. As we pull away from the curb, I tell myself that everything will be fine.

Somehow, though, I wish I could find myself more convincing.

CHAPTER TWENTY-TWO

Killkenny drops me back at my car. He was right; no one bothered to molest the Corolla. It sits there on the street, its windows open, begging futilely to be violated. I feel sorry for it as I climb into the front seat. 'I'll be in touch if I need anything else,' Killkenny says from his car.

'Let me know what you find from the other girls.'

'Right.' We both know he'll tell me what he wants to tell me, and nothing more. I suppose I can live with that.

I drive through the Back Bay, down Newbury Street, where the boutiques cater to the wealthiest of Boston's residents and the restaurants all have names that I can't pronounce. Soon I will be welcomed here with open arms, if I want. The proprietors of these exclusive outlets will make the effort to learn my name, and to memorize my likes and dislikes. Once NextLife goes public, and they have an idea of what I can spend, they will all act as though they have spent their lives waiting for me to show up. That is the fundamental nature of American egalitarianism: Everyone of equal wealth is equal; the source or timing of the wealth matters little.

From the Back Bay, I head down Massachusetts Avenue,

across the bridge and into Cambridge. Massachusetts Avenue runs from the river through the section of the city that is dominated by MIT, with its dorms and laboratories, and the large domed building that looks back at Boston like a curiosity. I try to remember what it was like to be here; to study here and belong to something. I can't remember, though. It seems too long ago.

I head toward the office and park right near where I was parked the night before – where my windows were smashed. It's daylight now, but there is still something that feels wrong about the area. It's as though the attack has polluted the area for me permanently.

As I get out of the car I can sense movement off to my left, and it feels as though the scene from last night is playing out again. I look over toward the sound, but see nothing. I take a few steps in that direction, wondering whether I'm willing to replay the scene, considering whether I'm willing to put the rest of the Corolla's windows at risk. The thought almost brings a bark of nervous laughter, but I stifle it. The alleyway where my stalker hid last night is only yards away. I could break into a run and be there in a matter of two seconds.

I take another step. 'Is someone there?' I call. I hang there for a moment before I decide that I'm imagining things and it's not worth the effort.

As I turn back toward the warehouse where my basement facility is located, though, I run straight into NetMaster's massive chest. It's shocking to me that a man of his size could possibly move quietly enough to sneak up on me, and it makes me wonder what other skills the man has.

'Shit! You scared the crap out of me,' I say.

NetMaster just stares at me.

'You need something?' I ask.

'You have not been at work,' he says in his thick accent. He looks and sounds like the perfect James Bond villain to me. 'Where were you?'

'I was dealing with other things.' I step to the side of him and head toward the building. I'm not in the mood to deal with his insanity. He puts his arm out to stop me. 'You really want to touch me?' I say. His advantage in life has always been that he's large enough to intimidate everyone he deals with. As a general rule I'm not easily intimidated, and I've dealt with guys bigger and more dangerous than him my entire life, so he and I have butted heads for our entire time at the company.

'Where were you?'

'I told you, I was dealing with other things.'

'What other things?'

I look up at him. 'I was fuckin' your mother.' When pushed, the street I grew up on comes out.

He looks confused. 'My mother is in Holland.' Apparently he's too literal to understand the game.

'That explains the fatigue,' I say. 'Jetlag's a bitch.'

'Boss wants to see you.'

'Pinkerton? Why?'

'Come with me.'

'Okay,' I say. 'I just need to check in with my people.'

'Now.'

'No, in a minute.' I take a step, pushing his arm out of the way. He keeps it firm, preventing me from getting around. I look up at him. 'Really?'

He looks down at me and gives a thin smile. 'You and I,' he says. 'We will have our time together. Do you understand?'

'Yeah,' I say. 'I do. But unless you want that time to be now, you're gonna move your fuckin' arm to let me by. Do you understand?'

The smile disappears from his face and he lowers his arm. I head into the building, and he follows.

I walk down the stairs and onto the basement offices. I pause, looking out over the floor. There are around fifty of my employees there, all sitting in their chairs, watching the LifeScenes of others play out on their screens, seeing what our users are seeing, feeling what they are feeling, delving into their psyches as the users open themselves, secure in their belief that what they do at their computers is safe from intrusion. The place looks the same as it has done for the past two years – since we started the project and I took over as project leader. And yet somehow it feels different to me now. It feels darker, more sinister than it ever has.

NetMaster is behind me, and I can feel him watching my every move. I walk onto the floor and make my way through the maze of stations, to the back where my office is located. Yvette is there, at one of the stations just outside my office. She's not GhostWalking, she is at one of the computer terminals, typing away in computer code at a furious pace. She is so engrossed in what she is doing that she doesn't see me.

I walk up behind her and tap her on the shoulder. 'Hey,' I say.

She jumps, startled. 'Shit, you scared me,' she says.

'We need to talk.'

'Yeah, we do,' she says. Her voice is excited. 'I think I've just about got it nailed.'

'In my office,' I say, cutting her off from saying anything more while we're still on the floor. She gives me a curious look, and I glance across the floor toward NetMaster, who is standing there, watching us. She looks over at him.

'What's he doing here?'

'In my office.' I jerk a thumb in the direction of my door. 'We can talk in there.' She gets up and follows me in.

'What's going on?' she asks.

'I'm not sure. But things aren't making sense.'

'How so?'

I take a deep breath and think for a moment. 'We met with Kendra Madison,' I start. 'She's the one who's in the LifeScene I've walked. The one with the black hair.'

Yvette's eyes narrow and she gives me a slightly annoyed look. 'That must have been very exciting for you,' she says sarcastically.

'You don't understand – this has nothing to do with me,' I say. 'But she said some things that were a little disturbing.'

'Like what?'

'She dated Pinkerton,' I say. I watch that sink in.

'Josh Pinkerton?' she says. 'How did that happen?'

'They met at the photo shoot. She says that she and he dated on and off for nearly four years. And that he ended up getting violent.'

'Josh? I don't see that.'

'That's what I thought too, but she swears, and she seemed pretty credible. She said that he brought in NetMaster and they started trying to control her life. When she pushed back, they pushed back harder, literally.'

'Well, I can certainly see that of NetMaster,' she says, thinking it over. 'Do you think this has anything to do with the murders of the three girls?'

I shrug. 'I have no idea. It could be a coincidence, but it's worth thinking about. It's certainly worth investigating.'

'So is Killkenny doing the digging?'

'I don't know. He didn't seem convinced. It didn't feel like it was something he was going to pursue. He actually accused her of being after Josh's money.'

She frowns. 'Killkenny wasn't convinced? Is it possible that she's not really credible?'

I think about telling her Killkenny's theory that Kendra Madison is running a whorehouse, but decide against it. There's no point in spreading that kind of a rumor without having any actual proof, and somehow I still feel protective of Kendra Madison. 'All I can tell you is what I saw and heard and, to me, she was very believable.'

'Are you sure you weren't listening with your dick?' Yvette has never had trouble expressing herself clearly.

'What?' I choke out. 'What are you talking about?'

She looks disappointed in me. 'Come on, Nick – it's me. I know you. I saw you when you were coming out of the GhostWalk that first time you were in *De Sade*'s Scene with this girl. I was in the room with you when you walked it for the second time. I saw your face, and I know you well enough to recognize infatuation when I see it.'

'And you think that's clouding my judgment?'

'I think it *could* cloud your judgment. I have no idea whether it is clouding your judgment, but it's clear that you came away with a different impression than Killkenny did. That raises a question mark for me. I mean, you tell her you're looking for a killer, and she tells you that Josh Pinkerton roughed her up. You've got to admit, that might give her leverage over Pinkerton to get something out of him.'

'Fair enough, but we hadn't told her about the murders when she told us about the violence.'

'Really?'

'Really. She thought we were there to investigate him for some sort of misuse of information. We didn't tell her anything about the murders until she'd already laid out her whole story.'

Yvette considers this. 'That's strange.'

'It is.' I rub my forehead, trying to make sense of all of it. 'Look, I'm not saying this is connected at all. I'm not even saying that she's telling the truth, but I find it all very disturbing, and we should look into it further, y'know?'

'Yeah, I hear you.'

'How about you? You said something about almost having this nailed? What did that mean?'

'It means I think I've isolated a whole bunch of LifeScene segments that all seem to be connected to *De Sade*, and it looks as though they may all originally have been created on computers actually on our network.'

'Computers, plural?' I ask. 'He's using more than one?'

'That's what it looks like,' she says. 'I'm still running the analysis. He's done a pretty good job of wiping his trail, but I think I've found the string. It should only take a couple more days, and I should be able to track it back to the source.'

'That's great,' I say. Looking at her, I can tell that she hasn't left the office. That means it's been days since she's been home. 'You need to get some rest,' I say. 'You look tired.'

'Thanks. A girl loves a compliment.'

'You know what I meant.'

'Maybe I do.'

'I'm serious. You need rest. This is too important, and we need to make sure that we don't make any mistakes, you understand?'

She glares at me. 'You think I don't understand how important this is? Why do you think I've been working as hard as I have been?'

'I know,' I say. 'I'd rather have you working on this than anyone else in the world. There's no one better at this kind of work. But you can't kill yourself over it, okay?'

'This is how I work best.' I realize there's no point in arguing with her on this.

I look through the window from my office out onto the floor. NetMaster is still there, watching us. 'I've been summoned to the boss's office,' I say. 'He's my escort.'

'Pinkerton's office? Why?'

'I don't know. I guess I'll find out. If I disappear, tell Killkenny where I was going.'

'Don't joke,' Yvette says. She's looking at me, and I can see the worry in her eyes. Suddenly I feel guilty for bringing her into this.

'It'll be fine,' I say.

'You think?'

'Maybe.'

She looks out at NetMaster, waiting impatiently for me.

'Nick, what do we do if I trace the LifeScenes back to their source, and it turns out it's Pinkerton?'

I take her by the shoulders. 'We'll deal with that if it happens. Don't worry, we just have to track this back to wherever it goes and then figure out the plan after that, okay?'

She nods. 'Okay,' she says. 'Be careful when you talk to him. I don't trust him.'

'You don't need to trust him. Trust me.'

'You know I do.'

NetMaster insists that I accompany him in his car to the NextLife building in Brighton, but I refuse and get into my own car. He glares at me as I put my key in the ignition, and only lumbers away when he realizes that I am not backing down, and that I am pulling out irrespective of whether he is ready. His car is only a half block away, and he hurries so that he can fall in behind me in the traffic. I can see him in my rearview mirror the entire way out west. At one point I deliberately slow down near the end of a green light and then speed through on the yellow, just to see how he will react. He hits the gas as well and flies through the red light, drawing a chorus of angry honks from drivers at the intersection.

He pulls into the parking lot just behind me, and I hear him slam the door as I walk toward the building. He catches up and we get on the elevator together. I can feel his stare like a laser on the side of my face, but I ignore him, and when the elevator reaches the top floor I get out ahead of him, leaving the giant huffing to catch up with me.

Pinkerton's assistant holds up a hand to me as I approach, but I ignore her. 'You can't go in there!' she calls to me.

'He asked for me,' I say. 'Don't worry.'

I push the door open, and I can see Pinkerton standing at the window, looking out toward Boston. He turns and sees me. 'Nick,' he says quietly. 'Come in.'

'Josh,' I respond. 'I'm already in.'

NetMaster comes through the door. 'I instructed him to come at once!' he barks, defending the time it took for him to produce me at Josh's office. 'He would not listen!'

'I understand,' Josh says. 'Not to worry.'

'He went into the Cambridge facility.'

'Of course.' He looks at me. 'I'm sure you had something to do that was urgent, no? Otherwise you would have come immediately, isn't that right, Nick?'

'Everything seems to be taking on additional urgency these days,' I say. 'I'm just trying to deal with it.'

He looks back at NetMaster. 'You see? It's alright. Would you mind letting me talk to Nick privately?' NetMaster looks incensed. He stands there, spluttering, but after a moment he nods – almost a bow – and backs out of the office. 'He's crude, but loyal,' Josh says. 'One of so many necessary evils that someone in my position must tolerate.'

'Are there many other evils you tolerate?' I ask.

He smiles at me, and I feel cold at the sight. 'Please, Nick, sit. Let's talk.' We sit on two incongruous, uncomfortable chairs set at an acute angle to each other. He leans forward, bringing his hands together, locking his fingers and resting his chin on his knuckles. 'I spent the morning talking to our people at Morgan Stanley,' he starts. He looks at me to see whether I'll have any reaction. I just stare back at him. 'Do you want to know what they said?'

'If it's something I should hear,' I say. At the moment I really couldn't care less. I know that's foolish; I have millions of dollars riding on what happens to the company, but it's just not what I'm thinking about at this point.

'Oh, it's something you should hear. They think we'll be ready to announce within the month. More importantly, they think the valuations for the IPO are going to go even higher than we originally anticipated. We initially had a goal of somewhere in the range of thirty-five dollars a share. That would be excellent. But looking over the numbers, and judging the interest on the street, our investment bankers are now thinking that the price is going to be over forty. Maybe as high as forty-five. Do you know what that would mean?'

'It means a lot of money for you,' I say.

'It would mean that we will have had the largest IPO in history. We will have done it! And, yes, it would also mean a lot of money, but not just for me. It would mean a lot of money for everyone at the company. Every single employee we have has some level of equity participation. I checked yours, and at forty-five dollars a share, you will be making over thirty million dollars. Can you imagine that?'

'I can't,' I answer honestly.

'I would think that would help to make whatever time your mother has left much more comfortable, wouldn't it?' I glare at him. 'Yes, I remember your mother, Nick. I met her when you first joined the company, and I remember that if it hadn't been for the opportunity I gave you, she would not have gotten treatment. Tom Jackson came to me and told me about this brilliant young man who was in a hard place, and he said you were exactly the kind of person who would be an exceptional asset to the company. He was right, you know? What you have created in your little black-ops section is remarkable. The research you are able to gather guides virtually all of the company's decisions on products at this point. You created that. No one else.' He leans back in the chair. It is awkward because the chair back is low and leans at an angle. 'You know, I think you may be even more talented than Tom himself. I've wondered recently whether you shouldn't be heading up our revenue development.'

'I'm not taking Tom's job,' I say firmly.

He shrugs. 'It was a thought. In any event, depending on what happens in the near future, I may have to move Tom out.'

'Why?'

'I'm not convinced that he is aggressive enough with respect to revenue generation.' He pauses. 'And recently I've started to have questions about his ability to judge the character of those he has hired.'

It hangs there between us for a moment, both of us fully cognizant of what he is implying. Then he leans forward again.

'How is this unpleasant investigation going, Nick?'

'It's going.'

'Is it? I understand that you met with Kendra Madison this morning.'

'How did you know that?' I ask.

He smiles icily again. 'Oh please, Nick,' he says. 'You wouldn't imagine that I would fail to stay informed about something as . . . sensitive . . . as this, would you?' I don't answer, and he looks away for a moment. 'She's a very disturbed young woman,' he continues. 'It's sad, really. She's very beautiful. Very

. . . sexy. I remember when I first met her, I was enchanted. She holds that power over men. Do you know what I mean?' This time it's my turn to look away. He chuckles. 'Yes, of course you do. I spent some time with her for a number of years. It was nothing serious, obviously, though I think she wanted it to be. She was a remarkably sexual creature, with very . . . unorthodox . . . tastes.'

'What do you mean?'

He hesitates, leans in and says in a conspiratorial tone, 'She likes pain.' I look at him, and he nods solemnly. 'She likes to inflict It, and to have it inflicted on her. I'm embarrassed to admit that I was intrigued by this for a time. I think it's a product of being successful, and still not feeling that I'm finished. I confess that I sometimes fall prey to idle specula- tion about the meaning of it all. All this,' he sweeps his arm around the room, 'what does it all mean? Questions like that have, on occasion, led me into unproductive behaviors. My time with Kendra was one of those times.'

I think about her. I have trouble drawing the distinction between the real woman and her incarnation in *De Sade*'s LifeScene.

'Do you understand why I'm telling you this?'

I nod.

'Good.' He grins. 'As you move forward, and as you and Detective Killkenny discuss these matters, I want you to have a full picture of who I am. I hope I have accomplished that.'

'I think you have,' I say. 'Is that all?'

The smile disappears. 'For now,' he says. 'But you should bear in mind what we have talked about here, and previously. You hold the future of all of those at the company in your hands. You must consider what the future will be as you move forward.'

'I will,' I say. 'You can count on that.'

I stop by Tom Jackson's office on the floor below before I leave the building. I trust Tom, and I've always been grateful to him for bringing me into the company. I'm hoping that he may be able to give me an unbiased perspective.

He is sitting at his desk, tapping away on his computer when I poke my head through the door. 'You got a minute?' I ask.

He looks up. 'Nick,' he says. 'Of course.'

'You working on the revenue generation?'

He smiles as he nods. 'Always. Not the easiest task.'

'No, I'm sure.' I'm not sure where to start. 'Tom, you know I've always appreciated what you did for me – bringing me in, making sure Ma was taken care of, all of it.'

'You don't need to thank me, Nick,' Tom says. 'I brought you in because I knew you'd help the company. I was right; you've proved that over the past four years.'

I sigh. 'There may be some who disagree at this point.'

'The investigation?'

I nod. 'I'm trying to do what's right.'

He smiles. 'You've always been better than any of us at that.'

'But what if that leads me into places that are no good for the company?'

'I'm not sure what you mean.'

I wave a hand in dismissal. 'Nothing,' I say. 'I don't mean anything. Listen, there was one question that I wanted to ask you. One of the girls who appears in *De Sade*'s LifeScenes is named Kendra Madison.' Tom sits up straight at the mention of her name. 'She said you were friends.'

Tom looks around, as though worried that someone might be listening in to our conversation. 'I don't know that I would call us friends,' he says.

'Don't worry, Tom, I already know about her and Pinkerton. I just wanted your view on what happened between the two of them. Josh says that she was into kinky violence. She says that he got out of line with her, and that you stepped in and helped her. I'm just curious for your perspective. It would be helpful.'

Tom shakes his head. 'I'm not comfortable talking about that,' he says. 'He's my boss, and she's . . . ' he pauses. 'Well, you've met her. I tried to help both of them. I'm still not sure I succeeded.'

'What do you mean?'

'Like I say, I'm not comfortable talking about it.'

He and I sit in silence for a moment. 'Okay,' I say at last. 'I get it.' I stand up and walk to the door.

'Nick,' he says before I can leave. I turn and look at him. 'You need to help the police track down the person who is doing these terrible things to these women.'

'I'm trying,' I say.

'Nick,' he says, his voice full of emphasis. 'I mean it. No matter where it leads, no matter what it takes. Do you understand me?'

'I'm not sure I do.'

'Whoever this is, he's going to keep doing it. We've provided a doorway for people to explore their darkest sides, and someone has walked through that door. He's gotten lost on the other side, and I don't think he's coming back. It's something I've worried about from the beginning of this company. So many people are unhappy with their lives, and then they find another life where they can be someone totally different. If you were that unhappy, would you come back?'

I think about it for a moment. 'Maybe not.'

'Now do you understand why he needs to be caught?'

I nod to him silently and walk out of his office.

CHAPTER TWENTY-THREE

When I get back to the office in Cambridge, my head is pounding. It's too much information for me to absorb, and none of it seems to make sense. I'm hoping that Yvette has found something that will bring clarity to it all, but those hopes are dashed when I see her face.

'I think I'm close, but I'm not there yet,' she says, her frustration evident.

'How long will it take?'

'I don't know, Nick,' she snaps. It's clear that she's going to need some rest soon, or she'll collapse. I don't care how strong she is, no one can keep going at this pace. 'I don't even know whether what I'm doing will work. I've written a program that should collect all the bits and packets that make up any LifeScenes that match *De Sade*'s profile and reside on the system, so anything that was created on a drive that is connected to the company should be found, but there's no guarantee that it's gonna work. And even if it does, I don't know that I'm gonna be able to put them back together in any way that'll be useful.'

'But you'll be able to identify which computer on the system was used to create the Scenes?'

'If I'm right, and they were created on the system, then yes, theoretically that information should be there. But I could be wrong.'

'Well, if you're wrong, I'm not sure where we go from there. We don't have any information about this asshole that will lead us to him.'

'I was thinking about that,' Yvette says. 'It's not really true. We actually have a fair amount of information.'

'Like what?'

'Well, we know what he's done to these girls. And we know that he's chosen *De Sade* as his username.'

'That doesn't seem like much,' I say.

'Maybe not,' she admits, 'but you never know. After my computer program started running and I had a moment to breathe, I started trying to put myself in this guy's mind.'

'Jesus, you really need to get some rest.'

'I'm serious,' she says. 'I started trying to figure out what's motivating this guy. Why is he doing what he's doing? What's the logic behind it?'

'You think there's logic behind this?'

'I think *De Sade* thinks there's logic to it. These killings are stylized. They're detailed and carefully planned. So the question is: what do these murders do for this guy? What do they get him?'

I think about this for a moment, but I can't think of anything other than that he's a psycho who gets off on murder. 'I've got nothing. You think you can figure it out?'

'Not yet. But I figured the more information we have, the better, so I did a little research on the real Marquis de Sade. I thought maybe that would lead us somewhere.'

'What did you learn?'

'A lot. I'm just not sure what it means. He was born in 1740 in France, and lived most of his life in Paris. He was a writer, philosopher and politician. When he was in his thirties he became known for a hedonistic way of life. He used to pay prostitutes to let him abuse them, and he would often take advantage of his servants.'

'Pinkerton apparently abused Kendra Madison,' I say.

'If you believe her. How do you know that she's telling the truth?'

'He confirmed it. He says that it's what she wanted – what she liked – and he just got dragged into it, but he admitted to me that he did get into that kind of scene with her when they were together. Maybe that was just the start. Maybe he decided that he liked it, and he wanted to take it further.'

'It's possible,' Yvette says. 'De Sade was rich, just like Pinkerton. That's how he got away with what he did for so long. He was able to pay people off, and keep people quiet. Maybe that's what Josh was trying to do with Kendra Madison.'

'What else did you learn?'

'Well, eventually De Sade's luck ran out and he was arrested. He spent a bunch of time in prisons and insane asylums. He was in the Bastille for six years, from 1784 through 1790. He was there when he wrote *The One Hundred and Twenty Days of Sodom*. That was his masterpiece – a 700-page story about four middle-aged men who exile themselves to a castle with forty-six victims and spend four months engaging in escalating degeneracy. They hire four women – brothel-keepers – to document all of the twisted things they do.'

'So who are the brothel-keepers here?' I ask idly.

'Maybe NextLife is all he needs. The system documents what he's doing; maybe that's all he wants.'

'Maybe. What happens in the book?'

'The sexual violence gets worse and worse, and more depraved with each consecutive month. Eventually they slaughter all of their victims. The things that De Sade describes in the book sound even worse than what our boy has done.'

'What sorts of things?'

'They flay the skin off their victims; they tear out their intestines and set them on fire; they use hot pokers to torture their victims in various different orifices. Things like that.'

'Lovely. Let's hope this bastard doesn't go that far.'

'You never know; the violence in the book apparently gets more and more brutal.'

'Did you come up with any connections that could be drawn with Gunta?'

Yvette shakes her head. 'Nothing that I could see. Though it's interesting that, even if we think the good doctor is gay, that wouldn't rule him out. The forty-six victims in the book are a combination of boys and girls, and De Sade himself apparently swung both ways. He was first jailed for sodomy with one of his valets.'

'What ended up happening to him?'

'He had an interesting life. He lived through the French Revolution, and was actually released from prison and elected to the French parliament for the ultra-liberal party. He was in the government during the Reign of Terror. When Napoleon came into power, he ordered De Sade to be jailed again, and his family arranged to have him transferred to an insane asylum and eventually released into exile on one of his estates. He spent the last eight years before his death having an ongoing, physically punishing affair with a girl that started when she was thirteen.'

'How old was he?'

'He was seventy-four.'

I shake my head in disbelief. 'And he was abusing a thirteen-year-old?'

'That's what the history books say.'

'What a sick fuck.'

Yvette nods. 'A brilliant fuck, too, though. He started the entire amoralist movement. People who took some level of inspiration from him included people like Friedrich Nietzsche and Sigmund Freud. Some historians trace existentialism back to him. Even Simone de Beauvoir, the feminist, relies on De Sade for some of her thinking. She wrote that his views on women were actually far more egalitarian than traditional religious doctrine.'

'Tell that to the women he tortured.' I look at Yvette. 'You don't buy any of this as a genuinely legitimate philosophy, do you?'

'Amoralism?' She stares at the wall for a moment. 'Not really, but I understand the attraction. I grew up watching the way the Church viewed morality. The heads of the Church sat on their hands as children were molested – they transferred abusive priests from parish to parish as they denied that anything was happening. I had a friend who was molested when he was thirteen; he was so afraid to tell anyone, he swore me to secrecy. He thought there was something wrong with him – thought it was his fault, because that's what he was taught.' She sighs heavily. 'He killed himself when he was nineteen. After that, it just seemed to me that the people I grew up thinking had moral superiority had no real legitimacy, so I figured everything was bullshit. I gave up on morality, and I just started doing my own thing – going by my own compass. I guess I believe morality exists; I just think it can be hard to find.'

'Do you have trouble finding it?'

'I do,' she says absently. She seems to shake herself and looks at me again. 'I've figured out enough to know that whoever is doing this to these women is a bad, bad person, and we have to stop him.'

As I nod, my cellphone rings. The caller ID is a number I don't recognize and I consider letting it go to my voicemail, but decide against it. I hit the answer button and hold the phone up to my ear. 'Hello?'

'Is this Nick?' I recognize Kendra Madison's voice instantly, and for a moment I think perhaps I'm having a dream.

'Yes, this is Nick.'

'Do you know who this is?'

I hesitate. 'Yes,' I say at last.

'I need to talk to you.'

'How did you get this number?'

'Information.'

'It's unlisted.'

'Will you meet me?'

I'm not sure what to say. I know that Killkenny will be pissed if I meet her, and I recognize that my objectivity is probably compromised by my obsession with the girl. I under-stand that it would be smart for me to avoid talking to her, and it's clearly a bad idea for me to see her in person. 'Yes,' I respond. 'Where do you want to meet?'

'There's a bar just off Warren Street. The Anchor. It's close to your house. Is that okay?'

'How do you know where I live?'

She ignores the question again. 'When can you meet me?'

I look at my watch and see that it's closing in on five o'clock. 'How about six?'

'That's perfect. I'll see you then.' The line goes dead. I take the phone away from my ear and stare at it briefly, wondering whether the phone call actually happened. It doesn't seem to make sense.

Yvette is watching me. 'Who was that?'

'One of Ma's doctors,' I lie.

'Everything okay?'

'I guess I'll find out. I'm meeting with him. Actually, Ma seemed better than I've seen her in ages today. Cormack stopped by, and she got all dolled up. It was a little freaky, actually.'

Yvette raises an eyebrow. 'You think there's something going on?'

'Maybe. I'm trying not to think about it.'

'Good for her.'

'She's sick.'

'Sick isn't dead,' Yvette says. 'If she can squeeze a little more pleasure out of life, why shouldn't she?'

'She's my mother.' I look at my watch. 'I have to go.'

She nods. 'Me too. It's gonna take a while for my program to run, so I'm going home to take a shower, maybe even lie down for a little while. I must look like crap.'

She's been up for two days, so she should look terrible, but she doesn't. Her eyes are clear, and whatever makeup she might have put on when she came to work forty-eight hours ago is long gone, but she's always looked better without makeup, I realize. I smile at her. 'You look okay.'

'Thanks.' She gets up and heads to the door to my office. 'Tell me what you find out about your mom, okay?'

'Sure. I will.'

She walks out, and I'm left sitting there by myself, wondering how I started lying to my best friend.

I stop by home on my way to the bar. Ma is sitting in the kitchen. She looks good, though she has the oxygen tube in her nose and she's breathing deep, as though storing up enough good air to last the evening.

'Cormack's taking me to dinner,' she says without my asking.

'You sure you're up to that?'

'Yeah,' she says. 'Beats the shit out of sitting around here, waiting to die.'

There doesn't seem to be much to say to that. 'I have to go out, too. I shouldn't be out late.'

'You meeting Yvette?' She is looking at me in that evalua-tive way she has – on the verge of judgment.

'No,' I say.

'Someone else?'

'I gotta go. I was just checking in.'

She breathes deeply through her nose, and it's like pure oxygen is a drug to her now. 'It's not my business, Nick, so I'll stay out of it. The only thing I'll say is that life is a hell of a lot shorter than you think it is, when you're your age. Wasting time just doesn't make any sense. You understand what I'm saying to you?'

'I gotta go, Ma. You have a good night, okay?'

I'm out the door before she can say anything else.

CHAPTER TWENTY-FOUR

I get to the bar at around ten of six. It's a place that's only a mile or so from my house, but not one that I frequent. The bartender is a guy who was a year behind me in school, and I nod to him as I walk in. He nods back. In this neighborhood that's practically a hug. I take a seat at a table toward the back, facing out, so I can see the entire place. It's a Thursday evening, and the place is relatively busy. It's not the crush of a Friday or a Saturday night, but there are plenty of people who refuse to wait for the weekend to begin drinking away the work-week. I recognize a few of them from various different stages of my life, but I stopped really belonging here years ago. I'm viewed as a bit of an oddity by those with whom I grew up. Few of them had aspirations beyond sustaining their position within the community. For most, that meant going into a trade – becoming an electrician or a carpenter. For the girls, that often meant passing the time as a waitress or a secretary while waiting for their boyfriends to propose. It's a good, hard-working lot, but no one ever told them that there was something better and, truth be told, they wouldn't have believed it anyway. Most like it too much in the neighborhood to think of leaving.

The door opens, and she walks in. For a moment I need to remind myself to breathe. She's wearing a red cotton sundress that looks like it was made to fit her body, and flat sandals. Her hair is swept back, and the satin choker she was wearing this morning is gone. Even dressed as simply as she is, though, she radiates a sensual aura. I watch as she looks over those in the bar and they look back. The effect she has on the place is unmistakable. Heads turn, some subtly, others not so much, as both the men and the women drinking their troubles away admire her. She catches my eye and heads to my table, takes the seat across from me.

'Thank you for meeting me,' she says. She seems sincere.

'How did you get my number?' I am not ready to trust her, and I'm even less ready to trust myself.

'I told you, I called Information.' She pretends to look for a waitress as she answers.

'I told you, my cell number is unlisted. How did you find it?'

'I'm resourceful.'

'No doubt. What are your resources?'

She stops pretending to look for someone to get her a drink and faces me. I can see her debating whether to tell me the truth. Finally she says, 'I called Tom Jackson.'

A waitress appears, looking us both over like we're an exhibit. 'What can I do for you?' It sounds as though she's propositioning us.

'I'll have a Scotch,' Kendra says. 'Neat.'

I nod to the beer that's three-quarters finished in front of me. 'I'll have another, please,' I say. The waitress heads back to the bar. 'You called Tom,' I say.

'I did.' She looks down at the table, and her hair falls forward. She brushes it back and looks up at me, her eyes wide. 'Should I not have?'

'I'm just surprised.'

'I needed to talk to you. Without the police listening.' She watches me, waiting for a reaction. I give her none. 'I'm scared.'

'Because of the murders?'

She nods. 'I think I know who is killing these women. And I think I know why.'

The waitress comes over and puts the drinks on the table. 'Can I get you anything else?'

Kendra gives me a suggestive look. 'Are you hungry?' Her tone makes me feel as though she can read my mind and she's aware of every erotic thought I've had about her.

'I think I'm fine.'

She shakes her head at the waitress, and the girl nods and leaves. I sit in silence, waiting for Kendra to continue. She looks like she's trying to decide where to start. 'Josh Pinkerton is a dangerous man,' she says. I don't say anything; I just continue looking at her, waiting for more. I get the feeling she's used to men simply accepting half of the story from her, and I'm not surprised. My silence seems to unsettle her. She gives me a sad smile. 'I think, when it started out, we both thought it was just business as usual,' she says.

'What kind of business?' I ask pointedly.

The smile grows sadder. 'This was never where I was supposed to end up,' she says, as though it's an answer to my question. 'I had plans, you know? I was smart. I got into Boston College – good school – and I went for a year. I was studying finance, and I was getting really good grades.'

'What happened?'

'I didn't realize how expensive a school like that is. I had enough for the first year, but after that, I couldn't pay the tuition. So I told myself I was going to take a year off and do whatever I had to do to get the money. One year – that was it. I said I was going to put my morals in a box for just long enough to get back to where I was. That's how it starts. You tell yourself it's just temporary, and then suddenly it's seven years later and somehow you've lost your way.' Her voice drifts off, and she closes her eyes. It takes a moment, and then she shakes her head and a tougher look returns. 'That's my own fault; I accept it. I'm not blaming anyone but myself, and I'm not looking for any sympathy. But this thing with Josh . . . '

'You met him at the photo shoot?'

She nods. 'That photo shoot was easy money for me at that point. A no-brainer compared to some of the things I was doing at the time. And when I was there, I could see him looking at me. I'd been working long enough to know that look, and to know how to take it from there.'

'It lasted for four years? Isn't that kind of odd for what it is that you gave him?'

'I'm good at what I do,' she says. 'Too good, as it turns out. I gave Josh a taste for things he'd never experienced before.'

'Pain,' I say.

'Pain,' she agrees. 'But it was never just about the pain. It's about the power. Power over another person, and the power to submit to someone else. It was easy with Josh; power is his driver. It's what he's always wanted, but he can never get it from money. I combined that need for power with eroticism.'

'A potent mix,' I say.

'More potent than any drug. And that's what it was for him – a drug. When I told him it was over, he refused to accept it.'

'Why did you end it? I assume the money was good.'

'The money was great. So great that I realized I had enough to get out, if I wanted to. One day I looked at my bank account and I remembered that promise I made to myself so long ago. And at the same time, I knew Josh was over the edge. He started pushing the boundaries, and I started to get scared. I told him I was done, and he reacted badly. He wouldn't let me out. He got his giant – NetMaster – involved. I was threatened; the friends I have who live with me were threatened. It got very ugly.'

'The friends who live with you are in the business, too?'

'Most of them. I rent the house, and they pay me to stay there.'

'You're a madam.'

She shakes her head. 'I don't make them work, and I don't take a cut of anything they make, if they do work. I just provide a safe place to stay, and take a cut of the rent they pay. That's it.'

'It's a subtle distinction.'

'Subtle distinctions are what allow us to live with ourselves, aren't they?'

'How did you get away from Josh?'

'I found out some things about the company. I used that information to scare him off.'

'What sorts of things?'

She shakes her head. 'It doesn't matter. It was enough to

get him to back off. I went to Tom, and he got Josh to leave me alone. At least for a while.'

'But you think you're in danger now?'

'I do. If Josh is behind these murders, it's only a matter of time before he comes after me. I know he's still obsessed with me. If he's crazy enough to take his lust for power to the next level, then he's crazy enough that eventually he'll kill me.'

'If he's the one who's actually behind the killings.'

'Who else could it be?'

I look at her, trying to read her face. I wonder if I'm being played somehow; whether she came here looking for information. That's not my impression, but you never know. 'Whoever created the LifeScenes that mimic the murders is a technological genius,' I say. 'The detail and the texture are . . . ' I'm looking at her, and I'm seeing her bound to the bed, I'm seeing her underneath me. I hope it's dim enough in the bar that she won't see my face flush. 'Well, let's just say they're impressive. Josh Pinkerton is a business genius, but he's never been the brains behind the technology. I'm not convinced he has the skill to create the Scenes I've seen.'

'Who, then?'

'That's the question.' I decide it's worth gauging her reaction. 'Did you ever get to know Dr Gunta?'

'Santar Gunta? I met him a couple of times. I told you he was at the photo shoot.'

'What was your impression of him?'

She considers the question. 'I think he's repressed,' she says. 'He could barely look at the girls when we were being photographed. And when he did, it was as though he wanted to be someplace else.'

'Do you think he could kill?'

She toys with the idea for a moment before answering. 'I don't know. It's not on the surface, but anyone who holds things in that tightly could be capable of anything, I guess. Why? Do you think it could be him?'

I shrug. 'I don't know. We talked to him today, and he seemed to be hiding something. And he's one of the few people I can see with the technical ability to create the LifeScenes that this killer has made. It's probably nothing, but he's a possibility.'

'Maybe,' she says. 'But I still think it's most likely Josh.'

'Could be. We'll keep an eye on him, one way or another.'

'Will you?' She seems grateful. 'Please. Like I said, I'm very scared. I'm afraid to go home.'

'There seems to be enough activity going on there that you're probably safe,' I point out. 'I'd be more worried if you lived alone.'

She shakes her head. 'It's the kind of place where people mind their own business,' she says. 'And it's not entirely unusual for people at the house to make a lot of noise. Scream, even.'

'I guess that kinda goes with the territory, huh?'

'Sometimes.'

'Well, if it's Josh, at least he knows that the police are looking into this. He's not likely to make a move at the moment.'

'How can you be so sure?'

'I can't. It just seems unlikely.'

The waitress comes over. 'You two ready for another?'

'I think just the check will be fine, thanks.'

Kendra seems disappointed. No, not disappointed, panicked. 'Will you have another with me?'

'It's been a really long day,' I say. 'I think I need to get home.'

'One more? Please?'

The sound of her voice – the sound of her reaching out to me in need – has a power that's difficult to describe. 'One more. That's it.' It takes only a moment for the waitress to bring back the drinks, and we wait in silence. Even after the drinks arrive there is an awkward silence.

She looks around the bar. 'You come here often?'

'That's a really old line.'

She plays back the sentence in her head and smiles. I wonder whether she has a smile that doesn't have the sadness in it. It seems unlikely. 'It wasn't meant as a line. It was just a question.'

'No. It's not one of my hangouts.'

'What are your hangouts?'

I realize I can't answer the question. 'I don't have any,' I say truthfully.

'A loner, huh? I got that impression. No one special in your life, either?'

'I've gotta go.'

'You still have half a beer. And I still have most of my drink.'

'I'm sure you won't be lonely for long.' Looking around the bar, I know it's true. There are a dozen men who continually glance over at her. If I leave, she'll be overrun. 'I'm just holding you back.'

She takes a large sip of her drink. 'Will you come home with me?'

I stare at her for a long time before answering. 'I don't think I could afford you.'

'Not like that. That's not what I want. I just . . . ' she looks down at the table. 'Like I said, I'm scared. And today, when we were together, I got the sense from you . . . ' She stops speaking. 'Never mind.'

I swallow hard. I know in my head that I can't go with her, but every other part of my body and soul is screaming out to take her home. It feels like my heart may explode. 'I can't,' I say quietly. They are the hardest words I can remember uttering.

'I know,' she says. She can't look at me. 'It's because of who I am. What I do.'

I shake my head. 'It's because of who I am, and what I have to do. I have to find whoever it is that's doing this.'

'I want you to.'

'I know. But if I take you home, I'll lose my perspective. I'll lose . . . ' As I'm speaking I see a tear run down her cheek, and I feel a physical pain through my entire nervous system. 'I'm sorry, I just can't.' I take out two twenties and put them on the table. I stand up. 'I'll let you know if we find out anything,' I say. I start to walk away.

'Nick,' she says.

'Yes?'

'Can I call you? If something goes wrong; if I need someone?'

I don't know how to respond. 'Why me?'

'Because I don't have anyone else.'

I walk out of the bar staring at the ground, feeling smaller than I've ever felt before. *Why me?* The question echoes in my head on so many levels.

I head up the block, toward my car, oblivious to everything and everyone around me. I don't even notice the figure in front of me until I am on top of him. My head comes up just in time to recognize NetMaster's huge bald head and see the fist swinging toward me. It's too late for me to dodge, and it catches me in the center of my torso, straight in the solar plexus, and all of the wind goes out of my body instantly. I am doubled over, gagging, wanting to throw up, completely incapacitated. He grabs me by the shirt and hauls me into a nearby vacant lot. He throws me against a round brick wall. I am just starting to get a drift of air back into my lungs when he hits me again in the same place. I think this time it may actually have killed me. If not instantly, I assume I'll suffocate shortly.

'You are a foolish man,' NetMaster says in his heavily accented voice. 'You will not listen. What do you have to say now?'

I'm doubled over against the wall, trying to protect my body, making sucking noises. I'm genuinely concerned that he may kill me, and I suspect that's the impression he intends to give. He grabs me around the neck and pulls me upright. My body fights against straightening, trying to stay curled in on itself, but it's useless.

'This thing you do – it is no good for anyone. Not good for the company. Not good for Josh Pinkerton. Not good for me.' He smiles and his teeth look small and sharp in his giant face. 'Not good for you.' He hits me again in the stomach. 'Do not see the girl again. Do not even speak to her,' NetMaster says. 'Ever. And if you speak to anyone of what I have said to you – the police, anyone at the company – I will kill you. Then I will kill your friend, the pretty girl with the strange hair, and I will kill your mother, if she is not dead yet.' He leans in close, so that I can feel his breath on my face. 'Do you understand?'

I still cannot speak, so I just stare at him, trying to force air into my body. He pulls his fist back and swings hard again, this time into my chest. He lets go of me, and I collapse on the ground. 'This is not your business,' he says. He spits on the ground next to me and walks away.

I lie there in the vacant lot coughing up blood.

CHAPTER TWENTY-FIVE

I'm not sure for how long I lie there in the rubble. There are no lights, and I'm tucked away out of sight from any passersby on the street. It's probably no more than fifteen or twenty minutes before I drag myself to my feet and make my way to my car. I pass a few people on the sidewalk, but they avert their eyes and offer no help. I don't blame them; I'm not their problem, and getting involved often leads to more headaches than most people are willing to reasonably put up with.

I drive myself to Massachusetts General Hospital, just across the river in Boston. The wait is shorter than I had expected, and they take X-rays to make sure I'm not bleeding into my lungs. Then they wrap my chest and tell me that I should stay in bed for a few days to let the ribs heal. I know that's not going to happen, but I don't tell the doctor that. It would only result in a protracted conversation that will do neither of us any good. When I arrived at the Emergency Room I was asked how I had been hurt, and I said that I tripped and fell onto a stairway railing. The doctor doesn't look like he buys it, but he has a waiting room full of other patients, so he leaves it alone.

I arrive back home at around midnight, feeling like shit. The lights in the house are out, and I open the door quietly and slip into the kitchen, switching on the lights. Cormack is sitting in the dark at the kitchen table, sipping whiskey out of a jelly glass. I'm startled, and sucking in a sharp breath sends shooting pains throughout my body. 'Jesus, Cormack,' I say, grabbing my chest. 'You scared the shit out of me!'

'Sorry about that. I was just having a quiet moment.'

'Is Ma home?'

He nods. 'We came home early. She had a coughing fit.' He takes a sip of his drink. 'She's not doing well, is she?' I shake my head. He looks more closely at me. 'You don't look so well, either. Who the fuck worked you over?'

I shake my head again. 'I'm fine.' Talking hurts so much it's hard to believe.

'Bullshit. It's your business, not mine, but bullshit.' He drinks again. It's clear it's not his first glass. Not his second or his third, either. 'I was so infatuated with her when I was a lad, you know that? We all were.'

'Ma?'

'Yeah. She was a fuckin' pistol. Tough, smart and a set o' tits on her that would cloud a young man's mind, if you don't mind me sayin.'

'No, by all means,' I say. I pull a glass out of the cabinet, sit at the table and pour myself a drink.

'No disrespect intended,' he says. 'Truth is truth. And your father was the one who got her. No one ever thought it would go any other way. What your father wanted, he got. That was the way of it, and God bless him for it. He was a stand-up man to the end.'

'That's what I understand. My memories of him are thin.'

'He was one of the best. I miss him still.' He raises his glass, and I meet his with mine. 'To a great man,' he says. We both drink. 'I hope you don't mind that I'm steppin' out with your ma,' he says in a serious tone.

'It seems to be doing her good,' I say. 'I'm more worried about you,' I joke. 'She's a tough broad. You better watch yourself.'

He laughs at that. 'Too true. But when I look at her, I still see the girl she was thirty years ago.'

I take out a prescription bottle of Percocet they gave me at the hospital, pour a pill into my hand, put it in my mouth and wash it down with the whiskey.

'Do you want to talk about it?' he asks me. 'I'll only raise it once, but if you want . . . '

'It's okay. I can deal with it.'

'Sure. But if you ever need anything – if there's anyone you ever need to talk to – I have resources that are at your disposal. In honor of your father, and out of respect to your mother. You should know that.'

'Thanks, I'll keep it in mind.'

He nods as though we've entered into a pact. 'Good. I'm going, then.'

'You okay to drive?'

He laughs. 'Unless they've redrawn the streets, I could do it from memory.' He puts his glass into the sink and looks back at me before he leaves. 'You keep what I've said in mind, hear? And you take care of yourself.'

'I will,' I respond. 'And thanks.'

CHAPTER TWENTY-SIX

I plan on getting into the office before daylight, but the Scotch and pain pills keep me under for a little longer than I anticipated. Dressing is an agony, and pain shoots through my entire body with every small movement. It takes twice as long as usual, and by the time I've thrown a piece of toast in my mouth and headed out to the car, it's already past seven. With a stop at the local coffee shop for the morning's caffeine, it's nearing seven-thirty by the time I arrive at the office.

Yvette is already there, sitting in my office in the back, going through the results of her computer scan. She looks up at me as I walk in. 'Holy shit!' she says. 'What the hell happened to you?'

I close the door to make sure no one is listening. 'Josh Pinkerton happened to me. Or, to be more accurate, Josh's muscle, NetMaster, happened to me. He used me for a heavy bag, and he's got a hell of a punch.'

'Back up,' she says. 'Tell me what happened.'

I realize I'm going to have to take some medicine in order to explain this. I sigh guiltily, 'I met with Kendra Madison last night,' I begin.

'Kendra Madison's your mother's doctor?'

'Funny. I don't even know why I didn't tell you.'

'I do.'

'No, it's not like that. Nothing happened. She needed to talk to me without Killkenny, to give me the whole story.'

'Why?'

'Because the whole story involves an explanation of what she does for living.'

'I take it she's not selling Avon door-to-door?'

I shake my head. 'Her services are a bit more personal.'

I can see Yvette processing this information. The doubt and concern are written on her face. 'Did you get a price list?'

'I told you, it's not like that.' She rolls her eyes at me, unconvinced. I press on. 'Apparently she hooked Josh on the whole domination scene. He kept at it for four years, and his taste for it grew. He got more and more violent, until Kendra had to get out.'

'Serves her right, seems to me,' Yvette says acidly.

'Maybe,' I concede. 'But that didn't end it. Pinkerton tried to force her to keep seeing him. He used NetMaster to threaten her, he threatened her friends. Apparently it got even more violent until she used the company to back him off her.'

'How?'

'She dug up some information that would have been damaging to him, or the company, and threatened to take it public. She said it was the only way he would back off.'

'How does all this explain what happened to you?'

'I met her at a bar in Charlestown. When I left, NetMaster jumped me. I never saw him coming.'

'Did he say anything?'

'Yeah, he told me never to see or talk to Kendra Madison again. He also said that if I told anyone that he'd attacked me, he'd kill pretty much everyone I know – including you – so you probably want to keep this to yourself.'

'You're not going to the police?'

'Not yet,' I say. 'Not until we have what we need on Josh Pinkerton. Once we can trace the LifeScenes back to him, we can make a move, and at that point NetMaster will have no backing and no real motivation to make good on his threats.' My optimism is almost enough to make me forget how much my ribs hurt.

'You're that sure it's Pinkerton?'

'Why else would he have sent NetMaster after me? Besides, Kendra spent enough time with Josh to be a pretty good gauge of what he might be capable of. She thinks he was over the edge by the time she got rid of him. He had such a taste for sadism that he could easily have taken it to the next level. That's why she was so scared, and why she wanted to see me. All we need to do now is show that the LifeScenes came from Josh's computer.'

Yvette shakes her head. 'Then we've got a problem, because they didn't come from Josh's computer.'

It feels like she's kicked me in my battered ribs. 'What do you mean?'

'I mean these LifeScenes weren't created on Josh Pinkerton's computer.'

A slight panic creeps into my chest. 'I thought you said you'd found enough fragments of the LifeScenes, and that it looked like they were created on a computer that was locked into the system?'

'I did, and they were,' she agrees. 'It's just that they didn't come from any computer associated with Josh Pinkerton.'

I stare blankly at her. 'How can you be sure?'

'The system tracks all activity on all associated computers – whether you're talking about a workstation in the office or a laptop that's leased for the employees. Whenever you log into the system on one of those computers, the system automatically makes a backup of everything you've done. This way, if someone is doing development work, the company can keep track, even if people are forgetting to actually upload their work to the centralized system. Every bit that's transferred is tagged with an IP address that identifies the originating computer, so even if you access it through the system, you can tell where it came from.'

'And the fragments of *De Sade*'s LifeScenes didn't come from any computer associated with Josh?'

She shakes her head again. 'I'm sorry, but no.'

'Are they associated with anyone's computer?'

She nods. 'They almost all come from Dr Santar Gunta's laptop computer.'

I let out a low whistle. 'You're kidding me.'

'Nope. Apparently the good doctor has quite a hobby.'

I rub my forehead. 'And there's no chance that Pinkerton redirected the signal somehow to fool the computers into thinking the material was coming from someplace else? Spoof the system, maybe?'

'I don't think it's possible.' We sit there for a moment without talking. In the light of my pummeling the night before, this complicates matters for me, and we both know it. 'What should we do?' Yvette asks carefully.

'Well,' I say, 'our first priority is to catch the man who killed these women. Like I said yesterday, we need to follow this wherever it goes.'

'That doesn't help you with dealing with Pinkerton and NetMaster.'

'No, it doesn't,' I concede. 'I'll just have to find a different way of dealing with that.'

'So what's our next step?'

I sigh hard enough to make me wince in pain. 'Our next step is to talk to Killkenny and make sure Gunta is arrested.'

Yvette and I drive over to the police station in the Back Bay where Killkenny has his office. We could have called and asked him to come over, but it seems a conversation better had out of earshot of anyone at the company. He's not in when we arrive, so we sit in the lobby on a hard wooden bench. At least it provides enough support to ease the pain in my chest. Some of Thursday evening's catch are being released. There are a couple of young men who look hungover, one of them being picked up by a mother who is cussing him as they walk out the front door, talking about how much bail cost and how the next time she'll leave his ass in jail. There are also a couple of streetwalkers, looking tired but still with their sense of humor, joking with the desk sergeants as they leave. The cops call them by their names and smile to them, wishing them a nice day. I'm always amazed at the way in which the police live in a certain symbiotic balance with so many of the criminals they deal with. It was certainly the case in Charlestown, growing up. The cops would chase the kids and hookers for show, but at the upper levels there were relationships that went beyond the clearly adversarial. In some ways, that's what kept the peace, and kept things running smoothly.

Yvette is watching one of the hookers flirt with a uniformed officer as she leaves. 'You weren't with her?' she asks.

I look up at the hooker as she walks out, and for a moment I think Yvette is talking about her. Then I grasp that she's asking about Kendra. 'No,' I say. 'I told you, I left the bar alone.'

'You also told me you were meeting your mother's doctor.'

It's a fair point. Trust, once lost, is hard to reclaim. 'I wasn't with her.'

'She's beautiful, though.'

'Yeah,' I agree unenthusiastically. Denying that she's attractive would only destroy what's left of my credibility. I've had women set that trap for me before.

'No one would blame you if you were with her.' There is no right response to that, so I keep my mouth shut. 'You remember Tim Murphy?' It feels like she's digging deep to protect herself now.

'Yeah,' I say. 'Your first.'

'My first,' she agrees. She watches as two cops bring a struggling suspect in through the doors. 'I knew how you still felt about me back then. Even after we weren't together anymore and we were just trying to be friends.'

I nod. 'I was never subtle.'

'Yeah, well, I just wanted you to know that I didn't do that to hurt you. That wasn't the purpose.'

'I never thought it was.'

'Yeah,' she says hesitantly. 'Here's the thing, though: I wasn't trying to hurt you, but I knew I was. I knew how you'd feel when you found out, and I knew you'd find out because you were still a friend, so I knew I was going to tell you.'

'Yup.' I remember that conversation as if it were yesterday. It's not easy to keep the supportive smile on your face when your heart is being ripped apart, but I did it. I sat there and relived her first time with her, even as every word from her lips was like a knife to my gut.

'And even with all that, I did it anyway. There was something about him, and about me at that moment, that made it something I had to do, and you understood that.'

'That might be an overstatement.' I smile at her, and she smiles back.

'Fair enough. But you dealt with it, and you were there for me when I needed you.' We both look up and see Killkenny coming through the door. She stands. 'Anyway, I just wanted you to know that I get it. I get why you've never come for me again. It makes sense.'

Before I can respond, Killkenny is walking toward us. 'What are you two here for?'

'We need to talk.'

'About what?'

'There have been developments.'

'Since yesterday?'

'Is there a place where we can talk?'

'We know who it is.'

Yvette spits it out even before anyone has taken a seat in the interview room in the back of the station house.

Killkenny takes a deep breath and sits in one of the chairs.

'You do,' he says. The skepticism in his voice is hard to miss. 'Just like that, you've figured it out.'

'I know it's hard to believe, but it's true,' I say. 'We have the proof.'

'Proof, too? This I can't wait for.'

'I traced the programming for the LifeScenes back to the computer they were made on,' Yvette says. 'We know whose computer it is.'

That gets Killkenny's attention as he realizes that we are not merely speculating. He sits forward in his chair. 'You told me there was no way to track the LifeScene back to the user,' he says. 'I asked you whether it was possible to do that, and you were clear – you said it couldn't be done.'

'And that's generally true,' Yvette says. 'Because the data for a specific LifeScene resides on the user's computer, our system can't access it. But there's one exception.'

'Which is?'

'If the LifeScene was created on a computer that is tied into the system in the first place – if it is a NextLife computer – then we can access it.'

'I don't understand,' Killkenny says. 'How would it be created on the company's computer.'

'There's only one way,' I say. 'It can only happen if it's created by someone at the company.'

'And you've already run these searches,' Killkenny asks.

'We have.'

'Why didn't you tell me about this?'

The question catches me off-guard. 'We didn't know whether it would work.'

He shakes his head. 'That's not it,' he says. 'You wanted to keep control over the process. You didn't want me running the whole thing, right?'

'No,' I say. 'That's not right. What does it matter, anyway?'

'It matters only because it will make it more difficult to make the evidence stick, because there was no police oversight. There's a chain-of-custody issue.'

'Are you serious? We tell you we can prove who this guy is, and you want to second-guess our methods?'

Killkenny stares at us, still angry. Eventually, though, his curiosity overcomes his annoyance. 'So, who is it?'

'The LifeScenes were created on a system laptop that is assigned to Dr Santar Gunta,' Yvette says.

Killkenny smiles. 'You see? I told you that guy was hiding something. I fuckin' knew it.'

'Yeah,' I say. 'Now we know it. So what do we do about it?'

Killkenny loses his smile. 'I'll tell you what we do about it; we take the asshole down.'

'Quietly,' I respond.

'What?'

'We take him down quietly. We had a deal; you're not looking to embarrass the company, remember?'

'Fuck that!' Killkenny says. 'I'm going in with a fuckin' SWAT team if I can get authorization.'

'No, you're not.'

'You really want to protect this guy?'

'If I wanted to protect this guy, I wouldn't have brought this to you.' I look at Yvette. 'We wouldn't have brought this to you. Neither of us has any interest in protecting Gunta. But I do have an interest in protecting the company. I also have an interest in knowing whether anyone else at the company had any idea this was going on.'

That suggestion stops Killkenny in his tracks. 'You think that's a possibility?'

'I don't know,' I say. 'All I know is that if you go in with automatic weapons and haul him out in handcuffs in front of everyone, anyone who might know something is gonna disappear. If you take him quietly and interrogate him, you may get more than you expect.'

He considers this. 'Okay,' he says. 'How do you want to do it?'

CHAPTER TWENTY-SEVEN

We arrive at NextLife's headquarters at a little after one o'clock. Killkenny brings two uniformed officers with him, and I install the three of them in a conference room on the third floor, near the Human Resources offices. I tell no one what is going on, and I leave Yvette with the police and head to the lab.

'He runs, I'll shoot him,' Killkenny says to me as I head out the door. 'Then I'll shoot you.'

'This will work,' I assure him. 'If I get any sense that he's not cooperating, I'll phone you immediately. I don't think it's going to be a problem.'

I go up to the lab and step inside. Gunta's there, at his raised desk, his nose nearly pressed against one of the gigantic computer screens, scrutinizing some line of code or obscure algorithm. His chief assistant programmer, Michael, is standing next to him. They seem to be discussing a programming problem. I walk over to him. 'Hey, Doc,' I say.

He looks up, but only for a split second before his attention returns to his computer screen. 'Hello, Nick,' he says. Michael continues to regard me with hostility. 'Are you here for more mischief?'

'Trying to prevent any more mischief, actually.' He tears his eyes away from his work and looks at me again. 'We need to talk again,' I say. 'Not here; someplace quieter.'

I get the feeling that he's thinking about telling me to fuck off, but he sees the seriousness in my expression and I think he understands that I'm not going away. 'My office?'

I shake my head. 'Not here. I've got a conference room down on the third floor. We can talk there.'

'Why not here?' I can hear the tension in his voice.

'You don't want to do this in front of the people who work with you. It may be a long conversation.'

He's looking at me the way a poker player evaluates an opponent who has just raised the pot, trying to figure out what I've got in my hand. It takes a moment, but eventually he folds. 'Michael, why don't you print this out and bring it down to the conference room? We can figure it out then.'

'Very well, Doctor,' Michael says. He's never taken his eyes off me, and I get the distinct feeling that, if he had the resources, he would try to do me serious harm. It's clear how loyal he is to the doctor.

Gunta gets out of his chair and steps down off the raised platform. He and I walk out of the lab and over to the elevators. As we stand there, waiting for the doors to open, he says, 'What's this about now?'

'What do you think?'

'Those girls?'

The elevator doors open.

'Yeah,' I say. 'Those girls.' I feel like punching him as we get in the elevator.

'Has there been another killing?' The question strikes me

as odd. After all, he should know whether there has been another killing. My blood goes cold as it occurs to me that he may have killed more, and he is just waiting for us to find the bodies.

'Not that we are aware of,' I say. I watch his reaction, and he seems genuinely relieved.

We get out of the elevator at the third floor and walk over to the conference room. I open the door and step back to let Gunta in first. He takes a step in before he sees Killkenny and the two other cops. Yvette is sitting on a chair at the far end of the room. Gunta stops, and I feel his momentum shift backwards, almost as though he's going to duck out of the room and make a run for it. I've positioned myself behind him, though, and I give his back a soft push. There is little resistance; I think he knows running would be futile at this point anyway.

'Detective,' Gunta says quietly. 'How good to see you again. And you've brought friends,' he nods to the two men in uniform. 'How nice.'

'Dr Gunta,' Killkenny says. 'We need to talk to you again, I'm sorry for any inconvenience. We just have a few questions that have come up, which you may be able to help us with.'

'No inconvenience at all.' He sits down. 'Fire away.'

The mock civility between the two of them is fascinating to watch – the homicide detective and the murderer, playing out a chess match, each trying to get into the other's head; each waiting for the other to show his strategy, to make a mistake.

Killkenny takes out a sheet of paper. 'This is a list of all the computers owned by NextLife and given to employees for their use,' he begins. He puts it on the conference table before Gunta. 'If you look midway down the page, you'll see there was an HP notebook that was given to you a year and a half ago.'

Gunta glances at the list, but I don't have the impression he's examined it closely enough to have actually seen the entry. 'That appears to be correct,' Gunta says.

'Do you know where that computer is?'

Gunta shakes his head. 'I don't.'

'You don't?' Killkenny looks at me. He wasn't expecting this answer.

'It was lost shortly after I received it,' Gunta says calmly.

Killkenny now glances back and forth between me and Yvette. Neither of us can give him any help. 'Did you report it lost to anyone at the company?'

'I don't believe so,' Gunta says.

'Why not?'

'I was embarrassed at having been so irresponsible. I was planning on simply replacing the machine myself, but I must have forgotten.' He looks at me. 'Nick, what is this all about?'

I say nothing, and Killkenny pulls out the printouts Yvette has prepared for him. 'The person who has been killing these girls has been practicing the murders on the NextLife platform before he actually does the murders,' he says. 'He goes by the name *De Sade*. Does that mean anything to you, Doc?'

Gunta is visibly shaken for the first time. His head drops and he says, 'No' so quietly I can barely hear it. It comes out less like an answer to the question and more like a lament.

'What was that, Doc?' Killkenny asks, pleased that he's finally made a dent in the doctor's facade.

Gunta picks his head up. 'No,' he says more clearly. 'It means nothing to me.'

'Really? Can you explain why the company's server records show that the LifeScenes where this man, *De Sade*, practiced these murders were created on the computer that the company gave to you?'

His face drains of blood. 'It's not possible!' he says indignantly.

'Why?' Killkenny asks, laughing. 'Because you used a fragging program to destroy any traces?' Gunta says nothing. 'Fortunately, others at the company are even better with computers than you are.' He nods at Yvette, and Gunta looks over at her. For a moment it seems like he's almost giving her a grudging look of respect. 'Well, Doc?' Killkenny says. 'Do you have anything to say to all of that?'

Gunta starts to open his mouth, then stops. 'I think I would prefer to talk to a lawyer, Detective.'

Killkenny nods. 'I expected that. We'll take you down to the station house and get you booked. Then you can call all the lawyers you want. You're going to need them.'

As agreed, we take Gunta out the back, where Killkenny and his boys have parked their cars. We walk out of the conference room, Gunta's hands cuffed behind his back, a jacket thrown over them to make the scene less conspicuous – as though a man walking with his hands behind his back, flanked by two uniformed cops, could ever be inconspicuous. It's the best Killkenny is willing to offer, though, and I can understand it. Gunta is, after all, a murder suspect.

We're coming out of the conference room when we run

into Michael, carrying a set of printouts. He looks at the two police officers holding Gunta by the elbows. 'What is going on here?' he demands.

'Don't worry, Michael,' Gunta says before anyone else can speak. 'It's all a misunderstanding.'

'You can't take him!' Michael protests. He drops his papers and gets in front of the group. 'You can't!'

'Get out of the way,' Killkenny says sharply. 'Or we'll make room in the cells for you.'

'Please, Michael,' Gunta says. 'Don't get involved. I will be fine.'

The younger man nods and backs off. As we pass by, he gives me a venomous look. 'You have no right,' he says quietly. 'You have no right.'

I ignore him and continue on with the group.

The parking lot out back is empty, and we hurry Gunta across the tarmac toward the awaiting squad car. For just a moment I think that we've gotten through the ordeal without any additional drama, but just as one of the cops pushes Gunta's head down to avoid him hitting it as he slides him into the back seat, the back door to the building opens and Josh Pinkerton hurries out, with Tom Jackson chasing after him.

'Nick!' Pinkerton shouts. 'What the fuck is going on?'

'Josh, come back,' Tom is pleading.

Killkenny steps up and holds his badge up. 'We're the police,' he says.

'No shit,' Pinkerton says. He's in a rage. 'I can fuckin' read!' he shouts, pointing at the lettering on the squad car. 'What the fuck are you doing to Dr Gunta?'

'We're arresting him,' Killkenny says.

'What for?'

'That's police business.'

'Nick!' Pinkerton shouts at me. 'What the fuck is going on?'

Killkenny shoots a look at me. 'Keep your mouth shut, Nick!' He turns back to Pinkerton. 'This is a murder investigation, sir. I can't share any additional information with you at this time, is that clear?'

'Who the fuck do you think you're talking to?' Pinkerton shouts at Killkenny. I know that's a bad move by Josh. Killkenny isn't the type to back down when challenged. If anything, questioning his authority only hardens his resolve.

'Josh,' I say, 'You need to go back inside. I'll explain this all to you later.'

'The hell you will,' Killkenny says.

'Tell me what's going on, Nick,' Pinkerton demands again. 'Don't worry about this asshole. I own people like him.'

Tom Jackson looks like he's going to have a stroke. 'Josh! We need to go inside!'

Killkenny takes a step toward Pinkerton. 'Let me tell you exactly who I think I'm talking to,' he says. 'I think I'm talking to an asshole who doesn't understand that money doesn't always buy you out of a jam. I think I'm talking to a guy who doesn't know what is good for him. And I think I'm talking to a guy who's about three seconds from landing in jail for the night, on a charge of obstruction of justice.'

'You wouldn't dare!'

'Try me.'

Tom Jackson is pulling at Pinkerton's arm, trying to get

him back into the building. Josh allows himself to be pulled for a few steps, and Killkenny starts heading back to his car. Suddenly, though, Pinkerton pulls out of Tom's grip and squares himself at a distance from Killkenny. 'You have no idea what real power is!' he screams. 'You can't even conceive of the kind of power that someone like me has. You'll never understand the kind of power I have over others. Never!'

It comes out as a bit of an irrational screed, and Killkenny looks over to me with an expression of disbelief.

'It's not worth it,' I say to him. 'You clear out, we'll catch up with you.'

Killkenny pulls out in his SS, the squad car following him. I'm left in the parking lot standing next to Yvette. Josh and Tom are standing about ten yards away. Pinkerton postures defiantly as he watches the cars pull away. Once they've gone, he looks at me and points his finger in my direction. 'This is your fault!' he yells. 'I trusted you, and you do this to the company?' He lets his hand drop. 'You've made a bad mistake, Nick.' He stares at me for another moment, and then turns and heads back into the building.

Tom is standing there, a look of disbelief on his face. 'I'll talk to him,' he says to me. 'He'll calm down. He'll realize it's not your fault, eventually,' he assures me. 'He'll forgive you. It'll just take time.'

He walks back toward the door.

'You think Pinkerton will understand in time?' I ask Yvette.

She tilts her head to the side to look up at me. 'I don't think there's enough time left in the universe for Pinkerton to forgive you,' she says.

'Thanks, that's helpful.'

She shakes her head. 'I don't think anyone can help you at this point.'

I drive Yvette back to the bunker in Cambridge. I'm half expecting to be met by security guards at the door, carrying a cardboard box full of my personal possessions. I wonder whether they will pick me up and physically throw me out of the building, just for effect.

Everything is quiet when we arrive, though. The floor is busy, with more than seventy GhostWalkers filling up their time cards, oblivious to the controversy that's swirling around the company. Yvette and I make our way around the work-stations, back to my office.

'What now?' she asks.

'Now, we let the police do their job. We go back to doing our job.'

'I'm not sure I can just go back to what I was doing. It feels . . . ' She's searching for the words. 'It feels wrong.'

'I thought you didn't believe in traditional notions of morality.'

'I don't,' she says. 'I believe in personal morality.'

'For all we know, so does Dr Gunta.'

'Yeah, well, his morality is fucked-up. I don't think there's anything anyone can do about people like that. And they exist in all religions and all moral traditions.' She sighs heavily. 'I don't feel like doing any work at the moment. You want to go grab a bite at the Diner?'

'Sure,' I say. 'Just give me a minute. I need to make a call.'

'Who are you gonna call?'

'I've just gotta . . . '

'Her. You're gonna call her.'

I'm sitting at my desk, and I pick up a pen and drag it along a piece of paper, trying to decide whether to lie. I know it's pointless, though. 'I just want to tell her that they've made an arrest.'

'Why?'

'Because she knows she was a potential victim. Wouldn't you want to know?'

'Yeah,' Yvette concedes. 'Okay, I'll go over and get us a table.'

'Sounds good. I'll just be a minute.'

'You sure?'

'Yeah, I'm sure.'

CHAPTER TWENTY-EIGHT

The phone rings four times before she picks up. 'Hello?'

'Is this Kendra?'

'Yes. Who's this?'

'It's Nick.' It's quiet on the line. 'Nick Caldwell.'

'I know which Nick it is,' she says. I can't tell whether there's anger in the tone or just disappointment.

'Did you make it home okay last night?'

'You mean did I make it home alone last night?'

'I didn't ask that. It's not any of my business.'

'No, it's not.' Now I can hear the anger. But there's something else there, too. Desire, maybe. Or maybe it's just the need to take on the challenge of rejection. 'I got home just fine. How about you?'

My heart is beating hard, and my ribs are giving me a constant reminder of my experience the night before. It occurs to me that I'm potentially risking my life just by having this conversation. Somehow that doesn't bother me. 'I made it home fine, too,' I say.

'Good.' She pauses, and then changes her tone. 'Listen, I'm sorry about last night. I just felt lonely.'

'It happens to all of us,' I say. I want to tell her how much I want her – how much I need her – but I can't. The desire is so strong it feels pathological.

'I shouldn't have put all that on you.' My mouth is moving, trying to respond, but no sound is coming out. 'Why did you call?'

'I just wanted to let you know that they made an arrest this morning in the murders we spoke about. I thought you'd feel better knowing.'

'They arrested Josh?' She sounds almost ecstatic.

'No,' I say. 'It doesn't look like it was Josh after all.'

'Who did they arrest then?' The ecstasy has turned to doubt.

'They haven't made an announcement, but it was Santar Gunta.' She says nothing. 'Are you still there? Did you hear what I sai—'

'They're wrong,' she says emphatically.

'What?'

'They're wrong,' she says again. 'It's not Gunta. I'm sure of it. I spent enough time around him to know what he's capable of, and what he's not. He's not capable of this. He's too much of a coward.'

'We have the evidence,' I say.

'The evidence is wrong.'

I'm not sure what to say. 'Well, it's in the hands of the police now, so I suppose they'll figure out whether they have the right person.'

'No, they won't,' she laments. 'They won't, because that's not the way the police work. Once they believe they have the right guy, they'll stick with that. It's the easiest way to deal with things. Anything that comes up that doesn't support their theory they will either ignore or they'll jam into a box that they can say makes sense.'

'Why do you think that?'

I can almost see her eyes rolling. 'I've dealt with the police before.'

'I'm not sure what you want me to do,' I say.

'Please, just promise me you won't let this drop. Maybe I'm wrong, and maybe it's not Josh, but I'm sure it's not Gunta. It just doesn't make sense. Will you promise me you'll keep looking into this?'

'It's not my job,' I say. In fact I worry about interfering in the investigation in a way that will get me arrested.

'I know it's not your job, but it's something you're good at. You're smart, and you're stubborn, and you don't like it when people get the better of you. What better traits are there for an investigator?'

'I'm not sure there's much I can do.'

'There has to be,' she says. 'There has to be, because whoever did this to those girls is still out there. And if he's still out there, it means he will do it again.'

I look at my watch and realize that Yvette has been waiting at the Diner for ten minutes. 'I've got to go.'

'Okay. Just please think about it?'

'I will.' I switch off the phone.

'That took a while.'

Yvette is sitting in a booth near the Diner's front door. The coffee on the table in front of her is half gone. She stirs what is left deliberately.

'Sorry.'

'Is she relieved?'

'No,' I say. 'She doesn't believe that Gunta killed the girls. She thinks it's someone else.'

'Pinkerton?'

I nod. 'She admitted that it could be someone else, but she's convinced that it's not Gunta.'

'Did she explain why?'

'Not really.' I flag down a waitress and order a coffee. Yvette orders another. I consider getting something to eat, but I'm not particularly hungry. 'She doesn't think he has murder in him.'

Yvette takes a sip of her coffee contemplatively. 'I can't say I disagree with her on that. I'm not a fan of his personality, but the good doctor doesn't strike me as a killer. And he certainly doesn't strike me as someone who would kill these girls in such a sexually ritualistic way. I just don't see it.'

'You think it's Pinkerton too?'

'Could be,' Yvette says. 'But that wouldn't explain why the LifeScenes were created on a computer that was handed out to Gunta. And I don't think he has the skills to create the kind of graphics that are used in *De Sade*'s LifeScenes.'

Our coffees arrive, and Yvette pours a huge dollop from the creamer on the table and chases it with five sugars. I drink mine black while I think about what she's said. 'What if it's not just him?' I ask idly. 'What if there's someone else who's helping him?'

'Like who?'

'What's your impression of Michael, the guy who works with him?'

'He's good-looking,' Yvette says immediately. 'He certainly wouldn't need to tie a girl up to get laid.'

'Maybe that's how they get these girls in the first place, you know? I mean, getting someone to go home with you without a struggle isn't necessarily the easiest thing in the world.'

'Speak for yourself.'

'I'm talking about someone like Gunta. Older, awkward with women and a little severe, you know?'

'A little?'

'That's my point. I haven't heard anything from Killkenny about these women being drugged, and it doesn't sound like they were attacked before they were killed – it sounds like they put themselves in these positions voluntarily. I have a hard time seeing Gunta being able to accomplish that on nothing but his own charm.'

Yvette tilts her head. 'It's possible, I suppose. But then, what does Gunta get out of it? What's he in it for?'

I shrug. 'Who knows? Maybe he just likes to watch.' I take another sip of my coffee and look around the place. It's mid-afternoon and the Diner is half full, mainly with college students and people in their twenties taking a break from whatever work they have. I notice that nearly every single one of them is tapping away at some sort of device: tablets, iPhones, BlackBerrys, iPads, smartphones . . . Everyone is sending out information about themselves over the Internet. Personal, intimate messages to secret lovers; sensitive business plans; credit-card information; missives to arch enemies. Few of them even look up to interact with the people sitting there in front of them. At that moment it strikes me how sad and lonely technology has made us. I think about the people on NextLife, passing their time in fantasies, unable to engage with the real world. 'We've become a nation of voyeurs, after all. Gunta was the one who created the NextLife LifeScenes in the first place.'

'Maybe. You think his assistant, Michael, is involved?'

'He gave me a look like he wanted to kill me as they took Gunta away today. He certainly seems like a guy who might be capable of murder.'

'How do you know, really? Do we know anything about his background?'

'No, we don't,' I admit. 'But I know a way we can find out.'

CHAPTER TWENTY-NINE

We're back in my office, sitting in front of my computer screen. 'I have an administrator's access to the company's employment records,' I explain. 'HR decided it was necessary because of the sensitive nature of what this department does. I need to be able to check on my employees to make sure there is no one who is a security risk.'

'Has anyone ever come up on the system as a legitimate concern?'

'Yes,' I answer honestly.

'Who?'

I look over at her. 'You.'

She laughs. 'Seriously?'

'Yeah. You have a history of hacking and at least one arrest for computer-related offenses. Remember, you hacked the WorldCom system and shut down all their financial records for three hours.'

'That was a prank! Everyone hated that company anyway. I was just trying to stop them from distributing any cash to their executives.'

'Yeah, but unfortunately it was while the Feds were

conducting their investigation, and it freaked the hell out of everyone.'

'That was just bad timing. I was never even charged with anything.'

'It doesn't matter – our system picks up everything that's out there. We have a full record of every interaction our employees have had with a government entity, every Facebook posting they've made, every bill they've been late on. It's all here.'

'Isn't that illegal?'

I shake my head. 'It's all available online, if you know where to look. Hell, most people regularly click website terms and conditions that give away all of their privacy without even reading them. We just go out and collect it.' I type in my administrator's password and navigate my way to the HR section. Once there, I pull up Michael's information.

'Anything interesting?' Yvette asks, looking over my shoulder.

'Nothing.'

'Well, I suppose it was a long shot,' she says.

'No, you don't understand, there's nothing here. There are no records of where he came from or what he did before he started working here. All we have is a social security number, and his date of birth. There are no recommendations, there's no employment history, no educational background. Nothing.'

'How can that be?'

'I don't know. I've never seen anything like this before.' I scroll through what few records there are, looking for anything that might give a clue to what happened to Michael's records. There is a link with no identifying information at the bottom of the screen, and I click on it to see what happens. The image on the computer flashes twice, and then links to an outside site.

'What's this?'

'It's the record site for the Massachusetts Department of Corrections.'

'The prison system?' Yvette looks in close. 'What the hell?'

The top of the screen identifies the Massachusetts prison-system records database, and the prompt asks me for an inmate number and security clearance. I try typing in Michael's name and hit return, but that just throws me back to the entry page with a red indication that the information I have entered is insufficient to allow access.

'At least we know he has a criminal record,' I say. 'That suggests there's a problem with him.'

'Bullshit,' Yvette says. 'I have a criminal record. For all we know, he's just another hacker who pulled something juvenile that pissed off the wrong people.'

'Fair enough, but there's no way at the moment for us to find out anything more.'

She shakes her head in disgust. 'You really don't deserve to work at a technology company. There's always a way to find out more. Move aside.'

I smile; it's the reaction I was hoping for. I slide my chair away from the computer and allow her to slide her chair in. 'You're gonna hack it?'

'Yeah, I'm gonna hack it.' Her fingers start flying across the keyboard.

'How long do you think it'll take?'

'Depends on what level of encryption they have on this puppy.'

'Is there anything I can do to help?'

'Yeah, shut up and get me a cup of coffee.'

Apparently the Massachusetts Department of Corrections on-line records system has a very sophisticated encryption system. Three coffees later, Yvette is still beating on the keyboard, obscene gerunds slipping quietly from her lips. I'm pacing at the back of my office, which clearly isn't helping her concentrate. Twice she turns and glares until I sit and force myself to be still. The second time this happens, I take out my phone and text Killkenny to ask him to call me. I'm curious about how the interrogation of Gunta is going, and whether he has learned anything that might help us.

Another half hour passes, and I think I may be losing my mind. I even consider going out onto the floor to do some GhostWalking, just to occupy my mind during the interminable wait. The thought of crawling around in other people's psyches, though, is no longer alluring to me. There was a time, particularly when we began the black-ops program, when I thought I had one of the coolest jobs anyone could imagine. The ability to peer into the minds of my fellow human beings seemed a power that any curious, adventurous person would kill for. Now it seems a tawdry, cheap parlor trick. I'm not sure I will ever view the company or my role in it the same way again, and I wonder what that means for my future. That kind of introspection, however, seems unproductive at the moment, so I put it out of my mind.

The room is silent except for occasional outbursts of Yvette's keystrokes. When she started, her rhythm was a steady stream.

Now it's sporadic and violent. 'How's it going?' I ask at one point.

'It'd go better if you'd shut the fuck up.' I hadn't said a word for over an hour, but I let it pass, and we lapse into more silence. Her keyboard acrobatics become shorter and are separated by longer periods of silence.

At one point she hasn't touched the keyboard for nearly five minutes. She's just sitting there, staring at the screen, not blinking. I wonder whether she's okay, but I keep my mouth shut. The tension is becoming unbearable. At that moment the deafening off-key computer melody from my phone shatters the silence, and both of us jump. Yvette turns on me and gives me a glare. I pull the phone out of my pocket and hold it up with an apologetic shrug of the shoulders.

'Yeah?' I say, answering the phone.

'It's Killkenny. You asked me to call.'

'I just wanted to know how it's going.'

'Nick, it's a police investigation. I can't very well give you updates.'

'No shit, it's a police investigation. Remember, you wouldn't have anything if it wasn't for the information we've been feeding you. I just want to know whether he's said anything that's helpful.'

'Like what?'

'Like has he confessed? Has he said anything?'

'He denies everything. When he got here he talked a little, but only to say he didn't know anything about the murders. He's lying, though. I'm sure of it.'

'How do you know?'

'Ten years as a cop.'

'That's it?'

'Yeah, that's it. Within a half hour of being here he lawyered up. We've gotten nothing from him since. You don't have to worry, though; my read on this is that we've got the right guy. There's no doubt in my mind he's lying.'

'Yeah, but lying about what?' I ask quietly.

'What?'

'Nothing. Okay, thanks. Let us know if you get anything else.'

'Us?'

'Me and Yvette. We're working on something here at the office.'

'Related to the case?' I say nothing. I can hear him breathing on the other end of the line. 'Nick, let me be clear about this. We appreciate the help you've provided, but at this point you two need to let us handle this. You start freelancing and you could weaken the case – make it harder for us to get a conviction.'

'I just want to make sure you convict the right guy,' I say.

'Whatever you're doing, you need to stop.'

'Okay, understood.'

'I mean it.'

'Okay, we'll talk later.' I press the phone off.

'Killkenny?' Yvette asks.

'Yeah. They've gotten nothing useful from Gunta. He denies having anything to do with any of this. Killkenny's convinced that he's lying.'

'Did he say anything else?'

'Yeah,' I say. 'He wants us to keep helping in any way we can.'

Yvette turns and looks at me, studying my face for a moment. Then she goes back to her work. 'You may be the worst liar in the history of mankind.'

'That bad?'

'It's one of your few endearing qualities.'

It's nearing midnight. Yvette has been hacking for more than eight hours. The air in the office is stale with sweat and coffee breath. The ventilation in the basement is awful to begin with, but my office is the worst. There are no windows, and only one HVAC vent. It's a tiny little mousehole of a space, and at this moment, for the first time, I regret not having made demands for better accommodation.

I'm sitting in my chair, leaning back far enough that my head is resting against the wall, my feet stretched out. I'm on the verge of falling asleep.

'I'm in!'

Yvette screams loud enough that I slip off the side of the chair and hit my head on the wall. She doesn't even seem to notice. 'I'm in,' she repeats. 'Holy shit, I did it!' She seems genuinely surprised. I'm not; I never had a doubt.

I roll my chair over to the computer and peer at the screen. We are inside the firewall for the Massachusetts Department of Corrections records website. There is a prompt asking us to put in the name of the prisoner we are searching for. Yvette types in *Michael* in the place for the first name. 'What's his last name?' she asks.

'François,' I respond. She hesitates before putting the name in. 'What's wrong?'

'I don't know,' she says. 'Somehow the name seems familiar.'

She shakes away the feeling and types in the name, hits return. An icon pops up showing that the server is being searched and the information compiled. It takes around two minutes before the results are displayed.

'Oh God,' Yvette says quietly as the results are displayed. There, before us, is a three-page list of arrests for sexual assaults of varying degree. There are only two convictions, both for aggravated sexual assault, though the records indicate that in both instances he was charged with the more serious offense of aggravated rape, and the charges were reduced in accordance with a plea agreement. There is also a record of his activities in prison, where he took extensive courses in computer programming. 'Jesus Christ!' Yvette says as she scrolls through the information. 'Why the hell would we hire this guy?'

'It looks like he was a wizard of a programmer, from what the instructors of his prison remedial classes say,' I point out. 'They say he has a real gift.'

'Yeah. A gift wrapped up in a rapist. It still doesn't make sense.'

I'm still reading through the information and I come to the end. 'That's why,' I say, pointing to the bottom of the last screen. There is a notion that he participated in an advanced pilot program to determine recidivism. The author and overseer of the program was Dr Santar Gunta, and there is a notation that the results clearly showed that Michael François was deemed highly unlikely to repeat his crimes. 'Gunta gave him a clean bill of health, based on his interactions on the NextLife system.'

Yvette sucks in her breath. 'Oh no!' she says.

'What?'

'I think I just realized why Michael's last name is familiar.'
'Why?'

She taps on the keyboard and pulls up another Internet connection and runs a search for *Marquis de Sade*. She clicks on the first historical website that comes up and stares at the screen. 'I came across it when I was doing research on De Sade,' she says. She pushes back from the screen so that I can get a better look.

I read the first line: *Marquis de Sade; born Donatien Alphonse François, June 2, 1740; died December 2, 1814.* 'It's the same last name,' I say.

She nods. 'It's the same last name.'

We sit here, staring at the screen in silence, wondering what to do next. My phone interrupts our ruminations, ringing in my pocket. I answer it. 'Hello?'

'Nick, it's Killkenny.'

My words come out in a rush. 'Paul, it's not Gunta – at least not alone. It's someone else!'

'I know.'

'How do you know?'

'Because we just found Taylor Westerbrooke.'

CHAPTER THIRTY

Neither Yvette nor I speak on the ride to Roxbury. A couple of times I start to say something, but when I play it in my mind before it comes out, it seems inappropriate. I finally settle for putting a hand on her shoulder when we're stopped at a light. She looks over and again I have the impulse to say something – anything to let her know that it's alright; that we did everything we could have done. But I know it's not alright, and I'm not convinced that we – that I – did everything that could have been done.

We pull up outside the building off Melnea Cass Boulevard in Roxbury, a rundown area of the city that's wedged between the fashionable South End and suburban Brookline. We're only a few miles from where Taylor Westerbrooke grew up, but I feel certain that she never spent any time in this neighborhood when she was younger.

There are several police cars parked haphazardly near the building, cutting traffic down from four lanes to two. Fortunately it's late enough that the pile-up seems to be causing minimal inconvenience to drivers. The locals who are awake and observing the process from a distance seem accustomed to the invasion of the law.

I park the car a half a block up the street, just past the last police car. We get out and walk back toward the building. A string of police tape stretches waist-high across the sidewalk, one end tied to a tree, the other to a car door handle. A young cop stands there, keeping the curious at bay. We walk up to the tape and I call out to him. 'Officer?' At first he pretends not to hear me, so I raise the volume. 'Officer!'

He looks at me, annoyed. 'Stay back, sir!' he barks.

'Detective Killkenny called. We've been helping with the investigation. He asked us to come.'

He looks at me suspiciously. 'You cops? Where's your badges?'

I shake my head. 'We're not cops. Just ask for Paul Killkenny. Tell him Nick Caldwell is here.'

'Caldwell?'

'Caldwell. Whatever, just tell him.'

The officer calls over another uniformed cop and talks to him, sending him inside. He turns and keeps his eye on us. It takes around three minutes before Killkenny pokes his head out of the building's front door. He shouts to the cop watching the small crowd, 'They're good!' and ducks his head back inside. The cop gives us a grudging look, but lifts the tape to let us through.

Killkenny is waiting for us just inside. The building is a six-story box structure with all the personality that early 1960s utilitarian architecture had to offer. The hallways are tiled, and the floors are some sort of industrial linoleum that looks like it was designed to be easily cleaned. 'It's a flophouse,' Killkenny says. 'Rentals can be anywhere from nightly to monthly. I talked to the manager, and the efficiency apartment Taylor's in was rented for three nights.'

'Where is she?' Yvette demands.

'Third floor,' Killkenny says. 'I'll take you up.'

We walk across the entryway and get into an elevator that creaks as it closes. The lights are dim, and even with just the three of us it's cramped. The pulleys grind and groan as we make the three-story climb. The buzzer sounds, letting us know we are at our floor, and the doors labor to open.

We step out, and it takes a moment for my eyes to adjust. The light in the elevator is dim, but at least there is some. The hallway lights on the third floor are out, and the hallway is crowded with cops. They bustle back and forth, some serious, others cracking macabre jokes. They quieten down when they see Killkenny. He leads us down the hallway toward the doorway that seems to be the focal point of the activity. He pauses ten feet from the apartment. 'It's not pleasant in there,' he says. He looks at Yvette. 'You don't have to do this.'

She gives him a hard look. 'Yes, I do.'

He nods, and leads us to the door. There are two cops in the doorway, just staring at the scene, blocking our way. Killkenny taps them on the shoulder and they part, clearing the way for us.

The vision is awful to behold. Taylor is undressed, hanging from the ceiling, a chain running from the back of her neck to a metal bolt above her. Her head is slumped forward, her tangled thicket of red hair hiding her face, her neck stretched, taking her weight. There are leather straps around her wrists, and they are secured to hooks in the ceiling so that her arms hang loosely out to her sides, like a marionette awaiting the puppet show. Her ankles are tied with straps that run to hooks in the floor, her legs spread.

I stand there, unable to move, unable to speak. Yvette described the scene from her GhostWalk, so I knew roughly what I was likely to see when I walked through the door, and I've had my own experience GhostWalking *De Sade*'s LifeScenes myself, but nothing prepared me for this. As perfect as we like to view the technology at NextLife to be – as close to real life as it is – it cannot capture the brutality of a scene like this. NextLife is pristine, a sanitized version of reality that leaves out the sting of the real world. The walls of the tiny apartment are streaked with water stains from past years, and the place carries the stench of desperation and fear. In short, there is nothing erotic about the scene before us. It is raw and dirty and obscene.

There is a crime-scene investigator who is working the body inch by inch, taking photographs with a large camera with an oversized flash that illuminates Taylor Westerbrooke's flesh like lightning in a horror film. As he moves up, he comes to her head and he takes several shots before he reaches up and grabs her by the hair, tilting her head back so that we can see her face.

Her cheeks are streaked with mascara, her lipstick smeared. For the first time, now, I can see the metal collar, a spiked monstrosity two inches thick, the joints digging into her skin far enough to draw tiny rivulets of blood down like a spider web toward her breasts. The worst, though, are her eyes. They are open, and they stare out at us with a profound agony, begging for the release that has already come.

Yvette takes a step forward, her expression set, tears running down her face. 'I'm so sorry,' she whispers to the corpse suspended before her. 'I should have stopped this.' She stands there for just a moment, and then turns and walks out without another word.

'I talked to her mother,' Killkenny says out in the hallway. We've moved away from the apartment doorway and stand toward the end of the hallway. A swarm of cops clot the dark, narrow passageway, like flies around meat that's been left out for too long. I can feel them looking over at us, no doubt wondering who we are. 'Apparently, she didn't take our advice. She went out with the cute boy she met at the bar a week ago. The coroner says she's been dead less than four hours, and Gunta's been locked up at the station house. Besides, no one's gonna mistake Gunta for a matinee idol, so that clears him. At least for this one. You said you think you know who did this?'

'We think we do,' I say.

'We know we do,' Yvette corrects me. There is venom in her voice.

'You waiting for my birthday to surprise me?'

'It's Michael François,' I say. 'He's one of Gunta's chief assistant programmers.'

'Okay,' Killkenny says. 'You wanna tell me how you know this for sure?'

'He's got the same last name as the Marquis de Sade,' Yvette says.

'That it?' Killkenny demands. ''Cause that won't even get me a warrant, much less a conviction.'

'No, that's not it,' I say. 'He was part of Gunta's experiments with prisoners using the NextLife platform. Gunta cleared him as a non-risk, and he was released in part on that basis.'

'He was a convict?'

'Yeah.'

'What was he in for?'

'Multiple arrests and two convictions for sexual assault. He's also a programming genius, so he has the skill to create the intricate LifeScenes *De Sade* used to practice the murders.'

'Okay, I'm sold,' Killkenny says. 'That'll get me the warrant, at least. The coroner says there's semen still in the girl, so if we find this guy, it's a simple test to prove whether or not he did this. God bless DNA.'

'How long will it take to get the warrant?' I ask.

'I'm phoning it in now. I need you two to come down to the station house to look over the affidavit before I sign it, but there's a Superior Court judge on call. We should be able to have it within an hour or so.' He pauses for a moment, thinking. 'So, you think this guy is actually a descendant of the Marquis de Sade?'

'Maybe,' Yvette says. 'Who knows? It's clear that he feels a bond with him. Maybe he just has the same last name, or maybe he changed his name at some point because he wanted to be like him. In the end it doesn't really matter, does it? All that matters is making sure he doesn't do anything like this to another girl.'

'Speaking of the other girls, should we warn them again? Be clearer this time?' I ask. I can feel Yvette's eyes on me, bearing down.

'I was pretty fuckin' clear the first time,' Killkenny says defensively.

'Taylor Westerbrooke didn't get the message,' Yvette points out.

'I'm guessing that girl wouldn't have taken my advice no matter what I said to her.' Killkenny sounds sure of himself, but he looks at the wall as he's talking, and I think I can see the doubt in his eyes. 'We'll call them,' he says. 'Not at two-thirty in the morning, though. We'll wait until the sun is up.' Yvette and I say nothing. 'I don't want to create panic unnecessarily,' he adds. 'The morning should be fine.'

'If it was your daughter, would you want the cops to wait till morning to tell you this?' Yvette asks.

He sighs heavily. 'We can call them from the station house while we're waiting for the warrant. Happy?'

'No,' Yvette says. 'I'm definitely not happy.'

The detectives' squad room at the police station is virtually empty. Other than us, there's one young detective there, clearly the low man on the totem pole, who drew the graveyard shift. He's sitting in his chair, feet up on his desk, sound asleep when we walk in. He opens one eye briefly, shifts his position and goes back to sleep.

'I'll have the affidavit ready in about ten minutes. I'll leave some blanks that you can fill in once you've looked at it, okay?' Killkenny says. We nod, and he picks up the files with the pictures and backgrounds on the models we've identified as the subjects of *De Sade*'s LifeScenes. 'There are phones on the desks. Dial nine to get an outside line. The phone numbers are in there. Tell them you're working with me.'

'What if they ask if we're police officers?' Yvette asks.

'Lie, if necessary,' Killkenny says. Yvette and I look at each other. 'What?' he asks. 'It's for their own good, right?' He walks over to a computer to start on his affidavit.

'You take three and I'll take three,' I say to Yvette.

'Deal.' She pulls off three files and hands them to me. I notice that she's included Kendra Madison in my pile, and I wonder whether that was intentional.

My first call is to one of the women Killkenny interviewed alone. I'm staring at her picture as I dial, so that I can put a face to the voice. It takes three rings for her to answer, and I relay the information, including the fact that the police have identified at least two suspects, one of whom has not been arrested and appears to be active. There is little more than sleep and confusion in the voice coming back at me, but I give a brief description of Michael François, and she assures me that she will call the police if she sees anyone who matches that description. I tell her to be very careful until she is notified that the second suspect is in custody, and hang up. My second call goes just as smoothly.

My third call is to Kendra. Her image from the file is in front of me on the desk, but I don't need it to conjure her face. The image is burned into my brain. At times I can't tell whether it comes from the LifeScene or from my time meeting her, but I suppose it doesn't matter; it's the same image in either case.

I'm expecting several rings before the phone is answered, and the same sleep-confused voice to come over the line. She picks up midway through the second ring, though, and her voice is clear and alert. 'Yes?' she says.

'Kendra?'

'Nick.'

'You're awake.'

'It's early yet.'

I look at my watch and see that it's two forty-one in the morning. I register her meaning, and a tiny part of my heart dies. 'I wanted to let you know that it looks like you were right,' I say, putting my feelings aside. 'It may not have been Santar Gunta who committed the murders. Or, if it was him, it looks like he didn't act alone.'

'Josh?'

'No. His assistant programmer.'

'Michael.'

'Yes, Michael.' I feel like there is so much I want to say, but I can't even bring myself to force the words out of my mouth. 'That's what it looks like.'

'I can see that,' she says after a moment. 'Are you sure?'

'Not one hundred percent, but ninety-nine.' I look across the room and see that Yvette is looking at me, still on the phone. 'Kendra, he killed another girl, and the police don't have him in custody yet.'

'Do they know where he is?'

'No.' I start to say something and then stop, trying to phrase it right. I realize there is no appropriate way to say it, so I give up on phrasing it perfectly. 'Kendra, I'm concerned you could be in danger.'

'Aren't you sweet?' Her voice is hard, but I press on.

'No, I'm not,' I say. 'I mean, with what you do, I'm worried that you're making yourself vulnerable.'

'Oh.' She says nothing for a moment. 'A girl's gotta eat,' she says at last.

'You said you had some money saved up.'

'I was being metaphorical, Nick.'

It's my turn now. 'Oh. About saving money, or . . . ? Oh.'

'Listen, you may not think so, but you really are sweet. You don't have to worry about me, though. I've always managed to take care of myself.'

'This guy's crazy.'

She laughs and it's filled with knowledge and understanding and sorrow. 'All guys are crazy.' The laugh comes again, and I want to reach through the phone line and take hold of her hand, tell her that she's wrong, that she's had a bad deal so far. 'I know what he looks like, Nick. I think I'm pretty safe.'

'Only if you see him coming.'

'A long time ago I decided that life was going to be what it was going to be. I'm too far along to change my stripes now, Nick. Trust me, I'll be okay.'

I'm searching my mind desperately for something to say that might convince her otherwise, but nothing comes. I look over, and Killkenny is standing next to Yvette. She has finished her phone calls and is filling in some of Killkenny's declaration for the warrant. 'I've gotta go' is all I can manage.

'I know.'

'I'll call. When all this is over, I'll call.'

'I hope so. I really hope so.' She hangs up without saying goodbye, and it's like a knife to the gut. I hold the phone for a few seconds before I hang up, trying to catch my breath. As soon as the handset is on the cradle, I hear Killkenny's voice. 'This is done, and I'm faxing it to the judge,' he says.

'Will he fax it back?' Yvette asks.

'No, we have to go pick it up at his apartment. He's in

Fenway. François lives out by Boston College, so it's on the way.'

'Boston College,' I say. 'Isn't that where one of the early victims was?'

Killkenny nods. 'The first was in Cleveland Circle. He started out hunting near his home. That's the way it starts a lot of the time.'

'This happens often?' Yvette asks.

'Not exactly like this, necessarily, but are serial killers common? Yeah, it happens more often than anyone would like to think. Some people just get a taste for it, and they can't stop.'

'You think that's what happened with Michael François? You think he just got a taste for it?'

'From his record, it looks like he was fairly predisposed. But, yeah, I'm guessing once he started, he found he couldn't stop.'

'All the more reason we have to find him,' I say.

'True,' Killkenny says. He walks to a gun cabinet hanging on the wall, takes out a shotgun. He grabs a box of shells and slides five rounds into the chamber, looks at us. 'Are you two ready?' he asks.

I look at Yvette, and she stands. 'We're ready,' she says.

CHAPTER THIRTY-ONE

Killkenny is in the judge's apartment for less than two minutes before he returns with the warrant. 'That's it?' I ask.

'That's it,' he says. 'It's a pretty convincing affidavit. Plus, at this time in the morning, judges tend to have fewer questions.'

We drive on to the Boston College section of Brookline. It's an area off Commonwealth, ten subway stops out from the center of the city, where the residents are split between students, young professionals and lifetime residents. Michael François' apartment is in one of the more rundown areas, where the residents appear to be primarily graduate students and twenty-somethings on the bottom of the employment ladder. It doesn't have the clear evidence of constant partying that accompanies the college set, but it also lacks the substance and permanency of more established residential neighborhoods. It looks transient in every respect.

François' building is a townhouse set off from the other residences in the area, with four apartments, each with their own external entrance. The building is dark, not only because the lights are off, but because it has that feeling of neglect that comes with short-time renters.

We park around the corner and wait for Killkenny's backup. He's called in three squad cars to assist in taking down François. 'You never know whether he's prepared,' Killkenny says. 'He may have been planning for the police from the beginning. If so, he's likely to be armed, and it's probably going to get ugly.'

The three cars arrive within minutes of each other, and the police officers get out and quietly begin preparing themselves for the invasion. They put on bulletproof vests with POLICE marked in bright yellow on them, and trade in their hats for helmets. I see three other shotguns passed around.

Killkenny puts on a vest, but leaves off the helmet. My guess is that his vanity would never allow him to wear the helmet. 'You two stay here,' he says to us. 'Once we have the all clear and we've arrested him, I'll send for you, okay?'

'Okay.'

'I mean it.'

'Understood.'

Killkenny rallies his troops and they head out around the corner, and Yvette and I are left waiting by his car. There are no street lights in this part of town, and all of the dwellings around us are dark. The moon would cast a decent light, but the clouds have gathered low in the sky, blocking out the heavens. We are shrouded in darkness. I can hear Yvette breathing hard.

'It's okay,' I say.

'Tell that to Taylor Westerbrooke.'

'That's not your fault.'

'No? Maybe not.' She doesn't sound convinced.

'You think he's in there?' I ask.

She looks in the direction of the apartment, following the

path Killkenny and his men took. 'François? I don't know. I hope so. I hope he's there, and I hope they kill him.'

'No trial?'

'No trial, no lawyers, no appeal,' Yvette says. 'He didn't give those girls any kind of justice. I don't know why he would deserve any himself.'

'I can see that,' I say. 'I want to know it all, though. I want to know how Gunta was involved, I want to know what this was all about, I want to know where this comes from. That can't happen unless he's taken alive.'

I see her shake her head slowly in the darkness. 'I don't care where this comes from. I just want it over.'

We hear the sound of wood splintering in the distance and shouts of, 'Police! On the ground!' Two shots ring out and there is an explosion of confused voices shouting over one another.

Yvette and I are leaning against Killkenny's car, and we both stand straight at the commotion. 'It sounds like you may have gotten your wish,' I say. She takes two steps toward the apartment, but I grab her arm and hold her back. 'He told us to stay here,' I remind her.

'I need to know what's happening,' she protests. 'I need to see it for myself.'

'I know,' I say, 'but we need to wait for them to come get us. We don't know whether he's dead or running. You go out there now and you're putting everyone in danger. Not just yourself, but the cops too.'

She looks at me, and all I can see is the silhouette of her face. In what little light there is, I can see fresh tears running down her cheeks freely. I put one hand on her shoulder, and with the other I brush the tears away. 'It's gonna be okay,' I say. 'You have to believe that.'

'Why?'

'Otherwise you won't make it through. Okay?'

'Okay.' She nods.

There are footsteps coming from around the corner, running fast, toward us. I turn and put my body in front of Yvette, shielding her. A dark figure rounds the corner headed straight toward us. He stops twenty feet from us, and I still can't make out any details.

'Who's there?' I shout.

'Officer Brody,' the outline calls out. 'Detective Killkenny sent me to get you. It's all clear; he says it's safe for you to come up.'

We follow Officer Brody back toward François' apartment. Outside on the stoop two of the other cops are standing, helmets off, smoking cigarettes in silence. I walk ahead of Yvette, both of us moving somewhere between a fast walk and a run. We come to the front of the apartment and I glance at one of the officers and see the distant expression on his face. 'How is it in there?' I ask.

He shakes his head and nods toward the door. 'See for yourself.'

I feel Yvette take my hand from behind me, and I walk up the stoop slowly, Yvette following. The interior is only dimly lit; there are few working lights. 'Killkenny?' I call. 'Where are you?'

'Back here,' he answers from deep within the apartment.

I move toward the back of the apartment. The place is barren. Some rudimentary furniture stands in a central living room – a table with two plain wooden chairs pushed underneath it. A stand-up lamp in a corner of the room with a weak bulb that, thus far, is the only source of illumination I've seen. There is nothing on the walls. No pictures, no paintings, not even a poster to break up the expanse of plain plaster. We pass the other three officers coming down a short hallway leading to the rear of the apartment. 'He's back there,' one of them says as he passes us. I catch a glimpse of his expression as he heads past me, and I think I can discern a smirk. As we continue down the hallway I hear murmurings from the cops, followed by stifled laughter.

Killkenny is in a back bedroom, examining the scene. There are no lights, and he is shining a flashlight from one corner to another. It's like something out of a horror film. The walls are covered with hooks, and hanging from those hooks is a wide assortment of implements of torture. There are leather straps and chains, and restraints of every possible variety. Whips and cat-o'-nine-tails are segregated in one area, knives and other sharp implements in another, ball gags and collars in yet another. There is a shelf on the far wall, and vibrators and strap-on dildos are arranged with near-military precision. In one corner there is a mannequin outfitted in leather – masks, vests, bustiers, chaps.

'Where is François?' I ask.

'Not here,' Killkenny says.

'But we heard gunshots,' Yvette says. 'Who was shooting?'

'Officer Brody,' Killkenny says. 'He was the first into this room, and it was dark. He saw the mannequin in the back and told it to get on the ground. When it didn't comply, he shot it.' Killkenny moves over to the leather-clad plaster statue.

'Twice.' He shines the light close in on the chest, and I can see two bullet holes there. 'Pretty good shots, really. It's too bad; I probably would have done the same thing, but he's never gonna hear the end of it. He's only been on the job for six months, and this is gonna follow him for a long time.'

'No sign of Michael?' Yvette asks. 'Nothing?'

'I'm not sure I'd say nothing,' Killkenny corrects her. 'It certainly looks like we've got the right man. This guy has one hell of an active social life, from the looks of things.' I'm moving around the room, looking more closely at the wide array of sexual implements. 'Don't touch anything,' Killkenny says.

'Right – like I'd touch anything in here.'

'Fair enough. I want to get our forensics guys in here, see if there's any DNA on any of this stuff that matches any of the dead girls.'

'You don't think you've got enough evidence yet?'

'So far it's all circumstantial,' Killkenny points out. 'It's all rational supposition, and it might even be enough for a conviction, but you'd be amazed what a good lawyer can do with a case if there's no direct evidence.'

'You mean even after you catch him, he could walk?' Yvette sounds despondent.

'Don't stress out too much. There's hairbrushes and tooth-brushes here, so we've got enough DNA to match against the semen in the Westerbrooke girl. That'll be enough for at least one conviction. I'm just saying I'd like to nail him down for all of these murders.'

I can see Yvette shiver at the callous way Killkenny refers to Taylor Westerbrooke. She's still holding my hand, and I give it a squeeze to remind her that I'm there for her.

'You're not gonna nail him for anything if you don't catch him first,' I point out.

'No shit, Sherlock,' Killkenny says. 'You ever thought about going into law enforcement?'

'So what now?' Yvette asks, cutting short the argument.

'Now we put out an APB on Michael François. We make sure that every cop in Boston has a good description of this guy. We get a picture from the company, and from the Department of Corrections, and we plaster it on every place we can, so if this guy pops his head up even for a second, we'll know about it.'

'That's not enough,' I say.

'If you've got an idea where this asshole might be, I'm all ears,' Killkenny says. I get the feeling that he's losing patience with my meddling. I don't care, though; if I can help advance the investigation, that's what I intend to do.

'I don't have any idea where he might be,' I say. 'But I know someone who might.'

CHAPTER THIRTY-TWO

'I don't like this,' Killkenny says. 'I don't like this at all. This asshole's got a lawyer, and if anyone finds out I'm talking to him without his lawyer here, they could have my badge. Or at least bust me down a rank or two.'

We're in an interrogation room at the Boston City Jail, tucked in an industrial section of the city back behind TD Garden, where the Celtics and Bruins play, and where *Disney On Ice* delights kids every Christmas. We dropped Yvette at home and told her that we would keep her informed if there were any developments.

'You're not talking to him – I am,' I point out to Killkenny.

'You're acting as an agent of the police. It's the same thing as if I were talking to him. Once he's lawyered up, nothing we get from him is admissible. It can't even be used to find anything else that might be admissible. It's known as the "fruit of the poisonous tree".'

'Colorful.'

'Lawyers are assholes,' he says. 'It doesn't matter, though – it's the law. If I learn anything that implicates him, even if it's something he tells you, there's nothing I can do with it.'

'You can use it to find François,' I point out. 'Even if you can't use it to convict Gunta, who cares? Right now, all we should care about is finding the guy who's out there killing these girls. And you know he's gonna do it again. Like you said, he's got a taste for it. If anything, he's only gonna pick up the pace.'

Killkenny knows I'm right; I can see it on his face. A buzzer sounds from an intercom on the wall. 'He'll be here in a minute,' Killkenny says. 'I'm not listening in; that way I've got some deniability. The only thing I want to hear when this is over is whether Gunta has any idea where François might be. That's it, you understand?'

'Yeah, I got it.'

He hesitates.

'You better get out of here if you want to preserve that deniability,' I say.

He nods. 'Buzz twice when you're done.'

The buzzer sounds again, and the door opens. Dr Santar Gunta stands in the doorway, shackled at both the wrists and ankles. It makes me think of the restraints at Michael François' apartment. He's wearing an orange jumpsuit and prison-issued slippers. He looks ten years older than he did the last time I saw him.

'Doc,' I say.

He looks at me, and looks at the guard behind him. The guard pushes him through the door and says to me, 'You've got five minutes.' I nod, and he closes the door.

I take a seat at the Formica-covered table. 'Sit,' I say, kicking the chair across from me out from under the table.

He stands there for a moment before, giving in, he shuffles over and sits across from me. 'How is it in here?'

He stares at me. 'Why are you here, Nick? What more could you possibly want from me?'

'The truth.'

'There is no truth.' His chin goes to his chest and he looks like he'd eat a bullet if he had a gun. I wonder whether I can use that to my advantage.

'He killed another one,' I say. Gunta looks up quickly, and I can see it in his eyes. He knows it, too – he knows I've seen it. 'Where is he?'

'I don't know what you're talking about.' His voice is desperate and he's shaking.

'Yes, you do. I don't even care whether you knew or you were involved, I just want to know where he is. I want to make sure he doesn't kill again. You want that too, don't you? You don't want him to hurt anyone else.'

He shakes his head violently, not in answer to my question, but as though he was trying to get something off him; as though he was trying to shake free from some sort of spell. After a moment he goes still. 'He was better,' he says. 'He was cured, I know he was. I tested him myself, and he . . . ' He looks up at me. 'He was so beautiful, and so smart. I've never seen someone so good with the technology. And when he was in prison we tested him again and again, to make sure he was right again – to make sure all his impulses were under control. He passed; he was cured.'

'He beat the tests. He wasn't cured.'

'He was!' Gunta looks off at the wall. 'But those in prison wouldn't let him out. There was a group in there that reveled in the violence, and they used him, and he couldn't let it go. That's why he's striking out, don't you see?'

'I don't care why he's doing it. I just want him stopped.'

'You want to put him back there. Don't you understand what that will do to him? He will be lost forever. He was cured, and now he'll be lost forever. I can't lose him like that. I can't.'

'Doc, you've lost him already. If we know where he is, we can find him, and stop him, and do it without hurting him. But if he continues, he's gonna end up getting killed by some cop. You see that, don't you? I need your help.'

He shakes his head. 'I cannot betray him.'

'You're not betraying him. You're saving him.'

Gunta looks at me, and I can tell that he's trying to decide whether to believe me. He's trying to decide whether to tell me.

'If you don't help me, you will be responsible for the next woman to die. You don't want that on your conscience, do you?'

'It's not my fault!' The desperation is back in his voice.

'No? The laptop he used to create these things was yours. It was never lost; you gave it to him, didn't you?'

'I did not know what he was using it for!' he pleads.

'Maybe not, but you know now. And you knew two days ago, when we first talked about this. If you'd told the truth then, at least one girl wouldn't have died.'

This concept seems to shake him back to reality a bit. I can see some clarity return to his eyes. 'I don't know where he is,' he says. 'I don't.'

'But you do have some idea where he might be.'

He nods slightly; almost an imperceptible movement.

'Tell me. I can help him.'

'You won't hurt him?'

'I'll make sure he's not hurt.' It's a lie, but a small one under the circumstances, I figure.

Gunta looks around him, almost as though he's worried that someone might overhear. I can see that the ordeal has broken him, and I wonder whether he can make it back from this. I doubt it, but that is the least of my concerns at the moment. 'He has a key to my house,' he says. 'I always said that if he needed a place to be safe, he could come there. We spent time there together. He was so beautiful. You understand, don't you?'

'I think so, Doc. If he's not there, is there any other place you can think of that he might be?'

He shakes his head. 'If he is not there, he is lost.'

I stand and walk over to the door, hit the buzzer twice. A moment later the door is opened by the guard.

'You done?' he asks.

'Yeah, I'm done.' I start out through the door.

'Nick!' Gunta calls to me.

'Yeah?'

'You'll make sure he's not hurt? You'll protect him, won't you?'

'Yeah, Doc. I'll take care of him.'

Gunta lives in a mansion at the northern edge of Hull, north of Nantasket Beach. It's only a few miles as the crow flies from downtown Boston, but to get there by land we have to drive all the way around Boston Harbor and it takes us nearly an hour. Hull is a seven-mile peninsula that sticks up from the south shore of Boston Harbor and curls like a hook back against the mainland. The beachfront is a honky-tonk with arcades and bars and seaside concessions selling fried clams and fried fish and fried dough. Killkenny's driving and I'm in his passenger seat, watching as the shoreline rolls by. It's too far out, and too much of a long shot, to have backup with us; we're on our own.

'How sure was he?' Killkenny asks.

'I don't know. He's not all there anymore,' I say. 'It's clear he and François had a thing together.'

'François is gay? How can that be?'

'I don't think he's gay, he's an amoralist. The Marquis de Sade didn't discriminate in his sexual tastes. He was originally imprisoned for sodomy with a young boy. His writings involve violations of both men and women. If François sees himself as the heir to De Sade's ideals, he would have no problem in using Gunta sexually and playing on the older man's obsession with him to get what he wanted.'

'So he likes boys and girls?'

'He likes violence. He likes control. He doesn't worry about who his victims are, one way or the other. He's looking to wipe away the constraints of morality.'

'He's been successful there,' Killkenny says.

We drive on, past the bungalows in the heart of Hull, where the population is hard and tired. Notwithstanding its proximity to some of the most beautiful beachfront in Massachusetts, Hull has largely withstood the onslaught of renewal. It's remote enough that its residents have stood in solidarity against interlopers.

There are only a few outsiders who have taken over some

of the large houses at the north end, looking out on Boston. Gunta's house sits on the cliffs that fall off into the harbor. It's a refurbished Georgian-style beach house with broad porches sweeping around the entire perimeter, and decks on the second and third floors. It's early morning when we arrive, and the sun is rising over the Harbor Islands to the east. There's a Mercedes M-Class sedan in the driveway, which is flanked by dune grass rippling in the breeze coming off the water. It looks like it's going to be a beautiful day.

'Does he keep his car here normally?'

I shrug. 'Sometimes, probably.'

Killkenny and I walk slowly up the broad wooden stairs that lead to the front door, looking around for any sign of trouble. 'It's quiet,' I say.

'You expected him to be having a party?'

'Doc may have been wrong.'

'Maybe, but we're here.' Killkenny reaches out and tries the doorknob. It's locked.

'Do we ring the bell?'

He shakes his head. 'Not unless there's someone else who's supposed to be here.'

'He lives alone, as far as I know.'

'Then we won't be bothering anyone.' He pulls out his gun, wraps it in a corner of his jacket and taps one of the small windowpanes near the doorknob. I'm amazed at how quietly he manages to take out the glass; he's clearly done this before. He reaches in and turns the knob from the inside and opens the door.

'You wanna go first?' he asks.

'You've got the gun.'

He nods and steps through the doorway.

The place is decorated like one of the places featured in design magazines, with lots of natural colors and sisal rugs. The art on the walls is high-end, oils and watercolors of ships and beach scenes. It's clear that the place was done by a professional; Gunta would have neither the time nor the style to achieve the effect. In truth, it feels like it's someone else's house – like the leverage he's taken from the value of his company holdings has been sufficient for him to slip on another identity. It's like someone's idea of who he should be, rather than his idea of who he actually is.

We walk into the living room, and I marvel at the view. It's an open space with a giant stone fireplace. The far wall is dominated by oversized windows and French doors that lead out onto the back side of the sweeping porch, with views of the ocean to the east and the Boston skyline to the north.

'Nice,' Killkenny comments quietly.

'Wealth has its advantages.'

'You think you'll get a place like this after the company goes public?'

It's the first I've thought about the company's future since this whole ordeal began. I really have no idea what will happen now. 'Not my style' is all I say.

'We should split up, clear the place floor by floor,' Killkenny suggests. 'It'll take less time, and be harder for him to get by us if he's here.'

'Says the man with the gun.'

Killkenny walks over to the fireplace and picks up the heavy iron poker, comes over and hands it to me. 'Now you're armed.'

I feel its weight and swing it a couple of times. 'Okay,' I say. 'You take the north side of the house.'

I head to the south side of the house, which is dominated by the professional kitchen and pantry. It seems safer than the other side, where I could see a library and den where there are more places to hide. I move around the kitchen, admiring the granite countertops, the high-end appliances and over-sized double sink. I hold my breath as I swing open the pantry door, the iron poker at the ready, but all that's in there is a heavy stock of supplies.

I head back out to the living room, and Killkenny joins me a moment later. 'Anything?' he asks.

'Yeah, I've got him in my pocket,' I say sarcastically.

'Upstairs,' Killkenny says, ignoring me.

The house is large enough that it takes us several minutes to clear the second floor – a warren of five bedrooms, each with its own bathroom. I check in closets and under beds, but find nothing. Every time I go into a bathroom I am convinced that François will jump out of the shower stall, or leap out of the toilet, but everything is in order, all of the rooms spotless. I wonder how much the maid charges to clean the place, and figure it's a pretty good deal. It's a big house, but I can't imagine Gunta makes much of a mess. He doesn't seem like the type to throw big parties.

Killkenny and I regroup at the stairway. He motions toward the last flight, up to the third floor. 'Last possibility,' he whispers.

He goes up first, and I follow. It's clear that the third floor was an attic prior to recent renovations. The ceiling is comparatively low, and the floor plan looks as though it was open, before walls were thrown up to divide the space into thirds. The center section, into which the staircase rises, is an open carpeted area with a large flat-screen television on the far wall. There is a pool table that looks as though it's never been used, and a couch in front of the television that looks as though it has never been sat in. The walls on the north and south sides of the room have doors that are closed, and Killkenny motions to indicate that he's taking the section to the south. I nod and move to the other end of the room.

I put my ear up to one of the doors, trying to sense any motion on the other side. It's pointless, I realize; even here on the unused third floor, the doors are solid wood that no sound can penetrate.

I take a deep breath and swing the door open, holding the fire poker above my head. It turns out, though, that the door is to a small empty closet. I breathe again, chastising myself silently for acting like a scared little kid. Moving over to the other door, I open it slowly, the iron poker still in my hand at the ready, though not raised as high. The open door reveals a bedroom that is large by normal standards, but small compared to those on the second floor. There is a bathroom at one end, and a single glass door leading out to a small balcony at the other. The view from up here is even more spectacular. On the third floor I am probably forty feet up, and the house is close enough to the edge of the cliff that it seems as though it is a 200-foot fall straight from the balcony to the water below. I'm rethinking whether I'd want a place like this, if the company still manages to go public. It's awfully nice.

I check the bathroom first, pulling the curtain on the nautical shower stall and poking my head into a small linen closet. There's nothing there, so I walk over and look out onto the deck. No one.

I turn and start to head back out into the common area. 'I've got nothing here,' I call to Killkenny, no longer worried about raising an alarm. 'If he was ever here, he's gone now.' Before I get to the bedroom door I notice a half closet next to the bed, and grab the doorknob just to make sure, though I have no thought that there is anyone hiding there.

As I pull the door open there is a blood-curdling scream from within, and the door swings open, hitting me in the face and knocking me backward. I'm rubbing my jaw as I look up and see Michael François coming toward me, his face twisted in rage. The fire poker is suddenly heavy in my hand, and I'm too slow in raising it. It's just above my shoulder when François hits me on a full run, his shoulder driving into my already bruised ribs, knocking the wind from me. I try to call out, but I can't breathe.

He continues driving me backward, and my feet struggle to keep pace and prevent me from sprawling on the floor. A moment later my back collides with the door leading out to the balcony, shattering the glass and sending us tumbling to the exterior decking. I catch a glimpse of his face, and it's truly a terrible sight; any semblance of sanity has deserted him. I am still clutching the fire poker and I'm swinging it wildly, trying to connect with him, but he has me by the shirt, his chest to mine, and I'm too close to generate any power. I'm still gasping, trying to get my breath, as he pulls me up so that we are standing. I try one swing, but I have no strength, and he ducks it easily. He screams again and runs at me, knocking me backward once more. This time my back collides with the railing at the edge of the deck, and I flip over, landing on the narrow sliver of roof just under the balcony. It's steep and I start to slide immediately. I flail out, grabbing onto the railing to keep from going over the edge.

'Help!' I scream, as my feet dangle from the edge of the roof. I'm frantically swinging my legs up, trying to gain a foothold, without success. My head is just above the decking for the balcony, and I see Killkenny in the doorway, his gun drawn.

'Don't move!' he hollers at François. François screams at him and Killkenny raises the gun, aiming it as his chest. 'Don't!'

François screams again, but he doesn't move.

'Help!' I call out.

'Hold on, Nick,' Killkenny says. 'Hold on!' He motions François over to the wall. 'Hands up against the house!' François looks at him, and it seems that he's debating whether to comply. 'Now, asshole!'

I'm still dangling, and my ribs are on fire. My hands are sweating in the heat, and I can feel my grip slipping. I look over my shoulder and see the sea below me. I know that there is a thin stretch of grass between the house and the cliff, so if I fall, I won't go all the way to the bottom. Still, the chances that I'll survive the three-story fall are not very good. 'Paul!' I call. 'I'm slipping!'

'I'm coming,' he shouts, a hint of annoyance in his voice. He is pointing his gun at François, and the two of them are at a stand-off. Killkenny begins moving slowly toward him. 'You still there, Nick?'

'Yeah,' I answer. 'I can hold on.' As I say the words, though, the railing pulls free at the top from the house and slams down against the roof, dropping me another two feet, so that everything from my waist down is dangling freely over the edge now. 'Fuck! Paul!' I shout. It's useless, I realize, as my fingers begin the final slip. I look over my shoulder again to see whether there is a bush or some other spot that might increase my odds of survival. Unfortunately, all I see is a flagstone terrace beneath me. 'Oh, shit!' I shout as my fingers snap open and I feel myself begin to fall. My fear of heights returns, like a full-throated roar in my ears, and I close my eyes, accepting my fate.

I feel a sharp slap against my wrist, and it takes me a moment to realize I'm no longer falling. I open my eyes and see a hand holding onto my wrist, keeping me from slipping. Killkenny is lying on the balcony, one hand holding me, the other grasping the side of the balcony from which the railing has pulled free. I'm so surprised I'm not dead that I just dangle there for a moment, until he screams at me, 'Climb up, for chrissakes!'

'On what?'

'Use the railing!'

'You think it'll hold?'

'It'll hold better than I can!'

I throw my other hand up and grab the broken railing. Using it as a ladder, I slowly crawl my way back up onto the balcony. By the time I make it up I'm gasping for breath, as is Killkenny. 'Thanks,' I say.

'No problem,' he replies, huffing away.

I look up and don't see François. 'Where did he go?' As I say the words, we both hear the car on the other side of the house roar into life. 'Fuck! He's getting away!' I yell.

'You'd rather still be on the side of the house?' Killkenny sounds annoyed, and I suppose I can't blame him.

'We've got to stop him!' I persist.

'Nice gratitude.' He pulls out his phone, dials. 'Hull Police,' he says after a moment. After another pause he says, 'This is Detective Paul Killkenny, BPD. I'm down at the end of Hull investigating a series of murders. The primary suspect just fled in a black Mercedes M-Class sedan. He has to be heading off the spit; can you set up cars on 228 and South Road?' Another pause. 'Great, thanks.' He puts the phone back in his pocket. 'There're only two roads out of Hull. He's not making it out.' He leans over and looks down off the balcony, mentally measuring the fall. He whistles. 'Long way down. You okay?'

'Yeah. Thanks.'

'No sweat.'

'I mean it. Thanks. If it wasn't for you, I'd be a pancake.' The reality of the danger sweeps over me for a moment and I shudder.

'Yeah, you would be.' He stands. 'Let's go get this asshole.'

An hour later we're leaning against the car at the mainland end of Hull, near a stretch of restaurants by the state beach. One of Hull's finest is pulled up next to us. 'He hasn't passed here or on South Road,' the cop tells us. 'We've got all our guys out there looking for the car, but he may have ditched it.'

'You think?' Killkenny says.

'How's he getting back off the stretch?' I wonder aloud.

'Won't take much,' the cop says. 'Boost another car, we won't know to stop him.'

'He could take the bus, for that matter,' Killkenny says.

'Where would he go now?' the cop asks.

Killkenny and I look at each other. 'We have no idea,' Killkenny says. 'This was our best shot.'

'He's gotta turn up somewhere,' I say. 'He's got a taste for it now, he's not about to stop.'

Killkenny nods. 'Now we've just got to wait for the next body.'

CHAPTER THIRTY-THREE

Killkenny drops me back at my Corolla, which is sitting in front of the police station in Boston, its windows still smashed out. There's a light rain starting, and I realize I'm going to have to have them replaced sooner rather than later. At least it's summer, and it's warm enough that I'm not freezing my nuts off, but the rain is going to soak into the seats, and mildew will sprout. I've had enough crappy cars to know that once the mildew sets in, you can never get it out.

I need to go home; I haven't seen Ma in a day and a half, and even though she's been looking better, I can tell it's not that her health has actually improved – it's a product of her attitude. The cancer hasn't given up; in all likelihood it's just regrouping for a massive offensive. I should check on her before I do anything else, but there's something I have to do before that.

I drive out through Cambridge and into Sommerville, park in front of the old painted lady of a house and just stare at it for a little while, trying to figure out what to say to her. Nothing comes to mind, but I figure I can't sit there for the rest of the day.

It's still raining when I get out of the car. Not hard; just a mist coating everything with a sheen. I walk up the stairs and stand on the porch, ring the bell. The door is answered by the same woman who answered the first time Killkenny and I showed up. She looks at me with an expression that falls somewhere between annoyance and amusement. 'Kenny!' she calls before I have the chance to say anything. 'He's here again!' She stands in the door, evaluating me as she waits.

'Hi,' I say, only because I feel awkward. Kendra doesn't respond, just stands there eyeballing me.

'Thanks, Janie,' I hear Kendra say, and the girl pulls away from the door. Kendra moves into the doorway. She's wearing a red silk robe with an Asian design on it. Her hair is undone, but in a way that seems natural and full. 'You're back,' she says.

'I thought I'd check on you.'

'I take it the hunting didn't go so well?' She seems curious, but not quite concerned.

'We found him at Gunta's house.'

'Good.'

'Not really. He got away.'

'Not good.' She looks at me more closely and sees the bruises on my face, reaches up to touch them. As she does, I pull back and wince at the pain in my ribs. She reaches out and feels the bandages wrapped around my torso. 'You're hurt.' I can't think of anything to say. 'Are you stopping by the houses of all the girls who are in danger?' she asks. I'm not sure what the right answer is, so I keep my mouth shut. I suddenly realize how tired I am. 'Why don't you come in,' she says. 'Just for a minute.'

I follow her through the door and head toward the living room that we spoke in before, but she touches my arm. 'Not there.' She leads me down a hallway to a small apartment in the back on the first floor. Two large rooms and a bathroom, decorated in a simple modern style at odds with the elaborate Victorian feel of the rest of the place. The outer room has a kitchenette, a dining table and a sitting area with clean white furniture. 'This is my private space,' she says. 'The rest of it I rent out.'

I peer into the bedroom. It has a bed and a dresser, and a mirror in one corner. The walls are white with a few stylish black-and-white photographs on the wall. 'So that's where the magic happens,' I say. It comes out without thinking, and I'm sorry I've said it, though it was exactly what I was thinking. I look at her, and for a moment I think I can see a flash of pain, but she covers it quickly.

'No,' she says.

'I didn't mean . . . '

'I have a room upstairs.' I move away from the bedroom door, feeling that I've transgressed. She motions me to the couch. 'Please, sit down.' I obey. 'Do you want to tell me what happened?'

I consider it. 'No.'

She sits on the couch next to me, close enough that I can feel the warmth coming off her. The feeling is enough to make me dizzy. 'Why are you here?'

'I wanted to make sure you were okay.' My voice comes out as a whisper.

She shakes her head. 'You knew I was okay. Why are you here?'

'I don't know.'

'Yes, you do.' She reaches out and touches the back of my neck, running her fingertips through the swirls of soft hair, massaging gently. It's like she's slowly pulling the pain out of my body from the base of my skull – like she has the power to take all of my troubles away. I close my eyes for a moment, and I'm back in the LifeScene. I can see her face against the white sheets, that look of ecstasy and trust, her eyes wide, the shards of gold and diamond sparkling in giant pools of blue. I turn toward her, and I can feel her breath on my cheek, warm and heavy and full of life. 'It's okay,' she says.

I open my eyes and look at her. The eyes aren't quite the same. They're blue, and beautiful, but they don't sparkle quite the way I remember. And yet she is still pulling the pain from me, making me whole. 'I have to go,' I say. I'm not even sure why, but I know it's true. If I stay, I may never leave.

She nods. 'It's okay,' she repeats. It's hard to believe that identical words spoken seconds apart could have such different meanings. She takes her hand away from my neck and stands. 'I have to get some rest anyway,' she says.

I look at my watch. It's not quite noon. 'I'll stop by this evening, just to check again.'

'You don't have to.'

'I want to.'

She tilts her head. 'I may be busy.'

I nod. 'I won't interfere.'

'No?' she sounds almost disappointed. 'No, of course not. I'll see you out.'

We leave her apartment, and it's like crossing over into a

different world. She opens the front door for me. 'It was nice to see you again,' she says.

'I'm sorry,' I say.

'For what?'

'I'm not sure,' I say. 'But I am.'

She touches the bruise on my face. 'You be careful, okay?' Then she steps back and closes the door.

'Where have you been?'

I open the door to Ma's house, expecting to find Ma sitting at the kitchen table, where she spends most of the daylight hours. Instead Yvette leaps up from the table, her face flushed with worry.

'We went out to Gunta's house, down in Hull. I met him at the jail, and he told me François had a key, so we figured it was worth a shot. We were right; it was worth a shot. He was there.'

Yvette's eyes go wide. 'Did you catch him?'

'No,' I respond. 'He attacked me, and things went wrong.' I can feel her eyeing the bruises on my face.

'Are you okay?'

'Yeah, I'm fine. He got away. They set up a police road-block, but either he got through it or he's still out on Hull. They're not gonna keep it up indefinitely, so it's safe to say he's free for at least a little while longer. I'm sorry, I should have called sooner; I didn't mean to make you worry, it's just that I was—'

Yvette cuts me off. 'It's not that,' she says. 'It's your mom.'

A bolt of panic goes through me. 'What's wrong?'

'She had a relapse. A bad one.'

'When?'

'Last night. Cormack found her collapsed on the floor. He took her to the hospital.'

My mind is racing. All of a sudden any thought I have of François or Kendra or my company melts away. No matter how bad things have been, I don't think I've ever really accepted the notion that the cancer would end up beating Ma. Nothing has ever beaten Ma; she's the ultimate survivor. *Me and the cockroaches,* she used to joke. *We'll still be here after the bombs go off.* I always believed it in my heart, even when my head was telling me that her time was limited. 'I've got to go,' I say. 'I've got to get to the hospital.' I start toward the door.

'Wait, Nick!' Yvette calls after me. 'She's not there!'

I turn to look at her. The horror of the only other possibility overwhelms me. I feel as though my legs have gone numb and I may collapse. 'She's . . . ?'

'No, don't worry. She's back here.'

'Here? This house?'

Yvette nods. 'It was touch and go, but she came out of it around two this morning. I guess they tried to keep her at the hospital, but she was having none of it. She refused further treatment and started throwing things.' Yvette smiles sadly at the thought. 'Even with one foot in the grave, she's still not someone to mess with.' For a moment she looks as though she regrets the way it came out. 'I'm sorry, I didn't mean it that way,' she says, coming over and taking my hand.

She's too close a friend, and I care too much about her, to take offense. 'Don't worry,' I say. 'It's true. All of it. I'm surprised they didn't declare her a danger to herself and commit her.'

'They wanted to.'

'What stopped them?'

'Cormack.'

'Ah.' It makes sense. I have no doubt that Cormack would be exceptionally persuasive in a situation like that. If any doctor tried to have Ma committed, he would have had a short, loud, definitive conversation with Cormack that would have left no doubt as to the inadvisability of such a move.

'But why wouldn't she stay?'

Yvette looks away, and I can see the tears forming in her eyes. 'She said she wanted to die here.' I nod and squeeze her hand. She looks up at me, the tears flowing freely now. 'I'm so sorry,' she says, a little sob escaping her throat.

I take her in my arms and hold her. She feels warm and soft and real. She's been a part of my life for almost longer than I can remember, and we fold into each other with a natural sense of understanding and silent communication. I hold her tight as we rock back and forth. It feels so good, in spite of the bleakness of the occasion, but after a moment I push away. She tries to hold on another moment, but I break free. She wipes her eyes. 'I'm so sorry,' she says again, and I wonder how she means it.

I touch her shoulder. It feels so impersonal, but it's as far as I'm willing to trust myself. 'It's okay,' I say. 'I'll be okay.' I realize that I'm crying, too, and I wipe away my own tears. 'She's upstairs?'

Yvette nods.

'I'm going up to see her.' I need to see Ma, but I'm also running away, and Yvette knows it. She looks so good standing there in Ma's kitchen, and there's a part of me that wants to crawl back into her arms, but I can't. I'm not even sure why not anymore, but I know that I can't. 'When did you get here?'

'They were bringing her in when I got back from . . . from seeing Taylor Westerbrooke.'

'You never went home?'

She shakes her head. 'Cormack said he had to put some things straight down at the docks, and he'd be back early this afternoon. I stayed with her.'

'Why didn't you call me?'

'Your mother wouldn't let me. She said you had your business to deal with, and she wouldn't have me taking you away from that.'

'You should have called me.' There is reproach in my voice.

'Maybe. But she said it wasn't my place to butt in. I thought maybe she was right. I thought maybe . . . ' Her voice trails off.

'Go home,' I say. 'Get some rest and I'll call you if anything happens.' I head upstairs, afraid to turn around and see her face.

I remember times, when I was younger, feeling petrified walking up the stairs in my parents' house. There were the times when I was a child and I'd done something wrong, and I was sent upstairs to await my father's punishment – my father was a firm believer in traditional parenting methods, which used corporal punishment to ensure that lessons were remembered. There were the times, after my father had died, when I was sneaking in after being out late at night and I knew for certain that Ma was waiting up to catch me – and my mother's version of corporal punishment made my father's whippings feel like backrubs. But I've never known fear walking up these stairs the way I feel the fear now. Ma's tough. More than that, she's hard, and her maternal love is a volatile phenomenon. And yet it's the only constant I've known in my entire life. A world without her would be a world unmoored. I would be adrift, and I'm only now realizing this. It is the most terrifying thought I've ever had.

Her door is closed and I have to inch it open. 'Ma?' I say softly. She doesn't answer. 'Ma?' I say a little louder. The door is open wide enough for me to see in now, and she's lying on her back in her bed, propped up on the pillows, the oxygen tube running to her nose. Her eyes are closed, and it doesn't look like she's breathing. 'Ma!' I say in a loud voice. She twitches and her eyes slap open.

'Jesus, Mother and Mary,' she says. The effort to talk brings a coughing fit that lasts for thirty seconds. 'Are you trying to kill me, boy?' she demands quietly. 'It won't take much.' She looks at me without turning her head. The years that seemed to have melted off her in recent days have returned and brought friends. She looks ancient and frail. I smile at her. 'Don't smile at me,' she orders. 'For Christ's sake, you'll make me think I'm dead already.'

'I heard it was a rough night,' I say, entering the room and taking the seat near her bed so that she can see me.

She looks at the bruises on my face and frowns. 'Not nearly as bad as yours, from the look of you.'

'My night was fine,' I say. 'It was the morning that sucked.'

She laughs. 'Me too. I don't even remember the night; as far as I knew, I was asleep. That wasn't bad – waking up was a bitch.'

'How're you doing, Ma?' I ask, striking a more serious tone.

'I've seen better days,' she says, matching my sobriety. 'But then, I've seen worse days, too.' She raises her hand, and I take it. I wonder when I last held my mother's hand. It's been at least a decade and a half, by my memory. It feels oddly intimate. 'I remember when your father passed. The boys came up here from the shore to tell me. They told me how good a leader he'd been. They told me there would be revenge.'

'Against the ladder?'

She gives me a confused look.

'It was an accident, right?'

It takes her a moment to get the joke. 'You knew.'

'I suspected.'

'Since when?'

'Fourth grade, I think.'

'You always were the smart one. Your father, he had street smarts. That's important, particularly in these streets. You've got those smarts, too, but you've got so much more. More than your father or I ever knew what to do with. Where you got your brains from, I'll never know, but it wasn't from either of us.'

'You're plenty smart,' I tell her.

'Don't lie to a dying woman.' She looks at me. 'You did right getting out of here. It would have been a waste. You're destined for something better.'

I shake my head. 'I'm not sure,' I say. 'My job . . . ' I can't bring myself to tell her everything. There's too much, and I wouldn't know where to start. Even if I could, I wouldn't want her to know the ugly truth of wading hip-deep through the swamps of the fantasies of the lonely. I wouldn't want her to know how tawdry it all seems now.

'Good God, not the job you have now, boy,' she says. 'They're a bunch of charlatans. Anyone can see that. This isn't where your greatness lies. You'll be great in spite of what you're doing now, not because of it.'

I'm not sure what to say. 'How did you know?'

'Street smarts,' she says. 'I've got them in spades.'

'Yeah, Ma. You do.' She gives me a tired smile, and it feels like a gift. 'Close your eyes and get some sleep, okay?'

'I will,' she says. Her voice is breathy. 'And I'll be downstairs for a drink with you before you know it.'

I rest her hand on her chest as I get up from the chair. I suspect she and I have shared our last drink, and the thought leaves me so lonely I can't put it into words.

CHAPTER THIRTY-FOUR

I'm back downstairs, sitting at the kitchen table, an untouched glass of whiskey in front of me. I don't know for how long I've been sitting here. Maybe twenty minutes, maybe an hour. The afternoon sun is still bright outside, and the heat is stifling in the little house. Last summer Ma finally broke down and let me put air-conditioning units in the bedrooms, which is a blessing, but the rest of the house feels like a sauna.

I take my phone out of my pocket and dial Killkenny's number. He picks up on the second ring. 'Yeah,' he says.

'It's Nick. I'm just checking in to see if anything's happened.'

'Nothing good,' he says. 'They found the Mercedes abandoned in the alphabet section of Hull. No sign of our boy.'

'Any cars reported stolen in the area that he might be using now?'

'It's Hull. Cars are stolen all the time.'

'Okay, I get it. Anything else?'

'Preliminaries came back on the Westerbrooke girl. Doc puts time of death at around ten. Looks like she was partying for at least five hours before that.'

'How can they tell?'

'Bar food in her stomach, partially digested. Also scored a point-two-three on the blood alcohol scale – nearly three times what would get her a DUI. Full toxicology will take another week, but Doc suspects from the other evidence that we'll find an ample amount of coke in her system. Last time anyone saw François was at the NextLife lab when we busted Gunta. Apparently he never even went back inside, so he had plenty of time to get things ready, meet the girl, ply her with drugs and booze and strap her in for her final ride.'

The callous reference to the murder victim offends me, but I suppose if you spend your entire life dealing with the sorts of things he deals with, you probably get pretty hardened to it all.

'What now?' I ask.

'We've got his description and headshots out on the street and up in the post offices.'

'Good, so if anyone went to the post office anymore, we'd have a shot at catching him?'

'Best we can do. We're also talking to people at NextLife to see whether anyone knows where François might hang out. He rented the dump where he did the Westerbrooke girl under a false name, so we're running that through the system, too, but the reality is that he could have another five apartments like that rented already.'

'Great. You're really cheering me up.'

'Don't worry, we'll get him. It may take another body or two, but he'll fuck up.'

'Spreading more joy.'

'I'll let you know if we get a line on any other information.'

'Okay.' I hang up and put the phone back in my pocket. The whiskey in front of me looks appealing, but I wonder whether it will actually make me feel better. I think probably not.

I get up and walk into the small living room. It's the place where I spent my boyhood, sitting on the floor playing with games while I listened to the adults talk about adult things. When I got older, I used to think about those times and marvel at the corruption of it all – the blasé manner in which my father and his friends used to talk about breaking the law. Now it occurs to me that the rest of the world has gone the same way, they just use prettier words.

Looking out the window, I can see a herd of kids playing in the vacant lot across the street, marauding in some game that seems like a cross between baseball and rugby, where it's clearly legal to tackle the runner. That's what people learn early, I suppose – it's more fun to make up the rules as you go along than to follow those that someone else has set down for you.

I hear the door open and close. 'Cormack?' I'm still standing there, looking out the window, when I feel the shadow of a figure cross the living-room doorway. I turn, expecting to see Cormack there, but he's not. Instead the entire doorway is blocked by NetMaster.

'You don't listen, Nick,' he says. His accent sounds as menacing as ever. 'I thought I was clear, but perhaps not.' I notice for the first time that he is holding a knife. I'm thinking quickly, trying to figure out whether there is a way past him. The door he's blocking is the only way out of the room. There are two windows, both half open to catch any breeze that might cool the house, but neither opening is wide enough for me to get through.

'I'm not sure what you're talking about,' I say.

'I think you are.' He takes a step into the room, toward me. It's a small enough room, and he's a large enough man that there is little space separating us now. Yvette mentioned that Cormack was coming back shortly. I need to buy time, I realize.

'Can I ask you something?' I enquire, stalling.

He steps to the windows and closes them. I assume it's to keep any shouting from reaching the streets. I could tell him it doesn't matter much; neighbors are slow to respond to commotion around here.

'The name – NetMaster – what's that all about? Are you auditioning for the role of a comic book villain?'

He smiles and I see those tiny, sharp rodent teeth again. 'Ah,' he says, nodding his head. 'You are a funny person. I like humor.' He's moving toward me again.

'Seriously, though,' I continue, backing up to the wall. 'Why?'

'My real name,' he says, 'I could not use anymore. It was too well known among the authorities at Interpol. That is why I came to this country. In this country people can start over – they can choose who they would like to be.'

'And you wanted to be a psychopath?'

He smiles again, and I remind myself not to make him do that anymore. 'Josh Pinkerton suggested that when he agreed to hire me. He sought me out, and he thought it would be . . . what is the word . . . intimidating.'

'And you believed him?'

He looks at me, frowning.

'He was fucking with you. You don't see that?'

He shakes his head, but I can see the hint of a doubt in his eyes. 'You are wrong.'

'You don't think he's laughing at you behind your back? Please . . . he's totally screwing with you. And now he has you coming out here to do what? Try to intimidate me again? That didn't work the first time, remember?'

'Who said I am here to intimidate you?' he asks. 'This neighborhood is not so safe, I think. Someone could break in to steal what you have.' He holds up the knife. 'They could kill you in the process. Then kill your mother.'

The mention of my mother sends me over the edge. I lower my head and run at him, taking him by surprise, driving into his stomach to knock the wind from him as I grab for the knife. He stumbles back, off balance, and for just a moment I think I have the advantage. He hits the wall next to the door, and I make a break for the kitchen, but he grabs me by the arm and it's like being caught in a bear trap. I try to pull free, but he gives a hard tug and I hit the floor.

I hear a noise from upstairs, and I wonder whether Ma has given up the ghost. A part of me hopes so; the chances that I'm getting away from NetMaster are slim, and I'd rather not have his the last face she sees as he makes good on his threat to kill her.

He's on me instantly, and I marvel at his quickness. He has me by the throat and he's holding the knife in front of my face. I wonder whether he'll actually go through with it, or whether this is intended to drive home the intimidation factor. If it's just to intimidate me, it's starting to work.

He brings the point of the knife close to my right eye, and

it looks as though he's made a decision. Just then, though, I hear the sound of a revolver being cocked. I can't see past the giant man hovering over me, but I can see the barrel of the gun pressed against his ear. At first I'm assuming that Cormack has returned, but then I hear my mother's rasp.

'Drop your knife and get off my son,' she hisses. She's winded and doubled over, but the words are clear.

NetMaster's eyes have gone wide, and he pulls the knife back from my face.

'Drop it. It would be a real pain in the ass to clean your brains off my nice floor, but I'll do it if I have to.'

NetMaster drops the knife and rocks back so that he's resting on his knees. My mother coughs, her arm twitching as her body convulses, but she never takes her eyes off NetMaster, her gun still wedged into his earhole. I can tell he's concerned that the spasm will cause her to pull the trigger, and I don't blame him.

The fit passes and she says, 'Nick, you okay?'

'Yeah, Ma. Thanks.' I stand up.

'Who is he?'

'He's the head of security at NextLife.'

'Yeah?' She leans in close to his face. 'I'm head of security at the Caldwell house, so I guess we got something in common. Why's he here?'

'I'm looking into some things that don't reflect well on the company. I think he's here to scare me away from that. Either that or he really was here to kill me.'

She glares at NetMaster as she steps back, repositioning the barrel of the gun from his ear to the center of his forehead. 'Well?' she asks. 'Which is it?'

He looks at her, genuine fear in his eyes. 'I was sent to scare him. That is all.'

'You believe him?'

'I don't know.'

'Should I shoot him?'

I don't answer right away, and I can see the fear grow in NetMaster's expression. 'Nah,' I say at last. 'He's not worth the hassle.'

'Police, then?'

'I'm working with Paul Killkenny. I'll tell him about this, make a statement he can keep so that if anything else happens, they'll know to go after him. I don't want to involve others right now; the company has enough troubles.' I look at NetMaster. 'Tell Josh I'm seeing this investigation through, you understand? And if I see you again, Ma will hunt you down and kill you. Won't you, Ma?'

'You bet your fuckin' ass.'

'Yes, I will tell him,' NetMaster says desperately. 'I will.'

'Good.'

'Stand up,' Ma says. NetMaster obeys. He's more than a foot taller than she is, but she still has the gun pointed at him. She reaches up and presses it hard into the soft folds under his jaw. 'Nick's not joking. If I see you again, I'll blow your fuckin' head off. You got that?'

He nods.

'Get the fuck out of here.'

She pulls the gun off and NetMaster backs away, toward the door to the kitchen. Once he gets a little separation, he turns and hurries out of the house. Ma and I are left standing there in the hallway outside the living room. I'm still breathing hard, and we look at each other.

'You're feeling better,' I comment.

'I am, a little,' she says. She looks at the gun in her hand. 'I could use a drink, though.'

I nod. 'I'll get you a glass.'

CHAPTER THIRTY-FIVE

Cormack is at our house an hour after Ma chased NetMaster from the premises. Ma's on her third whiskey, and looks better. I've had three, but I'm slowing my pace. There's a lot going through my mind, and I'd like to maintain some semblance of sobriety. I figure I've put everyone I know at risk, so I owe them an explanation, and I fill Ma and Cormack in on the situation. I leave out some of the details, particularly regarding François' attack on me, but give them enough flavor for them to understand the seriousness of the situation. The only part I leave out entirely is the part about Kendra Madison.

When I'm done, Cormack chuckles. 'I thought you went into the world of big business because it was safer than the rackets,' he jokes. 'Sounds like you'd have been better off on the waterfront. Less violence.'

'And a better class of people,' Ma adds.

'True,' Cormack agrees. 'By far.'

'This is an unusual situation,' I point out.

'You sure?' Cormack asks. I'm too tired to answer honestly, so I take another sip of my drink. 'Thought so,' he says.

The sun is down now, and I can see that Ma is getting tired

again. It's a miracle that's she's alive at all, but then Ma's a fighter. She's not giving in until the last punch is thrown. 'Cormack, I've gotta go out and take care of a couple things. Can you make sure she gets to bed?'

He nods. 'I'll make sure she's okay.'

'She needs her rest, so don't get any ideas, got it?'

'Wouldn't dream of it,' he says with a wink.

'Bullshit!' Ma says.

'I'm serious.' They look at each other, and I see a smile pass between them. 'I said I'm serious.'

'Aye, sir,' Cormack says with a salute.

'Go, Nick,' Ma tells me. 'I'm still strong enough to keep him off me, if I want.'

I'm defeated on that point. 'Okay, Ma,' I say. I get up and give her a kiss on the cheek. 'Thanks again. I'm not sure what I would've done if you hadn't made it down the stairs.'

She pats my hand. 'You'd have figured a way out of it,' she says. 'You always do.'

I sit in my car outside Kendra Madison's house, trying to decide what to do. My head is spinning with a thousand different questions. What if she no longer wants me there? What if she's with a client? What if she welcomes me in – will I take her to bed? Can I be with someone with her past? What is it about her that I find so compelling? Am I obsessed with her, or with the girl from *De Sade*'s LifeScene? Is there a difference? What do my feelings for her mean about my feelings for Yvette?

All of these thoughts swirl and dance and defy under-standing as I sit there, watching the house. I'm desperate for a glimpse of her – some confirmation, at least, that she has put off any potential business for the evening in the hope that I would arrive. I see a few girls moving from room to room, but none of them resemble Kendra. I ache to see her raven hair and slim body. No matter how many questions remain unanswered, one thing is clear: I need to see her. I have no option, really.

I get out of the car and walk toward the house. I'm looking up at the windows, toward the front door, still searching for her silhouette – I'm convinced I could recognize her in an instant.

The lights are off on the front porch, and as I reach the house and put my foot on the first step up to the door, I'm seized with panic. I cannot possibly walk up and ring the bell. I'm not concerned about being mistaken for a client, though I note the irony of being caught up in a raid. But I cannot bear the notion of being ogled by the other girls who might be there. The thought of standing there in the front hall, waiting as they search from room to room to see whether she is with another man; the indignity of possibly being propositioned by another girl eager to muscle in on a business opportunity; the shame of being pitied, if Kendra couldn't – or wouldn't – come to see me, are all too much for me to consider.

I take my foot off the step and retreat into darkness. My heart is pounding as I walk back toward my car, cursing my weakness; appalled by my cowardice. I'm halfway there when a thought occurs to me: there was a back door to the house off the hallway that led to her two-room private suite. If it's open, I could go in that way and avoid the gauntlet at the front of the house. It's risky; I would be mistaken as an intruder if I'm spotted – in reality I would be an intruder – but I would be able to explain my actions if necessary, wouldn't I? And the risk of being caught going in through the back entrance seems far less daunting than the certainty of being seen going through the front. It takes only a moment for me to decide, and I head around the side of the house.

The old Georgian-style building backs up to a hill, and as I move toward the rear of the house, the ground rises up so that the back door, which is at the same height as the front door on the raised porch off the street, is level with the back yard. The further toward the rear of the house I go, the more of the interior I can see through the windows. I realize as I'm moving my way through the side yard that the last two windows on the side are to Kendra's two rooms. A dim light is on in one of them, and I'm hopeful that means she is in there by herself. As I draw even with the window, I fight the inclination to look in. I feel like a peeping Tom, and it seems a serious violation of privacy to be sneaking around, peering through bedroom windows. It was bad enough when I was on the sidewalk in front of the house.

When I pass by the window, I shield my eyes – it seems the chivalrous thing to do (as though chivalry plays any part in my behavior) – and move quickly by. In spite of my efforts, though, I catch sight of some movement casting shadows in the room. The reality that she is there proves too great a temptation. I turn toward the window and I see her.

The sight stops my heart.

I'm at the window to her main room, but I can see through into the bedroom, and she is stretched out on the bed. Her legs lounge lazily, uncovered, and her head is turned in the other direction, so that I can't see her face. She is dressed for work in a bustier and panties, and she seems so relaxed and comfortable with her chosen profession that I have to fight back a retch. At the same time, though, I'm too excited to look away. I need to watch. I need to be a part of the scene.

Her client is there, too, clearly. He is out of my view, but I can see the shadows moving about in the bedroom, and she is watching him, talking to him – encouraging him, I'm sure. I wish it was me, and the thought that it could have been me, if only I'd had the fortitude to choose to do what was in my heart – to follow my needs – is enough to sap the strength from my legs.

I move in closer to the window; so close that my breath is fogging on the glass, and I wonder whether I want to be caught. I wonder whether I want her to see me.

At that moment she turns her head, and I can see her face. She has a red ball gag in her mouth, and I realize she wasn't talking to her client, she was moving her jaw to relieve the pressure. I also realize that I haven't seen her hands, and that her arms are probably bound above her head. I've GhostWalked fantasies in the past where gags were used with restraints and other implements, and I know that Kendra has been, at least at times, a devotee of bondage and sadomasochism, so I shouldn't be surprised by this. I remember what she said about Josh – that he had become addicted to the power of bondage and pain. Something about the scene before me, though, seems off. Kendra told me that she only entertained clients upstairs in one of the other rooms in the house – that she kept these rooms for herself. And there is something about her expression that I can't place. She turns and looks directly toward the window through which I'm watching. She sees me and her eyes grow wide, tears rolling down her face. I can see the fear in those eyes; I've seen it before.

A split second later her client steps to the foot of the bed, looking down at her. I recognize him instantly and pull away from the window so that I'm not seen. I have no option now; I have to go in.

I move to the back door as quickly as I can. As I run I take out my phone, and when I reach the back door, I dial Killkenny's number.

'Yeah?' he says, picking up.

'You need to get over to Kendra Madison's house now,' I say. 'Send backup, too. I'm already here.'

'Why? Is there a party going on?'

'No, *De Sade* is here.'

It takes a moment for him to speak. 'Wait until the cops get there, Nick. I'll send them now.'

'No time. I'm going in.'

'Nick, don't!'

'I have to. She's in danger.'

'She's not your responsibility, Nick!'

I look through the small window in the back door. The hallway off Kendra's rooms is dark and deserted. 'Yeah,' I say into the phone. 'Yeah, she is.'

The back door is locked, but not bolted. I take out a credit card and slip it into the crack in the door; it pops the catch immediately. The door opens and I step in quietly.

I can hear the sounds of people talking out in the front of the house. The echoes of flirtatious laughter waft throughout the house, and from upstairs I think I can hear the faint panting and grunting and groaning of girls working false magic on lonely men. There does not appear to be anyone in the back of the house, though, and I can hear no sound coming from Kendra's rooms.

I can't remember whether Kendra had a lock on her interior door. It wouldn't surprise me, given all the activity in the house, but I try the knob and it turns freely. As I push the door silently open a crack, I am relieved that there isn't a deadbolt.

I can hear him now. He is talking softly, in a tone that would suggest rationality, and yet I can hear the hint of violence and cruelty in it. 'You're wondering why, I know,' he is saying. 'Why am I doing this?'

I hear a hard slap, and Kendra gives a guttural cry of pain. I fight to keep myself from sprinting in on them, but I need more information. Does he have a weapon? Could he kill her before I even get to him? I have to hold myself back until I know more.

'You're lucky,' he continues. 'Most give their lives without purpose. So few can be consumed in the great conflagration of pleasure and pain and death. You are one of the few who will receive that gift.'

I lean forward and I can see her on the bed, and her eyes dart furtively to mine, warning me. I keep the door closed except for the inch through which I can see. He is not in my view, but I can hear him pacing, and if I open the door any wider, he'll see me. I know from the LifeScene how this should play out, if he follows his script, and that would mean that the danger for Kendra is not yet imminent. I sense from her glance that she will give me a signal when I can slip through the door without being detected.

'There are those who say that the Marquis de Sade had no morals,' he continues. 'But he had morals. He had greater morals than all of the so-called great religious minds throughout all time, because he had the morality of the truth. He did not hide behind the hypocrisy of what we would like mankind to be, but waded through the truth of what we are. He understood the reality of what God created – ' I see a flash of glistening leather, and hear the snap of the whip against Kendra's skin as she cries out again ' – that pain is a necessary part of pleasure, and that it is in our nature to do evil to be happy. To deny this is to deny not only God, but the fundamental nature of our existence.'

I push the door open another inch, but Kendra shakes her head almost imperceptibly and I stop, leaving the door where it is. I feel impotent and helpless, standing there outside the room, watching the scene unfold.

'Those who try to tell us about morality – they are the ones who do real evil. Take those priests who molest little boys in the choir rooms and confessionals. There is evil in them, not because they fondle their victims at such an age – that is the nature of man, and in that they are merely following the laws of nature. Their evil lies in the fact that they indulge in their natures while denying others that privilege!'

He comes into view, moving toward her from the foot of the bed. He is wearing jeans and no shirt, and his chest is glistening with sweat. His hair is wild and matted. He is holding a gun in one hand, gesturing toward her with it as he moves toward the head of the bed and sits beside her, caressing her cheek. She recoils, and again I have to force myself to wait. 'You've been my favorite,' he says. 'It's been perfect, and it could have been perfect now, but you knew, didn't you? Somehow you knew what I wanted, and you started out scared.' He reaches out and touches her. 'Was it the police? Did they tell you?'

She hesitates, then nods desperately, the apology in her eyes.

He nods back at her. 'It's okay,' he says. 'It can still be perfect. It will just be different.' He puts the gun down on the bedside table and picks up a large knife. I can see the point glisten from where I am crouched, and he runs the sharp edge across her skin. He holds the knife up and leans in, placing the tip of the knife just under her right eye, and smiles at her. 'It may just take a little more time, and it will probably hurt a bit more.'

I realize that he no longer intends to follow the script he created on NextLife, and the unpredictability makes the situation significantly more dangerous. He walks to the foot of the bed and stands before her, spreading his arms as he looks down on her. In one fluid movement he bends and pulls his pants down, revealing his erection. He smiles at her, and I can take no more. I fly through the bedroom door and launch myself at him, my shoulder colliding with his torso, sending him sprawling onto the floor. The collision sends a wave of pain through my entire body, starting from my bruised ribs and rippling out to every cell in my being. The knife is knocked from his hand and skitters across the hardwood floor.

We dive for the knife at the same time, but I'm closer and I reach it first. I'm on my hands and knees, trying to get turned around to face him, and I feel him climbing on my back, clawing at me. It feels as though his body is on fire and is burning through my clothes. He has me by the neck, and he's squeezing my windpipe closed. I can hear his breath coming hard on the back of my neck, and I feel the bulge of his penis against the back of my pant leg. I thrash and buck to get him off, but he holds tight.

'Give in to me!' he shouts at me. I feel a fist drive into my ribs and the wave of agony is overwhelming. I lose my grip on the knife and fall forward on my chin. 'That's it!' he hisses in my ear. I can smell the sweat off his body. 'You and I are the same!'

I'm losing strength as he rides me from behind, his fingers at my throat, his body pressed against mine. My vision begins to narrow and I realize that my time is slipping away. I'm tempted to let go and slide into oblivion. I feel tired and warm and relieved. They say that these are the sensations that a drowning victim goes through just before death takes them, and I understand it now.

As I drift off, I hear her in the background, screaming through the gag, begging me to fight. It is the only thing that keeps me tethered to reality, and it inspires one last burst of strength. I muster every ounce of remaining energy to swing my elbow back behind me.

François clearly believed that I had fully succumbed, and the thrash takes him by surprise. He slips from off my back and lands with a crash against the dresser. I gasp and suck in a lungful of air, and it's the most painful breath I've ever taken. The second breath is better, though, and I scramble up to grab the gun on the bedside table. This time I spin and point the gun at François before he climbs back on top of me. He is rubbing his head and trying to get to his knees. 'Stay there, motherfucker!' I scream at him.

He stops moving and looks at me. I fight the pain and get to my feet and he struggles to his knees. His hands are raised in front of him. 'I was right,' he says calmly. 'You and I are the same.'

Without thought, I raise the gun above my head and bring it down hard and fast across his face, ripping the skin over his cheekbone open. He topples over, falling against the dresser again. A set of handcuffs rests on top of the dresser, and as he lies in a groggy stupor on the floor, I clip one of the cuffs against his wrist and the other on the radiator pipe.

'That's right!' he shouts, smiling as he struggles to his knees again. 'You need me!'

I kick him in the chest and he tumbles back against the wall. The blood is pouring down his face from the cut I've opened.

'That's it! Take your revenge!'

Hearing his voice stokes my rage, and I point the gun at his head.

'You know the truth, just as I know the truth,' he coughs out, raising his head to look at me. 'You know it, because you have helped to create it! You wallow in it, don't you? As you crawl through the dark fantasies of those NextLife users who are just starting to search for the truth of who they are, you know that we are all evil – that we need evil to be who we are supposed to be!'

I plant my left foot and kick out with my right, catching him in the chin. To my surprise, it brings forth a ripple of laughter.

'That's right! Take my place!'

I grab him by the hair and hold his head up, driving my fist twice into his face.

'Yes, Master!' he screams. 'More, please!'

I can hear Kendra breathing hard behind me, and I turn to look at her. She looks so beautiful, and her eyes are flashing, her skin flushed.

'More!' François screams behind me, and I spin at him, kicking him again and again. I look back at Kendra, and she is breathing even harder, and she gives a nod.

I square myself to him and see that he is on his knees again, his back straight, his erection straining and twitching. I'm so disgusted; I raise the gun to his head again. 'Yes!' he screams. 'Do it!' I pull back the hammer on the revolver, and at the sound his body convulses and his face contorts in ecstasy as the orgasm consumes him. He lets out a primal groan that morphs into a scream. 'Do it!' he begs. 'Free me, and take my place! Please!'

I feel like I may throw up. My finger tightens on the trigger for just an instant. I think about the girls he's killed. I think about what he would have done to Kendra if I hadn't been here. He deserves it, I realize. No one deserves death more than him, but I can't do it.

I release the hammer on the gun and let my arm drop slowly to my side.

'No!' he screams. 'No! Fuck you! Let me go free!'

I throw the gun into the living room. His obscenity-laced tirade fills the air, but I block it out and walk over to the bed. She is lying there, her breathing evening out. I take the gag out of her mouth, reach up gently and release her wrists from the restraints. 'Are you okay?' I ask her. It's probably a stupid question, but I can't think of anything else to say.

She nods unsteadily. 'You?'

I don't bother to answer. She puts a hand up to the bruises on my face, pulls me in and kisses me.

I hear the police at the door and I'm aware of the commotion, but none of it penetrates – not fully, at least. For a moment I am found, and I give in to the feeling.

CHAPTER THIRTY-SIX

'He's fuckin' crazy.'

It's two hours later, and I'm sitting in an interrogation room at the police station in the Back Bay. Killkenny is sitting across from me. He shakes his head and pulls out a cigarette.

'I thought smoking was banned in the station house.'

'We make exceptions.' He lights the tip, takes the smoke into his lungs and puts the ash into a half-filled paper coffee cup.

'Can I get one?'

'I thought you quit years ago?'

'I make exceptions, too.'

He nods and tosses me a cigarette. It's been more than a year since I've had one, but the world feels lost to me, and at the moment smoking seems a trivial vice.

'He hasn't said a comprehensible word since he was taken into custody,' Killkenny says. 'He's talking – it's just that it doesn't make sense. It's all about divine retribution and the coming awareness. Gibberish!'

'He thinks the world is turning to darkness,' I say. 'He

believes that's the fundamental nature of man. It's the way we're supposed to be.'

'Like I said: crazy.'

I take a long, deep drag. 'Is it?'

'You don't think so?'

I shrug. 'I've seen the shit that people do online, when they think no one is watching; when they think it's all safe. You wouldn't believe where the mind takes these people. It's darker than you can imagine.'

'I'm a homicide detective. You don't need to tell me about the demons of our darker nature,' Killkenny says.

'Maybe not, but I still find it hard to digest.'

'Listen, having a few psychos online doesn't foretell a revolution.'

'It's not a few psychos. People like to tell themselves that, but it's not true. It's schoolteachers and librarians and doctors and waitresses. It's everyone at every age. Fifties, sixties – it doesn't matter. And the kids?' I shake my head. 'The kids are being raised on it now. They have 24/7 access to graphic visual images of sex and violence and depravity. It takes more and more to shock us – to turn us on, or put us off. People think nothing of putting online videos of themselves beating the shit out of other people. I remember a few years ago there was a video that went viral of this street kid. He cold-cocks this other guy out of nowhere – knocks him out with one punch as the guy passes him on the street. And as the guy is lying unconscious on the sidewalk, the kid pulls out his dick and pisses on him. And someone's shooting a video of this, and you can hear a bunch of people laughing in the background. And I thought to myself at the time: *who are these animals?* Now I'm realizing that those animals are all of us.'

Killkenny finishes his cigarette. 'You've had a bad day.'

'You think?'

'You'll feel differently in the morning.'

'I don't think so.' I finish my cigarette and throw the butt in the coffee cup. He and I both get up and walk slowly to the door. When we get there, he pauses.

'I actually had one other question I forgot to ask,' he says.

'Yeah?'

'François was pretty fucked-up. Beaten, I mean. Cuts on his face, bruises on his ribs. Shit, he was practically coughing up blood.'

'So?'

'You said in your statement that you fought with him, and that's when you hit him.'

'I did.'

'Was that it?' Killkenny's watching my face closely. 'You didn't hit him after you had him cuffed?'

'No,' I lie. 'It was just when we were fighting.'

'Okay.' He grabs the doorknob. 'Because, you know, no one would blame you if you took a lead pipe to the guy a little, after you had him down. The guy deserved it.'

'I didn't,' I say. 'It was just when we were fighting.'

'Gotcha.' He opens the door.

'Is Kendra still here?'

'Who?'

'The girl.'

'Oh, right, the hooker. No, we ran her home a little while ago. We asked if there was someone she could stay with, but she said there wasn't. Sounds like she's pretty much on her own. She seems pretty tough, though. I'm sure she'll be fine.'

'Yeah,' I say. 'I'm sure she'll be alright.'

I find her going through the wreckage of her apartment. François and I did enough damage on our own as we tumbled about the place, but it's nothing compared with what the police investigation has wrought. Fingerprint dust covers everything in the apartment. Drawers and closets and cabinets have been pulled out and searched and dumped. For what purpose, it's not clear. It's not as though there's any question who the perpetrator was. They did catch him naked and handcuffed to the radiator, spewing hateful venom, after all. Still, I suppose that the investigative gods must be placated with the formalities of police work.

The door to her little two-room mess of an apartment is open, but I stand at the doorway and knock anyway. She's bent over a table in the corner, picking up the shards of glass from what was once a lamp. She looks over at me, straightens up.

'Come to see the wreckage?'

'I wanted to make sure you're okay.'

She laughs bitterly. 'Who, me? I'm great. Haven't you heard? I'm resourceful.' She throws the glass into a trash can, sits down on the couch. 'That's what the cop called me. *Resourceful.* He said it in a way that made clear he was using it as a euphemism for *slutty*. Like it means I don't matter.' She looks out the window. 'Maybe I don't.'

'You do, though.'

'You're sweet, but everyone questions your judgment. Hell, even I do. Josh can't be happy with you, and you stand to lose millions if you can't patch things up with him. Some might say you've lost your objectivity.'

'Maybe I have,' I admit. 'Objectivity is overrated, though.'

'I'm not the one for you, Nick,' she says with a sigh. 'I know you think I am, but you're wrong.'

'Why not?'

She fights back tears for a moment, then composes herself. 'Because I'm a whore. It's time we use the word with each other, because it's a word I'll never escape.'

'You will,' I say. 'If you want to leave it behind you, you can.'

She shakes her head, but we both know there's nothing she can say. After a moment she looks at me. 'I thought you were going to kill him,' she says. 'When he was handcuffed, and you had the gun, I thought you were going to pull the trigger.'

'Me too.'

'Why didn't you?'

'I honestly don't know. Maybe because it felt like that would be letting him win. It would have been giving him what he wanted. I couldn't bear that thought.' I sigh. 'And I didn't want to believe what he was saying – all that stuff about man being evil, about us needing evil to be truly happy. I didn't want to make that true.'

'I sometimes wonder how wrong he is, though,' she says in a dreamy voice. 'Don't you?'

'Sometimes.'

She pulls her legs up underneath her on the sofa. 'You saw the LifeScene he created using me, didn't you?'

I nod.

'What was it like?'

I shake my head. I don't want to have this discussion.

'I need to know. I need to make sense of all of this.'

'I can't.'

'For me? Please?'

I sit across from her, trying to think of a way to avoid telling her. Nothing comes to mind, so I close my eyes. 'You look beautiful in it,' I say. 'So beautiful.' With my eyes closed, I conjure the images from that scene: the white ceilings, and the red door, and the canopied bed, with the curtains billowing. But most of all what I see is her, lying on the bed, the anticipation spread across her face. 'Your wrists are strapped to the headboard, and you look so turned on.'

'What am I wearing?' she asks.

'A choker.' It's the first thing I remember. 'A black satin bustier, garter and stockings.'

'No panties?'

'To start, but he takes them off.'

She is quiet for a moment, and my eyes are still closed. I'm pulling it all back. 'What happens?'

'The two of you have sex.'

'Is it good?'

I nod. 'It is. But as you get closer and closer, he puts his hand on your throat, cutting off your breath.'

'Asphyxiation heightens sexual pleasure,' she says matter-of-factly. 'It's far more common than you probably realize.'

'Maybe. I've never done it. In this case, though, he doesn't let go. He keeps squeezing and squeezing, until you both explode. And even then he holds on, choking you. And when it's over, you're gone.' I open my eyes.

She's watching me, and she looks flushed again. 'So that's

what he had in mind last night. He showed up and he wanted me to play along, but I wouldn't.' It almost feels as though she wishes he'd been able to carry it through. 'That's it?' she asks.

I nod. 'That's it. The plot's not particularly elaborate, and the staging is simple, but the graphics are overwhelming.'

'You seem pretty . . . affected . . . by it.'

'You're very beautiful. It would be difficult not to be affected by it.'

She stands up. 'I have a lot of cleaning to do.'

'Can I help?'

She shakes her head. 'I'm afraid I wouldn't be very good company tonight. The cop was right, I am resourceful, but that doesn't mean I don't feel things.'

'I know. I want to help.'

She nods. 'I have to find a place to go. A hotel.' She looks around the ruined room. 'I can't stay here. Not just yet. If I call tomorrow, will you meet me?'

'Anywhere.'

'Thanks.'

I stand and go to the door. 'I'll see you tomorrow.'

'Nick, one question?'

'Sure.'

'How did you feel when you were watching the LifeScene? Did it turn you on?'

It takes a moment for me to decide whether or not to be honest. In the end I figure we've been through enough that there's no point in lying. 'Yeah, it did. Particularly at the beginning. More so than anything I've ever seen.'

'And later?'

'I wanted to save you.'

'Were you still turned on?'

I have to think about that for a moment. 'Yes, I was still turned on,' I admit. 'Even at the end.'

She nods. 'Thanks. You saved me. Now you just need to find a way to let some of the darkness out. Let yourself be the person you are without worrying that it will overwhelm all the good in you.'

'That's what you want?'

She shakes her head. 'It's what you need.'

It's morning when I get home. It's been two days since I've slept, and the world has taken on a dreamlike quality. As I walk I can feel the cartilage in my joints, slipping over the bone. My eyes move faster than my brain can process, so my field of vision has a jerky, disjointed quality to it.

I walk up the steps slowly, open the door. Yvette and Cormack are sitting at the kitchen table. They both look up at me.

Cormack is the first to speak. 'You look like shit.'

'Shit would be a step up from how I feel.'

'Sit down,' Cormack says. He goes to the cupboard and gets a glass, pours three fingers of whiskey in it. 'Drink this,' he says. It's probably not what a medical doctor would recommend, but I've never really trusted doctors. I sip the drink. 'What the hell happened?'

'We got him,' I say. I figure I might as well lead with the good news.

'François?' Yvette says. 'They caught him?'

I nod.

'Where was he?'

'Kendra Madison's house.'

Yvette sucks in a lungful of air. 'And you were there, too?'

I look at her. 'I went over to check on her. I had a feeling . . . ' I can't hold her gaze, and so I glance away. 'Anyway he was there, getting ready to make her his next victim. I called the police. We got him.' It's the abridged version of the story, but I'm not convinced the detailed version will be particularly well received.

'So it's over?' Cormack asks.

'I'm sure the lawyers will try to have their say, but yeah, it's over except for that.'

'Hot damn,' Cormack says. 'Finish that drink up and get yourself some rest. You deserve it.'

'What about Gunta?' Yvette asks.

I shake my head. 'He didn't have anything to do with it, except that I think he knew that François was screwed-up. I don't think he was deliberately helping him murder anyone, though. I guess the cops will have to sort all that out.'

'So the company will be okay?' I'm surprised that Yvette would care about the status of the company, though I suppose – given the timing and the planned IPO – it's on everyone's mind but mine.

'Yeah,' I say. 'It'll take a PR hit, but it doesn't look like it's going to completely undermine the management team or prevent investors from being interested.' I take another sip of whiskey. 'Who knows, the publicity may even drive interest in the IPO higher.'

'Have you told Josh yet?'

I shake my head. 'Given that he sent NetMaster over here

with a knife just yesterday to have a talk with me, I'm not sure this news will sound best coming from me.'

Yvette nods, looks down at the table. I have a pretty good idea what she's thinking. 'Is the girl okay?'

'The girl?' I'm not sure why I'm pretending I don't know who she's talking about.

She rolls her eyes. 'Kendra. Was she hurt?'

I shake my head. 'It was a little ugly,' I say. 'He had her tied to the bed.'

'Nothing she's not used to, I'm guessing.'

I shoot Yvette an annoyed look. She looks back down at the table.

'I think I'll go check to see how your mother's doing,' Cormack says. He gets up and heads up the stairs.

'I'm glad she's okay,' Yvette says.

'I don't know that she's okay, but she wasn't hurt. It was pretty awful.'

'I'm sorry. Did you take her home?'

I shake my head. 'They let her go before they let me go. I stopped by when they let me out, just to see that she was alright. Her place was pretty badly messed-up.'

Yvette's ever-evolving hair is pushed back from her forehead, a single lock falling in front of her left eye. I know that she has barely slept in days as well, and yet she looks beautiful. Just being near her sends shockwaves through my body, and in my addled state I worry that I may be overcome. I'm in love with her, I realize. I'm as sure of that as I can be of anything at this moment. And yet, life is never that easy. There's something between me and Kendra that remains unfinished, and I know that I can't escape it. It's as though I've discovered some dark place in my soul – a corner I never knew existed – and I need to know what's there. I need to know how deep the darkness goes, and there is only one person who can show me. Yvette picks up my glass of whiskey, throws back what remains. 'Are you gonna see her again?'

We're looking at each other now, and I know I can't lie to her. 'Probably.'

'Is it love?'

I shake my head. 'I don't know what it is.'

'She's very pretty.'

'She is,' I agree. 'So are you.'

Yvette looks down into the empty glass. 'Don't patronize me.'

'I'm not.'

'What is it about her, do you think?'

'I wish I knew.' I'm staring at her, desperate for any words that might make sense of this, but there are none, and we both know it. She stands, and I do too. I move toward her, but she shakes her head.

'No,' she says. If she's fighting back tears, she's doing a good job. 'You need to figure this out for yourself.' She touches my cheek for just a moment before she heads to the door.

'You gonna be okay?' I ask her.

'Sure,' she says. 'I'm pretty resilient.' She walks out the door and calls over her shoulder, 'Get some sleep. You'll need a clear head to figure any of this out.'

She's right, and suddenly I feel more tired than I ever have in my life. I wonder whether I can even make it up to my room. As I turn to go up, I hear Cormack coming down the stairs.

'How's she doing?' I ask as he walks into the kitchen.

'She's okay. She's tough, too.'

'She is that.'

'She'd like to see you.'

'I'll stick my head in on my way to bed,' I say. 'If I don't fall down before I get there.'

'You'll make it.' He nods toward the screen door through which Yvette disappeared moments before. 'How's she doing?'

'Yvette?' I shrug. 'She's okay. She's tough.'

'She is that.' He puts a hand on my shoulder as he walks past me on his way out. 'Get some rest, Nicky. Things will seem brighter in the morning.'

I can hear my mother's labored breathing as I approach her room. 'Ma, you need anything?' I ask as I poke my head in.

She's lying on her back, looking up at the ceiling. She turns her head to face me. 'Not a thing,' she says. It comes out almost defensively. 'Cormack told me it's over.'

'It is.'

'Good. Everyone's alright?'

'More or less.'

She nods. 'You can tell me more in the morning.'

'Okay,' I say. 'I'm going to bed.' I pull my head out of her room and start down the hall.

'Nick!' she says quickly.

I turn back and stick my head in her room again. 'Yeah?'

She looks at me, and I have the sense that she's trying to make up her mind about something. 'I loved your father,' she says slowly.

'I know, Ma.'

'Let me finish,' she says sharply. She takes a deep, rumbling breath. 'I loved your father, but there were others. Before him, not after we were married – he'd have killed me if there was anything after he married me. But before that there were other men I loved. At least I thought I loved them.'

'I understand, Ma,' I say.

'Do you?' She shakes her head. 'I'm not sure. Eventually you choose. It's the way it has to be. Do you understand?'

'I do.'

'And once you choose, what happened before gets left behind.' She looks at me, her eyes clear, her expression serious. 'Do you understand that?'

'I think so.'

'I hope so. Because if you hold someone's past against them, it will never be right. Your father and I both knew that.' She turns her head back to the ceiling and closes her eyes. 'Good night, Nicky,' she says heavily.

I watch her for a moment. 'Good night, Ma.'

CHAPTER THIRTY-SEVEN

I sleep through the day and wake as the sun is starting to crest.
I stumble out of bed, throw on some jeans and a T-shirt, head
downstairs. Ma is sitting at the kitchen table, sipping some
coffee. She looks stronger, and that is a relief to me.

'I didn't want to wake you,' she says.

'I'm not sure you could have.'

'Last night sounds like it was bad.'

I sit at the table, pat her hand. 'It was, but now it's better.'

'Is it?' She passes a sheet of paper over to me. 'A woman
named Kendra called. Asked you to meet her at the Liberty
Hotel in Boston tonight at ten.'

I take the message and read it. 'Thanks.'

'Friend of yours?'

'Yeah.'

'The Liberty's the hotel they built in the old jail, right?
Pretty swanky, from what I hear. Ten seems awful late for a
date.'

'Mind your own business, Ma,' I say. 'I'm gonna go take a
shower.'

She raises her hand in surrender. 'You're right, not my

business. Yvette called too, just to see if you were alright. I guess that's not my business either, but I thought you'd want to know. She left no message.'

'Thanks, Ma.'

The Liberty Hotel is located on the back side of Beacon Hill, behind Massachusetts General Hospital, just across the river from both Charlestown and Cambridge. It's an imposing granite structure looming over the water, which for more than a century and a half was a prison that housed some of Boston's most dangerous criminals. In the late 1970s it was the site of a prisoner revolt, organized to protest against the deplorable conditions. A decade and a half later it was decommissioned, and the remaining prisoners were sent to more modern facilities.

The building sat fallow for many years, as the city and Mass. General, which had acquired the property for development, considered proposals for renovations. Eventually it was decided that the building would be converted into a new boutique hotel. The architects called in were careful to keep many of the original elements of the jail, including the prison bars and steel doors to give the place a mysterious Gothic feel. The restaurants all have themes relating to incarceration, and the hotel offers romance packages catering to the adventurous, including pleasure kits of handcuffs and restraints.

I've never been to the place before. It's only been open for a few years, and it's become a mainstay of the cutting-edge world of upper-class Boston. It's as far away from my little street in Charlestown as two miles can feel. As I walk up to the front door, the huge granite facade stares down at me in judgment. Stepping into the lobby, I am awed by the seven-story central atrium that was the guard station when the prison was in use. Looking up, I can see the catwalks that ring every floor. Four radiating wings split off from the central structure; these were the cell blocks where the prisoners were kept, and now they are used for the guest rooms. The feel of the place, with its dark-brick interior and fire-lit ambience, is a little overwhelming to me. All around the city's beautiful people move with a sense of belonging that I've never felt. More than one woman glances at me and gives a smile, but I can't seem to smile back. A man in a red vest approaches me. 'Can I be of assistance, sir?' he asks.

'I'm meeting someone at Clink,' I say.

'Yes, of course. It's the restaurant in the back.' He raises his arm to the left. 'This way.'

Clink is the main restaurant at the hotel, and it's in a warren of what used to be ground-floor cells. The bars remain, and the stone and brick walls give the place the feel of a refurbished castle dungeon. I walk through the place, peering into every nook, growing dizzy with the effort as the gas lights on the brick throw off moving shadows that flicker and disappear. I find Kendra tucked away at one of the private tables in a section just off the bar. She's sitting by herself, staring ahead, the expression on her face one of calm contemplation and subdued anticipation.

She looks perfect. She's wearing a red dress that clings to her in all the right places, black stiletto heels. It's a simple, clean outfit that doesn't look as though she's trying too hard. And yet as understated as the look is, she makes it look like an open invitation. Something about her breathes desire into the air, like a neurotoxin that paralyzes everyone around her.

I can see it in the people at the tables nearby; their heads are drawn to her with a sense of sexual fury.

I walk over and sit across from her. 'You look spectacular.'

'You look rested.'

'I feel better. I collapsed this morning and slept through the afternoon. It's been years since I got that much sleep.'

'It's awful, isn't it? I'm the same way; I haven't slept for more than a few hours at a time since I was in my teens. It doesn't matter how tired I am.'

The waitress comes over and I order us drinks. She's having Scotch, and I join her, ordering her a second. 'Thanks for calling.'

'I said I would.'

'I know. That didn't mean you had to. Are you staying here?'

'For tonight. Tomorrow . . . who knows?' The waitress returns and puts the drinks down. We sip them in silence for a few minutes. It's a comfortable silence, though. My mind isn't darting from one thought to another, searching for conversation. I am content just sitting there in her presence. She smiles at me. 'Tell me about your job,' she says.

'Small talk?'

'A lot can be learned from small talk. There's really nothing small about it, if you listen hard enough.' I wonder whether that's something she's learned in her professional life.

'Well, you know about my job. You dated Josh.'

'I know about NextLife. I don't know much about your role at the company.'

'I'm not allowed to talk much about what I do.'

'Because you're the black-ops end of the business, right? Like Josh's own little CIA.'

I'm caught off-balance for a minute. 'I thought you didn't know much about my role at the company?'

'Well, I know some. You'd be surprised what you learn when you date a CEO.' She makes a face at the thought of the time she spent with Josh Pinkerton, but shakes it off quickly. 'So, what's it like crawling around in people's fantasies all day?'

'I do less of that than I used to,' I say. 'I oversee the operation now, and we have a bunch of people who do the actual GhostWalking.'

'Still, you must do it sometimes.'

'Sometimes.'

'What's that like?'

I feel a little uncomfortable talking about this, but I push ahead. 'It's strange,' I start. 'Our users have the ability to live out their greatest desires. They can experience space flight; they can sit in a Formula One car as it wins a Grand Prix race; they can climb Mount Everest. The possibilities are limitless.'

'But what's the point?' she asks, frowning. 'That's what I've never really understood.'

'What do you mean?'

'Take Mount Everest. The whole point of climbing Mount Everest is to make the climb. The whole point is to accomplish something and actually have the experience. What's the point of doing that while you're sitting in a Barcalounger.'

'But the experience is almost the same. The graphics on our system are so advanced, it's literally hard to tell the difference.'

'Doesn't that make it even worse? It cheapens all of those things we've found important and thrilling for our entire existence.'

We pass our first uncomfortable moment. 'So what else did you learn about the company when you dated Josh?' I ask, just to move off the awkward conversational island we seem to have landed on.

'I learned plenty. Thank God.'

'What do you mean?'

She looks hard at me. 'Did you talk to him before you came out here tonight?'

'What? No. Why would I have?'

'You work for him. Maybe this is the way you get back in his good graces. Come out here and find out what I know; find out how serious it is.'

'I don't understand.'

'Knowledge is power, Nick. I have that power now; I'm not giving it up.'

I finally realize what she's saying. 'That's how you got away from him, isn't it? Josh isn't the type to give up something he cares about without a fight. Which means that you had to know something that would make him back off. Tell me what it was.'

'Why would I tell you?'

'Because you trust me.'

'You're pretty sure of yourself.' She says it with a smile.

'It's true. I saved your life, and you can see straight through me. Tell me I'm wrong.'

We sit there, looking into each other's eyes, neither one of us blinking. I can feel her fighting it, but she's losing the battle. The smile slowly fades, and I see the vulnerability she's shown only once before. 'I can't tell you you're wrong,' she says. 'I trust you. I'm just not used to that feeling, and it scares me.'

'I understand that. But it doesn't change how I feel. I'll protect you. I'll always protect you, don't you get that?'

She nods, and her eyes tear over. She uses a cocktail napkin to soak up the moisture before it spills over onto her cheeks. 'I know that.'

'So, what made Josh back off?'

'What's the greatest danger with a company like NextLife?' she asks rhetorically.

'Greater than a psychopath using the system to murder a bunch of women?'

'Much greater than that,' she responds.

I consider the possibilities for a moment. The company has grown so large, the possible ways in which it could be used for nefarious purposes are myriad. 'I don't know,' I say at last. 'There's lots of information on the system that could be used for ugly purposes, if you could connect that information to the individual users.'

Kendra nods solemnly.

'But that's why the algorithms are in place, to prevent that from happening.'

'As long as those algorithms aren't cracked, everything's okay then,' she says in an ominous tone.

'Are you saying they've been cracked?'

'I'm saying they're not as secure as NextLife likes to pretend. I'm saying there have been rumors about blackmail and identity theft on NextLife, which could only be happening if someone knew how to break through those algorithms.'

I let the implications marinade for a moment. 'If people knew about this, it would kill the company.'

She nods. 'Only a few people know. They've been able to

keep it quiet. That's why Josh backed off.' She takes another sip of her drink. 'The company was ultimately more important to him than his other needs.'

'What other needs?'

'The need to have complete control over someone, and to give in to someone else and allow them to have power over him for a time – to completely let go. That was what I gave him. That was what he needed, and what he tried so hard not to give up.'

'I wonder where that need comes from?' I ask idly. 'We see it all the time in the fantasies our users create.'

She's holding her drink just under her chin, and she breathes in the aroma. 'I think it comes from guilt. We all have these desires, these needs that we're taught from an early age are wicked – that will lead us into hell. And so, when we're in control, there's always this internal governor – the voice inside our heads – that tells us: *that's too far . . . you shouldn't be doing that*. If you give over control to someone else, literal physical control, the guilt goes away. We're not the ones satisfying these dark needs, someone else is. We're the victim – the plaything – and we're at someone else's will. If you're with someone who you trust, it's an extremely liberating experience.'

'Who do you trust that much?'

Her smile is defensive. 'I don't trust anyone that much. Not really. That's probably why I'm not naturally inclined in that direction. For me, it's a business proposition. I need to know what makes others feel good, if I'm going to be successful at what I do. It's not about me; it's about them.'

'That sounds lonely.'

The smile disappears. 'It is. If I could find someone to trust, it might be different.'

'Are you close, do you think?'

'I may be,' she says. 'You?'

'I don't know.'

She picks up her drink and swallows the last of it. 'Let's find out.' She stands and takes a hotel card out of her purse, puts it on the table. 'Room 813. Wait fifteen minutes and then meet me there.' She leans in close, brushing her cheek against mine. I can feel the soft flutter of her dress against my arm, and smell the subtle fragrance of jasmine. 'Trust me,' she whispers. She kisses my lips softly. 'Trust yourself.'

CHAPTER THIRTY-EIGHT

I'm walking down a long corridor with high ceilings, numbered doors on both sides. The second whiskey I ordered while waiting downstairs at the bar warms my extremities and lightens my head, making it feel as though I'm floating toward the door at the end of the hall. I can feel the pounding in my wrists, the blood sounding out a steady beat in my ears. It's all so familiar, my chest feels tight and I'm breathing hard.

I reach the end of the hall and I pause at the door, listening for the soft sounds on the other side. They're there, barely audible, tearing at the sinew of my heart as though to leave me powerless against them. I put my hand and cheek against the door and linger there for a moment, savoring what remains of my innocence, knowing that the last of it is to be sacrificed here, tonight – for what, I'm not yet sure.

I put the hotel card into the slot, listen for the electronic clicking and push the door open. It's a simple room, done in white. The furniture has been pushed to the side to give the impression that the only piece in the room is the king-sized canopied bed. There is a gauzy white cotton curtain hanging from the iron rods above the bed frame, rustling in the warm breeze that's slipping in through the open windows. Candles line a shelf on the nearest wall, the light flickering, casting shadows that dance on the walls.

I can see her outline through the canopy, lying on the white sheets, just as I'd described to her, just as I've seen in my head a thousand times. She is moaning softly, as though some ache is radiating out from the center of her being – as though a longing that can no longer be ignored has broken through the surface.

I move slowly, drawn by a force as irresistible as gravity. When I'm at the foot of the bed, I pull the curtain and stand there, gazing at her. Her eyes are closed at first, and her body moves as though in slow motion, the muscles flexing against the desire, turning her slowly, her legs rubbing together with a deliberate intensity. She is wearing white stockings over those perfect legs, garters running under lace panties, a ribbed bustier that runs out of fabric just below her small nipples, which are so erect they seem to be straining against the limits of her skin. A satin choker is tight to her throat and her arms are above her head, her wrists slipped through loose leather restraints wrapped around the wrought-iron headboard. She pulls on the straps, as if trying to escape.

She opens her eyes and looks at me, lets out a deep moan. I'm just standing there, barely breathing for a moment, my ears flooded with the blood coursing through my body. Her lips part, moist with her breath, she leans her back and writhes with greater urgency, the ache growing; the leather straps go taut as she pulls against them. Her legs run together once to the side, and then her knees separate. She groans with an encouraging nod.

I put my hands out, onto the bed, sliding up so that I am kneeling between her feet. My hands move along the silk sheets, closer and closer, until they are caressing her ankles. With that first touch, she lets out a moan and arches her back. My hands move up her legs, caressing her skin, kneading her muscles.

My body is responding now. I am breathing again, the air coming in great gulps, my lungs desperate for more. I take off my shirt and let my hands explore her body. She is mine, I realize. There is nothing separating us, and she is helpless before me. It is exactly as I have imagined it so many times.

I lean down and kiss her neck. She turns her head away with a sigh, to give me better access, and to keep up the charade of feigning resistance. I kiss her ear and work my way down her throat, across the choker, to her breasts.

She is panting now, and I push myself back up so that I'm kneeling again, and I reach out and slip her panties down. She lifts her hips to facilitate the process. I reach out again and undo the straps on the side of her bustier, pull it off, so that she is fully revealed before me. I caress her sides as I lean forward and kiss her breasts again, running my tongue over her nipples, gently at first, and then with greater pressure and sustained rhythm.

I kiss my way down her body, taking my time, savoring every inch of her skin. Her moaning is growing in volume, her anticipation becoming desperate. When I reach her hips, she raises them up to meet me, but I pull back, hovering over her, looking down into her eyes. Then I slide down and begin kissing her again, starting at the ankles this time and working my way up. She lets out a frustrated, feral groan, her body straining for my touch and my kisses.

Eventually I work my way up the inside of her thigh, pausing for just a moment as I listen to her breath coming in storm waves. 'Please,' she pleads. It is the first word she has uttered. 'Please,' she says again, her voice even more fervent.

I move my way up, and she calls out when my tongue touches her. 'Oh, God!' Her hips rise and churn with my rhythm, her moans becoming screams. I can hear the bed frame creak and she pulls hard against her restraints. I alter my speed to match the natural pace that her hips set. As her body begins to reach a crescendo, I pull away.

'No, please!' she calls.

I slip off my pants and move up so that I'm looking straight down at her. My hands touch her sides again, and I can feel myself pressing into her. She spreads her legs and lets out a groan as I move inside her. We rock together for what seems like an eternity, our bodies adjusting to each other, finding the perfect alterations of speed and intensity. My hands explore her entire body.

At one point I slide my hand up along her arms and then down again, so that my fingers come to rest at the base of her throat. We are still moving together, and our rhythm is gathering speed. Her face is inches from mine.

'Do it,' she whispers.

I frown, confused.

'Do it. I want you to.'

I am frightened – not because she would ask me to do this, but because I want to. I hold her in my hands, her body at my every whim, and there is a part of me that wants to make my will known. I move my hand up onto her throat and squeeze softly.

She nods, looking at me, and thrusts her hips up into me with determination, her legs wrapping around behind me. 'Trust yourself,' she says. 'I trust you.'

I squeeze harder, and her face contorts in ecstasy. 'Yes!' she chokes out, and both our bodies respond frantically. I watch as her face turns red, her mouth opens in a heavenly smile, her body drawing me in, as though it will never get enough.

We are reaching the end, and every muscle in both of our bodies strains and flexes. I close my eyes as my hand increases the pressure.

She climaxes first, her body spasming and bucking, her legs squeezing my torso. The restraints on her wrists are so tight now that the bed frame leans forward toward us, and I'm sure it's bent for good. My body responds to her orgasm in kind, my own climax building like a tsunami, the ache withdrawing like the recession of the ocean, then crashing forward in a wave that carries everything in its path with it.

My free hand is behind the small of her back, and I draw her into me as tightly with all my strength, as my body convulses over and over again, each successive wave cleansing me, carrying with it the hurt and the confusion of the past week. Even the obsession I have created around this woman I'm with seems to ebb from my soul. I can feel it leaving my body as I hold her tightly enough to make our two bodies one.

As the last of the spasms quiet, I am able to breathe again and I lift my head to look at her. I realize to my horror that my fingers are still at her throat, still strangling her. 'Oh my God!' I yell, taking my hand away. 'Kendra, are you okay?'

Her eyes are open, but she doesn't move, and I pull away, feeling like I may throw up. 'Kendra!' I scream.

It takes a moment, but she jerks and coughs and takes a labored breath.

'I'm sorry!' I say. 'Please, are you okay?'

The color is returning to her face. She gives me a weak smile. 'I'm okay,' she says. 'That was perfect.'

Looking at her as her breathing evens out, an expression of satisfaction on her face, I am even more sure I'll vomit. She reaches up and slips her wrists out of the restraints, and I realize for the first time that she was fully in control throughout the encounter. She could have released herself at any moment. I'm on my elbow, looking down at her face, my mind stuck in a feedback loop, unable to compute – unable to fully understand what has just happened.

She looks up at me, and her eyes are different. They aren't dead, the way they were in the LifeScene, but they lack the sparkle that was always at the heart of my desire. 'Are you okay?' she asks.

It takes a moment for me to answer. 'Yeah,' I say. 'I'm alright.'

She smiles again. 'How was it?'

I lie back next to her, looking up at the canopy. 'I don't know,' I say. 'I'm not sure what to think.'

'You're not supposed to think,' she says. 'That's the point.' She puts a hand on my chest and strokes my skin. 'It's there in all of us,' she says. 'It's okay to let it out every once in a while. It doesn't make you a bad person.'

I put my hand on hers. 'I know.'

She leans up on her elbow now, so that she's looking down at me. 'Do you?'

I don't answer. The truth is, I don't know.

It's four in the morning, and I'm in the shower in the room at the Liberty Hotel. Like everything else in the place, it has a prison theme, with high-end steel sink and toilet made to be reminiscent of the accommodation afforded to the former residents. The shower water comes straight from the ceiling, hitting the top of my head, running down my entire body. I stand there, feeling numb even against the scalding water.

I get out and dry myself off, put my clothes on. I turn off the bathroom light before I open the door, trying not to wake Kendra. As I make my way quietly to the hotel room door, I hear her voice.

'You're leaving.'

I'm caught off-guard. 'I have something I need to do at the office, and I need to check in with my mother first. She's been sick.'

'There's nothing for you at the office,' she says. She knows the truth. I suppose that kind of wisdom is an unavoidable by-product of professional experience.

'It's just something I need to take care of,' I say. 'I'll call you later today. Maybe we can do something tonight.'

I hear her shift under the covers. 'You won't call,' she says. 'It's okay. I'll be fine. I'm resourceful.'

'Why do you say that?'

She sighs. 'Because men who leave quietly at four in the morning don't call. It's something every girl knows in her heart, even when she doesn't want to believe it.'

CHAPTER THIRTY-NINE

I don't go home. Ma is the last person I want to see at the moment. In truth, the only person I want to see is Yvette. I'm not even sure why, but it's a need that I can't ignore. I consider going over to her house, knocking on the door, waking her up, but even I'm not that stupid. First of all, I have no idea what I would say to her. I'm not going to lie, I know that, but I have no idea how to tell the truth. The truth seems like an enemy, and I haven't figured out how to wrestle it to the ground yet.

There's only one place I can go at the moment: the NextLife offices in Cambridge. I feel a little like a traitor as I enter the place, like an informer stopping by to see the slaughter his betrayal has wrought.

It's not as bad as I thought it would be when I arrive, though. It's five o'clock in the morning, one of the quieter times in the office. There are fewer than forty GhostWalkers in their chairs, mining the darkness of our customers' imaginations for useful information that the company can turn into profit centers. I think I see one or two of them look up and glare at me, but I can't tell whether it's my paranoia. By this point everyone at the company has read something about Michael François and Dr Gunta in the papers, but it's had a lower profile than one might expect, thanks to the fact that Killkenny has kept his word and tamped down the sensationalism. As a result, it's still not clear what ultimate impact the whole episode will have on the company.

No matter what the impact, though, I've decided that I won't be around to see it. I cannot bring myself to stay after all that has happened. I'll never be able to troll our customers' fantasies again, and the thought of working for someone like Josh Pinkerton is too much to bear, no matter what the cost. I'll lose some of my shares if I quit before the company goes public, so I'll take a hit, but if the IPO goes forward, I'll still walk away with several million dollars. That's more than I'll ever need.

I'm at the office now for two reasons. First, I want to clean it out before anyone else has the chance to do it for me. There's not much there; like I said, I never turned my office into a personal homage to the person I wanted others to think I was. There are some correspondences and personal financial information in my desk, as well as a few personal items – pictures and postcards.

I take a moment to flip through a packet of images from a trip Yvette and I took a couple of years ago. We went down to Hyannis Port on the Cape. We spent the day walking around the shops, then caught a ferry over to the Nantucket, had dinner by the water. We stayed over in a little hotel – separate rooms – and spent the next day on the beach before returning. It was a good time. We're comfortable around each other, and there's always been the hint of possibility that neither of us has pushed. I'm not sure why; maybe it's just that our timing has always been wrong.

She's the second reason I'm at the office. I assume she'll be here at work eventually, and it's a more natural way to see her than just appearing at her house. I still haven't figured out what I'm going to say to her, but I know I'll find my way through it. She's my friend, above all else, and she'll understand what I've been through. She may not like it, but she'll be there for me.

I'm sitting at my desk, keeping an eye out on the floor to see her when she comes in. She doesn't keep anything approaching regular hours, but it's not unusual for her to show up around ten o'clock for a few hours of GhostWalking before lunch. By ten-thirty, though, there's no sign of her. I've run out of things to clean in my office, and I'm starting to think about leaving – biting the bullet and going over to see her at her house. I've just about made up my mind to get out of there, when the external door at the far end of the floor opens and I see NetMaster walk through it. I feel a wince in my ribs at the memory of my last encounter with him. They've been bothering me less and less, but I'm not anxious for another round with him. I figure it's unlikely that he'll do anything here in public, particularly now that François has been caught and the investigation is closed. Still, I decide to stay in my office and wait to see if he leaves.

He comes down the steps from the door and walks around the floor. Halfway across, he looks at the window to my office and sees me. I'm looking back at him, and our eyes meet. A thin, evil smile forms on his face. It gives me a sick feeling in my stomach, and I have little doubt that he is here to throw me out of the building in as humiliating a manner as possible. I don't really care; I'm beyond worrying about what those at the company think about me. But if he gets physical, I resolve not to back down. No matter how big he is, I know that if it's a fair fight, I've got a reasonable chance to take him out. I sit there, waiting for him to approach me.

He doesn't head to my office, though. He stands there for a moment, smiling his sick grin at me, like there's something he knows that I don't. Then he turns and heads back out the exterior door. His behavior is unsettling, and I'm curious about what he has planned, though I'm not willing to stay here just to find out. I stand and start heading for the door.

Before I can leave my office, though, the exterior door opens again and NetMaster walks back in. This time he's not alone. I'm relieved to see Paul Killkenny behind him, as well as two other officers. I know NetMaster is not going to try anything as long as they are here. I sit back at my desk and wait for Killkenny to enter. He does, and Net Master follows him in.

'Paul,' I say. 'How's the investigation going?'

'It's complicated,' he says. He looks at the box that I've packed with my belongings. 'You going somewhere?'

'Anywhere but here,' I say. 'I think I've stayed long enough.'

'You have stayed too long,' NetMaster says.

I look at him and give a derisive laugh. To Killkenny I say, 'I may be stopping by the station house to file an assault claim against this guy. Two, in fact.'

'He is a liar,' NetMaster says. 'We already know that. We know much about him now, don't we?'

'Shut up,' Killkenny says.

I'm starting to get a queasy feeling. 'What's going on, Paul?' I ask.

'I've just got to ask you a couple of questions.'

I assume he's going to ask about some aspect of the investigation into François. 'Fire away.'

'Where were you last night?'

I frown at him. 'Last night? Why do you want to know?'

He ignores my question. 'Someone fitting your description was seen at the Liberty Hotel last night around ten. You know anything about that?'

'Yeah, that was me. Why?'

'What were you doing there?'

'None of your business.'

'Yes, it is our business!' NetMaster yells. 'You tell!'

Killkenny wheels on him. 'Shut the fuck up!' He stares at NetMaster until the huge man lowers his head in submission. Paul turns back to me. 'Sorry about that. I do need to know what you were doing there. It's important to our investigation.'

I frown. I really don't want my liaison with Kendra to become public knowledge, particularly if it means that Yvette will find out from anyone other than me. Still, I suppose there's nothing I can do. 'I was there to see Kendra Madison,' I admit.

'Did you stay the night?'

'Yes,' I say. 'What's this about?'

'You need to come down to the station house with me to answer some more questions,' he says.

'Why?'

'Because a maid found Kendra Madison's body in a room this morning. She was tied to the bed and strangled, just as you described in the LifeScene you saw.'

I feel like a building has fallen on me. I start to say something, but no words come out. I feel like I'm choking. 'Dead?' I finally manage to say.

He nods. 'Raped and killed. We have a DNA sample.'

'She wasn't raped!' I yell, getting to my feet.

'Yes, raped! And then you kill her!' NetMaster shouts.

'Fuck you!' I scream at him. My world is spinning out of control, and NetMaster is standing there with a sick smile on his gigantic, twisted face. It's more than I can take, and I step forward and hit him in the face as hard as I can, snapping his nose. He screams out in pain, and it feels good. I hit him again and again. The two cops who accompanied Killkenny rush into my office to pull me off him. They pin my arms back and put handcuffs on me.

'I didn't do anything,' I scream. 'Paul, tell them to take these fucking things off me!'

'We'll take them off at the station house,' he says. NetMaster is standing again, his face a smear of blood, but with a smile on it.

A woman's voice comes from the office door. 'What's going on?'

I look over and see Yvette there, and my heart drops. 'Nothing,' I say. 'I didn't do anything!'

'We're taking him in for questioning,' is all Killkenny says.

'For what?' Yvette asks.

'He killed the whore!' NetMaster yells. 'He raped her and he killed her! What do you think of your boyfriend now?'

She turns to look at me, and I meet her eyes with mine. 'It's a lie,' I say. 'It's not true.'

She says nothing as the two cops take me by the arms,

practically lifting me off the ground as they drag me out of the office and toward the external door. 'It's not true, Yvette! You have to believe me!'

I'm trying to look back over my shoulder, but it's useless as they pull me away. I'm searching for something to say – something that will make her understand and believe, but there is nothing. Suddenly I realize that I am all alone.

CHAPTER FORTY

'You see my problem, Nick, don't you?'

I'm sitting in an interrogation room in the police station in the Back Bay. Paul Killkenny is sitting across from me. His boss, Detective Sergeant Tom Welker, stands against the far wall, watching. There's a mirror behind him, and I'm sure there are others observing through the glass. I'm still handcuffed and I sit uncomfortably on the hard wooden chair, leaning slightly forward to keep my hands from pressing into the chair back. Not that it would matter, I suppose; the handcuffs are so tight that they've cut off the circulation, and my hands lost feeling long ago.

I haven't spoken since I saw Yvette. The full implications of my situation are just beginning to set in. If what they are telling me is true, Kendra is dead – found strapped to the headboard on the bed in the hotel room where she and I spent the night before. There would be plenty of people who would testify that we were together the night before. The girl at the front desk might even remember me leaving early that morning, and I have no alibi until I was seen at the office. Plus there's the physical evidence, which will be overwhelming. My DNA will be all over the room, and all over Kendra's body. Hell, they'll even have bruises on her neck that match my hands. Based on the evidence, there will be no question that I killed her. That puts me in a difficult position, given that she was fully alive and talking when I left. I need time to think this through, and being handcuffed and interrogated by the police is hardly conducive to rational contemplation.

'My problem,' Killkenny continues, 'is that François is currently in police custody in the secure wing of the psych ward at Mass. General, undergoing observation. He's been there for more than a day. Gunta is still in custody, though we're not convinced he was actively involved in any of the killing anyway. They're the guys we've been assuming were responsible for all this. Shit, we know François did the Westerbrooke girl – his DNA was dripping out of her.' I wince again at the way he talks about the murder victims. 'Until this morning I was ready to put this whole thing in the win column and be done with it.'

He reaches into a folder on the desk and pulls out a picture. I've been here before, I realize, and I'm dreading it. 'Then we find this.' He flips the photo over, so I can see it. I don't want to look, but I can't help myself. She's there, in the room I left less than ten hours ago, in the same position she was in when I first entered the room, her wrists strapped to the headboard, the bustier back on, her legs spread. And yet, despite the identical position, the scene could look no more different from the one etched into my memory. There is no candlelight, no soft cries of ecstasy, no intimacy. Instead, her skin looks harsh and raw against the blare of the light. Her hair is mangled, tossed over her face like a death shroud. I can just make out her mouth, which lolls open, her teeth catching strands of her hair. Her breasts, so full of life the night before, lie flat to her chest. I want to look away, but I can't. After a moment I begin to wretch.

'Get him a trash can,' Killkenny says.

Welker reaches out with his foot and kicks a plastic trash can across the room. It comes to rest by Killkenny's chair, and he picks it up and puts it on my lap. Because my hands are still cuffed behind my back, I have to balance it on my knees as I spew the contents of my stomach. It feels like I may have separated a shoulder in the effort, and my ribs, which have only just begun to feel better, scream out in pain. My body convulses three or four times even after there is nothing left to come up. I cough and spit, trying to clear the vomit from my throat and sinuses. I'd like to wipe my face, but that's not an option in my position.

Killkenny takes the trash can and puts it on the floor, near enough to me that the stench is overpowering.

'It's not a pleasant sight, is it?'

I lean over and spit again into the trash can.

'You want to tell us what happened?'

I stare at him. 'I didn't do that,' I say after a moment.

'No?' Killkenny looks back at his boss. 'No one wants to believe that more than me, Nick. Trust me, my nuts are on the block here, too. I let you get involved in the investigation into the *De Sade* situation. If it turns out that you're somehow connected to that, I'll lose my stripes.'

'I had nothing to do with *De Sade*,' I say. 'You know that.'

'See, I agree with you there. I saw you on that investigation and, like I said, we've got François dead to rights on at least one of the girls. Once the DNA tests on the others are done, I think we'll have him for all four of the girls, other than the Madison chick. But we can't jam him up on her, 'cause we got a camera on him in a padded room, and he never moved last night. That's why I think this was probably an accident.'

I glance quickly at the picture, then look away. 'An accident?'

'Yeah, you know, an accident.' He points to the picture of Kendra. 'This chick had a history. Lots of arrests for solicitation, an established history of kinky sex. And she's a hot piece of ass, no doubt. Someone who looks like her asks me to tie her up, fuck the shit outta her – trust me, I'm all on board. I don't care what she's charging, y'know? No one blames you for that.' He turns and looks at Welker. 'Hell, even the Sarge here would be on board, and I'm pretty sure his wife cut his nuts off in the Nineties.'

Killkenny gives an awkward chuckle. I just stare at him, and Welker remains a statue.

'Thing is, once you go down the road she liked to go down, things can get a little dangerous. I figure that's what happened here, right? This was all consensual – I could see she was trying to reel you in when we first talked to her – and you're not so experienced in this. So she's okay with you choking her – shit, maybe she even wants you to, right? But you don't know your own strength, so by the time you let up . . . ' He shrugs and taps the photo. 'Am I on the right track? 'Cause if that's the case, you're looking at involuntary manslaughter at the worst.'

'That's not what happened.'

Killkenny takes a deep breath. 'Look, Nick, I know this sucks. But if we've got to go for a full trial and prosecution, the DA is gonna go for the whole shootin' match. Rape. First-degree murder. The whole ball o' wax. Life without parole. You take a plea, give us a story we can work with, you can be out in three – maybe less. Plus, it doesn't fuck up the case against François.'

'What do you mean?'

He leans back. 'You shittin' me? A defense lawyer for François finds out there's another murder that mimics one of these LifeScenes, which he knows his guy didn't do? He's gonna start thinking he can create reasonable doubt with a jury. We don't need that. Work with us here; I'll let the DA know how big a help you and Yvette were on the François thing, and maybe you can cut some time off with that, too.'

The mention of Yvette is like a sharp fist in the gut. 'I didn't do this, Paul,' I say. 'I'm not gonna say that I did.'

He leans back in his chair with a frustrated sigh. 'No? Then who did?'

'Josh Pinkerton.'

'Pinkerton? How do you figure?'

'You heard her before. She was with him for a couple of years and he couldn't take it when she wouldn't see him anymore. They were way into the bondage thing – the control thing. That's what Josh is all about. He didn't even like me talking to Kendra, and he sent NetMaster out to warn me, to beat the shit out of me, twice.'

'Why didn't you report that?' It's a good question, and I've been second-guessing my own thinking on that.

'He threatened Ma, too. And Yvette. I thought maybe it was about the investigation, and once we caught *De Sade*, they'd let it go. I was wrong. It was always about Josh's jealousy. He didn't like that I was spending time with Kendra – that's why they came after me. He must've been following her, or following me. Either way, he ended up at the Liberty Hotel and saw us. It must have sent him over the edge, and after I left, he killed her. It's the only thing that makes sense.'

'She wasn't tied up when you were with her?'

I say nothing.

'You didn't choke her?'

Again, I figure silence is the only option.

'This brings me back to my original problem, Nick. You're giving us an interesting theory about Pinkerton. The only thing it's missing is any shred of evidence. Unfortunately, all the evidence we have points to you.'

He's right, and I know it, but the evidence is lying. I just have to figure out how to make them see that.

There is a commotion outside the interrogation room. People are shouting angrily at each other. Suddenly the door swings open and a tall, thin man in his forties is standing there. He has dark hair, a handsome, thin face, and he's dressed in a dark suit and expensive tie. Killkenny looks at the man and rolls his eyes. 'Finn. What the fuck are you doing here?'

The man glares at Killkenny. 'I'm here to take my client out of an illegal interrogation.'

'Illegal interrogation?' Killkenny spreads his hands, the picture of innocence.

'Who are you?' I ask.

'I'm your lawyer,' the man says. 'Shut the fuck up.' He looks at Welker. 'You read my client his rights?' he asks. Welker looks away.

'You offer him a lawyer?' he asks Killkenny.

'This isn't an interrogation at all. He's speaking with us voluntarily.'

The lawyer looks at me, bent over in the chair, the pail of vomit next to me. 'With his hands cuffed behind his back and a bucket of puke next to him?'

'We're just trying to make him comfortable,' Killkenny says. He holds up the picture of Kendra tied to the bed. 'He's into this sort of shit. That's why we're having this conversation in the first place.'

'This conversation is over,' the lawyer says. 'Unlock the cuffs now. He's coming with me.'

'He isn't going anywhere,' Killkenny says. 'He's under arrest.'

The lawyer glares at him. 'Is he? You've booked him on charges? That would also mean you've read him his rights and advised him that he has the right to a lawyer, yes?'

The cops exchange a look that says they've been caught. 'We could arrest him now,' Killkenny says.

'Yes, you could, Detective. But if you do, I'll file a motion that lays out exactly what went on here. I'll put every detail of this illegal interrogation in front of a magistrate to get a ruling on the record. You know what happens then, right? He'll spend less than an hour in jail,' he looks at me sharply, 'keeping his mouth shut,' he says with emphasis, 'before Judge Taylor sees my petition and not only lets him go, but busts both of you down two pay grades for pulling this shit. Either that, or we skip that process and you let him go. Anything you learned here today is off-limits, but you're free to conduct whatever investigation you want. And if you think you have the basis for an arrest, you come see me tomorrow and we can discuss it. Am I being clear?'

Killkenny looks at Welker, who remains still. 'Yeah,' he says after a moment. 'You're being clear.' He stands and walks behind me, unlocks the cuffs. I pull my hands in front of me, trying to rub them together, but they're still totally numb, and they dangle like rubber from my wrists. 'But you better make sure your client doesn't skip town,' Killkenny goes on. 'We will be coming for him. If he's in Canada tomorrow, your ass is in a sling, Finn.'

'You're in no position to make threats, Detective,' the lawyer says. He takes me by the shoulder and leads me toward the door.

'I'm serious,' Killkenny calls. 'Don't leave town, Nick!'

The lawyer calls over his shoulder, 'Pull this shit again with one of my clients, Killkenny, and I'll make sure you're writing parking tickets for the rest of your career!'

'I didn't hire a lawyer,' I say once we're outside of the station house. The feeling is only starting to return to my hands.

'No, you didn't,' the lawyer says. 'Someone hired me for you.'

'Who?'

'Tom Jackson. He'll be at my office.' He walks over to an ancient MG convertible parked in a spot reserved for police vehicles. 'They don't tow my car,' he explains as he opens the door for me. I slide into the passenger seat. He closes the door and walks around to the other side and gets in, turns the ignition and the engine grumbles to life.

'Tom hired you?'

'Yeah. He seems to think you've been set up.'

'He's right.'

'Is he?'

I look at the man sitting next to me. He's looking at me without judgment, but also without sympathy. 'Yes, he is. I had nothing to do with this. Do you believe that?'

'I'm a lawyer,' he says. 'I don't believe anything.' He pulls out into the traffic, heads in the direction of Charlestown.

'I had nothing to do with this!' I shout.

He shrugs. 'Maybe not. I don't care whether you did or didn't. I care about what the evidence looks like. And I can tell you that, from what the evidence looks like at the moment, you're fucked.'

'Thanks.'

'My job's not to lie to you.'

I look out at the Charles River as we cross the bridge into Charlestown. 'Well, great. You do your job exceptionally well.'

The lawyer's office is on Warren Street in Charlestown. He parks in front of a brick-fronted building and gets out, leads me inside. Tom Jackson is waiting inside in a comfortably appointed office with two desks, expensive art, oriental rugs and a fireplace. He looks relieved to see me.

'Thank you, Mr Finn,' he says to the lawyer.

'Don't thank me,' the lawyer says. 'Just pay the bill when it comes. I haven't really done anything yet.'

'You got him out,' Tom points out.

'Only because they know the interrogation was illegal, and they were covering their asses. They'll have enough to charge him by the book by morning, and I don't know how successful I'll be in the future on this. A plea deal might be the best way to go.'

'I'm not taking a plea,' I say.

The lawyer rolls his eyes at Tom. 'You talk to him. I've got some other things to do. Ultimately I can't make him take my advice.' He walks out of the office, leaving me and Tom alone together.

'Why did you get me a lawyer?' I ask.

'Yvette came to see me. She told me what happened. She told me about you and Kendra, about everything Kendra told you about Josh. I knew you needed some help.'

'You're taking my side against Josh?'

He looks away. 'I knew what was happening with Josh two years ago when he was with Kendra. I saw it, and I didn't do anything about it. I didn't want to rock the boat, and I figured he'd get himself all straightened out once the company went public.' Now he meets my eyes. 'It was a mistake I made. I should have gone to the police right away. If I had, maybe none of this would have happened. Maybe Kendra would still be alive.'

'The same is true if I hadn't spent the night with her,' I point out.

He nods. 'We both failed her. What did you tell the police?'

'Not much. They weren't interested in listening.'

'That's not surprising. What will you do now?'

'I'm going to prove it was him,' I say.

'How?'

I shake my head. 'You don't need to be involved. You've done enough by getting me out of jail. I can handle the rest. I have people who can help me.'

'Like Yvette?'

I shake my head. 'I don't know whether she'll be willing to help me, after some of the things I've done.'

'You're wrong there,' he says. 'She loves you. She came to me for help, but even if I hadn't gotten you out, she was going to do all the digging herself to find out what really happened – to prove you didn't do this. She made that perfectly clear. Her determination and the loyalty she has for you were the reasons I got you out. They made me feel ashamed of just standing on the sidelines while a friend was in need. I figured the least I could do was get you a lawyer.'

'I appreciate that,' I say. 'But you shouldn't be involved from here on out. The company needs someone to run it.' I head out toward the front door. I need to get home. I need to find Yvette, and I need to figure out a plan.

'I've tried to find Josh,' Tom says, following me out. 'No one has seen him since Michael François was caught. I think he may have lost it.'

I nod. 'I definitely think he's lost it. But I'll find him. I'll spend a lifetime tracking him down, if I need to.'

CHAPTER FORTY-ONE

Ma is sitting at the kitchen table when I walk through the door. She stands and comes over to me. 'Jesus Christ, you had me worried, Nick,' she says. Something in her tone reminds me of the time when, as a child, I'd upset her or made her angry, and as she approaches me I assume that she's going to slap me. I wince as she raises her hand, but instead of hitting me, she reaches out and gives me a hug. 'I'm glad you're home,' she says.

I'm not sure how to react, so I simply hug her back. 'Thanks. I'm glad I'm home, too.' I wonder how much she knows. 'I'm in a little trouble,' I say. Always best to lead with understatement, I think.

She pulls back, looks at me and nods. 'Yvette was here earlier. She told me. I need to hear it from you, though.'

I sit at the kitchen table and put my head in my hands, overwhelmed at the notion of sharing the details of my situation with my mother. 'It involves a woman,' I say.

'Kendra was her name, I believe?' Ma encourages me.

'How much did Yvette tell you?'

'She told me the girl was a real looker, and that you've been . . . obsessed.'

I nod.

'She said you saw her in some sort of sex video when you were snooping around on that system your company has created, and you couldn't get her out of your mind. She told me about the prick who was killing the girls, and that you helped Paul Killkenny catch him. And then, after he was in jail, this girl – Kendra – was killed last night.'

'I was with her last night,' I say.

'Yvette told me that, too.'

'It was stupid.'

She waves her hand as though it doesn't matter. 'It was human. You're not a boy anymore, Nick. I know how the world works; I'm not looking to make you feel guilty about that. We need to focus on what to do to get you out of this.'

I'm not sure how to tell her what I need to tell her. 'Ma, you're gonna hear some things about what went on in the hotel room. Some things you may find . . . ' I'm not even sure what the right word is.

'Nick,' she says, 'if your generation wants to think you invented kinky sex, that's fine, but it's giving yourselves too much credit. You may be the first to share it on computers, but I've lived in a dark enough world that I'm not likely to be shocked.'

'I didn't kill her,' I say.

She smiles at me. 'I know that, Nick. I've known people who are killers – spent my life around men who are capable of killing, in fact. I can see when it's there and when it's not. It's not in you. It's not a part of your nature.'

'So what do I do?'

'You catch the man who really did this.'

'How?'

'First, you get someone involved who is capable of killing. I've always found that, in situations like this, that's a good start.'

I've always known that Cormack is connected. I've never truly understood how connected, though. I suppose, if I'd ever thought hard about it, I would have guessed. He's the owner of the largest tugboat companies operating in Boston Harbor and, as a result, has a hand in the delivery of nearly every large container ship that comes through one of the biggest ports in the country. He runs the union that covers not only the tugboat crews, but also the stevedores who unload the ships. If I'd ever thought hard about it, I'm sure I would have realized how crooked that makes him, but I've never had reason to think about it. Besides, I suppose that if I'd let myself think about that, it would also have implications about how mobbed-up my father was as well, and I never really wanted to deal with that.

I realize it now that I'm sitting with him, explaining my problems. I start by explaining what the company does, and what my role is. Then I describe the various players in the sick melodrama that has unfolded in the past weeks. I spend a fair amount of time describing Josh Pinkerton and his background, and give as many details as I can about NetMaster – which, frankly, are few. Cormack sits there, smoking a cigarette, taking it all in, with few comments. Occasionally he'll ask a clarifying question, but for the most part he just listens. When I'm done, he stands up and paces the room for a couple of minutes without speaking. Finally he sits down again, across the table from me.

'You think Pinkerton's the doer on this girl you were with?' he asks.

'I do,' I say.

'Okay. That means you've got to prove it. If you don't, the cops are gonna keep after you. From the sounds of it, they've got a pretty good case against you, and I've never known the cops to give up on a good case – even if it was against the wrong guy. Usually the easiest way to get the information you need would be to go right at Pinkerton. Grab him up off the street and work him over until he tells you what you want to know – until he admits to doing this thing. The problem is, we do that and then bring what's left of the man to the police, they're gonna know that we've beaten the shit out of him, and that's just gonna make them think you're even more guilty. If he recants, the cops will buy his story and discredit anything we've brought them in terms of evidence.'

'Not to mention the fact that Josh has apparently disappeared, so just finding him is gonna be a challenge.'

Cormack nods. 'If I'd just killed this girl and I was trying to frame you, I'd disappear, too. If no one's talking to me, no one's taking the cops' attention off you. So that means we need to find another way to come at Pinkerton that's not as direct.'

'You have any thoughts?'

He rubs his chin. 'From what you've told me, it sounds like this crazy fuck NetMaster was probably involved in some way, if Pinkerton killed the girl, right?'

'I'd assume. Josh sent him after me when he realized I was talking to her, and it's clear he's not squeamish about using violence. I don't know everything about Josh – I wouldn't have pegged him to be into the whole rough sex scene – but I don't see him as someone who has a lot of practice with murder. If he did want to go after Kendra, it wouldn't surprise me if he used NetMaster to help him.'

Cormack leans back in his chair. 'That's our way in then,' he says. 'We pick up this whack-job and get him to spill his guts on what happened. Once we know what actually happened, we'll be in a better position to figure out how to go about getting the evidence we need to get the cops off your back.' He leans in and looks at me seriously. 'Taking this bastard on isn't going to be pretty, though,' he says.

I nod. 'He's a pretty big guy. Picking him up off the street isn't going to be easy.'

Cormack dismisses my concern with the wave of a hand. 'I'm not talking about the logistics of getting to the man,' he says. 'I'm talking about the ugliness of getting him to talk. It may be that he's a coward and an easy talker. We can't assume that, though. We have to go into this believing that he's gonna be a legitimate hardass. That means it's gonna have to get rough and it's gonna have to get messy. Are you prepared to let me and my boys do what needs to be done to get the information out of him?'

I nod. 'Yeah.'

Cormack cocks his head at me. 'You sure? You've always been the compassionate type. When you start to see the kind of pain we may need to inflict, you may have a change of heart on this. I need to know that you're willing to follow through, before we start.'

'He didn't have any compassion for me or Ma when he

came to our house. And he and Pinkerton sure as hell didn't show any compassion for Kendra. I'm ready for whatever needs to happen.'

Cormack nods. 'Good. Okay, let's go over it all again, and this time tell me everything you know about NetMaster. No detail is too small. We need as much information as we can get.'

I shrug my shoulders. 'I think I've told you everything. I don't think there's anything more we can learn, unless you've got contacts in Amsterdam, where he apparently last worked.'

'That's the nice thing about working the docks,' Cormack says with a smile. 'You deal with influential people from every part of the world. If I have enough to go on, I can have people do the legwork for me.'

'Okay,' I say. I proceed to tell him everything I know about NetMaster again. On the second telling I realize that I'd left out some small details, and I understand why Cormack asked me to go through it again. 'You want to take notes?' I ask at one point.

He smiles at me. 'This isn't college, Nick. We don't take notes; we don't write anything down; and we don't tell anyone our business, you get that?'

'Yeah.'

He shakes his head. 'You need to say it. This isn't a game. I'll help you out of my respect for the memory of your father, and out of affection for your mother, but this is serious business we're dealing with now. We fuck this up, and people go to jail or get killed. Do you understand that?'

'Yes,' I say. 'I understand that. I won't fold.'

'Good. I have to spend some time on the phone to get the

information we need.' He looks at his watch; it's approaching three o'clock in the afternoon. 'It's mid-evening over in Amsterdam,' he says. 'My contacts at the port in Rotterdam will just be getting in to sort out the day's illicit activities.'

The door bangs open and Yvette is standing there, looking at us. 'I heard you got out,' she says.

Cormack nods at me. 'You two talk. I have my work to do.' He gets up and leaves, touching Yvette on the shoulder as he passes her.

Yvette stands there looking at me, her expression inscrutable. There's so much that I want to say to her; so many things that I want to explain, but I can't figure out where to start. Looking back at her, and seeing my failures reflected in her eyes, makes everything seem all the more overwhelming. 'Yvette—' I start. It ends there, though, and I've no idea where to go with it. She rescues me.

'I love you,' she says. She coughs the words out as though they'd been caught in her throat for some time, choking her. And once the words are out, she looks both relieved and surprised.

'What?'

'I said I love you.' She says it with more confidence and surety this time. 'I don't want you to say anything back to me right now. You've got too much going on and too many things to focus on, and if you told me that you loved me at this moment, I don't think I'd believe you – even though I believe it's true. I just wanted to tell you now, so that you'll understand. I figure if I can love you right now, with all the shit that's going on, it's gotta be real, right?'

I stand up and move over toward her slowly. 'Yvette, I—'

She cuts me off, putting her hand to my lips. 'Don't,' she says. 'Save it for later. Right now, we have too much to do.'

We're sitting at the kitchen table and I'm shaking my head. 'I don't want you involved,' I'm saying. 'I've already put you through too much, and it's gonna get dangerous from here on out.'

'You haven't put me through anything,' she says. 'The crazy assholes who run the company have put us through this. Gunta, with his technology and his dreams of rehabilitating a twisted fucker like Michael François, put us through this. Josh Pinkerton put us through this. And now it's time for us to make it alright.'

'I have Cormack helping. That's all I need. You can't help with that.'

'I can't help with what he's doing, but there are other things I can do that he can't.'

'Like . . . ?'

'Like hacking into Josh's files at the company to see what's there.' I blink at her. 'We need to see what's on his computers,' she says. 'If there's anything helpful, we need to know it.'

'Things like what?'

'He was together with this girl for close to four years, and he was obsessed with her even after that, right? What are the chances that he doesn't have a ton of stuff on his computer about her. He's gonna have emails and texts with her, from when they were together – and from what he's admitted, chances are some of them are gonna be pretty raw. You think that's not gonna be important in convincing the cops that he's the guy they want?'

I know she's right, but I can't accept it. 'It's too dangerous.'

'What's dangerous about it?'

'You and I both know that you're talking about starting on the system at NextLife and hacking into his personal data from there.'

'So?'

'To do that, you have to be at the company – physically at the office, sitting there working on the company servers. And for all we know, he's having the activity on the system monitored at this point. If he has visibility into what you're doing, who knows what he'll do?'

'You think I'm an amateur at this?' she demands, offended. 'I'm not going to do anything that anyone can track. Besides, I'm gonna be at the office, where there are a lot of people around, and from what I understand, Josh has disappeared, so it's not clear that he even has the means to find out what anyone at the company is doing anymore. I mean, hell – the rumors are already flying at the office and people are getting stressed. I'm not sure Josh is really in control anymore, and from what I've heard the IPO may be in jeopardy. Compared to what you and Cormack are going to be doing, this is a goddamned walk in the park.'

'I don't like it.'

'That's sweet, but I don't care. You need my help.'

I take a deep breath. I do need her help, but I'm not sure it's worth it to put her in any danger. 'If anything happens to you, I'll never forgive myself.'

She reaches out and takes my hand. 'That'll make two of us.'

CHAPTER FORTY-TWO

The next morning I get a call from Cormack, telling me to meet him down at a warehouse near the edge of the old Charlestown naval yard. I check on Ma, make sure she's okay and get her a cup of coffee before I head off. I peer through the kitchen before I walk outside, my head on a swivel as I make my way to the car. The lawyer bought me some time, but I know it's only a temporary reprieve. The cops will pick me up and haul my ass back to jail as soon as the forensics come back and show that my DNA is in Kendra Madison's body. I'm half expecting that I'll be taken down at any moment, but I make it to my car without incident, start it up and pull out.

The old naval yard is an area of redevelopment on the eastern side of the Charlestown peninsula. It used to be all industrial, with ship repair shops and storage and smelters, all of them falling into disrepair as the need for their services waned. In the 1990s a development company purchased most of the land, and vomited up luxury townhouses along the shoreline. To the extent that urban homesteaders and young professionals have made an organized offensive to grab land in Charlestown, the spearhead of that offensive landed here. The parking lot is filled with BMWs and Land Rovers and Audis. The kids from the projects refer to the lot as 'the car store', and auto insurance rates for high-end models in this area are higher than any other place in the country.

The development company didn't manage to get a hold of all of the property down by the waterfront. At the far end of the naval yard, several battle-scarred warehouses remain, like ancient barflies looking down with moral disdain on the pretty, manicured developments that have invaded.

I drive through the yard and exit at the far end, go through two large lots and pull up to a windowless cinderblock structure surrounded by a barbed-wire fence. I head to the gate in the fence and put in the combination that Cormack gave me over the phone. I open the gate, pull my car through and then get out to relock the gate.

The building is a chunk of concrete with a front door and a back door. There is nothing about it that would give any hint of its purpose – no signage, no identifiable heavy machinery in the parking lot – all it has is the number 142 in nondescript block lettering over the front door. That's the number Cormack gave me.

I walk up and knock on the door. I can hear metal slide on metal as a peephole is pulled open. No sound penetrates the steel, and after a moment the peephole is closed. The door is unlocked and Cormack opens it. 'Come on in,' he says with a smile, as though he's welcoming me to a garden party.

I step into the small building. It's around 20,000 square feet of storage space, mostly empty. At the far end there are roughly thirty large cargo boxes stacked to the twenty-foot-high ceiling.

The rest of the place is open space with a concrete floor. There are several chairs strewn about. Four of them are pulled into a small circle in the center of the building, and three of them are occupied by men in dark clothing.

'Who are they?' I ask.

'They're the boys. C'mon over and we can talk.' He leads me over to the men, who watch us approach in silence. 'Boys, this is the lad I was telling you about. Nick Caldwell, this is Toby Mickrick.'

One of the men stands. He's my height, with a full head of pure gray hair and a large mole on his neck. 'Knew your father,' he says with a nod. 'Good man.'

'This is Slim Putnam,' Cormack says. Another one of the men stands. He's short and stout, with a barrel chest and a bald head. I assume, based on his girth, that his nickname is the product of some childhood cruelty that stuck. He merely nods at me.

'And this, here, is Eddie Black.' The third man looks as though he may lift weights professionally, and he is at least two inches taller than my six feet. He swings his chair over toward me and invites me to sit, going over and pulling up a fifth chair. We all sit down.

'Boys,' Cormack starts, 'I appreciate your helping me out with this.'

'Like we had a fuckin' choice?' Slim mumbles.

Cormack looks sharply at him. 'No man needs to be here. This is a debt of honor from me to this man's father. If anyone feels their heart isn't in this, walk out now.'

Slim looks cowed. 'Sorry, Cormack,' he says. 'Didn't mean nothin' by it.'

'Ignore him,' Eddie Black says with a scowl. 'His heart is in it, or his heart'll be floating in the fuckin' Charles.'

Slim looks down at the floor. Cormack stares at him for another few seconds before moving on. 'I've given you all a little background, and you don't need much more. Our target goes by the name NetMaster.'

'Fuckin' poser,' Toby Mickrick scoffs.

'Maybe yes, maybe no,' Cormack says. 'I've reached out to our people in Rotterdam, and they say he had some juice over there. He was well known as a bit of a psycho and was making a name for himself when his name was Dieter Schlosser.'

'So why'd he give that up and come here?' Toby asks.

'It seems Dieter has a weakness.'

'Drugs?'

Cormack shakes his head.

'Women?'

He shakes his head again. 'Young boys.'

'Fuck!' Toby says.

'Motherfucker,' Slim agrees.

'He was dabbling in the sex trade, among other hobbies,' Cormack says. 'Moving lots of bodies, most of them young males. It seems one of them got away and made it to the authorities. He told them a whole lot of sick tales about what Dieter liked to do with the young boys.'

'And the cops chased him out of the country?' Slim asks.

'Not really. They played it smarter than that. They simply put the word out among their contacts. The Dutch are an open-minded people, but the majority of the bosses who control things on the dark side of the street still frown on child rape. He was done after that. Changed his name and headed here.'

'What do you want him for?' Slim looks at me. 'You know one of the boys he raped?'

I shake my head. 'He and his boss killed a woman I knew.'

'Sounds like a hell of a guy,' Toby Mickrick says. 'So what's the plan?'

'I've got an address in Brighton for him. We'll watch, and when we see our opportunity, we'll grab him up. Just understand: we need him alive. Damaged is fine, as long as he can still talk. We'll take a car and the van. When I call it, we go. Understood?'

Everyone around the circle nods.

'Good. With luck, we'll be done with this by dinner.'

NetMaster's apartment is in a weather-beaten shingled building just off Commonwealth in Brighton. Cormack is in a Caprice Classic parked a block up from the building, and I can see a trail of cigarette smoke twisting from his window. I'm in a solid-bodied white utility van with tinted front windows with the three other men. It's only seven o'clock when we arrive, but the day is already heating up, and by eight the van is sweltering. The place reeks of sweat and coffee and anticipation. No one talks; the men I'm with are all business, and I can see why Cormack chose them for this job. NetMaster generally gets to the office by nine o'clock, but the entire company is in turmoil, so there's no telling what his schedule will be like today.

He emerges from the apartment at eight-fifteen, looking tired and slightly disheveled. There's a bandage over his nose from the shot I gave him the other day, and he has two black eyes. I take some satisfaction in that. 'That's him,' I say.

'Big fucker,' Slim comments.

'Everyone looks big to you,' Eddie Black growls. I wonder whether he was the one who gave Slim his nickname.

'Too big to be buggering little boys,' Toby Mickrick says quietly.

'Amen to that,' Eddie agrees.

'What do we do now?' I ask. 'Do we take him?'

'Not until the Captain gives us the go-ahead.' Eddie looks out through the darkened windows in the rear door. 'Too many civilians on the street,' he says.

Just then the phone in his pocket chirps and Cormack's voice comes over the walkie-talkie function. 'Patience now, boys. Let's follow him.'

I'm expecting NetMaster to climb into his car and head to the office, and I'm worried that we will be sitting in the parking lot all day waiting for him to come out so that we can get another shot at him. He passes his car parked on the street, though, and heads over to a deli. He's inside for a few minutes, and emerges with a sandwich and a carton of milk. He stands on the corner for a moment, just looking around. A sheen of sweat covers his forehead, and the perspiration is starting to seep through his shirt.

He walks north slowly, away from both his apartment and his car, gets to the corner and heads east. 'Where's he going?' Slim asks me.

'I have no idea.'

The phone chirps again. 'I'm going up two blocks to get ahead of him,' Cormack says. 'I'll let you know where to go when he passes.' Cormack's car pulls out and rounds the corner around which NetMaster disappeared. We sit in the wheeled sweatbox, choking down unbreathable air. It feels like hours before Cormack chirps in again. 'He's staying on Elm,' he says. 'I'm parked two blocks up. Pull past me, and park another two blocks further on.'

Eddie Black is sitting in the driver's seat and he starts the engine.

'Crank the fuckin' air conditioning,' Slim says. Eddie blasts the blower and pulls out. We round the corner and head up the street. We can see the Caprice parked on the right side of Elm Street, the cigarette smoke still wafting from the window. A half a block on from that we see the hulking figure moving his way up the sidewalk. We drive past him and park on the far side of the next block, next to a small park with a circular fountain in the center. 'He's coming this way,' Slim says. I look out the back windows and I can see that if he continues his path, NetMaster will pass within a foot of the van – an easy grab. I look around, and I see several nannies and young mothers sitting on benches in the park, watching over children as they play in the fountain to relieve themselves from the unbearable heat. 'Still too many people,' Slim comments.

NetMaster continues up the sidewalk until he's a half block from the van. There he stops and takes a seat on a bench at the edge of the park. He unwraps his sandwich and puts it on the bench beside him, opens his carton of milk. He stretches his feet out and takes a bite of the sandwich.

'What the fuck is he doing?' Eddie asks.

'Eatin' his fuckin' breakfast,' Slim replies.

The horrid reality hits me. 'He's watching the kids,' I say quietly.

There is silence in the van as the other three men look at NetMaster, following his gaze across the park to the fountain, where a dozen children ranging in age from six to ten are frolicking in the water, jumping and running and laughing. They are in bathing suits, and the water beads on their healthy, tanned skin.

'Motherfucker!' Toby grunts. There is real anger in his voice – the kind of personal anger that suggests the scene has hit a nerve with him.

'Sick bastard,' Slim agrees.

'We should take him,' Toby says.

'It's too crowded,' Eddie says. 'And the Captain hasn't given the word.'

'Motherfucker,' Toby says again. I can see that every muscle in his body is tight.

Eddie's phone chirps again. 'Patience, boys,' Cormack says. 'We need to get him alone.'

NetMaster finishes his sandwich, crushes the wrapper into a ball and rolls it onto the ground. He takes a swig of his milk and goes back to his sightseeing. A moment later one of the older kids – probably around ten – shouts something to his friends and steps out of the fountain. He puts on a shirt and his shoes, waves to the others and heads out of the park. He turns onto Elm and starts walking toward the van. No adult accompanies him, which seems odd, but it's a quiet residential neighborhood, and if he's been playing with his friends it's not inconceivable that he's been let out of his apartment without his mother.

I watch NetMaster's head turn, tracking the boy out of the park. He looks around to see whether any of the nannies or other adults in the park are following the boy, and to see whether anyone is taking notice of his own movements.

'He's going after the boy,' Slim comments.

'He wouldn't,' I say. 'He's sick, but he's smarter than that. There's too much attention on the people he works with, and it's too big a risk.'

'Maybe, maybe not. If he's really sick, then he may not be acting rationally,' Slim says. 'Stress makes people weak. That's when they're most likely to act on impulse.'

'I'll fuckin' kill him,' Toby comments. 'I don't care if he's actually prowlin', or just lookin'. Run a fuckin' skewer through his heart.'

'Still too many people here,' Eddie says.

The boy is passing the van now, smiling in the carefree way that only a child can smile, full of pure joy. The giant man is twenty feet behind him, still watching the boy.

'This is bad,' Eddie comments, looking through his rearview mirror as NetMaster approaches the van.

'I'm taking him,' Toby says.

'The fuck you are!' Eddie says.

'Fuck you!'

As though he can sense the tension in the van, Cormack beeps in again. 'Not yet, boys.'

'You heard him,' Eddie says.

'And I don't give a fuck.'

NetMaster has passed the van now, and he's only a few feet away from us. He's still watching the boy, his lips curled into a twisted smile. He's so close I can see him swallow and lick his lips.

Toby opens the back door. He's wearing a wool ski mask

rolled up on the top of his head, and he pulls it down in a quick motion to cover his face. He steps out and heads after NetMaster.

'Get back here!' Eddie hisses.

Toby continues toward NetMaster. 'Hey!' he barks.

Both NetMaster and the boy turn. NetMaster looks mortified that he's been caught watching the boy, and it takes a moment for him to register the fact that the person who has caught him is wearing a ski mask in eighty-five-degree weather in Boston. By the time he's processed the absurdity, Toby is on him. He's carrying a hand-held Taser, and he brings it up into the huge man's chest. NetMaster gives a gurgling shout and bends at the knees, but doesn't go down. He brings his fist up, as though he's going to throw a punch, but Toby hits him with the Taser again and this time he collapses.

I hear shouting from the park, and I turn to see the adults there looking at us, screaming for the police. Cormack buzzes in again. 'Go!' he orders. 'Take him!'

The three of us left in the van pull our own ski masks down. Slim and I leap from the rear of the van and hurry toward Toby. Eddie pulls the van up so that the rear doors are even with the collapsed figure on the sidewalk. It takes all three of us to hoist the huge man and load him into the van, but we manage it in around three seconds. By then, several of the adults from the park are headed in our direction. They're moving at half-speed, though, their instincts to help fighting their instincts for self-preservation. We hop into the van with our cargo.

'Go!' Slim shouts.

Eddie hits the gas and we pull away. As we do, I look out

at the young boy standing on the sidewalk. He still hasn't made a sound; he's just watched the scene unfold. I wonder whether he understands how close he's come to an experience that could have destroyed him, and likely left him dead. Probably not.

Toby reaches out to close the rear door and, as he does, he looks at the boy. 'You owe me one, kid,' he says.

The door closes, and we are gone.

CHAPTER FORTY-THREE

We are back at the warehouse in the naval yard. NetMaster is still unconscious, but now he is tied to one of the chairs, stripped to his underwear, with a pillowcase over his head. A 120-watt spotlight is set on a tripod three feet from him, pointing at his face. Cormack and his three men and I are standing behind the spotlight, still with our masks on. We've discussed how the interrogation is going to go, and it's been made clear to me that I am to keep my mouth shut. That's fine with me; these men clearly have done this before, and they know what is effective, and what is not. One key, they tell me, is to keep the subject off-balance – to never let him know what information you are actually looking for. Disorientation is a powerful weapon, even with the hardest men.

We're standing there, watching him, waiting for him to show some signs of consciousness. Eventually his head starts to bob as the fog lifts from him gradually. Just at the moment when it looks like he may be able to keep his head up, Cormack switches on the spotlight, and Toby steps forward and removes the pillowcase.

The effect is dramatic. NetMaster reacts as though he's been punched in the face. His head pulls back and he tries to raise his arms to ward off the light. His eyes squint shut as he attempts to figure out what's happening. The noises coming from his throat are pained and unintelligible grunts. He is still not fully conscious, but his body knows enough to recognize the assault on the senses. Toby steps forward again and waves smelling salts under the man's broken, fleshy, bulbous nose.

Again, the reaction is instantaneous. NetMaster's head shoots up straight, and his eyes flap open for just a second before slamming shut again when the light hits the pupils. 'Wat in hemelsnaam?'

Toby steps forward and slams his fist into NetMaster's nose twice, causing the man to scream out in pain. 'Stoppen! Wat is er gaande?'

'Shut the fuck up!' Toby tells him, punching him in the face one more time, just for good measure.

'Good morning, Dieter,' Cormack says. 'You don't mind if I call you Dieter, do you? Would that be okay?'

'Who are you?' NetMaster demands, switching to his accented English.

Toby hits him again, this time in the cheek, hard enough to knock his great jowly face to the side. 'Shut up and answer the fuckin' question!' Toby yells.

'Do you mind if I call you Dieter?' Cormack asks again. 'It seems so much more personal than NetMaster, don't you think? And trust me, we are going to get to know you on a very personal level.'

'Answer!' Toby screams. He doesn't hit the man this time, but NetMaster flinches as though he has been hit anyway, letting out an anticipatory shout.

'Yes, yes! You can call me Dieter!' As he gets more nervous, NetMaster's accent becomes more pronounced.

'Thank you, Dieter,' Cormack says. 'This will all go much more quickly if we're cordial with each other.' He nods to Slim, and Slim retrieves a rolling table from against the wall. The table has on it a car battery with several wires running off the leads. One runs to a small hand-held dial. Two others run to small metal clips. A fourth ends in a wire loop the diameter of a tennis ball. Slim rolls it up so that it is next to NetMaster, only a couple of feet away, close enough for him to see it. His eyes go wide with fear. 'You have probably seen something like this before,' Cormack says. 'From what we understand, you were pretty tied in back in Amsterdam, and it wouldn't surprise me if you'd even operated something similar to this yourself.'

NetMaster turns away from the battery and squints into the light. 'What do you want?'

'Answers.'

'About what?'

Cormack gives a low chuckle that sends a chill through my spine. 'About everything, mate.'

Slim takes one of the wires with the metal clips on it and fastens the clip onto NetMaster's left nipple. It takes several tries before the clip will stay, and NetMaster twists and struggles to get away, making pained noises as the metal digs into his skin.

He is breathing hard now, and – truth be told – just watching the scene, my heart feels like it may explode. I've always thought that I would have excelled as a criminal, but I'm starting to have second thoughts about that as I watch what these men are willing to do. I suppose it comes with the territory, and I remind myself that they are doing it for my benefit, but it still makes me feel like I may throw up.

Cormack walks over to the table, where NetMaster can see him in his mask. 'You understand how this works,' he says. 'It will be such a relief to work with a professional such as yourself. It should make everything go smoothly.' He takes the dial at the end of the wire off the table. 'This controls the voltage. We'll start with a low setting. Every wrong answer you give, the voltage will go up. Do you understand?'

'What do you want?' NetMaster demands. He is trying to seem tough, but his voice breaks, which ruins the effect.

'Of course you understand.' Cormack folds his arms. 'Your name is Dieter Schlosser, correct?'

'Yes, yes, that is my name.'

'You are from Amsterdam?'

'Yes.' Sweat is pouring off NetMaster's body now. The cinderblock storage facility has no windows, and no ventilation system that I can identify, so the place has gotten hotter and hotter. 'From Amsterdam, yes.'

'Good,' Cormack says. 'See how easy these things go when everyone involved is reasonable?'

'Yes, reasonable,' NetMaster says. He tries a smile, but it comes to his face as a grimace.

Cormack leans in toward the naked pile of flesh. 'You were going to rape that little boy earlier, weren't you?' he says quietly, as if he's trying to get NetMaster to share a secret.

'No, I was just watching!'

Cormack holds up the dial and presses the button, and the current from the car battery travels through the wires into

NetMaster's body via his nipples. His body goes into spasms that I think may break the chair. All of his muscles contract, and the fat on his belly quivers and shakes. Cormack holds the button down for around three seconds and then releases it. The slight sickly-sweet smell of burning flesh hangs in the air. NetMaster's body goes limp and his head lolls to the side, a long string of spittle going from his lower lip to his chest. He is still conscious, though, and Cormack leans in to whisper into his ear.

'I was there, mate.' He holds up the dial. 'That was setting two, of ten. I'm going to three now. Do you want to try again?'

NetMaster nods listlessly.

'Good. You were going to rape that boy this morning, weren't you?'

NetMaster manages a second weak nod. 'I wanted to, ja. I don't know whether I would have been able to, but if I could have, ja, I would have.' He sobs at the thought. 'It has been so long.' He breaks down and weeps openly.

'So much better,' Cormack says. 'Hopefully we won't have to resort to this too many times again.' He holds up the dial.

I step out of the building for a moment twenty minutes into the interrogation, pulling off my ski mask and breathing deeply to clear the stench of the warehouse out of my nose for a brief moment. Cormack hasn't even started asking NetMaster about the girls and his role in the *De Sade* murders. I'm growing impatient, but Cormack has made it clear that he wants to establish that NetMaster is telling us the truth before he starts asking questions about the things we really need the answers to. His contacts have given him enough information about

NetMaster's illicit activities in Amsterdam for it to be clear when he's reached the point where he's no longer willing to lie and take the risk of another shock. I know it's going to be another ten or fifteen minutes before we get there, and the sight of the torture is beginning to wear on me. In addition, I want to check in to see whether Yvette has discovered anything in her hack into Pinkerton's NextLife computers.

I dial her number and she picks up on the first ring.

'What's happening?' she asks without greeting.

'You don't want to know.'

'Is it bad?'

'It's not good. What's happening there?'

'I'm working in a corner of the floor to try to keep out of sight,' she says. 'I don't know what people know. I think they're aware that things are fucked-up. They all saw you being walked out of here in handcuffs, and the police have taken everything out of your office – computer, desk, everything.'

'Great.'

'I don't know whether people know about Gunta and François. This place is pretty well removed from corporate, so they may not have any idea how screwed-up things really are. The one thing that people are starting to hear is that Josh has gone into hiding. It's freaking everyone out.'

'Is anyone bothering you?'

'No, everyone is pretty much keeping their distance. I feel a little like a leper, but I'm fine with that. I don't have any interest in talking at the moment, and if I had to deal with questions, I wouldn't be able to get anything done.'

'Have you been able to get into his servers?'

'Yeah. I've cracked his security both on his desktop and

his laptop. I have pretty good visibility, but it's taking me a little time to get through everything. I'm surprised he didn't do a better job of protecting things, but I suppose it's better for us.'

'Is there anything related to Kendra's murder?'

'Not that I've been able to locate yet, but like I said, it's taking a while to get through everything. There are a ton of emails from when they were together, but I haven't read them all. There's a bunch of other stuff on his system, too.'

'Keep looking. If we find anything, I'm in a lot better shape.'

'I know. I will.' Something about her voice raises an alarm in my head.

'Is there something you're not telling me?'

She hesitates. 'I did find something on Josh's laptop,' she says in a whisper.

'Something about Kendra?'

'No. But it's . . . '

'It's what?'

'It's similar to the *De Sade* LifeScenes. But this one doesn't use the *De Sade* name. It's got Josh's personal identifier, and Josh is the star in it.'

I'm leaning against the cinderblock side of the warehouse, looking out at the water. There is a huge Liquid Natural Gas tanker going by. It's so big it seems as though you could walk across Charlestown harbor on it and never touch the water. Its housing is nine stories, and that's on top of the deck, which must be 200 feet off the water. It's more than 500 yards long, surrounded by armed coastguard boats. If a terrorist were able to mount a successful attack and blow up one of these tankers, the damages-estimates suggest that all of Boston would be leveled. It makes me think about how fragile everything we take for granted really is, as I watch my life collapse.

'What's in the LifeScene?' I ask.

'It's a little like the others. There's a girl, and she's in what looks like a dungeon. She's all suited up in leather and chained to this wall with leather padding. He's having his way with her, and then he strangles her.'

'Sounds fairly simple.'

'It is. It doesn't have any of the creativity of the other *De Sade* LifeScenes.'

I think through what she's telling me. 'Is there anything else about it?'

'Yeah,' she says. I can tell that she's debating whether or not to tell me something. 'There's someone else in this one.'

'Someone else?'

'Yes. It's another man. He is chained to the wall, too, just a few feet from the girl. He's watching what Josh is doing to the girl, trying to pull away from his chains. Josh kills the guy after he strangles the girl.'

'How?'

'He stabs him slowly with a long sword.'

'That can't be fun.' My mind is racing as I try to figure out what it all means.

'It gets weirder. Once he's done killing the guy, he steps back and jerks off to the whole scene while auto-asphyxiating himself to heighten the sensations.'

'Jesus! Sounds like Josh has gone completely around the bend. Did you recognize the models in the Scene?' I ask.

'I did,' she says. Her voice is so quiet now, I can barely hear her. 'The guy is you,' she says. 'The girl is me.'

It feels like I've been hit with a charge from the car battery. The sensation is so powerful it shoots pain throughout my body. 'Listen carefully, Yvette,' I say, trying to keep calm. 'I want you to get out of there. Get out of there now, and wait for my call. I'll find you as soon as this is done here.'

I'm back in the warehouse, the ski mask pulled down, hiding my face, standing behind the light, out of NetMaster's sight. I'm watching everything as it unfolds, but it's like I'm not really there anymore. I feel completely removed from my body. I'm floating, as though someone else is in control of my actions. Things feel less real than when I've GhostWalked others' LifeScenes.

'Tell us about the girl,' Cormack is saying. He is standing over NetMaster, looking down on him. Toby now has the dial in his hand, and he's taking his orders from Cormack. The setting on the dial is up to seven, and NetMaster looks like he can't take any more. His skin is gray, and from the smell I'm pretty sure he's shit himself at least a little. That stench is nothing compared to the pungent sting of fear that clouds the air.

'What girl?' he asks.

Toby holds up the dial, as though he's going to press the button, but Cormack waves him off.

'I tell you, but what girl?' NetMaster pleads. He's so worn out now, his English is barely passable, and his accent makes it difficult to understand him.

'Your boss's old girlfriend.'

'The whore?' NetMaster asks. 'She was murdered.'

'What did you have to do with it?'

I can read the confusion on NetMaster's face. 'Nothing,' he says. 'I have nothing to do with that.'

'Your boss, then,' Cormack presses. 'He relies on you; surely he told you something.'

'No, he have nothing to do with it. Ask police; they arrest someone for that already. Caldwell. Nick Caldwell. He kill her!'

I can feel the eyes of the other men in the room on me.

'That's what the police think,' Cormack says. 'But that's not the truth, is it?'

'Yes, it is truth!'

Cormack nods at Toby, and Toby looks at NetMaster malevolently. He presses the button and keeps it down for close to five seconds. The giant's body twitches and quivers like it's a chunk of bacon on a griddle. I can smell burning hair, and I'm watching as his face twists, his tongue sticking out like a slab of meat.

'That's enough!' Cormack shouts.

Toby allows a beat before he takes his finger off the button.

NetMaster is having trouble catching his breath, and he is doubled over. 'It is truth!' he pants. 'I know nothing else. My chest!'

'Tell us,' Cormack yells back at him. 'Tell us, and we can let you go!'

'I don't know nothing. Nick Caldwell! He kill!'

'Tell us!'

It's too much for me to take. I have an image of Josh torturing Yvette in my head, and as awful as the thought of him torturing Kendra was, the thought of the same thing happening to Yvette is unbearable. Combined with the doubt that I can see in the eyes of the other men in the room as they look back and forth between the two of us, it feels as though my head may explode. Before I know what's happening, I am moving toward the gasping man strapped to the chair.

'You're lying!' I scream, as I punch him in the face. 'You're a fucking liar! Tell the truth!'

'I tell. I tell!'

'You're a liar! Tell us about Pinkerton.'

'No, not Pinkerton. Caldwell! I tell the truth!'

I'm hitting him repeatedly now. Blood pours from NetMaster's broken nose, and his lips are sliced to ribbons, but I keep swinging, no longer fully in control of my actions. 'Tell the truth! He killed her!' I pull off my ski mask, grab him by the ears and stick my face right in front of his. 'Tell me, you motherfucker, or I swear I'll kill you right here and now!'

His eyes go wide as he recognizes me. 'You!' he screams. 'You! You kill girl!'

'Liar!'

'You kill girl!'

I am punching him again, holding him by the throat, his blood and sweat sticky in my hand. I am aware of the other four men in the warehouse moving behind me, talking – saying something to me – then screaming at each other. Out of the corner of my eye I see Toby hold up the dial. I hear him echoing my own demands of 'Tell us!' I hear Cormack scream, 'No!'

A split second later it's as though the world has caught fire. I feel like the wrath of the gods has been visited upon me through NetMaster. It's running from my hands, up my arms, into my shoulders and spreading throughout my body. I'm looking him in the eyes, and they are burning into me. Both of us are shaking. I can hear Cormack somewhere far off, screaming through miles of cotton candy, muffled and barely audible. 'Turn it off! You're fuckin' killing them!'

It stops and I fall to the concrete floor, the world sliding onto its side as I lose consciousness.

CHAPTER FORTY-FOUR

My eyes open slowly, and with great pain. My vision is blurred and I can't seem to move. It's as though every nerve in my body has been shorted out. I try to lift my head, but it feels like, if I do, it may separate from my body.

'Easy there,' a voice says. I have the sense that I recognize the voice, but it's muffled, and I can't be sure.

'Where?' I choke out.

'Where are you? Union office, down on the docks.' My vision clears a little, and I can see Cormack standing over me. 'This here's our sickroom. Bed's pretty comfortable. It seemed the best place to take you. Couldn't very well admit you to the Emergency Room. Too many questions, you understand. And I didn't want your ma to see you in the condition you were in. She's got enough to worry about.'

'What happened?'

He moves back, sits in a chair a few feet away. 'Toby let his anger get away from him,' he says. 'Stupid fuck. He cranked the dial to ten and hit that fat fuck with the maximum juice. You were holding onto his neck, so the current went straight through him and into you. For a moment I didn't think you were gonna make it. You looked like a fuckin' hot dog that'd been left too long on the charcoal. Lookin' a bit better now.'

I flex my arm and manage to push myself into a sitting position. It still feels as though all of my extremities may fall off the rest of my body. 'NetMaster?'

He shakes his head. 'I'm not sure he would've made it much longer anyway. You carry around that kind of weight, it takes a toll on the heart. He certainly couldn't take the last jolt, though. He was belly up before you hit the floor.'

'Where is he?'

'You don't need to worry about that. Toby's in charge of disposal. He has experience, and it's his punishment for fucking up. Toby had a difficult childhood, and I think he let that cloud his thinking on this job.'

'That's it?'

Cormack shrugs. 'Not like the world's the worse off for not having the likes of that man in it. There's not a child in a twenty-mile radius that isn't safer now than they were this morning. And I can't imagine there's anyone who'll miss the bastard. It's not how I planned it, but it's part of the risk when you start in on a business like this.'

'We didn't get anything from him.'

'No, we didn't.'

'He wouldn't give Josh up.' Cormack looks away. 'What?'

He looks me in the eye. 'I've seen a lot of men pushed hard during interrogations. I'm not proud of that, but it's a fact. I've got a pretty good eye for when a man's gotten to the point where they'll give everything up, no matter what the consequences.'

'And?'

'And that worthless pile of pig shit was well beyond that point. He was telling the truth. I have no doubt.'

'So you think I killed Kendra?'

He shakes his head slowly. 'I'm not saying that. I'm saying that he believed you killed the girl. He certainly wasn't protecting his boss. He would have said anything we wanted to at that point, but he was genuinely telling us what he believed was the truth. When you were out of the warehouse, he copped to all sorts of ugly shit. Trafficking in children, rape, all manner of crimes against God. He was done, and he knew it. He wasn't holding anything back anymore.'

I shake my head, and the motion sets off a firestorm of neurological distress as my nerves learn how to function properly. 'It's hard to see Josh doing this without involving NetMaster.'

'I'm only giving you my honest view.'

I'm stumped. 'How does a guy like that end up here with Pinkerton?'

'Well, it's logical actually,' Cormack says. 'The sex trade was moonlighting for Dieter. His real money came from working on the Internet.'

'The Internet?'

'Yeah. When he was in Amsterdam, his specialty was cybercrime. Identity theft, electronic extortion, things like that. It's a huge business these days. Very organized and well funded.'

'And that makes him a good fit for NextLife?'

'If you want to protect your system, the best people to have working for you are the people who would know how to compromise that system, so they can figure out ways they can prevent others from getting in. It's logical. Lots of banks and top Internet companies seek out the rebel types and hire them to be on their team.'

'I guess that's right,' I concede. It does make some sense.

'Frankly, I've always thought that was why your company hired Yvette. I know there's no one better at hacking than her.'

The mention of her name sends a new kind of pain crashing through my nervous system. 'Yvette!' I exclaim, bolting painfully to my feet. 'Where is my phone? I need to call her.'

'I called her when we were on our way here. I left a message.'

'She didn't pick up?'

'No, but maybe she didn't have her phone with her.'

'How long ago was this?'

'A few hours. You've been out for a while.'

'And she hasn't called since then?'

He looks a little unsettled, but it's nothing compared to how I feel. 'She hasn't. I didn't give it any thought. Why? What's wrong?'

I pick up my phone and check for messages, but there's nothing. I dial Yvette's number and it rings four times before I get her voicemail. I leave her a message and hang up the phone.

'What's wrong?' Cormack asks again.

'She's in danger,' I say. 'Serious danger, and we have to find her.'

Cormack drives me to pick up my car at the warehouse. The mere sight of the place is enough to make me feel sick. I wonder how Toby disposed of NetMaster's body, but I would never ask. I assume he was probably chopped up and mixed with chum and is currently being dropped bit by bit into the

Atlantic several miles offshore. That's one of the advantages of being on the water as a leader of organized crime. There's never any real problem with disposing of bodies.

I head to Yvette's place, with Cormack following me. It's after ten o'clock, and dark outside. No lights are on in the house. I know where she hides a key behind a gutter in the back of the house, so I retrieve it and we go in.

There are only a few rooms in the place – two bedrooms and a bathroom upstairs; kitchen, living room, dining room and half bath downstairs – so it doesn't take us long to go through the place, but there's no sign of her. I try her cell again, but with no luck. I leave another message. Cormack calls the Cambridge office and asks for her, but he's told that she left several hours before. I call Ma's house, just to make sure she's not waiting for me there, but Ma says she hasn't heard from Yvette. Getting off the phone with Ma is a challenge.

'What's happening?' she asks.

'I don't know. That's what I'm trying to figure out.'

'The other thing? The part that you and Cormack were handling? Did anything happen there?'

'Nothing helpful, Ma. I can't really talk about it.'

'I understand. Is Cormack there with you?'

'Yeah.'

'Okay. Is there anything I can do?'

'I don't think so, Ma.'

'I can still be useful, y'know.'

'I know. I'll call you later.' I hang up.

'Your ma okay?' Cormack asks.

'Stressed.'

'I guess that makes all of us.' We're in the living room, and he paces for a moment, looking through the bookshelves for nothing in particular. 'Is there any other place where she might go?'

'Not that I can think of,' I say. 'And certainly not any place where she wouldn't have her cellphone with her.'

My cellphone buzzes and I grab it out of my pocket. It's a text message from Yvette. 'It's her,' I say.

'Thank God,' Cormack says. 'Where is she?'

I read the message on my phone screen, and it sucks the breath out of my lungs: *I have her. Marblehead. Midnight. Simple swap: you for her. Tell no one. Someone is watching you; come alone or deal's off, and you can live with the consequences. J.*

'What does it say?' Cormack asks.

It takes a moment for me to get enough air into my chest to speak. 'It says she's fine, and she'll be home soon.'

CHAPTER FORTY-FIVE

I'm sitting in Ma's kitchen. Ma's upstairs asleep and I don't want to wake her, so I don't even bother turning on the lights. I'm staring at the wall, thinking through my options. There aren't many. Josh Pinkerton is a man of endless resources, and there is no question that he could easily have someone keeping an eye on me, making sure that I'm acting alone. If that's true, then if I let anyone know what's happening or where I'm going, he'll pull the plug and I have no doubt Yvette's body will be found sometime in the near future, violated in ways I can't even bring myself to think about. For all I know, he's even got my phone tapped. I don't trust him to follow through on his promise to let Yvette go if I show up; but I have no question that he'll follow through on his threat to kill her if I don't. It's a bad situation any way you look at it.

I glance at my watch for the twentieth time in five minutes; it's ten-forty. Marblehead is on the North Shore, around twenty miles from Boston. I've been to Josh's house for dinners and company parties several times, so finding the place won't be a problem. At rush hour it could take more than an hour to get there, but at this time of night I'm pretty sure I can make it in a half hour or so. I'll leave at eleven, just to be sure.

I'm sipping a glass of Scotch. I figure it can't hurt; particularly in light of what could possibly happen to me later tonight. I've thought about the LifeScene Yvette described with the two of us in it, and the mental image of being run through with a sword as I'm chained to a wall is not an appetizing picture. The drink doesn't fix that, but it makes it a little easier to bear.

The light flashes on, and I turn to see Ma standing in the doorway. She's looking a lot better, and I wonder whether there may be a bit of a remission in the cancer. Oddly, I have mixed feelings about the possibility. On the one hand, I'm thrilled at the prospect that she might be around for a few more years. On the other hand, given what may happen to me in the next few hours, and the possibility that I may be convicted of murder even if I make it through the night, the thought that she might have to live those years carrying my shame is less than pleasant.

'Sitting in the dark with a drink,' she says. 'Not a good sign.'

'It's fine, Ma.'

She sighs heavily and sits next to me at the table. 'Nick, you've never been a decent liar. I take it you didn't get what you needed from that disgusting mountain of a man?'

'It's worse than that.'

'How much worse?'

'Yvette's in danger. Josh has her, and it looks like he's planning on . . . doing things to her.'

Ma takes a sip of my drink. 'Is there anything Cormack can do?'

I shake my head. 'Josh has got someone watching me. If I bring anyone into this, he'll kill her. After what happened to

Kendra, and everything she told me about Josh, I don't doubt it.'

'So, what are you going to do?'

I take the drink back and gulp down a healthy swallow. 'He says that if I show up at his place, he'll swap her out for me; let her go.'

'Do you believe him?'

'No. But I have to take the chance.'

She nods. 'You're a good man, Nick. Better than any I've ever come across; even the ones I've loved. Your father would be proud of you.'

'What would he do if he found himself in this situation?'

She shrugs. 'I honestly don't know. He'd surely kill someone, but that would be as much out of anger and pride as anything else. I don't know whether he'd have your courage – to walk in there and give himself up for someone else?' She shakes her head. 'In the spirit of Christian charity for the dead, I'd like to think that he would. But in reality, I don't know.'

'Do you think I'm doing the right thing?'

'Do you love her?'

'Yeah, Ma. I do.'

'Then there's no question about it. She'd be lucky to have you. And I feel lucky to have been your mother. Take my gun, okay? I'll leave the light on in front. Make it easier to get in when you get home.'

It's still warm out, even at eleven o'clock, when I walk back out to my car. A light mist is trying to decide whether it's rain or fog, slipping back and forth between the two. As I reach for the handle on the car door, a figure emerges from the mist at the end of the driveway. I can see only the outline of his body, but there is no question that he's moving toward me. I start to reach for my gun, but I see he has his drawn before I can even get my hand in my pocket.

'Tests came back,' he says. 'Looks like I get to arrest you a second time.' Paul Killkenny's face materializes in the place of the silhouette that is moving closer. 'Hands on the hood of the car, Nick.'

'You can't do this,' I say, not moving.

'I have to do this.'

'I didn't kill her.'

'DNA says otherwise.'

'DNA doesn't say shit. All that says is that I was with her. I never denied that.'

'And then she was found dead. Coincidence?'

I shake my head. 'You're a cop. You don't believe in coincidences.'

'That's right, I don't.'

'And this wasn't a coincidence; I was set up. Don't you see? He followed me there. He planned this all along.'

'Who did?'

'Josh Pinkerton. He knew about François' LifeScenes. He knew about me and Kendra. He'd never gotten over her, so he used me. He followed me and saw that I'd stayed the night, and then when I left, he went in and he killed her. He set it up to look like I was the one who did it. It all makes sense.'

I can see that I've caught Killkenny's attention. 'Maybe,' he says. 'And you've got a hell of a lawyer working for you now, so he may just be able to get a jury to buy into all that. To be honest, there's a part of me that hopes you do beat this. But I've still got to take you in. Hands on the car.'

'I can't do it. Not right now.'

Killkenny laughs. 'You don't have a choice.'

'He'll kill her,' I say.

Killkenny frowns at me. 'He'll kill who?'

'Yvette. He's got her. He's offered a swap: her for me. I'm going.' He stares at me, his gun still drawn, and I can tell that he's debating whether or not he believes me. 'You've known me for a long time, Paul,' I say. 'You know where I'm from and what I'm made of. Do you believe I killed Kendra like that?'

'I don't know anyone well enough to know what they're capable of doing.'

'That's bullshit, and both of us know it. You know I didn't do it. You know it, and you're going to stop me from preventing him killing Yvette. Is that really what you're willing to do? I'll come right to the police station when this is over. I'll turn myself in, and we can let the justice system take it from there.'

He's still thinking it over, trying to find the right thing to do. 'I'll tell you what I'm willing to do,' he says. 'I'll go with you. If you're telling the truth, then I'll know it and I can help you.'

I shake my head. 'He said he has someone watching me. If you leave here with me, he'll kill her. Just by standing here with me, for all I know it's already made him decide to go ahead and kill her. I'm leaving. Just me. If you follow me, you'll be signing Yvette's death warrant. Understand?'

'This is a joke, right? You expect me to let you walk, just like that?'

'You do what you want, but if you want to stop me from leaving, you'll have to kill me.' I open the car door.

He raises his gun so that it's pointed at my head. 'Don't!'

'Do it,' I say. 'Because if you're not going to let me do what I need to do, you're as good as killing me anyway.'

I hear the action pulled back on Killkenny's gun as I slide into the driver's seat. I don't turn around; if he's going to shoot me, I want it to be in the back of the head – let him try to explain that.

'I said, don't!'

I fire up the Corolla's engine, thankful for a dependable car, even if it's starting to smell of mildew and doesn't have windows in the back, and put it into reverse to back out of the driveway. 'I'll be back as soon as I can be. Don't follow me. I'm serious about that.'

I pull away and only look back when I'm halfway down the street. In my rearview mirror I can see Killkenny still standing there, pointing his gun at my car as it gets further and further away, probably still debating whether to pull the trigger.

CHAPTER FORTY-SIX

Marblehead is a point of rocky terrain sticking into Salem Harbor, where the shores fall violently into the churning water. Originally settled as a plantation that was a part of Salem, it split off from the main town early in American history. Over time, it became known for its maritime skill and wealth. It was the birthplace of the American Navy, and of American naval aviation. The small town is still known as a mecca of yachting, rivaling places like Newport and Watch Hill to the south.

Today, Marblehead is also one of the wealthiest towns in Massachusetts. Starter homes cost more than a million dollars, and mansions along the water can run well into eight figures. Josh Pinkerton's home there is one of the most expensive. Two years ago, when it was clear how successful NextLife was going to become, he purchased an old colonial on the top of the cliffs at the end of Ocean Drive, in a spot with six acres of trees and enough privacy for any recluse. It took him just over a year to tear the house down and erect a huge stone mansion designed to rise from the shoreline rocks like some Bavarian mountain retreat. Turrets and stone balconies along the shore side reinforce the impression he wanted to convey of unceasing power. The local Brahmins shake their heads at the influence of 'new money' in the old New England town, but there's little they could do.

I make my way up Route 1A, through the working-class towns of Revere and Lynn just north of Boston, then peel off onto the local shoreline drives. As I make my way north, I worry that whoever was watching me – assuming Josh was telling the truth – has already gotten word to him that I talked to the police. Certainly my conversation with Killkenny could have been seen as a breach of Pinkerton's conditions, and it's possible that he's made good on his threat.

I pull into the private driveway at eleven-forty. I turn off the lights and the car crawls slowly through the trees toward the mansion at the edge of the water. There are no other cars that I can see, and no lights on in the house. The driveway ends in a semicircle, with an offshoot leading to the five-car garage that is designed to look like the castle's stables, with three-bedroom guest quarters above. I turn off the engine and sit in my car for a few minutes, not sure what I'm waiting for. I guess I expected someone to come out and greet me. What that greeting would consist of, I have no idea. I feel as though the rules of physical reality no longer apply, much less the formal conventions of etiquette.

After five minutes I decide that there's no point in waiting anymore. I open the car door and step out onto the driveway, which consists of crushed white seashells. They crunch beneath my feet as I make my way toward the front door, looking in every direction, expecting an attack of some sort at any moment.

I reach the steps to the front door without incident and

start up. The steps are rough-cut stone, to blend both with the dwelling's rock walls and with the outcroppings of ledge that jut their way up through the lawn like reminders of nature's supremacy. The steps wind their way in a curve that mimics the broad arc of the central turret into which the front door is carved.

I am about to ring the bell when I notice that the front door is ajar – just enough for me to peer in through the crack. The lights are off, though, in the entryway, and I can see very little. 'Josh?' I call out hesitantly. 'It's Nick. I'm here.'

There's no answer and I push the door open a little more.

The fog is thicker here than it was down in Charlestown, and any light from the moon and stars is completely blocked, so even with the door opened wider, I can see very little. I step inside the house, waiting to be hit with a baseball bat, or tackled, or Tasered. Anything is possible at this point, and I realize that I'm really ready for none of it, but I have no choice. I can't leave Yvette to this monster.

'Josh,' I call a little louder. 'You can come out! Let her go! That was the deal.'

There is no sound in the house and, with the fog outside, even the natural rhythm of the shoreline, which is normally ever-present, is muffled. The air feels heavy, like it is pressing in on me, and I start to sweat a little.

I move slowly through the place, with its spectacular artwork and furniture, all seemingly designed to bridge the interior-design gap between a twelfth-century fortress and an eighteenth-century sea captain's mansion. It's a yawning chasm from a design standpoint, but I give credit to those who worked on the place – they've made an admirable effort, and on the whole the pieces they've chosen complement rather than compete.

The foyer opens into a huge living room with three sitting areas looking out on the water. I move into that part of the house, staying in the center of the room, so that I may be able to detect any motion coming at me. The house is still, though. Not just still – dead. That's what it feels like. It feels like any life the place might once have held has been sucked out of it. I worry again as I stand there in silence that my worst fear may have been realized. Josh may have caught word that I spoke to the police, and he may have fled with Yvette.

I'm starting to move into one of the galleries that lead off the main living room when I finally hear something. Well, not *hear*. It's more like I feel something, underneath my feet. It's faint and barely perceptible, but it feels like the heart of the house is somehow beating below me. It makes no sense, and I wonder whether I am imagining it, but that's the way it feels. I'm reminded of the old Edgar Allan Poe story, 'The Tell-Tale Heart', and it crosses my mind that perhaps the guilt of putting Yvette in danger has driven me insane.

I think back to the tours Josh gave at his parties, and recall the 'man-cave' he had built into the rock-cliff foundation. The stairs down were located off the kitchen, which is on the east side of the house, so I head in that direction. The swinging door to the kitchen is closed, and I put my ear up to it, but hear nothing, so I push it open slowly. 'Josh?' My voice is quiet, and I have to force myself to take each step.

Ma's gun is heavy in my waistband, digging into my skin, so I take it out. I wasn't planning to show it until I absolutely had to – I was planning on trying to talk my way out of whatever Josh had in store for me, as stupid as that sounds – but I'm so freaked out now that I figure having the gun handy isn't a bad idea.

No one is in the kitchen, at least no one I can see. Instinctively I raise the gun and point it into the corners of the cavernous room, which is outfitted with more professional appliances than most restaurants. Nothing is moving, and there is still no sound – only the intuition of sound, tormenting me.

Satisfied that I'm still alone, I move toward the door that I recall leads to the downward staircase. It's there, and I pull it open.

As I stand at the top of the staircase I strain to hear some sound – any sound. There is nothing, though. And then, just as I am getting ready to start down, I hear it. It's a rhythmic beat that's low and steady, like quiet rumblings at the very bottom edge of the auditory spectrum perceptible to the human ear. I hold my breath to make out more, but there's nothing. There's a part of me that wants to flee – to turn and run, find the nearest police station and bring them back here. That's no option, though, I know. Not only would it put Yvette's life in greater jeopardy, but no cop would listen to me now. There's a warrant out for my arrest for murder, so any conversation I have with the police will be brief and pointless.

I feel the weight of the gun in my hand, take a deep breath and start down the stairs.

It takes me a few moments to make it to the bottom of the stairs. Josh's recreational center is in a basement, carved out of the natural bedrock. There are no windows, so the place is almost pitch-black. I have to feel my way along the curved, rock-walled stairway. I remember what the room looked like the last time I was down here. It's an open space with a pool table and seating for a dozen before a theater-sized television screen, outfitted with an HD projection system with access to both television and Blu-ray movies. A bar runs along the back wall, fully stocked with every imaginable top-shelf alcohol.

As I stand at the bottom of the stairs, I can just make out the outlines of the furniture that I remember. It's all in place – nothing has been moved. The place is empty. I swing the gun around, desperate for a target, desperate for something to happen – *anything*. The stillness is far worse than any violence I can imagine. I search for a light switch and find a set of three against the wall at the bottom of the stairs, but when I flip the switch, nothing happens. Either the circuit breaker has been flipped or the power has been cut to the entire house.

The sound is louder down here. I can hear the rhythmic thumping, and feel the stone shaking ever so slightly around me. It's enough to give me a slight case of vertigo as I feel my way along the basement walls, searching out the source. I assume it's coming from the massive bass amplifiers that are a part of the home-theater system Josh has had installed. But when I work my way to where I can touch them, I realize I'm wrong. The sound is coming from the bar – or more specifically from behind the bar.

I move my way over there slowly, feeling along the walls, until I'm standing behind the bar, still searching for the sound. I can't find it, though. It makes no sense; I've run out of places to look in the basement. I know the sound is here, but I can't find its source.

The heat in the basement is oppressive, and I put the gun

on the bar for a moment, so that I can wipe the sweat pouring from my forehead. I lean against the back wall, trying to clear my mind – to think through the possibilities. As I do, I realize that the sound I hear is coming from behind the wall. I turn and put my palms up against the smooth flat surface, and I can feel the beating, and I realize that there must be another room behind the wall – one with some sort of a hidden doorway. It would be consistent with Josh's personality, I know.

My hands fly across the wallpaper, looking for a hinge or a knob, but there's nothing there. I put my ear up to the wall, and I can hear the low pulse more clearly. I can hear something else as well. It sounds like screaming, or more accurately *screeching* – like metal dragged across metal, or a cat having its claws pulled out with a pair of pliers. It's a sound that – even as faint as it is – cuts through my eardrum and crawls down my spine. Every muscle in my body tenses as my imagination plays out all the horrors to which Josh may be subjecting Yvette. I fly into a panic and search the wall again, prodding and pulling at every inch of it.

'Yvette!' I call out, no longer worried about being discovered. The only thing I can think about is her, and doing anything I can to keep her alive and safe. 'Yvette!'

I've searched the wall as best as I can without the benefit of light. It occurs to me, though, that there could be a flashlight or matches under the bar. I turn my attention there and start opening the drawers and cabinets, my hands shaking as they fumble over tumblers and mixers and glasses, desperate for anything that might supply some light. I find them in the third drawer I pull open – *matches*. I feel the distinctive cardboard of kitchen safety matches and, when I pick up the box,

I hear the familiar rattle of a full pack. I pull out a match and feel for the strike pad, slide the match across it. My hands are sweating so badly that the first match slips from my fingers and falls to the floor. I curse myself and pull out a second match, strike this one more carefully.

The flame from the match casts a light that feels, in the utter darkness, as bright as the sun. I look around the basement and confirm that I am alone, and that the place is as I remembered it. By the time I've adjusted, the flame is down low enough on the wooden match that it burns my fingers and I drop it into the sink. I pull out another match and light it.

I get down on my knees and let the match lead me through the cabinets beneath the sink, hoping to find a candle that I can light to provide more consistent illumination. I see nothing useful, and go through two more matches in what seems a fruitless effort.

There is only one cabinet I haven't gone through, and I use my fifth match to look through that, the steady rhythmic beat from behind the wall keeping half time with my heart, and the screeching setting my every nerve on end. This cabinet seems bare, except that there is a switch deep along the side. I wonder whether that might control the power to the basement, and I flip it, hoping for the best.

For a moment nothing happens, and I curse my luck. Then I hear something behind me. It's like the whoosh of a pneumatic seal being broken, and there is a rush of air that rustles my hair. At the same time the volume of the beating and screeching increases tenfold, and my hands go to my ears defensively. Another second later, a faint light glows from over my shoulder.

I pull back from the cabinet, slamming my head against the frame, and turn to look at the wall behind me. There is a crack at the far corner, like the wall has come unsealed, and the light and noise are coming from behind that crack.

'Yvette!' I scream.

I don't hesitate. I'm on my feet, scrambling over to the narrow opening, clawing at it with my fingers, trying to pull it wider. The door is heavy and it takes several seconds for me to get it to budge. Eventually, though, it begins to move. It's agonizingly slow, and I can barely breathe. 'I'm coming!' I scream, no longer fully rational. Eventually I force the door open wide enough that I can squeeze through and I slide my shoulders in, petrified at what I might find.

CHAPTER FORTY-SEVEN

I'm in a room that's roughly twenty feet by thirty. The walls are rough stone, carved out of the earth's natural ledge, and there are electric torches hanging every ten feet, casting a flickering light throughout the place. Against one wall there is a variety of whips and chains and torture devices. The noise I've been following is coming from two black speakers that blare a recording of what sounds like disjointed machine sounds. It's like background music from some twisted dream. The details of the place barely register with me, though. There's only one thing I can focus on.

She's there.

She's stripped to her underwear, her wrists bound in leather-buckled restraints, raised high above her head. Her knees are slightly buckled and she's dangling, her entire weight borne by her arms, her shoulders twisted at an awkward, lifeless angle. Her head is flopped forward and her hair covers her face. She isn't moving.

'Yvette!' I scream.

Nothing. I sprint to her and take her body in my arms.

Her head flops back, loose on her neck, and I pull it forward again. 'Please,' I beg her. 'Say something!'

She doesn't move, doesn't speak, and I can feel my heart beat so fast I think I'm going to pass out. 'Please,' I say again, this time not to her, but to a God I've never actively acknowledged before. 'Let her be okay.'

I put my head to her chest, listening for a heartbeat, but with the soul-shattering music I wouldn't be able to hear anything even if she was alive. I lean her back against the wall and feel her throat, but my hands are shaking so badly it's useless. Finally, I put my face up to hers and close my eyes, trying to feel her breath on it. There's nothing, and all hope rushes out of my body. 'No!' I cry. 'No, please!' The tears run down my cheeks and I lean into her, hugging her with what strength I have left. I have no idea how long I stand there, probably only a few seconds, but it seems an eternity. And then I feel it. A tickle along the damp tracks on my face. I don't even realize it at first, but then it feels stronger, and I pull back and look at her.

'Are you alive?' I'm holding her head now, putting my face close to hers again, making sure that I'm not imagining it. 'Are you breathing?'

She says nothing, but her head moves and I can see a flutter in her eyelids.

'You're okay,' I say, willing it to be true. 'You're okay,' I say again. 'You're going to be okay. I promise, I'm getting you out of here!' I bend down and unhook the buckles around her ankles. I stand up, and support the weight of her body by wrapping my arm around her again and lifting her from under her arms. Her head is forward now, her mouth lolled open against me.

'Josh,' she mumbles into my shoulder.

I'm so startled to hear her voice that I pull my arm away and drop the full weight of her body back onto her shoulders. She lets out a soft groan.

'It's Nick,' I say. 'You're going to be okay.' I grab her again and lift the weight off her. With my other hand I straighten her head, so that I'm looking into her beautiful face. Her eyes are struggling to open. I can see that her pupils are fully dilated. She's been drugged, I suspect. 'Yvette? Are you okay? Stay with me. I'm getting you out of here!'

She's coming to, but slowly, mumbling something I can't understand. 'Don't worry,' I say. 'I'm here. You'll be okay.' I continue to hold her weight with one arm and work on the wrist restraint with my other. It isn't locked, but the buckles are pulled tight, and it's difficult to get them free with one hand. 'Can you stand?' I ask her.

She's still trying to say something, and as she wanders further and further toward consciousness, her ramblings become more urgent. 'Josh!' she blurts out.

It suddenly dawns on me for the first time since I saw her dangling against the wall that we are probably not alone. 'He's still here?' I ask her.

Her eyes are blinking open, but she can't focus. 'Josh,' she says again.

'Where is he?' I hold her head, trying to let her focus. Her eyes dart past me, over my shoulder, and I spin, expecting to see him there. We are alone, though. I look back at her. 'Where?'

Her eyes are still looking toward the other side of the room, toward the wall along which a series of sadomasochistic tools hang. There, in the middle, is a large upright box. It's black, around six feet high, narrow. Positioned as it is in the room, it looks as though it must contain additional implements, perhaps even more grotesque in nature, but it is large enough for a man to hide in it.

I look back at her. 'In there?' I ask.

She nods, and then her head collapses forward onto me again. 'Josh,' she repeats.

She's awake enough that her legs are starting to come back to life a little. I'm pretty sure she wouldn't be able to stand, but she can lean against the wall to take some of her weight. I prop her up and approach the box.

There is a knob on the door that forms the front of the box. It's studded and ornate, and something about it makes me shiver. If he's inside, I wonder what he's waiting for. I wonder whether he can see out, and it occurs to me that he may be gauging the moment when I'm close enough to leap out at me. I reach into my pocket for Ma's gun, but realize I've left it on the bar in the other room. I look around me and see a wooden paddle hanging on the wall, almost large enough to be a cricket bat. I grab it off the wall and hold it in my right hand as I reach out with my left.

I touch the knob, and it's cold. I take a deep breath and turn it, as I pull the door open in one swift motion.

The sight sends a shock through me. Josh is in there, staring back at me, dressed in leathers, a horrid look on his face. Before I realize what's happening, he's coming after me, leaning forward, his features twisted and anguished. I raise the club in my hand as his head hits my chest. I scream and swing at him. It feels like I've barely made contact, but he goes down at my feet. I jump back, raise the club again, staring at him, waiting for him to spring up at me.

He lies there, motionless.

I move forward a little and poke him with the club. He shifts slightly, and then comes back to rest as he was, when I take the club away. 'Josh!' I yell at him, but he doesn't react.

It doesn't feel as though I've hit him hard enough to knock him unconscious, and I keep the paddle raised high as I reach down with my free hand and roll him over.

He stares up at me, his eyes meeting mine and yet missing me somehow. It takes a moment for me to realize that he's dead. Looking more closely, I see a thin red line around his neck.

A thousand thoughts run through my head – and as many questions bombard my brain – flying at me with such speed that I can't separate them. I stand there for a moment, just staring down, trying to make sense of what I'm looking at, but I can't. Finally I remember where I am, and that Yvette is still in the room with me. I turn and look at her. She's awake enough now that she can keep her head up, though not steadily, and she's looking at me. 'It's him,' I say. 'It's Josh. He can't hurt you anymore.' It's all I can think of to say.

She shakes her head, and I can sense the frustration in her. 'No!' she groans. 'It's not Josh!'

I hurry over to her. Now that she can stand somewhat, I can use two hands to work on the wrist restraints, and using two hands makes it quicker work. 'It's okay, he's dead. Trust me.'

'It's . . . not . . . Josh!' she says. Her voice is still shaky, but she says it with emphasis.

'I'll get you out of here,' I say. The first wrist restraint comes free and I start working on the second.

Suddenly there is a voice behind me that I recognize. 'She's right,' the voice says. 'It's not Josh. It's me.'

CHAPTER FORTY-EIGHT

'Tom.'

I say his name even before I turn around, but I have to see him to believe it's true. I turn slowly to face him. Tom Jackson is standing in the door that leads back out to the rest of the basement.

'Nick,' he says.

'What are you doing here?'

'I'm sorry it has to be this way.'

I still can't comprehend what's going on. 'I don't understand,' I say. 'What way?'

'This way,' he says, taking a gun from behind his back and pointing it at me. 'I never wanted you to be involved. Not you or Yvette. I like you both. But sometimes things don't turn out the way we planned.'

The pieces are swirling, trying to find their place in the puzzle, but they don't form an image that makes sense yet. 'The way you planned?' I ask. 'You did this?'

He nods. 'I'm afraid so.'

Another thought nearly knocks me down. 'You killed Kendra, too?'

'I had to. I had no choice.' He moves toward me. 'Step away from Yvette,' he says.

'Why?'

'Because I'm telling you to.'

I shake my head. 'I mean, why did you kill Kendra?'

'She knew too much,' he says.

'What do you mean?'

He points the gun at me, motions for me again to step away from Yvette. 'She was smart, you know? She should never have left school; she would have been great in business.'

'What did she know?'

'When she was with Josh, she went through some of the company financial records and figured out that some of the revenue wasn't legit.'

None of this makes any sense to me. 'Not legit?'

'We were booking revenue that didn't align with the actual purchases online. The company had revenue streams that hadn't been allocated to any source at all.'

I almost don't want to ask the question. 'Where was the revenue coming from?'

'Some of the company's more illicit activities.'

'Such as?'

He shrugs. 'NetMaster really is a master,' he says. 'Josh knew what he was getting when he hired him, but he thought if he paid NetMaster enough, he'd change and only do what he was told. A man like that doesn't change.'

'Where was the money coming from?' I demand.

'Extortion,' he says flatly, as though it's nothing. 'Identity theft. Various sales of illegal substances. Knowledge is power, and it can be used in an infinite number of ways, if you know how.'

'How did NetMaster get the information?' I stare at him. 'You cracked the algorithms.'

A beam of pride lights up his face. 'I did,' he says. 'Josh always underestimated what I was capable of.' He looks down at Josh's body and his expression goes dark. 'Not anymore.'

'Why?' I ask. I can't believe what I'm hearing.

'At first it was to try to raise revenue for the company, to make myself look better. I was under so much pressure, I didn't know what else to do. Once we were able to connect the information on our users from their activities across all of the company's platforms, a world of possibilities opened up. I knew NetMaster had the connections to make it work. When I saw how much money we could make, I started to wonder why I would give it to the company. For a while, it was perfect. We were making more than Josh could even have imagined.'

'But Kendra found out what you were doing,' I say.

'Some of it. She was trying to find something to get Josh to leave her alone, and she realized that there were . . . irregularities in the finances, shall we say? She thought Josh was responsible for what was going on, though, so she came to me to warn him off.'

'And you never told Josh at all, did you?'

He shakes his head. 'I couldn't. He had no idea what NetMaster and I were doing. Oh, I convinced him to stop seeing Kendra, but that wasn't particularly difficult. He wasn't nearly as obsessed with her as she assumed.' He raises his eyebrow. 'He was less obsessed with her than you were, Nick. He was obsessed with power, and with his money he could find an endless string of women willing to play with him in this twisted little dungeon. He didn't need Kendra for that anymore. But even after they stopped seeing each other, I knew that she presented a risk – one that I couldn't leave out there forever.'

'So you were *De Sade*?' I ask, my head still spinning.

He scoffs. 'Of course not.' He looks around the room with disgust. 'You really think I'm like these perverts?' He moves toward me and Yvette. 'That was François, the sick bastard. So much for Santar's hope that he can rehabilitate people like that. But I needed to get rid of Kendra, and when I found out about it, it gave me an idea. When I discovered she was one of the models in François' LifeScenes, I hoped François was going to take care of her without my ever having to get involved. But then you had to interfere. If it had taken another day or two to figure out that François was *De Sade*, he would have killed Kendra, and none of us would be here. I had no idea what I was going to do, until I realized that you and she were going to end up together. You always had a savior complex, y'know that? I wish it had been someone else. But I had to take the opportunity when it presented itself.'

'So you killed her and framed me.'

'I killed her. You framed yourself.'

'And this?' I waved my arm around the room.

'This is the way I put all of this behind me,' he says. 'This is Josh's little hobby room. I knew neither one of you would go away easily, particularly her,' he nods at Yvette, who is still groggy. 'She wasn't going to let the man she loved go to prison without a fight, and she's a hell of a hacker. This way, I give the cops their easy solution. They'll find the LifeScene I planted on Josh's computer and assume Josh killed you both, and then accidentally killed himself while jerking off. Auto-asphyxiation can be a tricky business.'

'So here we are,' I say.

'Here we are,' he agrees. 'I'm not happy about it, but I have no choice.' He reaches into his pocket. 'Fortunately for you, I'm not cruel, and I like you.' He tosses a bottle of pills at my feet. 'Take those, and you won't feel a thing.'

'What are they?' I ask.

'Rohypnol. It's a high concentration – the same thing I gave her,' he nods again at Yvette. 'If you hadn't been early, she would never have been aware of any of this. Seriously, who comes to something like this early?' He laughs at his own joke. 'You always were the conscientious one, weren't you?'

'You didn't . . . ?' At this point I'm not sure even why the answer matters to me, but it does.

'Touch her?' Jackson smiles. It's the first time I've really seen the evil in his eyes. 'This isn't about sex for me, Nick. This is about money and power. With the information that NetMaster and I have access to, through the system, we can make more money than even Josh could have imagined, and the amount of power we have is immeasurable.'

'He's dead,' I say.

Tom hesitates. 'Who is dead?'

'NetMaster. I killed him.' It's only partially true, but I'm trying to rattle Tom as much as possible – trying to buy some time. By the look on his face, I have.

It takes a moment for him to respond, but he regains his composure. 'An inconvenience, to be sure. But I have access to his networks, and it's the information that matters most.

People across the world log onto our system, and give us their names and their identification numbers and their credit-card numbers. They let us watch as they surf for porn, and email old lovers and order hookers. And all the while they assume that their information is safe. Why? Because we tell them it is. They're willing to stick their heads in the sand because we offer them convenience – one-stop shopping for everything they want to do. They believe their information is safe because we tell them it is.'

'You have stock in the company,' I say. 'Why would you need this?'

'I want both. And I wanted the ability to tell this ass-hole to fuck off.' He points his gun briefly at Josh Pinkerton's corpse. 'You never had to deal with him very often. His idea of a management strategy was to humiliate those who worked hardest for him.' He looks around the room at all the imple-ments of torture. 'Apparently that was a theme that ran through his private life as well. He had no idea what was happening anymore, right up to the point where I came up behind him.'

'You don't have to do this,' I say.

'Yes, I do. Now take the pills.'

'No.'

He walks around me, brandishing his gun the entire way, moving over toward Yvette. She is still chained to the wall by one hand, still wobbly. Her free arm dangles loosely at her side, and she's leaning heavily against the wall. He puts the gun to her head. 'Take the pills, or I'll kill her now.'

'You'll kill her anyway.'

He cocks his revolver. 'Now.'

'Okay!' I shout. I lean down and pick up the pill bottle. I

open it and take one out, pop it in my mouth and swallow. I look at her. 'I'm sorry, Yvette.'

'It's not your fault. Are you ready?' She's slurring still, and for a moment I don't understand what she is saying. I give her a curious look. 'Are you ready?' she asks again. Suddenly she straightens up and her free hand grabs for the gun pointed at her head. 'Now!' she yells.

Her attack takes both Tom and me by surprise. Tom's arm jerks upward and the gun goes off. I can hear the bullet ricochet off the rock ceiling, and feel a rush of air as it passes close by me. I dart toward the two of them, my shoulder lowered, driving into his chest. He is thrown back into the leather-covered wall, loses his gun. It clatters across the floor to the other side of the room. I pull my fist back and I hit him hard in the stomach, knocking him to the floor. I'm on top of him, pummeling away at his face and torso.

'Get him!' Yvette screams. I can see her, frantically trying to free her other hand from the wall, but with only one hand to work on the straps, it doesn't look like she's having much success.

Tom is so shocked by the instant turn of events that it takes him a moment to react. Once he does, though, he fights back hard. He manages to block two of my blows in succession and lands two of his own, right in my face. I'm knocked back and hit the wall, stunned. It's odd – they were decent punches, but they seemed to have a greater impact on me than I would have expected.

I flail around, trying to grab something to fight with. My hand grasps something long and thin and metal, hanging from the wall. I pull it free and get to my feet, holding it like a spear.

Tom is struggling to get to his feet, his face bloodied. He looks for his gun and sees it across the room. I swing the pole at his head and hit the mark – the point opens up a gash above his right eye. I bring the pole back and ready myself for a second swing, but as I do, my vision blurs, and the momentum of my backswing carries me to the floor. I try to get up, but my legs don't seem to be working. I realize that the drug is taking effect, and the recognition makes my struggle to control my muscles more desperate. I feel like a fish on land, though, as I flop and toss myself to try to get vertical.

Tom sees my distress and clambers to his feet. He walks steadily over to his gun and picks it up, walks back to me and looks down at me.

I can no longer move. I am lying on the floor, my eyes open, just taking it all in. The drug is so powerful that I no longer even care, really, and I am willing to accept my fate.

Tom points the gun at my head. 'I'm sorry, Nick. I really am.'

Behind him, I sense movement, and even in my haze I'm curious about what it could be. Tom's mouth opens wide, as though he's going to say one last word to me, but no sound comes out. He looks so odd, just standing there in silence, his gun raised at me.

I see it come through his chest. It pokes out at first, like a worm trying to get out of his shirt. The fabric tears and I can see the sharp point as the red stain on his chest appears and grows. The tip grows and gets longer, sticking out of his chest like a horizontal flagpole. Then it withdraws and disappears. Tom still stands there, looking at me as a dribble of blood runs from the corner of his mouth.

He collapses, and once he does I can see behind him. Yvette has managed to free her hand, and she is standing there with a sword she's taken from the wall. She's holding it like a warrior, the blood running down the blade.

I smile at her. 'You're a remarkable woman,' I say. 'Can I say it now?'

She nods.

I take a deep breath. 'I love you, too,' I say.

The world narrows and fades to black as I pass out.

CHAPTER FORTY-NINE

I open my eyes and she is there, lying next to me in her bed, half covered with the sheet. I can see the soft curve of her shoulder and the undulation of defined muscle where her shoulder rolls into her triceps. Her back is lean, her skin smooth, marred only by a two-inch scar where she cut it on a fence when she was thirteen. I remember when it happened; I was there. She and I were drinking down by the old junkyard by the water, sipping some God-awful Mad Dog she'd boosted from the bottle that her dad kept under the kitchen sink. It was one of those nights that sticks in the memory like a marker in time. Our lives have moments like that – primary moments – from which everything else flows. The day my father died . . . the night I lost my virginity . . . the day I left MIT: these are the turning points that tie the other events together. Everything else is before or after. That night with her in the junkyard is one of those nights.

I can still remember exactly how she looked just before she leaned in to kiss me. My heart was beating so hard it felt like my ribs might shatter. And the moment her lips touched mine and I realized that she would let me touch her – that she *wanted* me to touch her, and that she *wanted* to touch me – was a moment of discovery and awakening as powerful as any other in my life.

When we saw the police lights we immediately assumed that her father had sent the cops after us, and we ran. Clambering over the chain-link fence at the back of the property, she let out a little gasp, but we kept moving until we made it back to my house. Ma was out, still trying to drink off the pain of my father's death years before. There, in my bedroom, I cleaned the cut on her back, put butterfly bandages and Band-Aids on it. She probably should have had stitches, but neither of us was anxious to explain to anyone what had happened. We spent the next hour there on top of my bed, exploring and touching and kissing. That bond of flight and excitement and discovery has never left us.

I reach over and touch the scar. She lets out a soft, tired moan and her back arches. I run the tips of my fingers along her skin, up over her shoulder blades and to the back of her neck, down the sides of her arms and up her sides.

Her body responds to my touch. It's been nearly a month since that night at Josh's, and there was a brief time when I thought we were both too damaged ever to let anyone touch us like this again. That fear lasted for about ten seconds after we were alone for the first time together. We fell into each other's arms with a desperate passion, clawing at each other as though we could use one another to cleanse away all the darkness of the past. It worked, too, at least for a little while. In the end we both know that some of the darkness lives within us and always will. That's okay, I suppose, as long as we understand it and learn to control the desires.

She rolls over and kisses me, trailing her fingers across my chest, down my stomach, between my legs. I close my eyes and let out a satisfied sigh as she kisses my chest, nipping softly at my nipples and moving her hands teasingly between my legs.

She kisses her way down my body, dwelling for a few moments on the more interesting topography, then slides back up so that she is straddling me, her hands on my chest.

She lowers herself onto me, and I watch as she closes her eyes, her face straining in exquisite pleasure. I want to hold her. I want to take her in my arms and bring her into me, but I can see that she wants to be the one in control at the moment, and that's okay. It's a game we enjoy that hints at the darkness, without diving in too deep. She is rocking slowly, sitting up so that I see her entire beautiful body, and the sight drives my need to take her in my arms. It is becoming a yearning that must be satisfied.

'Please,' I say softly, breathlessly.

She opens her eyes and looks down at me, smiling. 'You want permission for something?' she asks, the sexiest lilt in her voice I've ever heard.

'Please,' I say, again.

She is still rocking slowly on top of me, and I've never felt so alive. 'Yes?' she asks. 'What is it?'

'I want to hold you,' I say. 'Please?'

She gives me a mischievous smile. 'Do you think you deserve it?' she queries. 'Have you been good?'

'Yes,' I say, looking deeply into her eyes. 'I've been good. We both deserve it.'

Without breaking rhythm, she reaches down and takes my

hands, bringing them up to her. I wrap them around her body, pulling her to me, holding her as tightly as I can, kissing her hard as our bodies meld into one, the frantic passion gathering desperate speed until neither one of us can hold off anymore.

The meeting at the police station should be a mere formality at this point, but I am still nervous. The past few weeks have reinforced the lesson I should have learned long ago: nothing is as it seems.

Finn, my lawyer, is with me. I wonder who is paying him at this point; his agreement to represent me was with Tom Jackson – Tom needed a top lawyer to get me out, so that he could try to take care of me, Josh and Yvette at the same time. I'm sure Tom agreed to pay a pretty pile for that to happen, but Tom's dead now. Maybe Finn plans on collecting from Jackson's estate. That would be satisfyingly ironic. If not, I'll pay the fees; I need a good lawyer right now, and from what I understand, Finn is the best. A good guy, too, if most in Charlestown are to be believed.

Killkenny's there, too. He's the one who found us that night. After I'd left him on the street in Charlestown, he looked up Pinkerton's address and headed up, in the hope that that was where all the action was going down. The action had already played out by the time he got there, but it was still helpful to have someone familiar with the back story leading the Marblehead cops through the investigation. I'm sure they're good men, but the swanky neighborhood doesn't see too many double homicides. Throw in the S&M angles, and I have a feeling the Marblehead Police Department would have been overwhelmed if Killkenny wasn't there.

Sitting next to Killkenny in the interrogation room in the Back Bay station is Detective Sergeant Tom Welker. I still haven't heard him speak, but at least he's regarding me with less hostility than in the past. I suppose that's something.

Standing behind Killkenny and Welker are three men. One of them I recognize as the Suffolk County District Attorney. The other one has been introduced to me as the Police Commissioner. Apparently this matter has garnered the attention of all the VIPs in local law enforcement. Every one of them wants a piece of the glory, now that it looks as though it's been solved.

'I just want to be clear,' Finn says, taking control of the gathering. 'My client is being granted immunity from prosecution for anything he tells you about, with respect to the investigation he conducted into these matters, is that correct?'

'For anything excluding murder,' Killkenny says. He means it as a joke, but it's not to me. I've posed the hypothetical to my lawyer: I participated in the kidnapping and assault on NetMaster, and he died as a result. That makes me guilty of felony murder. The fact that I wasn't the one who turned the dial on the battery up, and flipped the switch, is irrelevant. So is the fact that NetMaster was a pederast scumbag who deserved to die. I'm just going to have to leave that part out of my answers to any questions, and rely on the competence of Cormack's men in disposing of the body. If I have some sleepless nights over it, I suppose that's a mild penance.

'Do you have the written agreement?' Finn asks.

Killkenny slides a sheet of paper over to Finn. He reads it, nods to me.

'What do you want to know?' I ask.

'We've dug through the computer files at NextLife, and we think we have a good handle on how all this went down, but we want to make sure it lines up with your understanding.'

'Okay,' I say. 'Where do you want to start?'

Killkenny shrugs. 'How about the beginning? How did this all start?'

'Some of this I'm guessing at,' I say. 'I obviously wasn't there at the beginning.'

'I understand. Anything you can tell us would be helpful.'

I take a deep breath. 'Tom Jackson was a friend,' I say. 'There was a time when he was a good guy, and he was always a brilliant mind. He was tasked with raising revenue for the company while not upsetting the "organic" nature of the services we provide. It's not an easy task. I'm guessing he started out thinking that if he could break the algorithms that protect people's identity in the system, he could use that information to generate research on how people were spending their time and money on the site. That would help him drive revenue.' I'm thinking about those first days at MIT when I met Tom. 'I don't think he started out planning anything illegal.'

'So, how did that turn?'

'I don't know. But I would guess that it's such a huge amount of information that, in the aggregate, he probably wasn't even able to break it down. On the other hand, he would have noticed certain people engaging in unethical – maybe even illegal – activities on the site. He could have thought that those people deserved to be targeted, and he probably started by dabbling in identity theft and online extortion. It's fairly easy and low-risk. And he used that money to prop up the company's revenue.'

'And then?'

'Well, he would have realized pretty quickly that there's a huge revenue opportunity, if that kind of behavior could be regularized. He wouldn't have had the resources or knowhow to do that, though.'

'So he convinced Pinkerton to hire NetMaster?'

'He admitted that much to me,' I say. 'But then Josh started seeing Kendra. And when Josh started getting too aggressive, she started looking for something to keep him at bay. Apparently she managed to get a look at the company's finances, and she realized there were things going on that weren't quite kosher. She thought Josh was behind the whole thing, so she went to Tom Jackson and told him. Of course she had no idea that Tom was behind it. At that point, he realized that he had to find a way to make her disappear.'

'So he got Michael François involved?'

I shake my head. 'François didn't have anything to do with Tom. He was just a psychopath who was using the system to practice murders. He was one of the subjects in the pilot programs that Gunta was running. I'm guessing he seduced the good doctor and convinced him to tell the parole board that François was cured – that he was not likely to repeat the sexual assaults that landed him in jail in the first place. Once out, though, François picked up where he left off, but this time he escalated the violence and started killing people. When I started investigating, Tom found out about François. I'm sure he went onto the system and figured out that Kendra was one of the likely victims.'

'So he killed her.'

'Not right away. I think at that point he just hoped that

François would get around to her, and his problems would be solved without him ever having to lift a finger. I think that's why he set NetMaster on us, to keep us from being too quick to solve the murders.'

'The car that almost ran you down in front of Yvette's house?'

I nod. 'And then breaking my car windows. I think that was all intended just to scare us – convince us that we didn't want to be looking into these murders. As long as there was no connection to the company, François would have been able to continue his killing spree and it was just a matter of time before he killed Kendra.'

'They were right about that,' Killkenny says. 'If you hadn't been stalking her, she would have been killed that night you found her at her house.'

'I wasn't stalking her.'

'Right.'

Finn puts a hand on my arm to tamp down my anger. 'Let's just get this over with,' he says.

'Anyway, things got more serious when they realized that Kendra was starting to talk to me about NextLife. That presented a much greater danger to them. Just scaring me wasn't enough anymore. They couldn't afford to have her giving me any more information.'

'So NetMaster beat the hell out of you,' Killkenny says.

'Yeah. And he showed up at my house with a knife.'

'Do you think he would have killed you?'

'I don't know. All I know is that he's lucky Ma didn't kill him.'

Killkenny smiles. He has genuine admiration for Ma. 'He was lucky about that. Though maybe she caught up with him.'

I look at him uneasily. 'What do you mean?'

'NetMaster has disappeared,' he says. 'We're looking for him, but it's like he's vanished into thin air.'

'Really?' I work to keep my face neutral, my voice calm.

He nods. 'NetMaster's not his real name, either.'

'You don't say.'

'Dieter Schlosser. That's his proper name. He was a real scumbag over in Europe before he became a real scumbag over here. We're assuming he was involved in the murder of the whore.'

I hate that word. It punctures me like a spear through my chest. 'She wasn't a whore,' I say with quiet ferocity. I can feel everyone in the room looking at me, as the room goes silent for a moment. 'She was a girl.'

Killkenny looks around at the other faces, gauging their level of offense. He looks back at me and shrugs, making clear that he doesn't really care how I'm feeling. 'Fine. We're assuming that NetMaster had something to do with the Madison girl's murder. Does that make sense to you?'

I have in my mind the image of NetMaster strapped to the chair in that warehouse, his eyes burning into me, convinced that I had killed Kendra. Unfortunately it's a visual that will likely never leave me. I've thought about it a lot, and I've come to the conclusion that Cormack was right. NetMaster wasn't lying; he genuinely believed that I had killed Kendra. I shake my head. 'I think Tom did that on his own. I think it was a crime of opportunity. He may not even have told NetMaster.'

Killkenny looks surprised. 'What makes you say that?'

'I don't know. It's just a hunch.'

He shakes his head. 'I don't buy it.'

I'm staring at him. 'You don't buy what?' I'm trying to figure out whether I've said too much.

'I don't buy your hunch,' he says. 'I think NetMaster must have been involved.'

I shrug. 'You may be right. You'll have to ask him when you find him.'

'You don't have any idea where he is, do you?'

'How would I know where he is?' I'm trying not to sound defensive, but I suspect I've failed.

'I don't know. You weren't close, but you worked at the same company. Maybe you heard about where he goes, that sort of thing.'

I shake my head. 'Like you say, we weren't close.'

Killkenny drags the silence out for a few more moments. 'I think that's all we've got,' he says. 'You'll let us know if you think of anything else you forgot to tell us?'

'Of course.'

Finn stands up. 'I'll expect to see the dismissal of all charges against my client filed today, correct?'

'It'll be filed,' the DA says. He and the others file out of the room. No one thanks me or shakes my hand or offers an apology. In their eyes, I'm still guilty of something. Maybe they're right.

Finn and I make our way through the station house and out onto the street. My Corolla is parked there. The windows are still broken, but they can be fixed. It's a reliable car, and there's nothing quite as comforting in this world as a dependable car.

'I'll give you a shout when the papers are filed,' Finn says. 'Congratulations.'

I get into my car. 'Thanks.'

'You celebrating tonight?'

'Not really. Just a dinner.'

'A few close friends?'

I nod. 'Something like that.'

The little brick patio out the back of Ma's house is large enough only for a barbecue grill, a cooler and an old wooden table big enough for six or seven people. That's bigger than we need for tonight. Cormack is standing over the grill, looking like he's in control of a supertanker as it heads out to sea. Ma and I are sitting at the table, sipping beers. It's cooled off a little bit, but the patio traps heat and keeps it like a warming tray, so I've got a layer of perspiration over my forehead. That's fine with me, though; it's a healthy sweat. Not a drop of anxiety.

The screen door slams and Yvette steps out with a tray of steaks and marinated chicken breasts. She's wearing a short skirt and a tight white shirt that looks perfect on her, and she catches me staring at her. 'Thanks,' she says with a smile.

'For what?'

'For noticing.'

'Hard not to.'

'Over here, lass!' Cormack bellows. 'The coals are ready and waiting, and I'm starved like a man coming home to shore!'

She squeezes past the table and puts the tray down next to the grill, grabs a beer and comes to sit next to me. 'Nice day,' she says, kissing me on the cheek.

'Best day,' I say.

'I like what you've done with your hair,' Ma says, looking over at Yvette.

I study her hair for a moment. It's funny: because it's always a tangled, multicolored mess, I stopped noticing her hair a long time ago. But looking now, I notice that it's muted – a rich auburn with understated highlights. It's also neatly brushed, which may be a first. 'I like it, too,' I say.

'Thanks. Trying something a little different,' she says. She seems almost uncomfortable with it.

'Are you done?' I ask her.

She nods. 'They let me in this morning to get the last of my things. I'm not going back.'

NextLife has been shut down for two weeks as the cops and the Feds and the IRS agents crawl through the system trying to figure out where the mess ends. I'm not convinced that it does end.

'What happens to the company now?' Yvette asks.

'I'm not sure,' I say. 'The website has been shut down, which probably means that it's dead as a portal. The Internet generation isn't known for its patience, and the publicity over all this is a killer. No one is ever again going to trust NextLife with their personal information.'

'Charlatans,' Ma mutters. 'I always told you there was no good at that place. No way to make an honest living there.'

'You were right, Ma,' I concede. She looks good. Stronger again, and I wonder whether she might just beat off this cancer for a while.

'So the company's dead?' Yvette asks.

'Well, it's safe to say that the IPO won't be going forward. Still, there's a good deal of value in the technology. My guess is that the investment bankers will be able to put together a private sale to some private equity group, and they'll be able to make a ton of money licensing the technology to other companies.'

'You still have your stock?'

I nod. 'It's not gonna be worth the twenty million it once was, but I may still get a few hundred thousand. Maybe more. It'll take a year for all that to shake out, though.'

'Not bad,' Yvette says.

'Blood money,' Ma mutters.

'As opposed to what Dad used to bring home?' I chide.

'Your father, rest his soul, made an honest living,' Ma says sharply. 'He may have been on the wrong side of the legal ledger at times, but that didn't make it dishonest.'

'Easy, old girl,' Cormack says from the grill. 'Morality's a slippery fish, if you try to hold it too tightly.'

She waves her hand at him. 'Bah! Fool.'

'I am that,' he agrees. He brings the first installment of charred meat over and puts it in the middle of the table. 'Don't wait for the chef.'

We tuck into the food, and a few moments later Cormack joins us with some more. He sits down and starts eating. After gorging for a few minutes, he sits back with a satisfied look on his face and takes a swig of beer. 'So, what will you do now?' he asks.

'I don't know,' I answer honestly. 'I'd like to get back to school at some point, but I don't have the cash for it at the moment.'

He regards me and Yvette pensively. 'You could be useful to people like me,' he says, an air of philosophy in his voice. 'Both of you.'

'That's nice,' I say, 'but I've never really wanted to head in that direction. No offense, of course.'

'I'm not suggesting anything illegal,' he says, shaking his head. 'But the two of you together did a remarkable job running this thing to ground. Investigating it using a whole range of skills that few have.'

'What's your point?' Yvette asks.

'No real point,' he says. 'It's just that there's room in this town for competent private investigators. And you can do that on the right side of the law – at least most of the time.'

It's an interesting idea. 'We'd need licenses, wouldn't we?'

He nods. 'You'd need to know someone with reasonably decent connections to get that. I wonder if you're acquainted with anyone like that.' He winks.

Yvette looks at me. 'What do you think?'

I lean over and kiss her. 'I think I don't want to think about the future at the moment,' I say. 'Right now, all I want to do is enjoy the afternoon.'

Acknowledgments

It has often been said that writing is a solitary endeavor, and there is some truth in that. The process of editing and publishing, however, is very much a group effort. I have been fortunate to have a great team to work with, and much of the credit for any merit in the final product goes to them. At Macmillan, the leader of this team, whose insights and suggestions were invaluable, is Trisha Jackson. Other crucial members include Ellie Wood, Ali Blackburn, Natasha Harding, Stuart Wilson, James Long and Tom Skipp. Thanks so much to you all, and to the wonderful people at Macmillan who have been such a huge support. To Aaron Priest, Lisa Erbach Vance, and those at the Aaron Priest Agency, as well as Arabella Stein in London: Thank you for always believing in me and for all your love and support.

Finally, thanks to my family: My wife Joanie for all she does, Reid and Samantha, Mom and Dad, Ted, and so many wonderful people in my extended group of family and friends, without whose support I would never be able to write.